Balance

The Divine, Book One

M.R. Forbes

ISBN-13: 978-0615775197

DEDICATION

To My Angel, for always believing. Thank you.

Chapter 1

There was something about the way she moved; the feline grace of her body, the softness of her steps. The way her arms swayed languidly back and forth as she sauntered past me. She had black hair that fell to her hips in a single silken flow, blue eyes, olive skin, a pair of tights, a fitted red sweater, and a something extra that put her at the top of the 'out-of-your-league' Christmas wish list. What's more, she was in a Museum! By herself! Yeah, I stared. No, she didn't notice.

It was my second week on the job at the Museum of Natural History, my first job post-incarceration. It was a long story, but the short simple version had to do with being a too-social computer geek and other people's credit cards. I had been lucky to get such cake work. Normally the Museum didn't hire ex-cons, but they'd imported a special 'first time ever outside the Vatican, limited time only!' exhibit of ancient Catholic relics, prompting them to beef up staff. The nature of my crime hadn't been violent or physical in any way, shape, or form, so they were willing to look past it. My job was simple, stand around and make sure nobody even tried to breathe funny on the artifacts.

Today, I was guarding cups. Excuse me, chalices. One in particular, a simple wooden one that sat at the end of the exhibit hall on a special pedestal surrounded by a rope, ten feet of space, tamper-proof, bullet-proof glass, and surveilled by every type of technology you could imagine. They said it was the cup Jesus drank out of at the Last Supper, the Holy Grail. It looked like it had come from 'The Last Crusade'. Lucas hadn't been off by much.

So far, the job had been as boring as I had assumed it would be. Every day from nine to twelve and one to close I would stand at the entrance to the exhibit room, watch the people go in and out, and occasionally wander up and down the aisles to make sure nobody got fingerprints on the glass enclosures. My greatest adversaries in this new career were children. They liked to touch things.

A particularly ambitious offender caught the corner of my eye, and I was forced to stop staring at the girl, who was approaching the wooden chalice at the end of the room. She seemed really interested in it. Very sexy.

Annoyed by the interruption to my creepy stalking, I walked over to where the little boy was standing, his hands and face pressed up against the glass. I peeked down at the label, *Diamond Chalice, 771 A.D.* There was more, but I didn't need to read it, I already had over a hundred times. It was a fancy piece of work that had been gifted to the Pope by Charlemagne. It tended to be a favorite with women, and even more so with kids. My guess was that the 'ooh shiny' part of his underdeveloped mind had taken over.

"Excuse me young sir," I said, kneeling down to get my face at a level with his. "The rules clearly state there will be no touching of the glass."

He looked at me, and I pointed my finger over at the 'DO NOT TOUCH' sign. He laughed and ran off to find his mother, who had moved on with little concern for the location of her brood. I watched him go, skirting through the line of adults and latching onto her hand. She looked down at him, and he pointed back to where I was still crouching. She gave me a Medusa look and yanked the little tattletale forward. What was with parents these days anyway? God forbid their kids actually follow the rules. Wait... did I just say that?

I was contemplating the human aging process and that weird phenomenon that occurs when we somehow begin to turn into our parents, when a collective murmur caught my attention. I stood and looked around for the source. Damn!

The cutie with the black hair was inside the rope line! Not really that impressive I know, but this was a major infraction in the Museum Guard handbook. At least it would give me an excuse to talk to her. I began pushing my way through the gathering crowd, who were complaining of course that she was obstructing their view.

"Excuse me, miss," I said to her back.

She had reached the tamper-proof, bulletproof glass, and was standing there in a very thoughtful pose, her left hand up to her chin, her right tapping on her hip. She ignored me, which was about what I would expect from someone like her. I picked up my radio and called for backup. I didn't have the authority to move her. Only the senior guards could do that.

"Hey Jimmy," I said. "I have a little situation over in the chalice exhibit. There's a girl here who thinks she has exclusive viewing rights to the Last Supper cup." There was a short silence before the reply.

"Chalice, Landon. It's a chalice. I'll be right there." He sounded like I had woken him up. I probably had.

I broke the rope barrier and approached the girl. She still didn't move. "Miss, are you okay?" I asked.

Better to play it sensitive. She didn't react at all to the sound of my voice. I didn't expect much attention from someone like her, but to treat me like I wasn't there? That was a little much. I flicked my eyes back towards the entrance. It should only take Jimmy a minute to get over from the office. When I looked back at the girl, she was cutting through the glass with her fingertip.

"Uhh..." My mind lost a step at the sight, tripping over itself and sending the rest of my body into a spastic overload. Does not compute. I picked up the radio again.

"Jimmy, where the hell are you," I yelled, my voice going up an octave. I looked again. Her finger appeared more like a claw now, and it really was cutting through the glass; the bulletproof, tamper-proof glass. The alarm started ringing.

Jimmy finally trundled into the exhibition hall, his breathing heavy as he pulled up next to me. Old... check. Overweight... check. Out of shape... did you doubt? He was your standard issue Museum guard.

"Geez Landon," he said. "You didn't tell me she was hot." He reached out and put his hand on her shoulder. “I’m sorry miss but you’ll have to go back behind the rope line.”

There was a blur of red, and the next thing I knew, Jimmy was on the floor sans one appendage. Chaos entered the building.

The crowd that had gathered to watch the show began to scream. I began to scream and backpedal as the girl turned and looked at me. Her eyes were yellow; her teeth were elongated into fangs. It was straight out of an issue of Fangoria. She growled, blasted the rest of the tamper-proof, bulletproof, glass into dust with her fist, grabbed the Grail, and ran towards the spectators - all in the space of three seconds.

Still backpedaling, my legs hit the rope and I tumbled backwards. The last thing I saw was the devil-girl dropping a package that looked all too familiar from any number of action movies. There was a loud pop, and a lot of heat. As I felt my life slipping away, I could hear the screams and smell the cooked flesh. I wasn't the only one who died that day.

Chapter 2

I came to, if you could call it that, with my face literally buried in the sand. My head was pounding and my heart was racing. Wasn't I supposed to be dead? I clearly recalled the white light, the fading away of my senses, and an overwhelming sense of freedom.

I picked my head up and looked around through the sand that was stuck to my eyelashes. I was lying on a beach, wearing a pair of board shorts. I was alone. If this was Heaven, it was going to be a lonely eternity.

Who was she, I wondered, forgetting my predicament for a moment. The girl had killed me, but I was still thinking about her. Did that make me crazy? I pushed myself to my feet and began brushing off the more tenacious grains of sand, then took a deep breath and tried to think. Okay, so I had just died in an explosion, I was standing on a beach completely alone, and for some reason I wasn't afraid. In fact, other than the headache, I felt pretty darn good.

"Landon Hamilton." The voice was old, deep, and smooth as jazz. It scared the crap out of me. I spun around.

The man had appeared out of nowhere. He was a good six inches shorter than me, middle-aged, gaunt but muscular, and bald. He had a short white goatee and pale blue eyes. He was wearing a tailored black suit.

"Are you God?" I asked.

He gave me a 'you're an idiot' smile. "Thankfully, no. You can call me Mr. Ross. I'm the Collector."

Oh. "I am dead right?" I asked.

He nodded.

"A beach?"

"Look around son," he said. "Earth, water, air, fire; the feel of sand between your toes, cooling off in the water from the heat of the sun. The fresh salt sea air... Where else does humanity so perfectly merge with the most basic natural elements?"

It made sense, in a nothing-is-really-making-sense sense. "Okay. So, I'm pretty sure this isn't Hell, unless you're tricking me into thinking this isn't Hell, and then it turns out it actually is. If this is Heaven, I don't know... don't take this personally but, it's kind of a bummer."

Mr. Ross sighed. "You may not be much, but if you're all we've got I guess we'll have to make a go of it. Now, please try to stop making a fool of yourself. Let's go."

He started walking. I followed behind.

"Wait a second. Where are we going?" He didn't answer. "Mr. Ross!" Nothing.

What did he expect? Two minutes earlier I had seen a beautiful woman turn into some kind of monster right before she blew me to smithereens. I was dead, but I was standing on a beach with one of the Blues Brothers. It had left me a little disoriented, confused, and giddy. I was finding it hard to calm down, so I was getting a little stupid.

We were walking, but I couldn't see where we were going. Ahead of us was a large sand dune, over it the clear blue horizon. There still wasn't another soul around, and Mr. Ross wouldn't say anything. He led. I followed. Until, for no apparent reason, he stopped.

"It'll be okay son," he said. "It happens to everyone. Just let it."

"What happens?" I asked.

Then it did. The reality. The crushing weight of what had actually occurred, the cold realization that I was no longer part of the land of the living. That my mother was going to be hearing from the police sometime soon that her son was a casualty of some kind of terrorist attack, disgruntled employee, or major nut job. That I was never going to get married, have children, graduate college, or travel to Europe. Heaven or Hell, I was out of the game.

That's the simple description. The pain that ensued was a hundred times worse. Regret, guilt, anger, envy, I think I went through every single human emotion in the space of a couple of minutes. I curled up on the beach and cried my eyes out, the maelstrom of feeling overwhelming my senses and leaving me there for ten minutes, an hour, a month? There was no way to measure it except through pain. It felt like it lasted another lifetime. Mr. Ross just stood there while it happened, waiting for it to pass, as I was sure he had done plenty of times before.

When it did, the resulting reality was cathartic. At least I still had something. Something I could build upon, strive for, be challenged with. I may have lost my vessel, but the soul was still sentient. I got back to my feet, wiped my eyes with my hand, and looked at Mr. Ross.

"I'm ready," I said. He didn't say anything, but he looked pleased, as if I had passed some kind of test.

When we reached the top of the sand dune, we were greeted by nothing but white, empty space. Who knew that nothing could be so amazing? I gawked.

"I've seen this at least a million times," Mr. Ross said. I believed it. "I'm still amazed by it every time."

"What is it?" I asked.

"Think of the beach as a staging area. I'm the Collector. I pick you up here. From staging, you can go to any number of places depending on how you've been assigned. Most people get moved on to a secondary staging area where they're met with by an acquaintance if we have one available. We try to find somebody who's already learned the ropes to help them with the transition. If they don't know anybody, or maybe nobody ever liked them, they get moved on to orientation, which is divvied up by religious belief. A few get reassigned up or down, usually because of a 'clerical error'." He actually did the air quotes. "You're a special case. You get to meet the Boss."

Special case? Up or down? Boss? Too many questions, but I never got to ask them. He put his hand on my back and shoved me into the nothingness.

When we came out on the other side, we were standing on a busy city street that reminded me of New York. It was an instantaneous thing, a smooth transition. Right foot forward to land on the sidewalk, left foot still planted in the sand. Thankfully my clothes matched the environment, a pair of jeans, black t-shirt, and a leather blazer. I bet I looked cool.

"New York?" I asked.

"You tell me," Mr. Ross replied. "You made it."

"What do you mean?"

"I'll let the Boss explain it to you." He motioned me towards the building we were standing in front of. I looked up at the huge mass of glass and steel stretching as far up into the sky as my neck would crane. A hundred stories, at least. As we slipped through the revolving glass door, I noticed a small sign etched in the glass in a really fancy script.

Alighieri Corp.

The inside of the building was incredible. A huge reception area with a ceiling that easily reached two hundred feet, a solid wall of glass to the left and right, and a massive tapestry hanging behind a semi-circular reception desk where a young brunette was typing something into a computer. On either side of the desk were two pairs of elevators. Mr. Ross swerved left and hit the 'up' button. I took a closer look at the tapestry while we waited.

It looked familiar. A man in the foreground wearing a red robe and a funny hat, holding open a book. To the left a bunch of naked people dancing their way downward towards a fiery pit and the Devil. To the right a walled city, and in the background a spiraling mountain that led upwards to a ribboned sky.

I turned to Ross. "Is that?" I didn't get to finish. The elevator doors opened and he pushed me inside.

"The Boss," he mumbled, telling me to keep quiet and save the questions. The elevator doors binged closed and we started rising, slowly at first but I could feel us building speed. I tried to organize my questions into some kind of logical order, but logic was failing me and besides, the ride was too short. I felt my stomach lurch as we decelerated way too quickly. Could dead people vomit?

The elevator doors opened and I stepped out, feeling the softness of thick carpeting beneath my leather boots. That was nothing compared to the view. The entire floor was surrounded by what seemed like a solid pane of completely invisible glass, and I could see out for miles. The angle was no good to look down on the city itself, but I could see now that tall mountains, with snow-covered slopes and plenty of jagged peaks, ringed us. At the foot of the mountains was a thick forest, and before that the tail end of the city, just as dense as I imagined the area around this building to be. There were no roads leading out of the city, at least not that I could see.

About fifty feet forward, directly in front of the elevator was an ornate mahogany desk. Sitting behind the desk in an equally ornate chair was a tall, thin man with short white hair. He was turned so I could only catch his profile, but I could tell even from here that he was wearing a finely tailored suit, and a heavy gold Rolex dangled from his bony wrist. Mr. Ross led me over to him.

The man spun the chair to face us as we approached. His lips spread in a tight smile and he leaned himself onto the desk to drag himself to his feet. He was shorter than I had thought, standing a full head below me. He stuck out his hand.

"Buongiorno, Signore," he said. I took his hand in my own, making an effort to be firm, but not break anything. He felt like he would crack under the slightest pressure. "My name is Dante."

He had a soft Italian accent, but it was different than I was familiar with. By that I mean, not like in the Godfather. "Landon Hamilton," I said. I was sure he already knew that, but I didn't know what else to say.

"Of course," he said with a laugh. He dropped my hand and waved me to a chair that hadn't been there a second before. "Please, take a seat." He looked at Mr. Ross. "Thank you Mr. Ross. You can go. I believe you have another pickup."

Mr. Ross looked at his watch. "Yes," he said. He didn't leave by elevator. Instead, he just vanished.

Dante eased himself back down into the chair. "Now, where were we? Ah yes, you are surely wondering what is going on? Would that be a good estimation?"

"Dead on," I said. He stifled a grin.

"I'm sure you've already surmised that you have left behind the state of existence often referred to as 'being alive'. You did so in quite a violent manner in fact, being blown to bits by a certain 'hottie'." He stifled another grin. At least he was amused. "Believe me when I say you should be glad for the fact that it was quick. Better to come to a sudden end than to suffer."

That might actually be true, but I was twenty-three years old. "Better to live another, I don't know, fifty, sixty years," I said.

"So you think," he replied. His jovial expression faded somewhat. "Things are not as simple as they may seem from that side of the coin, Landon. Not simple at all."

"I really have no idea what you're talking about," I said

"No, you wouldn't. Are you familiar with the Catholic Church?" he asked.

Familiar? My mother dragged me to Church every Sunday morning for most of my childhood. I had spent my adulthood teetering between a healthy fear of God and a complete lack of belief in anything special. Considering that second part had already been proven wrong, maybe I should reconsider the first.

"I spent a year as an alter boy," I replied.

Dante stood up again and began pacing the room. After a few trips back and forth behind the desk, he spoke again.

"It's a lie," he said.

"What?" I wasn't sure I had heard him right.

He took a deep breath and sighed. "It's a lie, Landon. Not a total fabrication of course, there is a God, and as you may have determined Heaven and Hell are real. So is the place in between."

That was one question answered. "So I'm in Purgatory?" I asked.

"You're in Purgatory," he confirmed. "But it's not what you think. None of it is."

I had a feeling he was going to say that. Who knew it took eternal sleep to be woken up? "Do you care to explain?"

Dante resumed his pacing. "It is difficult to explain, Signore. We are speaking of thousands of years of history. I will start with the simplest description." He paused, trying to think of how to say what he wanted to say so I would understand.

"In all things there is balance," he said. "It is the single most important law of the Universe. If something expands, it must contract, if it goes up, it must come down. Even God must adhere to this law, because it transcends even Him. This is the reason for Purgatory. It is necessary for the balance of goodness, and evilness. When God created mankind, and named it good, he tried to push this balance to his own ends. Such things are not to be."

I knew some of the stories in the Bible. "The serpent."

"Yes," he shouted, smiling and clapping his hands together. "Not a serpent of course. That is just a story in a book, a representation of the truth, a simplification much as I am attempting now. Mankind could never have been inherently good, or inherently evil, because the Laws of Balance would not allow it. To use an analogy you may understand, the more he pushed these boundaries, the more feedback he received. He created the seraphs, the angels, to try to steer us back on the path of righteousness, and they began to fall."

"The Devil?" I guessed.

"As he is known in some circles," Dante said. "He was an angel once, but he was corrupted by temptation. He sewed dissent amongst the ranks of the angels, making false promises and filling their ears with believable lies. He gained immeasurable power before God realized his one and only mistake, the only one he could ever make. God restored the balance by giving Hell to the Devil. He then created Purgatory to put some distance between the two, in order to minimize the damage that could be caused by shifting tides. So it was for many thousands of years."

"But..." I knew there had to be one. There always was, wasn't there?

Dante sighed again. He walked over to the window and gazed out at the mountains. "The Devil and his minions thrive on chaos. He gains nothing from balance, and lusts only for power. He twists mankind to his will when he can, and forever hopes to tip the scales in his favor.

For many years this was as expected, and thus the balance was held steady. Two thousand years ago, a problem arose.

God decided to get back in the game. He was unhappy with the status quo, unhappy to have been denied in anything. The war began anew with the birth of His son."

I rose to my feet and went to stand at the window with Dante. His eyes darted over to look at me, and a surprised expression spread across his face, and then vanished.

"Jesus was crucified," I said. "Wouldn't that have rebalanced the equation?"

"Crucified yes, but also martyred. His death created the underpinnings of the Catholic Church, the most powerful of God's armies. I was once a staunch ally of the Church. I fell in love with an angel, and was granted a rare opportunity to visit all three realms. Heaven is a wondrous and beautiful place, incredible to behold, and Hell is just as opposite."

Now I was really confused. "So why not stay in Heaven?"

"There is a war going on, Signore. It may seem that there are only two sides, but there is a third, and it has very few soldiers. If the Devil gets his due, the world of man will fall into chaos and ruin. It will be ruled by violence, death, and famine. All of humanity will be hunted to extinction by the creatures of the Underworld."

"So we root for good right?" I asked.

He shook his head. "It is certainly tempting to do so, but if the world is overwhelmed with good then God will have leave to do as he wishes. You have heard of the Rapture?" I nodded.

"He will take only his most faithful servants up to Heaven, and he will destroy everything else in order to make right his miscalculation. Do not think badly of Him for it, Landon, it is not for any ill will to us, but because that is His nature. He does not understand that there is something greater than Him, and as such He will lay challenge to this universal law. He cannot see that He is destined only to fail in this. In any case, this is why there must be a third side, and this is why we fight for it. If either good or evil wins, the world as you know it will cease to be."

It was a scary thought, and a hard one to accept. My mother had spent my entire life teaching me to be good, to obey the word of God, to hold the moral high ground. Okay, I hadn't exactly mastered it, but I tried to be a decent person overall. My incarceration was for identity theft and fraud. I had tried to cheat the system, not hurt anybody. Yet, now I was being told that by doing good I was threatening all of humanity?

"How can it be wrong to do good in the world?" I asked.

"It isn't wrong, for the balance must be maintained. For every old lady you help with their groceries, there is someone being teased for their appearance. For every prayer you send to God, there is a curse being uttered. Such things are of utmost importance, and thus the infinite circle continues."

It made sense in a way I did not completely understand, but was able to accept. The more I thought about how the world did its business - war, humanitarianism, greed, philanthropy, stealing and charity, the more I came to understand the pattern. I moved to stand directly in front of Dante, so I could look him in the eye. I squeezed in between him and the view.

"Okay, so everything is in balance, and God and Beelzebub are duking it out to see who can take home the whole pie. So then, here you are trying to get in the middle of it and prevent a clear winner?"

He seemed uncomfortable having me so close. He backed up a few steps. "Yes. Exactly."

Something was out of whack with the story. “But if the Universe forces all things into balance, then shouldn’t it be able to take care of their attempts to tip the scales on its own?”

Dante smiled wearily. “The Universe works on its own time, not ours. A victory by either side will throw the balance, and the Universe will put it back in place. When? How? That is not for us to know, and it will matter to us little, for we will all be gone.”

It was time for the million-dollar question. "How many people know about this?"

He knew the question was coming. He didn't want to answer it. He knew I wasn't going to like the answer.

He did another one of those big sighs before he replied. "Other than the angels and demons?” he asked. I nodded. “Counting you and I... four."

Mr. Ross had said I was special. What made me so special that I got to know this anyway? "Why so few?"

"Please, Landon, let us sit again." He waved me back over to the chair and returned to the desk. I was hesitant to follow him, but I needed answers. It was like an itch that started at my feet, ran up my legs, and disappeared deep into my soul. Once I had plopped down into the chair, he picked up a remote control and faced it towards the window in front of me. It became a gigantic screen. Depicted on it was Dante, looking much the same as he did today. The video relayed the scene to me exactly as he described it.

"For me, it was an accident. I was never supposed to stay in this place. The caretaker at the time had tired of the fighting, and wanted to get out. He could never leave Purgatory of course, but he could escape his memories of all that had occurred. As I traveled through this realm, he reached out and touched my arm, and by doing so passed all of his knowledge on to me. Once I knew the truth, I could not abandon the mortal world to the end I knew would otherwise come."

The scene in the video changed. It showed Mr. Ross lying naked on a beach. The same beach I had arrived on.

"Mr. Ross is the next," he said. "He told me he was a tax collector for King Henry the Second. In those days new souls had to find their own way off the beach, but he came straight to my front door so to speak. He knew who I was, I don't really know how. He started asking me questions about Heaven, and about Hell. Nobody else had ever asked me these questions. Everyone else lands on the beach, suffers their Regrets, and moves on to spend their eternity much the same as they lived their lives. I was so grateful for someone to share this burden with, I told him everything I knew. Ever the Collector, he felt there was more information out there, something more that I didn't know."

Now the scene shifted to Mr. Ross torturing a tan, golden haired man. It was disturbing, and I couldn't bear to watch it. "He knew how to get information. As a Collector, he could collect anything. He found out that we did not have to be bystanders in this war, that there were others that could accept the truth. That there were others who could possibly even prevent total annihilation." He paused and took a sip of water for a cup that had just appeared on the desk.

“Thirsty?” he asked. I shook my head, so he continued.

"We waited over a hundred years for the first to arrive," he said. “Mr. Ross collected every single soul in order to be sure not to miss her. When she came, we knew her right away because she wasn't naked."

Not naked, of course. "What?"

Dante let himself grin this time. "Almost everyone who dies comes to the afterlife unclothed. I did, Mr. Ross did. She didn't. Neither did you." He paused dramatically, or maybe so I would make the connection. Special. Me. Right. "What it meant was that she was Aware. Not on a conscious level at first, but Aware just the same. She could exert her will upon Purgatory itself, and it bent in response. She didn't want to be nude, and so she wasn't."

I looked down at the clothes I was wearing. "Mr. Ross said I had made this," I told him, waving my hand at the room.

"That is somewhat true," he said. "But not completely. Everyone who dies experiences Purgatory in a different way. It has no specific shape or form, but rather is consumed by each individual according to what they believe it will be. For me, this place is typical to 14th Century Italy. The others here are peasants, merchants, and farmers. In my mind you would normally be a knight, however your will has changed this place to something you are more familiar with. While you are here I am a CEO, sitting in the penthouse of a modern skyscraper. You have made this my reality. If you went outside the people around you would find themselves in this city you have created, and many would suffer some level of disorientation before they would be able to adjust to the change."

I looked out at the city again with new eyes. This was all a figment of my imagination? "How far does it reach?"

He shook his head. "There is really no way to know. It could be all of Purgatory has changed because you are here. Most of the inhabitants here will not remember the change once you have gone."

I wanted to test this. I wanted to have some proof that what I was hearing was true, to see what Dante saw. I wanted to be in his world. I tried to picture a medieval castle, a throne, and a large timber table. Nothing happened.

"You don't have control of it," Dante said, as if he had been reading my mind. "Not yet. Your mind created this because it was familiar. It will hold onto it tightly until you can convince it that it doesn't have to."

"I feel like Neo," I said.

"Hardly," Dante replied.

Something was nagging at me. Something he had said before I tried to turn this place into Camelot. "Once I've gone? Isn't Purgatory, you know... forever?"

"No," Dante said. "Purgatory is never forever, unless you choose it to be. It is where the souls who have not chosen a side or who have not earned a place in either Heaven or Hell are sent until such a time as they do. Time is not observed the same way here, so such endeavors can take many hundreds, if not thousands of Earth years. And yes, you will leave this place if you choose to accept who and what you are."

There it was again. "Who and what am I?"

"You are a diuscrucis, a crossbreed of angel and demon. Not directly of course, but somewhere in your lineage, buried deep within your roots. The blood of the creatures of dark and the creatures of light flows through your veins. Moreover, the balance of this mixture is precise, or you would not be here now. Almost all diuscrucis are inherently good or inherently evil, depending on which side is more dominant. But you... You are a perfect balance of every variable in the equation. The odds are so infinitesimally small, that it has happened twice in a millennia is beyond words."

I was expecting something grandiose, after all Dante had said there was only one other like me that he had ever met. This went beyond grandiose though. This went deep into impossible. You would think a guy would know if his grandma were Satan's handmaiden. If my day had gone any differently, I would never have believed it. I did though. There was something telling me that I should.

Dante had read my expression, and he watched me curiously as I worked through acceptance of my family tree. "You would know if I was lying Landon," he said. "That is one of the traits you inherited from your good side. It is what allows me to tell you all of this, and know that you will accept it and believe it."

I did know he was telling me the truth. "If that side helps me to recognize lies, does the other make me better at telling them?"

It was part of the balance. That deviousness had led me to hacking, to stealing, and ultimately to my arrest. The thought bothered me.

"Wait a second," I said. "You speak of balance, good, and evil as if we have no choice in the matter. Are you saying that every decision I make is predetermined in order to keep me right in the center?"

When I asked the question, Dante flinched as though he had been struck. His wide eyes narrowed and dimmed, and he took on a look of sadness. "Everyone has the freedom to choose their own path. Charis did."

"Charis?" She was the other one like me. I knew it by his reaction. "What happened to her?"

He paused before he answered. "She made a choice. She isn't with us anymore."

I could tell by the way he said it that it was all he wanted to say. There was no reason to push him. I had gotten what I wanted.

"Then I guess the burning question is, what exactly am I doing here?" I asked.

Dante's demeanor changed again, turning him back into the energetic and lighthearted man that had greeted me.

"You are in a unique position, but as I have said it is your choice. The battle between good and evil rages on; the angels want the perfection that God had envisioned, and the demons aim to mangle the world to satiate their desire for chaos and destruction. Mankind has been caught in the middle, and they have no one to fight on their side. No one to assure that the balance is maintained so that they may continue to have control of their own future."

"So you think that I can help humanity deal with this somehow?" I was doubtful. Maybe I could spot a lie and dress myself in cool clothes, but I had a feeling that wouldn't help much against Satan or Saint Michael.

"I know you can, Signore," he said. "You are stronger than you know. Shedding your mortal skin has opened your being up to all of the power that it is due a diuscrucis." He leaned up over the desk and looked me right in the eyes, a look that delved deep into me. "ALL of the power." He seemed very satisfied.

I would do this. I had to do this. The need was an unbreakable iron grip on my soul. It was what I had been born to do, had died to do. It was frightening, exciting, and impossible to resist. It wasn't about the power that Dante believed I had. It was about nature. My nature. How many people ever get to find out where they stand, and connect with it so completely? According to Dante even God Himself was being driven by His basest nature. I had asked about choice, discovered I had none, and realized that it was okay, because I didn't care.

"So what happens next?" I asked.

Dante smiled. "When someone who leans to good leaves Purgatory, they go to Heaven. Someone leaning evil goes to Hell. Someone who doesn't lean at all, they go..."

He didn't finish. He didn't have a chance to. The solid glass window I had been enjoying looking out of earlier exploded inward, showering us both in glass. I backed away and raised my arms to cover my head. Dante didn't move at all, he just turned his head to watch the interlopers make their entrance. The glass seemed to bounce off of him. It took me a moment to realize it hadn't hurt me either.

The interlopers looked like angels, but I knew on my new instinct that they weren't. Maybe once upon a time before the greedy promises and lies had changed their hearts, but not now. They may have been brothers, both with long silver and white hair, ebony skin and sharp red eyes. They were wearing matching leather dusters with black leather vests over purple shirts and dark wash jeans. Each was holding what looked to me like a samurai sword. They glared at Dante with disgust, and looked at me as if I were nothing more than an ant to be stepped on.

"You have no rights here," Dante said to them. He shifted over to put himself between them and me. "If any harm comes to me you will be in breach of the Treaty."

The two dark angels stepped forward as one. "We have no intention of harming you Alighieri," the one on the left said. "We only want him."

I felt my heart jump into my throat. What was this frail old man going to do to keep those swords from taking my head? This was turning really bad, really fast.

Dante turned his back on them and leaned in close to me. "I don't know how they found about you already," he said. "Take this." He handed me a... cellphone? "Mr. Ross will get you out of here."

"Wait... what am I supposed to do?"

Dante whispered something and put his hand to my forehead. The entire room started spinning. One of the dark angels pushed Dante out of the way. The other raised his sword and smiled, taking pleasure in his killing strike. I closed my eyes so I didn't have to watch myself die for the second time in one day. I wondered how that was even possible, sure I was about to find out.

I felt a pair of arms wrap around me. I smelled something burning. The blow never came. I opened my eyes. I was standing on the torch of the Statue of Liberty.

Chapter 3

I stood there for a few minutes, trying to make sense of everything that had happened within what had felt like only a couple of hours. Somehow, I had been brought back to life. I worried first that I was one of the undead, a zombie or something, but I could feel the pulse beneath my fingers, and I was cold in the night air. I was still wearing the same clothes, which I was grateful for, because it was REALLY cold. Hadn't I died in the summer? How much time had passed? What was I supposed to do? Where should I start?

I looked at the phone Dante had given me. It was a newer model, a smartphone. I lifted it up to my chest and turned it on. Along with the standard assortment of apps was one titled 'Landon'.

I thought about opening it there, but I was freezing. I edged my way around the torch to the small door that led down into the main stairwell. Please be open. It was. I slipped inside and closed the door; glad to be out of the bitter winter wind. Not that it was a whole lot warmer inside, but at least I was out of the elements. I descended the ladder and made my way out to the staircase, then sat down on a step and opened the app.

Buongiorno Landon,

I'm sorry that you will have to learn in this way. It means that we've been compromised to Mephistopheles, and his Collectors have come for you. Be thankful that I had suspected a traitor in our midst, and have prepared this guide to help you on your journey to discovering your full potential and making good on your promise. I will speak with you again once I can be assured that it will not lead them to you. In the meantime, if you do nothing else, read the entry titled 'Rules'. Following the rules within will keep you alive. Yes, you are 'alive', although not in the manner you are used to. You are Awake, and a full member of the Divine, with all of the rights, privileges and power that comes with it. You will find out what that means in time. Stay safe my friend.

Ciao,

Dante

There was a menu item at the bottom that said 'Rules'. I pressed it, and read them.

1. *Check the inside pocket of your jacket.*
2. *Find somewhere safe to read the rest of this guide.*
3. *Do not travel at night.*

4 Stay aware of your surroundings. You will be able to recognize the Divine. Most of the Divine will also be able to recognize you. Only the weakest will be fooled by glamour.

5 When in doubt, hide. They will know what you are, and they will try to kill you. You have no allies.

6 Both sides have human allies. The agents of good are called the Touched. The agents of evil are called the Turned. They have some power that has been transferred to them by the Divine, but they are still mortal. They will try to kill you, but will not recognize you so easily.

7 You can kill an angel with anything that has been cursed.

8 You can kill a demon with anything that has been blessed.

9 You cannot kill a Divine with anything that is not Divine.

10 Do not lose hope and do not give up. You are special.

That was it. A few bits of advice that read more like instructions, and a few helpful tips that may or may not keep me alive. That part about killing angels and demons; I couldn't even fathom the concept, but if they really were going to be out to kill me, I guess I wouldn't have a choice.

I reached into the pocket of the blazer, grabbing onto a large wad of paper with a familiar feel. I unfolded it and a wedge of blank plastic the size and shape of a credit card fell out. What was I going to do with a blank card? I tucked it back into the pocket and spread the cash. It was mainly twenties and hundreds; four thousand dollars. That wouldn't last me too long, at least not in the Big Apple, but it was better than nothing.

Rule one taken care of, now what about rules two and three? It was nighttime, and Lady Liberty seemed safe enough for now. The problem was, come morning this place would be crawling with people and I didn't know if I should be afraid of that or not. How many Others were there? Did they mix in with the population, or keep to themselves? What about their allies? I could just picture Joe Blow the Tourist laying eyeballs on me and literally unleashing Hell. Of course, I was on Liberty *Island*. There was zero way I was going to get out without getting on a boat. There was no way I was going to get on a boat without any other people on it.

Decision made, I figured it best to at least head towards the bottom of the Statue, so if nothing else I'd be set to make a break for the ferry right away. Once I had gotten off the island I would find a hole in the wall somewhere and stay there until Dante got back to me with some useful information.

I was cold, slightly confused, and really scared. Through some strange twist of the Universe I had been granted a second life. It occurred to me that this was not the kind of second chance I would have imagined, and I doubt one that too many people would have jumped at. What would have become of me if the dark angel's sword had made contact? Dante hadn't had the chance to tell me what the downside to this was, but I could guess. I couldn't go back to Purgatory, and the other places didn't want me. Could a being just cease to exist completely? Could I be erased from the Universe?

It was a long way down, but to my surprise I didn't tire. I pounded onto the steps with gusto, hopping two at a time and expecting to become winded with every drop. I wasn't a total sloth, but I wasn't exactly Tony Horton either. I kept my body in shape, but it was more of a visual in shape than an actual efficiency in power and endurance. When I got to the bottom without even breathing hard, I began to question Dante's assertion that I was alive. He had called it being Awake. He claimed I had power. Maybe this was part of it.

I didn't see any guards, but I assumed that one of America's national treasures wouldn't be completely deserted. I pushed open the door to the stairwell, trying to prevent any squeaks or whines from the hinges. The coast was clear. I slipped away from the stairs and looked around. I assumed the outer door had to be alarmed, so that was a no-go. What I wanted was the men's room.

I circled around the entire area, past the old torch, up the steps and around the exhibits. I had only been the Statue once before, and I never realized that there was no bathroom inside the pedestal. I would have to find somewhere else to hide out.

The somewhere else turned out to be a small janitorial closet out of the way of the main traffic lanes. I was fortunate in that the door was unlocked, hanging open about a quarter of an inch when I spotted it. It was your standard maintenance room; shelves with cleaning agents, buckets, mops, and so on. I turned on the light hanging over the center of the room, found a comfy looking box to sit on in the back corner of the small space, flipped the phone over to face me, and opened the 'Landon' app again, pressing on 'Guide' in the menu.

****

What is written here has been collected through over five hundred years of exhaustive research, along with a number of interviews conducted by Mr. Ross, and through direct verbal interviews with Miss Charis Stone, the first true diuscrucis to be granted access to the mortal realm. Miss Stone's first hand experience is the most vital part of this guide, as it will give you a common insight into what it means to be what you are, and to take on the responsibility that you have. Read these words and take heed in every message contained within. Do not expect that being Awake will be easy. It is a difficult yet rewarding existence.

The assumption has been made that you have already read the rules, and are hiding out somewhere safe so that you can read this guide. In order for you to be prepared to survive the coming days, you must learn to control the universe around you. This will not be an easy task, but I believe you will find it most beneficial.

You may be wondering what this means. When you were in Purgatory you had the ability to change your surroundings at your will, although only subconsciously. You hold this same power in the mortal realm, albeit to a lesser degree. How much less, I cannot say. Your ultimate strength rests within yourself. Since you are still wearing clothes, you have your first physical proof of this power.

To control it, you must above all things believe in it. This is not a simple task, as you must let go of every natural law that you have ever learned or experienced. These laws do not apply directly to the Divine, as the Divine originated from the Creator to help guide the world He created. This does not mean you will be able to fly, or walk through walls, or any such nonsense because abuse of these laws can have catastrophic consequences on the fabric of the universe that you are manipulating. The more you push, the more resistance you will encounter. You do not have unlimited resources. You will become fatigued and could lose consciousness if you push too hard, leaving yourself open to your enemies, of which there are many.

Read this first exercise, then close the Guide and practice it. Once you are able to succeed in producing the desired effect, move on to the next page. Do not give up, no matter how difficult it may seem.

Make It Rain

1.Close your eyes, try to relax

2.Think about rain

3.Open your eyes.

4.Focus on a spot directly in front of you

5.In your mind, command the water vapor to condense in the air, creating rain.

****

I turned off the phone and put it in my pocket. After what I had been through already, how hard could it be to reject the laws of nature? Was there any reason I couldn't make it rain? At the same time, it just felt silly.

I closed my eyes and tried to relax, but even that proved difficult. I didn't feel like I was any different now than I had been before. True, I had just hiked down the Statue of Liberty without a sweat, but that was physical. I opened my eyes and focused on a spot just in front of me. Rain! Nothing happened. Rain! No dice. Dante had known this wasn't going to be easy.

Anyway, what else did I have to do while I waited for daybreak?

"Rain," I said out loud. I felt a small touch in my mind, as if I was actually using my brain as a muscle to physically push something. Nothing happened. I concentrated on that feeling, tried to duplicate it. Nothing. I took a deep breath and started over, closing my eyes and slowing my breathing. When I opened them, I was face to face with a vampire.

Her face was only inches from mine. Her fangs were bared in the scariest, most malicious smile I had ever seen. She had come out of nowhere, and hadn't made the slightest sound. Her skin was a lifeless white, her hair and eyes black. I could feel the animosity pouring off of her. Even if she had been a little girl smiling at me and offering me candy, I would have known her intent.

"Oh crap," I cried as I leaned to the side and started flailing like a fish, desperate to get off the box and away from the thing.

The force of her strike put chips in the wall where my chest had just been. The momentum of my flailing sent me off my seat and onto her, shoving her back and onto the floor. I fell on top of her, and by her expression I could tell she was surprised by the maneuver. I guess she had been expecting someone who actually knew how to fight.

Recovering from her shock, she grabbed my shoulders and literally threw me off of her, sending me slamming against the wall next to the door. I looked at it longingly, but who was I kidding. There was no way I could outrun or outfight this thing. I was done before I had even gotten started.

She hopped to her feet, not even using her hands to help push up. I got a good look at her now. She looked to be between eighteen and twenty two years old, five and a half feet tall, an athletic build, and a small face with high cheekbones. Her eyes had changed from all black to a more human looking, and quite striking blue. She was wearing a cropped leather jacket over a pink tank, a short black skirt and medium-heeled black boots that cut off just below the knee, accentuating her pale, well-toned legs.

She stood there and looked at me. If she hadn't been a demon-spawn who was about to kill me, I might have been thinking about asking her on a date. Why wasn't she finishing the job? I was the mouse and she was the cat. It made sense.

"What are you?" she asked me.

I hadn't expected her to speak. It caught me off guard. "Wh... what?"

"You smell like a seraph," she said, "but you fight like a human."

I didn't know what to say. I figured either way I was about to become a meal, so I went with the truth.

"Just part, actually," I replied. I inched my way towards the door while I spoke. She just stood there. Why should she be worried? I was pretty sure she could close the gap in half a second or less. "Part angel, part demon, part human. I just found out today."

"A crossbreed?" she asked. "You?"

Okay, maybe I wasn't much in a fight, but the way she said it was just insulting. I glanced over and saw I had almost reached the door. As I had thought, she noticed. She was on me in two strides, her long delicate fingers gripping my throat and pulling me to my feet. She put her face right into mine, and then leaned into my neck. I could feel the heat of her breath against my skin, and I prepared to be food.

Instead, she pulled her head back and looked into my eyes. It was the same look Dante had given me, the one that I had felt deep within my soul.

"Indeed," she said. She let go of my throat and backed up a few steps. "How did you get here?"

I was shocked enough by the fact that she hadn't bitten me. Now she was engaging me in conversation? "I was dropped off here," I said. "I haven't been Awake for very long."

She laughed. "That much is obvious. Today is your lucky day crossbreed. I only hunt pures. Sometimes humans when I need the sustenance, but angel blood tides me over longer, and to be honest it's much more tasty." She looked me over like she was trying to pick out a pastry. "I can't be sure if you'd be more like a chocolate bar or a clove of garlic." She smiled, showing off her fangs. She started to step around me to get out the door.

"Wait a second," I said. That was one of the oddest and most stomach churning things I'd ever heard anyone say, and she scared the heck out of me, but since I had limited sources of information I had to see what I could get from her. "I was told your kind would rip me apart without a second thought."

"Most of my kind would," she replied. She gave me that condescending look again that made me feel like I was less than dirt. "You're no good to feed on, and you're no sport at all; maybe in a few months when you've had time to adjust. My name is Rebecca. Perhaps we'll meet again."

I started to form another question, but before I could get it out she was through the door without a sound. I sat there motionless for a few minutes, trying to absorb all of the signals being rushed to my brain. Vampires were real!

It was a hopeless endeavor, and I stumbled over to the corner just in time to dry heave. Once that was over, I started shivering, the adrenaline withdrawing and leaving me to pick up the pieces. I sat down on the floor. I didn’t care anymore if someone found me here, as long as they were human.

I reached into my pocket to retrieve the phone, and then groaned in dismay. What I pulled out of my pocket didn't resemble a cellphone at all. It was just a mess of wires, circuit boards, and glass. As if things couldn't get any worse. I leaned back against the door so I wouldn't be surprised again, and went to sleep.

Chapter 4

I woke up to someone shoving at the door behind me. Still groggy, I was ready to let whatever it was come right in and eat my soul. I groaned and rolled out of the way, putting my hand on the floor so I could climb to my feet.

"What the hell?" The janitor looked down at me, hands on his hips and a sour expression on his face.

"Sorry," I said. "Drank a little too much yesterday, I must have passed out in here."

He glared at me, and then looked up at the rear of the room. I hadn't noticed, but one of the shelves had been knocked askew during the fight.

"You wait right here," he said. "I'm going to get the guard."

Like I was going to wait right here. I jumped to my feet and went out the door. It was still early, but the island was open for business. There were some tourists wandering around, but more importantly, the alarm was off and the doors were open. I looked across the area to where the janitor stood with a guard, pointing in my direction. They both started walking over.

I hoped they didn't see me, but I couldn't imagine how they wouldn't. There weren't enough other people here for me to blend in, and I wasn't exactly inconspicuous at six feet tall, brown hair, leather blazer and blue jeans. I was going to have to either accept getting caught, or somehow fight my way out.

I tensed as they approached, still undecided on which play I should make. They were still talking to each other, the janitor motioning like he was describing the damage to the wall. They looked over at me.

"Good morning sir," the guard said. Then they walked right by.

I turned around to watch them. I saw them go into the closet. A second later the guard came out, shouting into his radio and running for the door. I knew I should leave, but I had to know for sure. I walked back over and peeked into the closet. The janitor was standing by the damaged shelves, staring at what I assumed was the chipped wall.

"Looks like someone made a mess," I said to him.

"You can say that again," the janitor replied. "Some drunk asshole busted the door and barfed in that corner over there. Not to mention he knocked over all this crap."

I was curious about something. "Hey buddy," I said. "I just got my hair dyed to cover up some grey. What color does it look like to you?"

He gave me a funny look. "Black," he said. That was just what I wanted to hear.

"Thanks man," I said. I took one last look back at the closet and beat a path out of there. I was on the ferry within the hour.

I sat all the way in the back, not that it mattered. It was early enough that the majority of people were still headed towards Liberty Island, not away from it. We were pretty well spread out, and I appreciated the opportunity to relax a little bit. Even if I couldn't consciously exert my will on anything, at least my subconscious was helping me out. It seemed like as good a time as any to practice the Rain exercise.

I fixed my focus on a small spot below the seat in front of me, and tried to force the rain. The first few efforts were as effective as my attempts in the bathroom stall. Retrain my mind. That was what Dante had said. There is no spoon.

For some reason, my mind wandered back to my encounter with the vampire. Rebecca, she had said her name was. It was strange to think of a blood-sucking creature of the Devil and put a human name to it. It was stranger still to be thinking about the way she looked in that outfit. According to Dante, this was the face of my enemy. Well, one of them anyway. After all, she lived to feast on my kind. In fact, she couldn't live without feasting on my kind. Or angels, I remembered. She said she preferred to drink the blood of angels. That was really creepy.

I looked out at the water breaking off the back of the ferry. I had smashed the phone, and in doing so lost any hope of getting more information about what exactly I should be doing. Would Dante even be able to find me now? Maybe he couldn't, but I had a feeling Mr. Ross could. I had a feeling Mr. Ross could find anyone, anywhere.

Watching the waves became hypnotic, and brought me to a state of mind that I hadn't experienced before. Here I was, sitting on a ferry in the middle of New York Harbor, I had one set of clothes and four grand in my pocket, the bloodlines of angels and demons, both sides itching to put an end to me, and for the first time I felt like I was actually coming to life, or maybe waking up.

I turned my head back to my spot under the chair and willed it to rain. Not with a huge push, an overexertion. I willed it gently, fitting the force of my will to the strength of my desire. I felt the tug in my mind. I felt it grab on like a hook and pull towards me. Water vapor condensed and began to fall in droplets onto my boots. I had told the universe to make it rain, and it had acquiesced. It wouldn't save me from hungry vampires, but it was a start.

By the time I had arrived at Battery Park, I was able to reproduce the raindrops on at least half of my attempts. It was becoming easier to recognize the mental focus that signaled success, and more familiar to feel the pull on my energy. Dante had been right about limits. The few successes I had made had left me feeling a bit drowsy, and super hungry.

As I walked, I kept a watchful eye on all of the people around me. I had no idea who might be playing for one of the other teams, and who thought I was just another average guy going about his business. It would have helped if I could have at least known if they would react, or if they would run off to tell their superiors that they had spotted a diuscrucis wandering around.

Catching the delectable scent of coffee, I diverted myself across the street and into "Gino's Diner" in search of something to stop the rumbling in my stomach and the growing fatigue caused by bending the universe. The place was pretty empty, but I paid close attention to its inhabitants as I entered. Nobody even bothered to look up at me. I love New York!

Susan led me to a table and handed me a menu. I waved it away. "Two western omelets, a cup of coffee, and a slice of cherry pie if you have it. Whatever pie you do have if not cherry."

She looked down to check the size of my stomach. "You one of those competitive eaters?" she asked me.

"Nah, just hungry," I said. "I feel like I haven't eaten in months."

She didn't say anything, heading off to put in the order. She returned a minute later with the coffee. As she put it down, she looked me in the eyes.

"Can I help you?" I asked.

She looked away. "You just have really pretty eyes," she said. "You need anything else?"

"I'm fine, thanks," I said.

It was weird, but she hadn't been lying, and I didn't get that feeling from her that I'd gotten from Rebecca. I figured I needed to be cautious but not paranoid, or I'd destroy myself without any intervention necessary from the powers that be.

"Actually," I said. "Do you have a newspaper?"

The date was November 19th. I had been in Purgatory for nearly five months. How many had I spent curled into a ball 'suffering my Regrets', as Dante had called it? I thought about my mother for the first time since I had been killed. I wondered if there were any rules about going to see her. Would she recognize me? Did she know our history? Which side of this war would she be on? I knew the answer to that one; she was a devout Catholic. That raised a more important question. If she could see me, would she see me as her son, or as an enemy? Maybe I was being a coward, but I wasn't willing to risk knowing the answer to that. Better to let dead sons stay dead.

Susan dropped off my two omelets and a peach cobbler. I guess it was the closest thing they had to pie. I downed the eggs in record time, polished off the cobbler, and still felt hungry for more. I decided to satiate myself further somewhere else, in order not to arouse any kind of suspicion. I left forty dollars on the table and walked out while Susan was occupied with another table.

As soon as I got outside, I found the nearest street corner and hailed a cab. I had lost Dante's 'Guide to Being Awake', so I needed to start educating myself.

"5th Avenue Apple Store" I said, climbing in.

I would pick up an iPad so I could get online, then take it to a cheap hotel room somewhere and hole up until I heard from Dante. Combing the dark corners of the Internet was one of my specialties after all, and if there was any mortal information about the workings of the Divine I was sure I would be able to find it there. It might not amount to much compared to what I had lost on the smartphone, but it was better than what I had right now.

"Sure thing pal," he said.

He had a strong accent. Polish maybe? He was definitely European, with a black peach fuzz and a chiseled face. I could see him look me over through the rear-view mirror. I thought I saw his eye twinge as he looked at me, but didn't make much of it.

I sat back on the rear bench seat and took a deep breath. I was still hungry, but the headache had gone away, and I was more eager to start learning than I was to continue eating. I was going to start by finding out everything I could about vampires, werewolves, and any other demonic creatures I could branch off to from there. My feeling was that the evil team was bound to be more dangerous, and there was also something in my gut telling me that they were winning this war.

A war I could never win. Everything had happened so fast, I hadn't stopped to think about that simple truth. I was joining the fight for the continued existence of mankind. My goal was to keep things from becoming too evil, or too good. I couldn't snuff one out, or the other would triumph. Would I be spending the rest of eternity like this, or was there a limit to my Awakened life force? The thought was depressing.

When I looked out the window and saw that the cabbie had pulled us off into an abandoned housing project, I realized that I had broken rule number four. I had lost track of my surroundings, and now I was in a place where nobody would hear me scream. I looked up at the driver, who was turning his head back and forth, looking for something himself.

I saw him at the same time the driver did, a lone man in a fine pinstriped suit, sitting on the steps of one of the condemned buildings. When he saw the cab he stood and reached behind his back, retrieving a sword that even from the distance looked similar to the one the dark angel in Purgatory had almost halved me with.

"I don't suppose I can talk you out of dropping me here?" I asked.

"Go to Hell," he said. He stopped the cab at the sidewalk in front of the building. The door opened of its own accord. I wasn't about to get out.

"No sense in making this difficult," the man in the suit said. "My associate has already marked you as a demon."

A demon? Dante had said that they would be able to recognize me. That only seemed to be half-true, as both Rebecca and now this guy had seen me only as their direct opposite. I wasn't going to escape, so I slid over and got out of the cab. As soon as I was clear the door slammed shut, and the driver took off.

"That's better," the man said. He looked at me curiously. "You took quite a risk being out during the day. You must have some pretty important information to deliver."

Information? He had taken a look at me and judged me to be no more than a messenger. I did my best to play the part.

"Like I would tell you, asshole," I said.

His eyes narrowed. "Mind your tongue, worm. You can tell me what you know, or I can spit you like a pig."

The eyes. They were brown, simple, human. He wasn't an angel. This had to be what Dante had referred to as the Touched. I decided to change tactics.

"Do you take me for some kind of minor spawn," I shouted. "You have no idea who you are dealing with. The light means nothing to me."

I forced my will, just enough to make my eyes flash red like they do in horror movies. I didn't know if it would work or not, but the tug told me I had been successful. The Touched man's eyes widened and he held the sword up to defend himself. I could tell he felt overmatched, now all I could do was hope he wouldn't call for backup.

He did the other thing I had hoped he wouldn't. Fight or flight, he decided to fight. He came at me in a rush, committing himself and all his power to a single downward cut. Even as unskilled as I was, the desire to not be cut in half was more than enough for my brain to move my body out of the way. I danced to the side as the blade slammed into the cement, throwing up chips of concrete.

He surprised me by adjusting and getting back into a defensive posture. The trouble was, I hadn't even considered attacking him back. His maneuver left him a good four feet away, out of sword reach. It was my turn for fight or flight. I turned and ran.

I had six steps on him before he overcame his surprise and started giving chase. I dashed up the stairs and into the abandoned building, catapulting up the inner stairwell at a speed that I didn't know I had. I could hear his shoes landing on the steps below me, getting fainter and fainter as I rose at a pace he couldn't match. I was winning the footrace, but where was I going to go? The building was a bad decision, because I was going to run out of up, and I couldn't get back down without passing Samurai Joe. All too soon, I pushed open the door at the top of steps and found myself out on the roof, fifteen stories up.

"God dammit," I cried, seeing that there was nowhere to hide. If the building had ever had an air conditioner it had already been removed. The rest of the rooftop was solid cement. I spun in a three sixty. There was another roof about twenty feet away. No way I could jump that. I was considering other options when he emerged from the stairwell in a smoothly executed roll and came to his feet. He had been expecting an ambush. The moment he spotted me, he charged again.

All I could think as I raced towards the edge of the rooftop was that everybody falls the first time. Except here, there was no rubber street to bounce me back up. Here, if I fell... I wasn't actually sure if I would die, but I didn't want to find out. I willed myself to make it across, and I almost shouted with joy in midair as I felt my mind get tugged and my body soar across the gap. I watched the empty street pass under me, and then get replaced by cement. I hit the ground, hard.

I wasn't prepared for the momentum I had built up. I slammed onto the roof and fell, my body bouncing and rolling along the hard ground. The pain was immediate and intense, registering from a dozen places. My shoulder was broken. It had to be. So was my ankle. I may have gotten away from my attacker, but I had completely messed myself up in the process.

Once I had stopped moving, I started trying to assess the damage. I lifted my head and looked down at my splayed out carcass, saw a lot of tears in my clothes and blood trickling out through them. If I could bleed, I could die. I needed to figure out some way to stand up, to start moving, to get myself to a hospital. I needed to do it fast, because there was nothing preventing the man in the suit from going back down the steps, and coming up here.

I heard a faint rustle, and then the familiar sound of Italian leather shoes walking towards me. So the Touched had some mojo. I wish I had known that before my leap of faith. I looked at him. He was smiling broadly, confident of his triumph.

"Care to talk now, worm?" he asked me.

I coughed up some blood in response.

"Guess not," he said. He stood right over me and raised his sword two handed, prepared to bury it like Excalibur. I caught a hint of motion behind his right shoulder.

"Wait," I said, raising my hand. He hesitated for just a fraction of a second. It was the longest fraction of the rest of his short life.

She was on him in a blink, yanking the sword from his hands and throwing it across the rooftop, then spinning him around so he could see her face before she buried her teeth in his neck. His body writhed as he was overcome by the assault, a soft groan of pain, or was it pleasure, escaping his lips. As she fed, she looked up at me and winked.

I didn't know if I should be relieved, or more afraid. What was Rebecca doing here? I had a feeling she was following me, but why? There seemed to be more to this than I understood. Watching her drain her victim, my body wracked with pain, I could feel my stomach churning again.

She was finished within a couple of minutes. As the last of the life force left the poor saps body, she dropped the empty shell to the ground and carefully wiped the excess blood from around her mouth with a handkerchief. She was wearing a lot more clothes now; a form hugging long sleeve hooded sweater that dropped over a pair of black tights, knee high boots and long black gloves. She looked just as good, but much better protected from the sun. She pulled her hood up over her head before she spoke to me.

"Looks like your luck is holding out, worm," she said. I guess she had heard the way the Touched had referred to me.

"You're following me," I said. "Why?"

I was too beat up to be afraid. If she had wanted to take me, she would have done it already. I suppose I should have been disgusted by what I had just seen, and in the back of my mind I was, but she had just saved my life. I could be really forgiving for that.

She waved her arm towards the sun, shining down on the rooftop with a ferocity that was sure to be unpleasant for her, despite the attire.

"Can we talk somewhere else?" she asked.

"I'm a little indisposed at the moment," I replied.

"Come off it diuscrucis," she said. "You did a great albatross impersonation, but you should be fine by now." She came over and grabbed my arm, pulling me to my feet with a harsh jerk.

I had expected it to hurt. I had expected to see stars. It twinged a little where my ribs had broken, but otherwise I was feeling a lot better. I rotated my ankle, tested my shoulder.

"I'm healed," I said.

"Seriously, I know you said you were new in town, but didn't they teach you anything?" She let go of my arm and walked over to where the Touched's sword had landed. She scooped it up in a gloved hand and tossed it to me. "I think you might need this," she said.

I caught the sword, and then held it out so I could take a look at it. It looked like a Japanese katana, with a narrow, slightly curved blade and a guard less hilt. There were symbols running along the entire length of the steel, symbols I couldn't read.

"Do you know what these mean?" I asked.

I was so busy looking at the sword I hadn't noticed that Rebecca was standing by the doorway to the stairs, waiting impatiently to get out of the sun.

"Sorry," I said, and ran over.

We went down a couple of flights, then busted through a locked door into a dilapidated apartment that had been stripped bare of almost everything except a bed, an empty fridge, and a couch. Rebecca hopped up onto the couch and perched on the back, her legs bent and spread like a roosting gargoyle. The stillness of her form in that position was more than a little intimidating. Fighting back the reflex to run again, I sat on the far arm of the couch facing her. She started to speak, and I raised my hand to quiet her. Fear was one thing, but she was right - nobody had taught me anything. I wasn't about to let her dominate the conversation. She was following me. She wanted something from me. I wasn't about to provide it without some info in return.

"Question for a question," I said.

She furrowed her brow. "I don't understand?"

"I ask you a question, you answer it," I said. "Then you can ask me a question, and I'll answer it. Deal?"

She sat motionless for long enough that I started to think she really had turned to stone. "Very well," she said. "You have a deal. What is your question?"

"Why are you following me?"

She was thoughtful before answering. "I'm curious about you."

"Curious?"

She raised her hand and chided me. "You got your answer. It's my turn." She had a point. I started to feel like I may have suckered myself with this deal. "Where did you come from?"

If she was going to be obtuse, I could play that game too. "I grew up in New Jersey, but I was born in London, England."

There was a hint of frustration in her eyes, but she smiled. The game was afoot. "Why are you curious about me?" I asked.

"I've been nesting in the Statue for over fifty years. No one has ever gotten onto the island at night without me knowing it. Yet, there you were. Out of nowhere." There was something about my appearance that was bothering her. I could tell by the way she spoke about it. "How did you get onto the island?"

I spent a few minutes thinking about the best way to answer the question. While I thought, I looked into her eyes; so blue, almost gentle looking. Captivating. I suddenly had the bright idea to try to look into her the way she had tried to look into me. I felt the tug in my mind, and then my body slammed into the wall behind the couch. She had hit me before I had even seen her move.

"Don't do that again," she said. The blow had knocked the wind out of me. I stumbled to my feet and sat down in my spot on the couch.

"I'm sorry," I said. "Your eyes are beautiful."

It caught her off guard. So much so that she slipped from her crouching position and had to scramble to rebalance herself. I could have pressed the issue, made some other smart remark. I answered her question instead.

"I was dropped off there, on the torch, by a man named Ross." I watched her closely to see how she reacted to the name drop. Her eyebrows raised just a smidge, but it was enough. "What can you tell me about him?"

She got super uncomfortable. "I'm not supposed to speak about those things," she said. "I'm not allowed to say that name."

I pressed her. "We had a deal."

I didn't think vampires could sweat, but she did. She was fighting the war between her fear and our deal.

"Please," she begged. "Ask me something else."

I wanted to push her further, but I didn't have the heart. Maybe if I had been a little more evil, but then I wouldn't have been here.

"What did you just learn about me?" It was a similar question, but it would let her off the hook.

The relief was palpable. "I know where you came from. I know why you are here. There was another like you. Please don't ask me, because I'm not allowed to speak of her either. I had a feeling after we met that was your purpose. I wanted to know for sure. Do YOU know why you are here?"

It was my turn to be caught off guard. I started laughing. Rebecca looked at me with a confused expression.

"I have the thousand mile overview," I said. "But as you saw, I'm completely unprepared for this gig. How do you intend to use this information?"

She pursed her lips, then ran her tongue along her teeth. I waited while she fought with herself over how much to say.

"You may not understand how our kind is organized," she said, "but you will if you live long enough to learn. I'm from the demonic species nosferatu. In relation to humans, we are supreme. In the hierarchy of demons however; we are somewhere near the bottom."

I understood enough of that to understand that I was screwed. She was calling herself a weakling, and she could kick my ass three ways to Sunday before I even saw it coming.

"Have you considered what will happen to the nosferatu, should this world fall to the chaos of evil?" she asked.

I hadn't. I could put two and two together though. "No more food?"

She nodded. "That's part of the problem, but one that I hope will be overcome. There are members of the community who have been working on a synthetic."

I don't know why, but she tilted her head and sat very still. After ten seconds or so, she started talking again.

"No," she continued. "I believe there is a worse fate that would await us. Once the humans and the seraphim are gone it will be survival of the fittest, with no other prey to distract the stronger species. My fear is that nosferatu will be hunted to extinction. Unfortunately, I'm unique in that perspective. It's the reason I nest alone." She looked sad. "To answer your question more succinctly, I want to know all of the players so I can make sure I end up on the right side. Do you have another question?"

It didn't sound very loyal to me, but I had a feeling there was more to it than that. Plus, she had just given me a free question. I had so many, but I wanted to get right to the point. "Do you want to be on my side?"

She laughed at me. I don't know why, but the derision was painful. I guess I was looking for someone to validate my existence, because I felt so outmatched and uninformed. I could feel the heat rise into my face, turning me beet red. She stopped laughing, and even looked apologetic.

"I will not be against you," she said. "Which is more than I can say for a great deal of the Divine you will come across. I will not be with you either. Not yet. By the way, do you have a name, or shall I continue calling you 'worm'?"

"Landon," I said, feeling sheepish. It was time to change the subject, to get something with a little more direct substance. "What can you tell me about this sword?"

I held it up with an awkward grip so she could see the symbols running along it.

She didn't need to see them. "It's a standard issue weapon. There is nothing special about the materials, but the sigils are written in the original language of the seraph, and then blessed by a pure angel. You can't kill a demon without such an instrument."

I guess the wooden stake thing was a myth. Now I wished I had watched more Samurai movies when I was a kid. Or at least played a sport, or done something that would have improved my hand eye coordination. Learning to use a sword was a tall order, especially since I had nobody to teach me. I was waiting for her to ask her next question, when she tilted her head again and floated to her feet.

"We're out of time, Landon," she told me. "There is a demon coming, a messenger. He is no threat to you even in your pitiful state. It's likely they intercepted the messages being sent between the Touched agents that brought you here, realized you weren't one of theirs, and sent him to investigate." She walked over to the window, smashed it with her boot, and leaned out. "I can't be seen with you, it would mean my end. Good luck, worm." She jumped, and by the time I got to the window, she was gone.

If I was going to be receiving visitors, I figured I ought to play it cool. I lay down on the couch with one arm behind my head, leaving the sword in easy reach on the floor next to me. Within thirty seconds the demon appeared, a small mass of leathery flesh and wings that swooped into the room through the window Rebecca had exited. His beady black eyes caught sight of me, and he landed on the opposite arm of the couch, his taloned feet digging into the padding. He was about three feet tall with a stooped humanoid body that rippled with muscle, and a small elongated snout that shimmered with teeth.

"Master saysss findsss you, and findssss you I did," he said. His head bobbed back and forth as he spoke. "Master sayssss 'why is there another demon in my domain'." His voice rose to an almost comical pitch when he mimicked his master. His snout quivered as he took in the scents. "I wonderssss... smellsss like vampiresssss." He looked as if he was deep in thought. "Now I knowsssss why you are here." He snickered and winked at me.

"Yeah," I said.

I wanted to get him out of here. Even though he was diminutive in stature, he was still the first demon-looking demon I had ever seen. He could be ten percent the killer Rebecca was, and I didn't think I would stand much of a chance. Like the man lying dead on the roof, he seemed to recognize me as a demon, or at least a Turned.

"You scared her off," I told him.

He thought his perceived interruption of our tryst was the funniest thing he had ever heard. His laughter was like scraping Styrofoam.

"I thinkssss you wouldn't have liked the afterssss," he said. "I tellsss the Master why you come, but you needssss to go backssss to your domain. I thinksss you should thanks me for savingsss..." His head turned, and his eyes bugged out. He was looking right at the sword.

"Oh crap," I said, reaching down and grabbing the hilt. I pushed myself up to my knees and swung it awkwardly at the demon. He bounced skyward, avoiding the blow.

"Me doesss notsss understand. Smellsss like demonsss, but has angel'sss stick." He was talking to himself, halfway between the window and me. I got off the couch and approached him, readying the sword for another swing. It was just like hitting a piñata, right?

"Ooh, mastersss rewardsss me well to knowsss about you." He dodged my next two swipes, then retreated out the window. I leaned my head out to watch him fly away. I really needed to learn how to fight.

Chapter 5

I beat a hasty retreat from the abandoned building. As I walked, I tried to find an inconspicuous way to hold a four-foot samurai sword. Without some different clothes, it would be impossible. I considered ditching it, but Rebecca thought I would need it, and I tended to agree. Maybe I could even get lucky and hit something with it. With nowhere obvious to hide it, I held it downward and leaned on it as if it were a cane. I focused my will on it, hoping my desire to disguise the weapon as a harmless walking tool would be successful.

Rounding the corner and making my way back into the throng, the lack of surprised faces, looks of fear, or other signs that I was a psychopath wandering the streets with a sword comforted me. Yeah, this was New York after all, but I figured there had to be some kind of limit, if not from the regular denizens, than from any tourists that I happened by.

I decided it would be a bad idea to try a cab again, so I made my way across town on foot, finding a growing appreciation for my new endurance. I made it to the Apple store in good time, stopping outside the glass cube to take stock of my surroundings before I went anywhere with limited exits.

People going about their daily life engulfed me, and it occurred to me how ignorant we all were. Sure, we had this shallow understanding of the Divine, putting a face to it through religion, telling stories about angels, demons, and the supernatural. We had books like the Bible, or even Dante's classic poetry that attempted to describe that which our living minds seemed to be able to feel, but never truly see. We understood only through the periphery, out of the corners of our eyes, like when we said a prayer before going to sleep at night, or when we just knew there was a monster in the closet or under the bed. To find out it was all real... it was all true... maybe ignorance WAS bliss?

I descended the stairs into the even more tightly packed masses of humanity, threading my way over to a blue-shirt standing near the tablets.

"Can I help you sir?" he asked as I approached. I pointed at one of the iPads.

"I just need an iPad, color doesn't matter."

The clerk laughed. "A man who knows what he wants, I like it. I'll be right back."

He tucked his own device under his arm and headed off to the storeroom to fill my order. I stole glances wherever and whenever I could, keeping a constant vigil for anything out of the ordinary. If I had been spotted as a demon in an almost abandoned diner, the odds of being outed as non-mortal here seemed exponentially higher.

My sight landed on a young girl who was chatting with her friend. She was maybe fourteen, with short brown hair and a plain face. She was wearing a white down jacket that hung open to reveal a white dress with white leggings underneath, silver moon boots and a knit hat that resembled a panda bear. She was pointing at a phone and gesturing like she wanted it real bad. I wondered if her friend knew she was an angel?

I hadn't known how I would know before I knew. There was no halo or anything like that. In fact there was no visual sign of anything out of the ordinary. It was more like a radar signal getting sent from my eyes and bouncing back saying 'Divine dead ahead, captain!'.

The sight of her made me anxious. She was just a kid! I turned my back, but it seemed once contact had been made, line of sight was no longer required. I could FEEL where she was, what she was doing. I realized that facing the other direction wouldn't help me any more than it helped her. She didn't have to see my face. She would get a feel from my soul. That was it, I knew. I was reading her soul, just as she would be able to read mine. The only other question was would she see an angel, a demon, or a diuscrucis?

I spotted the clerk coming back over with the iPad in his hands and I decided to meet him halfway. I reached into my pocket and pulled out the wad of cash, counted out seven hundred dollars and shoved it into his hand. He gave me a look of suspicious disbelief when I told him to keep the change, but he didn't argue, and he didn't fail to give up the merchandise. I was almost at the steps back to street level when I felt her.

"*Fellow, why do you not announce yourself?*" The voice came from all around me, and ran right through me.

I felt immediate warmth and my whole body began to tingle. I flipped my head back to get a look at her. Her body was still manipulating the phone, her mouth still chatting idly with her friend, but her eyes were on me. Rich, golden eyes that held a soft glow like a single flickering candle. It was mesmerizing. I had to force myself to look away.

I didn't know what to say in response, or how to project it silently the way she had. I did the only thing I could think of, turning back and winking at her before beginning my ascent. It probably wasn't the smartest thing to do. Heck, it probably wasn't a smart thing to do at all, but at least I would know how she was seeing me by the way she gave chase.

There was a rush of cool air, and then she was beside me on the steps, walking alongside me. I peeked back to see her friend looking around, trying to figure out where her companion had run off. She headed towards the laptops.

I didn't say anything, and neither did she. We climbed the rest of the steps together in silence, and then I led her off towards Central Park. Even without speaking there seemed to be an understanding between us that transcended normal human communication. When she had spoken to me, she had made a direct line soul-to-soul phone call, and the more I probed the feeling, the more I recognized that she hadn't hung up. We were silent because there was no need for words. Not yet anyway.

I found a lightly populated part of the Park and settled us down under a bare oak tree, resting the sword against the trunk and placing my package next to it. She sank to the ground as if on a pillow of air, perching cross-legged on the grass. I sat opposite her in the same position.

"*I do not recognize you fellow,*" she said.

Her lips didn't move, but her eyes were incredibly expressive. There was curiosity there, friendliness, and sadness. I knew she had taken me for an angel. I was pretty sure the sword had at least a little bit to do with that.

"My name is Josette," she said aloud. Her voice was small and raspy. "Are you recent to our family?"

I didn't know what that meant, but I assumed she meant becoming an angel. If I said yes, I would need an excuse for being here without her knowledge. It felt safer to tell a bold lie.

"Not to the family," I said. "I've only recently returned from a pilgrimage in the Holy Land. My name is Paul." That had to be a safe angel name.

Her eyes widened, and she threw her arms around me. "Paul. Welcome! You have been to the Holy Land?" she asked. "There has been little news since Astrel was killed."

I breathed a sigh of relief. I could lie to an angel and get away with it. "We're losing," I said.

I hadn't thought about it before, but as I said it I knew that it was true. Whatever mojo came from my crossbred lineage, it was clear in that regard. The balance was tipping heavily towards evil.

"The dark gains reach every day," she agreed. "Since we lost John Paul, it has been difficult to keep an even footing. Even here, Reyzl has grown powerful beyond my ability to contain him."

Reyzl. It had to be the name of the demon that the messenger had flown off to squeal to. "I had a run-in with one of his messengers," I told her. "He escaped and intended to tell Reyzl about my presence here."

Her eyes held deep concern for my welfare. I was starting to feel bad for lying to her, and also beginning to wonder if I could do what Dante had asked. It wasn't much of an issue right now, but who knew what the future would hold. Would I be expected to kill this beautiful creature one day? If so, would I be able to do it?

"I do not mean to intrude, but what business brings you here?" she asked.

She reached forward and took my hands in her own. They were small, but so soft and warm. Her whole being exuded peacefulness. I felt like I could tell her anything. I could tell her the truth, and it would be okay.

"To be honest, I'm not sure," I said. "I've only arrived very recently, but I had a run-in with a vampire, and lost my phone."

My mind was beginning to feel as if it were mired in a pit of mud. Clarity was escaping me, replaced with this overwhelming need to tell her everything. All I could think about was the warmth of her hands, the softness of her voice, her shining golden eyes, and the connection between our souls.

"I used to be a computer hacker," I said. "I went to prison for credit card fraud."

It had been so easy to manipulate people. So easy to get the information I needed to get into databases, e-mail accounts, you name it. So tempting. It was a victimless crime, I had told myself. The credit companies had plenty of cash. They wouldn't miss a little bit here and there. I had gotten too bold, a friend had blabbed, and it all crumbled around me.

Two years in a low security facility, another year of probation, and banned from owning or using a computer for three more. I still didn't always feel remorseful for what I had done. I was more sorry I hadn't been more careful, and had gotten caught.

It had all started pouring out in a torrent, and I was drowning in the truth. I could tell by the way her golden eyes flared that she knew what I was. I could feel the warmth of her hands turn cold, feel the peacefulness turn to violence and anger. It was only then that I realized she had used her power on me, so subtly that I hadn't even known it. She must have suspected me from the beginning. I yanked my hands away and got to my feet. She rose, her sword appearing in her hand in a flow of swirling mist.

"Diuscrucis," she cried. "You seek to deceive me!"

I started to reach toward my sword, but decided against it. "Wait," I said, holding up my hands. "I don't want to fight you."

She had taken an aggressive posture, with her sword cocked and ready for the battle that I refused to start.

"I just want to talk," I said.

Seeing that I wasn't going to fight her, she let the sword dissipate back to wherever it had come from.

"*Speak*," she said, her voice powerful in my mind. She was showing me her strength, sending me a warning.

"The balance is tipping," I said. "The end of days are coming if it isn't restored. We should be fighting together, not fighting each other. You know, allies?"

Her golden eyes narrowed. "Allies? Seraphim Law states that I should strike you down where you stand."

This wasn't going well. "What benefit would that be to you? You're losing Josette. I think you need all the help you can get."

I started inching away, closer to the sword. We both knew it wouldn't harm her, but at least I could make some kind of feeble attempt to defend myself if she decided to follow her laws. She stood motionless, undecided.

"I can help you defeat Reyzl," I said, trying to convince her of my value, even though I knew I had none. "If he's grown beyond your control, it's only a matter of time before he comes for you."

Our souls were still connected, and I felt her demeanor shift again. It seemed even angels had a sense of self-preservation.

"Very well," she said. Her eyes were cautious. "There can be no alliance, our Laws forbid it, but I will not destroy you today. In return, you will seek out Reyzl and either destroy him or weaken him so that I can finish your work. I do not care if you live or die completing this task, but know that I will seek you out again one week hence to see you to your end if you do not hold up this bargain. I will not come alone."

I didn't need to ask what the other option was. I had only bought myself a week, but a week was better than nothing.

"We have a deal," I said.

The feeling of heaviness in my gut was immediate. It was if a chain had been clamped down onto my soul, an awareness of the power of the contract I had just verbally signed. Josette hung up the connection, and the sudden sense of loss nearly overwhelmed me. I had been tapped into some of her power through the bond, and had drunk from it like an alcoholic. I could feel a small piece of it within me.

“What is that?” I asked.

"So I can find you again," she said. "Do not think to double-cross me, Landon. You will speed us closer to these end of days if you do." She had said my real name. What else did she know? Why didn't Dante put 'never touch an angel' into his short list of rules?

"I'll see you in a week then," I said, trying to sound a lot more confident than I felt.

With the connection broken, Josette nodded, then turned back in the direction of the Apple store, most likely to return to her friend. I was bending down to grab my iPad when a massive wave of heat crashed into my senses. My mind didn't have time to process it, but my body reacted.

I dove to the left and rolled to my feet, somehow managing to escape the path of a black, jagged edged blade that buried itself deep in the trunk of the tree we had been sitting under. There was a growl of frustration, then the sound of pounding feet running toward me. I looked up just in time to see the demon make his leap at me, his long sinewy frame carrying him an impossible distance at an impossible speed. I moved faster than I could think, shifting my weight and dropping to the ground just underneath its outstretched limbs, escaping being raked by eight-inch claws.

The beast landed and turned, small black eyes looking right at me, a snout full of razor teeth bared. It had a humanoid frame with grotesquely long limbs that ended in those sharp claws, leathery skin, and bones which protruded at awkward angles from various points on its body.

"Reyzl sends his greetings, newcomer." Its voice was gravel, and its words dripped with disgust.

I got to my feet and reached over to where the sword was leaning against the tree. My instinct seemed to be doing a good job of keeping me from being destroyed. As long as I didn't think too much maybe I could get lucky.

I had forgotten about Josette. The demon didn't seem to have noticed her either until we both saw a white blur darting in at us. It raised its paw just in time to deflect her first strike, causing a shower of energy to reverberate against the air around us. She pressed the attack, her sword a blur of stabs and swipes that was matched by the demon's blocks.

Their attention diverted, I took a more defensive position behind the tree and peered out from the side to watch the battle mature. I looked around and saw the area was deserted of people, as if something in their minds had told them to stay away from this part of the park. Was this how the Divine war raged on with humans none the wiser?

The waves of energy from the clashing enemies filled my senses. Josette was a whirlwind, her down jacket flowing out behind her as she spun and twirled, the sword an extension of her arm that danced and pricked at the demon. It roared in pain and anger, lashing back but finding only empty air. She continued to press the attack, forcing the demon to retreat backward.

A few more quick jabs and she was past those massive claws, her body slipping inside the demon's reach, her sword being pushed up into its chest. She yanked the weapon free and leapt backwards a good ten feet, leaving the demon on its knees, doubled over as it's body expelled a viscous mess of thick black blood.

I stepped out from behind the tree and started moving towards them, wanting to get a closer look. Josette turned to glance at me for just an instant, then resumed her vigil of the demon's demise.

Something happened then. Something Josette clearly hadn't expected. The demon's wound closed over, and with a razor sharp grin it pounced forward, slamming her with its hand and sending her torn body thirty feet through the air. She bounced against the ground a couple of times and came to rest against a distant tree. The demon turned to face me.

"What are you staring at seraph?" it asked. "Have you never seen a Great Were before?"

Never seen, never heard. I only had a second to wonder if by were it meant werewolf, when it leapt at me for a second time with a speed that I couldn't match. There was an explosion of pain that blossomed throughout my entire body when the sharp claws dug into my flesh and rended it from the bone, ripping into me like no more than a piece of meat. My vision blurred and doubled as the Were lifted me to eye level.

"Pathetic," he said, throwing me across the lawn.

Another round of agony greeted me as I hit the dirt and slid face down. I lifted my head just enough to see the demon. I watched it transform in the space of one step to the next, shrinking in mass and gaining hair, skin, and clothing. It became a man with long raven hair in skinny jeans and a worn t-shirt, like a werewolf for sure. He exchanged his claws for a jagged black dagger that he pulled from the back of his pants. He was walking towards Josette, who I could see was fighting to rise to her feet.

As he approached her, he reached under his shirt and produced a necklace with a red stone. He held it up to her, showing it off. "Have you ever seen one of these seraph?" he asked. "It removes the poison from your blows. I don't suppose you have one of your own, to do the same to mine? No? A pity."

I could feel the pain in my body subsiding as it worked to heal itself. I looked down and watched in fascination as new skin grew to replace the shredded mess above it, new muscle regenerating beneath. Fascination gave way to anger. I'd had enough of this punching bag routine.

The Were was almost on top of Josette, his posture oozing confidence and superiority. He was oblivious to me, and to my change in health. I couldn't take him out head on, but there was more than one way to skin a big ugly monster cat.

I got to my feet and looked for my sword, finding it a good fifty feet away. No good. I looked back at Josette and saw her weapon was on the ground next to her. Not great, but better. I took off towards the demon at a run, willing myself to be faster than I had ever been. I was rewarded with a burst of speed that left the ground no more than a blur beneath my feet. In less than a second, I was leaping towards the Were, reaching out to will the angel's sword to my hand.

It all happened in the space of an instant. I should have been destroyed, because the sword didn't come at my call. I found myself airborne, rapidly approaching the back of the demon, and weaponless. There was no time for an alternate approach. I had sunk my efforts into this one desperate move. I could see the demon's head begin to turn towards me. I could see Josette's golden eyes flare as she sensed my approach.

The impossible happened then. The seraph took hold of her sword and threw it towards me with perfect precision, my hand caught it and my arm drew back. The Were completed his surprised turn, and I sank the weapon into his heart as I slammed into him. We both tumbled to the ground, the force of the impact throwing me away from him again. I rolled to my feet and watched him gather himself, rise to his feet, and pull out the sword a second time. He looked at me with a shocked yet satisfied smirk on his face, until he saw that I had his necklace in my hand.

"Who are you?" he growled as he went back to his knees. "You should be dead."

I got up and approached him. Whatever magic was in the angel's sword, it was doing its thing. The demon was disintegrating from the point of the wound outward. There was a smell of frankincense, and smoke began wafting from the hole in his chest. Where a moment ago there had been a gloating beast in man's clothing, there was now just a dying lamb.

"Pathetic," I said, turning my back on him, pocketing the necklace, and walking over to Josette. I didn't watch the demon finish his final death. I didn't need to.

Or maybe I did. I wanted to check on Josette, to see if I could help her. After all, despite her disdain for me, she had just helped me. Whether or not it was to aid her as well, that didn't matter right now.

I had almost reached her when I felt a coldness at my back. Before I could turn around, a black cloud encircled me, whipping around like a mini-tornado, spinning tightly in a maelstrom of energy. It smelled like sulfur, and in it I felt power. It overwhelmed me, and I fell to my knees unable to breathe. I opened my mouth to gulp in air and the black cloud forced its way inside. I choked on it, my mouth filling with the acrid taste of the stuff pouring into me. As it completed its forced entry, I leaned over and vomited.

"Diuscrucis." Josette stumbled over to stand next to me. Her clothing was hanging in shreds, and her bloody face had a deep gash across the cheek.

"What just happened?" I asked. My stomach told me it was getting ready for round two. At the same time, I felt different in a way that permeated much more deeply into my being.

"The demon tried to take your soul," she said, her breathing labored. "He didn’t know what you were, and has trapped himself. He can give you power, but not without cost."

I wanted to ask her what she meant, but her golden eyes dimmed and she fell back to the ground. Not gone, but seriously injured. I couldn't leave her here. I bent down and lifted her in my arms, surprised by how light she felt. I put her over my shoulder, and then retrieved her sword and my iPad. After a small bout of indecision, I grabbed one of the demon's daggers too. There was a part of me that was sure I was making a mistake by taking Josette with me. I ignored it and made my way out of the park, willing the world around me to see a man carrying a baby on one shoulder, a folded up stroller over the other. It was a little too domesticated for me, but it would have to do.

Chapter 6

The punk-slash-emo guy running the front desk at the Belmont Hotel didn't even give me a second look when I lumbered in holding two large duffels. I was getting more accomplished with altering my outward appearance, and had dressed down for the occasion. My hair was long and greased, I had three days growth on my chin, and my clothes were worn and dirty. On the walk over, I had also discovered how to repair my inward appearance, fixing the rips and tears in my clothing so I could see and sense myself with some semblance of physical dignity.

"How much for your best room?" I asked, approaching the desk.

Punkmo shrugged. "It's twenty-five per night, all the rooms are priced the same." He reached under the desk and produced a padlock with a key. "Just find an empty room and lock the inside. When you leave, lock the outside."

The modern world sure made being limited to cash a frustrating proposition, especially when trying to find a place to hunker down for a while. Most upscale hotels required holding a credit card on file, which meant bypassing anything a person might want to spend any amount of time in, and instead making do with something that someone could spend time in if they had to. I had to. I turned my back on him so I could count through my stash without him being able to see how much I was carrying. I handed him three hundreds.

"Good for twelve days, right?" I asked.

He furrowed his brow and looked at me. The math was a little too much for him. "Sure man."

He snatched the cash a little too eagerly and pushed the lock forward. I put down the sword to pick up the lock and stuck it into my jacket pocket.

The Belmont. The name made me laugh out loud. The place was about half of a step above the condemned projects where I had watched Rebecca drain a good guy. I was sure it had been a fine place a hundred years ago or so, but it seemed like it hadn't been renovated since, well, ever. The interior was old, drab, and dirty, with peeling faded wallpaper and either missing or busted furniture. The rooms weren't much better, decorated with ripped sofas, old mattresses stained yellow from all kinds of bodily fluids, ancient fridges of which maybe fifty percent were functional, and a varying but always present amount of mold. Every room had roaches. Only two of the rooms I passed had people. The place was more for quickies with hookers and drug exchanges than living in, but I didn't have too many housing options.

I settled into 7G, a room on the top floor in the southeast corner. It gave me a decent view of the streets below through small grimy windows that would hide my own visage from anyone looking in, and a mattress that had a better than fifty percent chance of not housing an STD.

I gently slid Josette off of my shoulder, placing her on top of the bed. She was still unconscious, but her breathing was steady. Her wounds continued to ooze blood, refusing to close over, and the gash on her cheek had some nasty black spider veins reaching out across her face. I had no way to judge the effect of a demonic wound on an angel, but going by what had happened to the Were when I stabbed him, she was suffering from damage that wouldn't heal on its own. When I put my hand to her forehead, I could feel that she was burning up, maybe literally.

"Josette," I whispered.

She didn't respond. That raised the question - how do you heal an angel who was wounded in a fight against a demon? Answer - holy water. Maybe it wouldn't work, but it seemed like the best option and I didn't have much to lose. I wasn't going to let her die, not like this. She had spared my life, and I was going to return the favor. Maybe she'd even be grateful. If she wouldn't let me out of our deal, the act of kindness might be enough to convince her to at least offer some measure of help in completing the task without having my soul destroyed. Not an alliance, but maybe information.

"I'll be back," I said to her prone form as I ducked out of the room, put the padlock on the door, and headed out to find a church.

The sun had vanished behind dark, heavy clouds, and it started pouring while I walked. I needed a vessel for the holy water, so I dropped in on a liquor store and bought the cheapest bottle of wine they had, which I dumped on the pavement outside. I got into a small argument with a passing vagrant about wasting heat, and then resumed my hunt for a house of God. When I pushed through the twin doors of Our Blessed Lady Mary RC Church I was soaked to the bone, the water dripping off of me creating a slippery mess on the cold marble floors.

"That rain's right devilish."

I had been hoping to avoid running into a priest, but he was already mopping the floor when I walked in. He was an older man with short reddish-white hair, a fair complexion, and a kind smile. He wore the wisdom of age on his face and the creases around his eyes. Irish, if his accent was any indication.

"It sure is Father," I said, not making eye contact. "I'm sorry for the mess."

There was an expanding pool of rainwater gathering at my feet. He looked down at it and chuckled.

"Don't ye worry yerself child," he said. "Ye look like ye could stand bein' outta the rain."

I had disguised the empty wine bottle as an umbrella. He looked at it, then looked at me, then looked back at the umbrella.

"Might've helped ye a wee bit if ye had used that thing," he said, a strange look on his face. "Then again, an empty wine bottle ain't much help in a rainstorm, is it?"

He could see right through my glamour. Were all priests Touched? There was no point being ambiguous.

"I need your help," I told him. "Holy water."

"What does someone the likes of you need with holy water?" he asked. "More like to poison you than heal you crossbreed."

I had to know. "How did you know? Are you Touched?"

He laughed then, an old, wise, hardened laugh. "I didn't just come out of the potato field laddie," he said. "And I don't need the blessin' of a pure angel to make my eyes work proper. Ye may fool some of 'em, but I'm a humble servant of the Lord, and I know me own. Besides laddie, what darn fool carries an umbrella, but isn't using it to keep himself dry?"

Dante was proving to be a little unreliable when it came to who could and couldn't sense my true nature. Here was a self-proclaimed plain ordinary mortal, and he saw right through the glamour, past the blood and lineage, straight through to the truth.

"It's not for me Father," I said. "I have a friend who was injured by a demon, a Great Were." I didn't know how much he knew, but I figured if he were familiar with angels and crossbreeds, he would know demons too.

The priest rubbed his hand along his chin. "A Great Were eh? That's a nasty beastie to get into a scuffle with. How many seraph were involved?"

"Just one," I told him. "You know about weres?"

"Aye, of course I do laddie," he said. "Always a treat to watch a werewolf movie, and laugh at how weak they portray those foul creatures ta be. A Great Were, now that's a hundred times nastier than your nastiest werewolf. Mean and smart, they are. Did you say one?"

I shrugged. "Well, one and a half I guess."

"Aye, a half," he said, his tone harsh. "The seraph was injured, and ye're here for holy water to heal it?"

"Is it so hard to believe father, that I would try to heal an injured angel?"

My voice was rising, and he put his finger to his lips to shush me, motioning with his eyes to the few scattered people kneeling behind the church pews.

"Actually boy-o, it is," he said.

He grabbed my arm and pulled me off to the left, through a door and into his private office. He closed the door behind us, then let go of my arm and reinstated his direct glare. "Look here laddie, it takes at least three seraph to take down a Great Were on a good day. Ye're saying ye helped one seraph do it, and not only did ye win, but the angel survived?"

I hadn't known what we were fighting, and now I realized that was probably a good thing. If I had thought about how powerful it really was I probably would never have made my kamikaze move against it.

"That's right," I said. "Although, I can't be too sure about the part where she survives unless you decide to help me. I would think you would be eager to see one of yours back to good health."

"It's not a matter of what I want boy-o, it's a matter of trust. Do ye even understand what ye are? Ye don't have a side but fer yerself. Ye can cross back and forth on a whim. Ye can employ all manner of trickery and deceit to meet yer aims, and only the most astute of the Divine will even have an idea they're bein' double-crossed. Ye can cause all sorts of mayhem, discord, destruction for no other reason than because it suits ye, all while smellin' like roses and gettin' all the blessins' of Heaven."

His face was turning beet red, and his anger was growing beyond reason. Without thinking, my hand shot forward and wrapped around his neck. His eyes widened in surprise, and he stopped talking.

"Listen to me Father," I said then, my own anger stewing. "My aim is only to heal the angel. She saved my life, and I intend to return the favor. Don't make it at the expense of your own."

I let go of him then, drawing back in a shock of my own at the violent outburst. I had never been like this before. A wave of guilt washed over me.

"I'm sorry Father," I said, lowering my head. "I'm pretty new at this gig, but the one thing I know is that I'm not your enemy." I turned to leave.

"Wait," he said, rubbing his neck with his hand. I looked back at him, feeling doubly foolish for almost choking him to death. "Why do ye think the seraph survived?"

I hadn't expected the question, especially after what I had just done. "Excuse me, father?"

"A Great Were can kill an angel with one blow," he said. "Why didn't he?"

I didn't know enough about weres of any kind to know the injury was uncommon. I told him about the fight. I gave him all the details. When I was done, he took the wine bottle and left the room. When he returned, he blessed it himself. He didn't speak again until he handed it back.

"He was gloatin'," he told me then. "He let the angel run him through so he could do it, and made straight sure not to kill her with his first cut. He didn't know what ye were. He didn't expect ye to recover. Ye got lucky killin' him." He walked over and held out the bottle. "I don't like ye laddie, and I don't like yer kind or whom ya be workin' fer, but if helping ye helps a seraph, I'll do it this once. Darker days are comin' when a demon lets himself be stabbed, and Lord knows we need all the help we can get. Now go, and don't ever show yer face in my church again."

Chapter 7

Josette was still unconscious when I returned to my room at the Belmont. The bedding under her was red with her blood, still running out through the wounds on her face and chest. I didn't know how much blood an angel could lose, but judging by the coolness of her forehead and the shallowness of her breathing, it couldn't be much more.

As I stripped off her shredded clothes so I could treat the wounds, I had to remind myself that even though she appeared to be in a child's body, Josette was not a child. Even so, it felt so wrong to be undressing her this way, but I had no other choice. Her flesh underneath was pale grey, and the same lines of black veins that I had seen on her face were also spreading from the cuts on her body.

The linens were already ruined, so I used the sword to cut out strips of cloth, dipped them in the holy water, and placed them over the gashes. The affected areas hissed and steamed as I did so, causing Josette to let out a soft moan and the familiar scent of frankincense to fill the room. Almost immediately some of the color began returning to her skin, and I could see the black lines receding from under the edges of the cloths. I went over to one of the empty hotel rooms to get a sheet to lay over her, then grabbed the box for the iPad and sat down at the side of the bed.

I slid the device out of the box and turned it on, then kept my eyes on Josette while it booted up. The cut on her face was super deep, and had taken two cloths dipped in the holy water before it had stopped bleeding. I wasn't sure if it would ever heal completely. Otherwise, she was looking a lot better already, her face flushing as the blood returned to it.

Wi-Fi was pretty ubiquitous in Manhattan, and I didn't have any trouble finding an open connection I could leech off of. I started with the basics. I typed 'how to kill a demon' into Google and hit enter. It didn’t surprise me that all of the results were filled with media fed, superstition based thoughts on destroying evil beings, without a hint of truth to any of them. Holy water, wooden stakes, garlic, blah, blah, blah. I hadn't thought I would come up with anything there. I needed better sources.

At the height of my illicit dealings in credit card numbers, I had belonged to a message board called 'SamChan', so named after Samuel L. Jackson, motherf**cker. If anyone knew anything real about the war between angels and demons, I could probably get a line to them there. The channel was filled with all types of hackers, crackers, conspiracy theorists, and other assorted societal chafe that would buy and sell any data they could get their hands on. I wasn't too sure I should try to use my old account, but getting access wasn't as simple as entering an e-mail address and password. If anyone noticed they'd probably think my credentials had been compromised, which would result in a good laugh for all involved. That was assuming my account was still active. It was.

I was eyeball deep in a thread posted by a guy who was looking to sell or trade a video he claimed was of a real vampire when Josette woke up. I wasn't looking at her at the time, but I could just feel her presence change. It reminded me of a butterfly bursting from a cocoon - one moment there was this ugly emptiness, the next a fullness of spirit and beauty that caught me off guard. When I turned my head to check on her, her golden eyes were open and alight with an internal sparkle, and she was smiling at me.

"Thank you," she said. I hadn't known what to expect, but gratefulness was a good start.

"I should be thanking you," I told her. "If you hadn't tossed me your sword, we'd both be dead right now. How do you feel?"

She took a moment, shifting in the bed a little bit. "The poison has been purged. The wounds are healing, but I still feel a little weak. Why did you save me?"

"Like I said, you saved my life."

She shook her head. "I saved my life, diuscrucis. You may have benefitted from that, but it was not an act of benevolence."

No, I suppose it wasn't. Had I really thought she was doing me a favor?

"Whether it was intentional or not, you did. Look, whatever you think of me, I'm not a bad guy. I'm just trying to make sure that mankind is allowed to govern its own future. Letting you die would have been a negative on the scorecard, and besides I don't think you deserved to go like that."

Her eyes turned thoughtful, the sparkle shifting inwards.

"You must understand, Landon," she said. "This isn't about whether or not you are a nice guy. This war has been going on for thousands of years, and now after spending centuries gaining ground we are beginning to lose, and badly. There was another who came here making the same claims as you. She earned our trust and respect even as our enemy. She fought against us, and she fought with us, but we believed she would never seek to deceive. We were wrong."

"You mean Charis?" I asked.

The name kept coming up. Was she the reason my inception here felt like such a disaster?

Josette nodded. "She used our trust to trick us, then gave us up to Reyzl. She knew the outcome would shift the tide of the war, would go against everything she claimed to be fighting for. She said we didn't understand the bigger picture. We lost a dozen angels and countless mortal allies in the nights that followed."

As she spoke, tears began rolling down her face. She winced in pain as one slid under the bandage and touched the wound there.

"What happened to her?" I asked. Dante had said she was gone. He hadn't bothered to mention that she was a traitor. Why not?

"She disappeared," Josette said. "We have heard that Reyzl double-crossed her, and stabbed her in the back while she was enjoying the fruits of her betrayal."

I was being racially profiled, except as far as I knew there were only two of us. It figured this Charis had to go and ruin it for me.

"We may have similar bloodlines, but we're not the same person," I said.

"It is unjust I agree," she replied, "but you must consider our perspective. Unlike demons, it is very difficult to replace a lost seraph. Heaven is a wondrous place, and few enough are willing to give it up to fight a war that has no definitive end. To lose so many in such a short time was an event that none of us can bear to see repeated. So we do not trust those who are not of our kind, and we forbid alliances because the gain of an ally cannot compare to the potential devastation that could follow."

She put her hand on the sheet to hold it in place and sat up. When she dropped the sheet, she was wearing a white leather raincoat over a plain white blouse. A large diamond cross hung from her neck. She reached up with small, delicate fingers and pulled the bandage from her face. As I had feared, the wound had left a thin black scar along her snow-white cheek. She ran her finger over it, her eyes dimming in sadness.

"I should have known it was a trick," she said. "I have to go. You have my gratitude for saving my life."

She moved to head for the door, but without thinking, I stopped her. I put my hand to her face, surprised by how small and soft it was in my hand. She didn't resist my touch.

"We both should have died today," I said, looking her in the eyes. "We got lucky. I won't keep getting lucky forever."

Her lips were trembling as she waited to hear me out, and to see what I intended to do with her. Her wounds might have been healed but I could tell she was still weak.

"If you can't or won't be my ally because of your laws, I can accept that," I said. "But please don't leave without giving me the one thing that can help us both stop this war from being won by the demons."

"Wh...What is that?" she asked. Her voice was soft, scared.

I didn't know if it would work, but I had to try. I focused my will on my hand the way I had focused on the air to make it rain. I tried to feel the damage to her face, to pick out every molecule of imperfection that was marring the otherwise flawless surface. I ordered the damaged cells to disconnect, pulling the remaining demonic filth into my own body, and removing it from hers. She shook as I did it, her eyes glowing brightly in surprise.

"Knowledge," I said, pulling my hand away.

With the dirty tissue cleaned she healed without obstruction, and in moments the scar was gone.

She stared at me then for what seemed like ages. Her eyes were locked on mine, and she was still as a statue. Her breathing evened out and her face flushed red. I could feel the tension between us while I waited for her to decide what to do.

"Very well diuscrucis," she said. "You saved my life, so I will try to help you. Know that we are not allies, and never shall be. I am simply repaying my debt, which is well within the tenets of our laws."

She smiled then, a big, wild smile that told me she had made up her mind, that she was throwing her caution to the wind, and that she still didn't trust that I wouldn't crush her with it. It was the kind of smile that comes from the strength of willful disobedience and the underlying fear of the consequences.

"Now, grab your sword and follow me to the roof," she said. "I shall call this class Demon Fighting One-o-one."

I went over to where my sword was resting by the window. I noticed it was dark outside. "Josette," I said, remembering Dante's rules.

She bounced over to where I was standing. Her whole demeanor had changed, and she looked a lot more like a fourteen-year-old girl to me. She peered out the window.

"What is it?" she asked.

"It's dark out," I told her.

"Yes," she agreed. "The sun has in fact set." She stepped back and looked at me, her brow furrowing inward. "You destroyed a Great Were, and you are fearful of the dark?"

I could feel the heat of my flush rise up through my cheeks. "Dan..."

"Do not," she cried out, interrupting me. When she was sure I was done talking, she lowered her voice. "Do not say his name." Serious Josette had returned.

"Why not?" I asked her.

"He is the only person ever to volunteer to leave Heaven for the Middle realm," she explained. "His name is to be forgotten and unwrought for all time, as is that of his servant. That is our law. It is the only law that both Heaven and Hell have ever agreed to. If you absolutely must make reference, he is known as the Outcast."

Wow, that was a lot of hate. I could understand why Heaven may have been cross with him, but what had he done in Hell to cause such disdain?

"How old are you anyway?" I asked Josette, trying to turn the conversation away from things she wasn't allowed to mention.

The seriousness faded, and the adolescent exuberance sprang back into view. "That is your non-sequitor, Landon?"

The way she giggled changed her from plain to almost pretty. My face flushed again. Everything I said was making me feel dumber and dumber.

"I know you aren't fourteen." It was all I could think of to say.

She laughed louder. "You are concerned about this physical manifestation?"

"I'm more concerned about having undressed your physical manifestation," I said. "I'm sorry for that, by the way. I didn't have any other choice."

It was her turn to be embarrassed. It seemed she hadn't realized the efforts I had to go to in order to heal her.

"Do not fear Landon, I have been a member of the Order of Seraph for over seven hundred years. I did die as a young lady, and have chosen to remain that way because I find it comfortable and familiar. The same goes for the underlying personality, although I do find it increasingly difficult at times to hold onto the joy and innocence of youth."

Seven hundred years? So much she had seen and done; centuries of war and fighting and killing. Did she regret her decision to become an angel? I didn't ask, for fear of spoiling her mood before she had taught me anything.

"Well then grandma," I said. "Let's hit the roof."

The rain had stopped some time earlier, but the roof was still slick from the downpour, and the dropping temperature was already turning it into a sheet of black ice. My footing was unsteady, and I was shivering from the cold as we walked out towards the center of the rooftop. Josette didn't seem to notice it at all, her knee high white boots moving her effortlessly across the surface despite their four-inch heels. When we reached the center, she materialized her own sword and held it up in front of me. She noticed how much I was shaking and cocked her head to the side.

"What are you doing?" she asked.

"It's freezing out here," I told her, crossing my arms and rubbing my shoulders. I guess I could have changed my shirt into a parka, but I had never seen any movies where the samurai wore heavy, puffy coats.

Josette laughed at me again. "Landon, you are Awake. Divine. You do not need to feel cold unless you choose to."

"You make it sound so simple," I said through chattering teeth.

"Your human mind believes you should be cold, and so you are," she said. "Don't listen to it. That is lesson number one."

Don't listen to it. Right. Don't listen to it. I tried to distract myself from the cold. I imagined being on a beach in Florida, feeling the warm sun on my face. For a moment, I almost thought I might not feel cold. No, I did. It was freezing.

"Can't do it," I said.

The sword vanished again, and Josette walked over to where I was standing. She took my face in her hands and pulled me down so I was at eye level with her.

"You are standing on a rooftop, with your face three inches from an angel," she said. "In the last six hours you killed a powerful demon, and swallowed its soul. You also healed from wounds that would kill any mortal. Now, tell me why you are cold."

While she spoke, her golden eyes sparkled as though they contained all of time and space. She was using logic on me, and I was falling for it. I took a deep breath and nodded. She broke her gaze and stepped back.

"Well?" she asked.

I bent down and put my hand on the icy cement. I could feel the sensation of the freezing surface in my fingers, but it didn't make me feel cold. Cold was a mortal sensation, and I was no longer mortal.

"I'm ready now," I said, standing back up.

Josette smiled and her sword reappeared in her hand.

"How do you do that?" I asked her. It would make moving around a lot easier to not have to manage the four-foot long blade.

"Sorry Landon," she replied. "You have your own abilities, but that isn't one of them."

"Why not?" I asked.

She rolled her eyes, making me feel dumb again.

"Excuse me miss seven-hundred-year-old-seraph, " I said, "but I've never been to the School for the Divine."

She giggled again and dismissed her weapon.

"Okay, I guess I need to give you at least a tiny bit of background before I start beating your brains in," she said, kneeling down and motioning for me to join her. "Most people talk about Heaven and Hell as if one is up there in the sky, and the other is somewhere near the core of the Earth."

She scratched out a rough globe with a cloud above it for Heaven and a flame below it for Hell. I tried to be nonchalant about the fact that she was using her fingernail to make the scratches in the blacktop. She put her hands outside of the pictogram and squished them inward, so that the three scratches all sat on top of each other. How did she do that?

"In reality, we're all on the same level, but we're not in the same... dimension, I guess," she said.

She was squinting as she tried to come up with a good description. It was adorable.

"It's not really a dimension," she continued. "It's more like a state of being. Our souls can travel these states, but our shells can't. Of course, its not like we can just go anywhere we want. There are rules, and that assures that Heaven is never overrun with sinners or demons."

"And that the moderates are given a chance to prove where they belong?" I asked.

She nodded. "That came much later, but yes. Purgatory is the buffer, the demilitarized zone if you will, but you must already know about that. It's the reason you and I can never be friends."

I don't know why, but when she said that, it hurt. More than it probably should have, I hardly knew her after all.

"You think the Rapture is a good thing?" I asked.

Josette looked up at me, and her eyes flashed in anger, but she covered it up quickly.

"Let us not get into that, Landon," she replied. "We will never agree. That is the nature of who we are, and it is best that we accept it and move on."

She had a point.

"So," she continued, "if Heaven is right here, but in another state of existence, than it is no large matter for a being such as myself who resides in both states to move from one to the other, at least in part. In essence, I can reach through from one dimension to another, where I know I left my blade."

"Neat trick," I said. "But why can't I do it?"

"Two reasons. The first is that you aren't powerful enough, not yet anyway. It took me five hundred years to learn how to reach through the dimensions. The second is because you don't exist outside of this state," she said.

"You're saying that Purgatory is part of Earth?" I asked.

"Yes. And no." She stood up and swept the scratches away with her boot.

"How can that be?" I asked, rising to join her. "How could millions of souls be living here, and nobody has ever seen them, heard them, or knows that they exist?"

"We are Divine, Landon. We decide what mankind knows about us. We control them, in order to protect them."

Like in the park. The area where we had fought the Great Were had been deserted even though it was the middle of the day.

"Why do the demons control them?" I asked. It couldn't be to protect.

"To use," she said. "As you have already discovered, information is the highest form of power and control. People are easily corrupted by promises of knowledge that will give them an edge." The same way I had been. "Now put up your sword."

She spent the next hour instructing me on how to hold a sword without cutting myself on it. She said I was a natural, but she said it sarcastically. By the end of the hour I could almost hold the thing steady, but it felt heavy and awkward in my hand, and I had no confidence at all in my ability to use it. We took a break, and I grilled her a bit more.

“What happens when a Divine dies?” I asked. We were sitting cross-legged in the center of the rooftop facing one another, our blades resting across our legs.

She shook her head. “Dying as a Divine is like dying as a mortal. Nobody knows for sure what happens, only that we do not return to where we came from. As my Lord has no knowledge of this end, I have always thought that we cease to be.”

"I’ve been making the same assumption,” I said. “Demons can be killed by..." I hung the end of the sentence, waiting for her to finish it.

"A seraph's blade, as you have already learned. Many demons also have a weakness to one of the four elements of life. Which one depends on the type of demon. Lesser demons like werewolves are susceptible to earth. All Divines can be killed by decapitation. Including you."

Decapitation was not a pretty thought, but I had assumed as much. Once the head and body were separate, which one was going to grow back? I could picture myself like a hydra, duplicating every time something lopped off my noggin.

“Silver, wooden stakes?” I asked.

“It can slow earth sensitives down, but won’t kill,” she replied. “You’ve seen too many movies.”

"Part of it is true,” I said in my defense. “What about holy water?"

"Ineffective as a weapon,” she said, “but it can heal any demon inflicted wound. It helps us to counter our greatest weakness."

"Which is?" I asked.

She started to speak, then thought about it. "Our greatest known weakness I mean. We need blessed blades to kill a demon. All demons can harm us with little more than a fingernail. As long as they break the skin, their touch is poison."

"So what about mine?" I asked.

"Yours?" She was confused.

"My touch," I said.

I had posed the question innocently enough, but her face flushed again. She stammered out her reply. "I uh... I really don't know. I haven't... I haven't been in that situation before. With a diuscrucis."

"You sure are demure for a seven hundred year old," I said, trying to keep the conversation light. I found her reaction intriguing, but I wasn't about to press her on it.

Josette conjured her sword and pointed it at me. "Shut up and fight," she said between laughs.

She spent another hour teaching me basic technique, which meant how to swing the blade without losing control of it, and how to get myself back into position to either attack again or defend myself. The night was wearing on, and the weather was getting colder, so I appreciated the fact that I was now immune to temperature changes. The earlier rain returned as snow, falling in heavy flakes that clung to everything they landed on, including us.

"Seven hundred years would mean you lived in the middle ages," I said.

We were taking another break, and I had decided I wanted to know more about my teacher than I did about anything else. I was getting a little tired of demons and fighting, and it was the closest I could get to so-called normalcy.

Josette nodded. "I was born in Paris. My father was a wealthy merchant who had close ties to the Catholic Church. I grew up in a privileged household, and wanted for nothing. It was not always an easy life, for my parents were very religious, and punished my brother and I severely for our sins. Still, it was a good life, especially for those times. You may think I was perfect because I am a seraph today, but I was not always the most well-behaved child."

"Good enough for Heaven," I said. "Besides, what child can ever avoid making a little mischief?"

"Yes," she agreed. "Good enough. My brother and I, we used to go down into the city dressed in rags and act as beggars. We would take the money we collected and spend it on sweets."

Her eyes were alight with the pleasure of the memory, and I could feel the warmth of her radiating and soaking into my skin. She was silent for a moment while she reminisced, and then her mood changed.

"When our parents found out, they took us out to the barn and tied us to a post, then used a riding crop to give us ten lashes each," she said. "Afterwards, they made us work to earn back all of the money we had stolen from the real poor, and go out to the city and distribute it to them."

I couldn't believe it. "Are you kidding me? Your parents sound like monsters."

She shook her head. "Do not misunderstand me, Landon. My parents could be as loving as they could be cruel, and the pain they inflicted served to teach us to be humble and always remember that service to God means caring for the less fortunate. I hated my parents for a time, because of what they had done, but after I had passed to Heaven, I realized what they had taught me."

"I'm sure there were less violent ways to teach a child a lesson like that," I said. I was getting angry thinking about it. Not that there was anything to do. I reminded myself that it had happened hundreds of years ago.

"You are right about that," she said. "My parents spent many years in Purgatory due to their treatment of their children. In the end they proved that their souls were essentially good, and they were misguided in their faith. They sought me out as soon as they entered Heaven, and begged for my forgiveness."

That cooled my anger a little bit at least. "What about your brother? It sounds like you two were very close."

Her eyes dimmed so completely it was as if they had gone black. So much emotion in those eyes, it was an amazing thing to experience, though it seemed to amplify her feelings to the point that I was experiencing them too. It felt as though a ten thousand pound weight had been dropped on my chest as a mixture of sadness and fury.

"He did not respond as well to my parent's teachings," she said. "He became violent, angry, and withdrawn. He left home when he was sixteen."

Tears started rolling down her cheeks, and I could tell there was more she wanted to say, but wasn't able to. The answer was written in her eyes, in plain sight to me. He had killed her.

"Josette, it's okay," I said, reaching out and putting my hand on her shoulder. "You don't need to talk about it. I can see it in your eyes. I'm so sorry."

Those same eyes widened when I said that, and she turned her head away from me. She hadn't known I could read her like that. Not knowing any better, I had just assumed it was normal.

"Thank you," she said. "No matter how many years have passed, the memory is a torment on my soul."

I didn't think, just acted. I reached out and put my arms around her, wrapping her small body up into a hug. She stiffened at first, not expecting the maneuver, then melted into my arms.

"Seven hundred years, Landon," she said between open sobs. "Yet it still feels as if it happened yesterday. I joined the Order of Seraph because I didn't want such a fate to befall anyone else. I have saved hundreds of innocents from the hands of evil men and demons alike. Men that you will help one day."

She just had to say it. Maybe it was just due to her emotional state, but I didn't appreciate it. I pushed her out of the embrace, holding her at arms length.

"I'm all for saving innocents, Josette," I told her.

She smiled at me, wiping away my anger in an instant. "I believe that about you. And right now you can do so without consequence. What happens when the balance is restored, should good begin to triumph? That is the nature of who you are, and the mission that you have accepted. For all the good you may feel and show today, there is a devilish side to you, or you would not be what you are."

I didn't know what to say. She wasn't completely right, but she wasn't completely wrong. I had choked the Priest when he had resisted giving me what I wanted. I knew there was a part of me that could harm innocents if it meant achieving my goals. Admitting that to myself was difficult. It scared the crap out of me. Admitting it to her, impossible.

"I guess I'll worry about that if and when it happens," I said, letting go of her. "I have a lot of good work to do in the meantime." I went over and picked up my sword from where it was resting against the rooftop ledge. "Show me something else."

She didn't respond right away. She looked at me with a mix of fear and admiration. Her eyes told me as much. When she realized she was telegraphing her feelings to me, she turned away again.

"Please stop," she said.

"I'm not doing it on purpose," I told her. "Your eyes shift and change with your emotions. For whatever reason, I understand what the variations mean."

"You shouldn't be able to do that," she said.

"What does it mean?" I asked.

"I don't know," she replied. "It's making me uncomfortable though. I feel naked in a way that goes so far beyond the physical."

I understood her perspective, but the selfish part of me didn't want to give up watching her eyes. The experience of seeing her emotions that way was intoxicating.

"I'll try not to look at your eyes," I told her. "But you should know they are incredibly beautiful and expressive."

She reddened again, but didn't say anything. Her sword materialized in her hand. "Shall we?"

"Thank you for doing this Josette," I said.

"I am repaying a debt to you fellow," she replied. "Nothing more."

I didn't want to look at her eyes, but I couldn't help stealing a glance. There was a hint of brighter golden flecks at the edges, which danced along the outer rim. She was lying. It was enough for me that I knew. I didn't call her on it.

"Still," I said. "Thank you."

The moment was broken by a scream that sent a shiver down the base of my spine. I felt an almost primal pull towards the source of the sound, a few blocks away from the rooftop where we stood. Josette had sensed it too, and she turned and began running along the rooftop in the direction of the noise. I stood frozen in place, watching her as she bounded onto the ledge of the building and leapt, landing on the opposite rooftop twenty feet away and continuing forward with ease. I knew what I had to do if I was to follow.

"Crap," I said, breaking into a run, following in the angel's footsteps.

I made the leap without a problem, and this time I decided to do a controlled roll, pitching my shoulder forward and flipping over and back to my feet as I hit the snowy ground and lost my footing. I was rewarded with a half success, my arm blossomed with pain as my shoulder dislocated, but I managed to get back up and start running forward again without losing too much momentum. By the time I pulled myself through the jump across to the next rooftop, my arm was healed.

I caught up to Josette leaning over the ledge of the building, peering down into the alley. I pulled up beside her and looked down. Two girls stood shivering together in a corner, holding each other for support while six men blocked their escape out of the alley. The girls were wearing short, tight skirts and down jackets, obviously heading to or from a club or party of some kind.

"Watch me," Josette said, "And try to learn something."

With that, she was over the ledge, dropping forty feet to the ground and landing ever so gently behind the men and the two girls. She didn't have her sword, not yet.

“Leave them alone, or I’m calling the police,” she said to them, getting their attention. All six turned to face her at once.

"What the hell is this," I heard one of the men say to the others.

"Are you lost little girl," another one said, laughing.

"You know what?" the first one asked his friends. "Now there's more to go around." They all laughed then.

The first one stopped laughing when Josette's foot connected with his face. There was an audible crack as his jaw crushed under the force, and a few of his teeth went flying from his mouth. He dropped like the sack of crap he was.

The second attacker fell before he could overcome his shock, a heeled boot to the groin creating more misery than he could handle. He lay on the ground twitching, and Josette turned her attention to the other four.

Knives had been pulled, and one of the scumbags had a gun. There was a loud pop, and Josette's arm was shoved violently back as blood sprouted from her shoulder. Two more pops, two more sprays of blood, and she fell backwards onto the ground.

Panicked, I jumped up onto the ledge, prepared to drop myself into the fray. I shouldn't have bothered though. I had forgotten a simple lesson that I already knew. As the gunman approached Josette to pour a few more rounds into her, she shot up at him, slamming him in the face with her palm. His head bounced backwards, his neck broken, and he fell to the ground.

I had thought seeing her leap back into action like that would have sent the remaining attackers running. Then I noticed that the first guy was back on his feet. His fingers had grown out into claws, and a set of fangs hung out of his mouth. Vampires!

He leapt up and clung to the side of the building across from me, circling around Josette while she was distracted by the other attackers, who had also revealed their true nature. I saw Josette reach for her sword, preparing to engage them. She didn't know the first one was getting the drop on her. I took that as my cue.

I flexed my legs and focused as I sprang from the rooftop, pulling myself across the gap and down onto the sneaky son of a bitch. It was a formless maneuver, but it worked. My body slammed into his, and we both plummeted to the ground. Luckily for me, he broke my fall. He hissed and growled beneath me in a mixture of anger and pain. I rolled off, more so I could get my bearings than in response to his protests.

He was one ugly dude, his features lumpy and twisted, his fangs crooked in his mouth. He rolled onto his knees. I didn't need any kind of special perception to know what came next. I ducked under his leap, and then turned to track him. I saw Josette out of the corner of my eye, her sword a blur as she twirled through the rest of the demonic mass. The second vampire had regained his senses and rejoined the fray as well.

I would have loved nothing more than to watch her and learn, as she had requested. Instead, I was preparing for the vampire's next move while wishing I had some silver on me. Heck, I would have settled for a wooden stake or some garlic and taken my chances. I crouched into the position Josette had taught me, even though I had neglected to bring my sword along for this ride. If nothing else it would help me react faster to my opponent's offensive. I hoped.

He eyed me cautiously, unsure of my position in the fight. He jerked left and right a couple of times, trying to judge my reaction time. Then he smiled, and I felt each individual nail of one of his buddies' hands slice its way down my back. I fell forward onto the ground, wondering what had happened to Josette that one had gotten past her. I listened for the sound of battle, but heard nothing. This was bad.

The wound healed quickly enough, but I decided to play injured while I got a better feel for the situation. I focused on my hearing, taking in the sounds around me. The shuffling of feet as the vampires rounded up the two girls, who were crying in between prayers. A body being dragged along the ground, the leather of her boots making a distinct noise against the pavement. The two assholes that dropped me were beginning to lean in to check on my health. I needed a plan, and fast.

Not enough time. They were on me in an instant. The vamp that nailed me from behind rolled me over, grabbed my throat, and lifted me up as high as his arm could reach. I couldn't think of anything else to do, so I spit on him.

He didn't like that very much. He responded by rearing back and throwing me at the side of the building. My face slammed into the brick, my nose shattering from the force. I hit the ground and rolled over to face them, my vision fuzzy. I could make out the two girls being tied up together. I could see Josette's prone form leaned against the building opposite me. My attackers had lost interest in me, either taking me for dead or just not feeling at all threatened. I coughed out some blood and rose to my feet.

I looked over at Josette, and my anger flared. I didn't seem to be able to control much of my power yet, but it seemed to have a way of making itself known when I got pissed or beat up. I could feel it now in the base of my spine, strength I couldn't tap into in calmer moments. It called to me, begged for release, a siren's call to accept what was offered. All reason vanished as my human mind faded into the background, replaced with clear burning purpose.

I knew myself, but lost myself. My mind became an engine to a singular goal, my emotions devolving into chaos. I could feel every vein and muscle in my body. I could hear the roar of my blood vessels pumping energy into me. I heard my clothes tearing as my body shifted and changed, into what I didn't know and in the moment couldn't care. I let out a roar so loud it shook the entire alley, breaking the lower windows of the buildings around me. This got the vampires' attention. As one they turned to look at me. I could smell their fear. It was intoxicating.

I heaved myself forward with unexpected speed and ease, leaping the distance between the vampires and myself. I grabbed the nearest one in both hands and easily ripped his head from his torso, taking pleasure in the sound of the tearing, the end of his existence. I rounded on the others, lashing out and cutting another from head to toe with my razor sharp claws. Their confidence was shattered, their fear ruling their actions.

They moved as one to get away from me, breaking off down the alley at a run. I crouched and leaped, landing on another vampire's back and ripping his head from his shoulders. I pounced again and shredded the fourth. Moments later I had dismembered the remaining attackers and turned back to where the two girls were standing, silent and motionless, hoping I wouldn't notice them.

I bounded down the alley on all fours, stopping in front of them. I looked down on the pitiful creatures, my eyes drawn to the shadowy darkness at the center of their chests. I shifted back into my human form, dressed in a pair of black pants, a white shirt with a vest over it, and a long leather morning jacket. I had a small dagger in my hand, and one thought on my mind.

The girls trembled as I approached them, drew back in fear as I raised the dagger. I brought it close to the taller one. She had long raspberry blonde hair and smelled like lemon. I pressed it against her chest, then slid it down to begin cutting through her blouse.

My heart thudded in my chest, and my mind was overwhelmed by every sense of them - the sight, the smell, the anticipation of the taste and touch. A small voice in my mind told me to stop, but I couldn't. I wanted this so much. My mind was mired in an evil place, no longer completely my own. I had traded control for power, and the power filled me with a primal lust.

I don't know what would have happened if Josette hadn't come to. I don't know what I would have done to those girls if she hadn't stopped me. One moment I was preparing to do vile things to them, the next I was skewered on the end of her sword.

She ran it through my stomach and used it to pull me back, away from the girls. She produced a dagger to cut their bonds, held her hand up to them, and whispered something in a language I didn't understand. They gained this blank, confused expression and fled from the alley. Josette turned me on the sword and slammed me back up against the wall.

"Landon," she said.

I didn't know who Landon was... yes, I did. I was Landon. Wasn't I?

"I warned you about the cost of using the demon's power," she said.

Demon's power. I tried to make sense of the words. They sounded like little more than moans through mud. It was slow, but the pain helped me stay focused on it. The power. I could still feel the source of it, pulsing in my spine, reveling in the chaos and destruction, screaming out in agony at the blade that was piercing my flesh.

Chaos. Destruction. Demon. My mind started to put the puzzle pieces together. The process was slow and agonizing, but I wrested back control, forcing the power to subside. All the while, Josette held me against the wall, her golden eyes fearful and sad.

"Josette," I said. "It hurts."

She knew I was back. I don't know how. She pulled the sword from my gut and took a shaky step back. Her own energy was exhausted, and she was bleeding from her temple. The second the blade was free. I fell to the ground, first to vomit, and then to sob. What had I done? What had I almost done? What had I become? It was all too much for me to handle. My body quaked as I cried.

Josette knelt down next to me and put her hand on my shoulder. She didn't say anything. She just let me know she was there. I appreciated it. It was something sane and peaceful for me to grab onto, to identify myself with. The pain took some time to subside, the pace of my healing seemed to be affected by the source of the wound.

After what seemed like hours I was able to calm myself, to stop the flow of tears, to roll to a sitting position. When I looked at Josette, I saw that she had been crying too.

"Let's get out of here," I said to her.

She nodded, and we helped each other to our feet. I tried to ignore the disintegrating bodies of the vampires as we made our way out of the alley. Sure, they were demons. Sure they were evil, at least in the greater hierarchy of the Divine. It didn't make the act of killing any easier.

We carried each other back to my room at the Belmont. Once we got there, I doused another rag with holy water and put it over the wound on her head. She smiled at me as I did it, placing her hand over mine.

"The demon will try to entice you with promises of power," she told me. "Do not give in. What he seeks is to own you, or to destroy you so that he can be set free."

"I never meant for this to happen," I said. "How do I stop it?"

"I will teach you," she said. "But not tonight. Rest now, Landon. You have earned it."

She took my hand and kissed it, my body electrified by the warmth of her lips. I had intended to crash on the couch, but I didn't make it that far. One moment I was awake, the next I wasn't. When morning came, she was gone.

Chapter 8

The sun was doing its best to get through the crud covered windows when I woke the next morning. My eyes opened slowly, and I experienced a moment of euphoria at the fact that I was alive, until I remembered with certainty that I wasn't really. Until I recalled what had transpired a few hours earlier. If there had been anything in my stomach, I would have expelled it. Instead I dry heaved off the edge of the bed for a minute before gaining enough of my senses to get control of my repulsion.

I scanned the apartment looking for Josette, but I knew right away that she was gone. She had told me she would teach me, and she hadn't been lying, so I just assumed she would be back. I went into the bathroom to look at myself in the mirror. I was still wearing the clothes the demon had put me in. I couldn't get them off fast enough. I tossed them in a pile and jumped into the shower, enjoying the cleansing feeling of the water as it rained down onto me. It didn't matter that it was tinged orange with rust, or that it sputtered and choked its way out of the pipe. My requirements were simple, and it fulfilled them.

Afterwards, I spent a bit of time trying to will myself some new threads. Meeting only failure, I resigned myself to wearing the bloodstained mess of clothes I had discarded. Once I had put them on, I discovered that while I couldn't create cloth from thin air, I could rearrange the existing material. I put myself in a black collared shirt and blue jeans, with silver tipped black boots. I didn't know if the silver was real or just a facsimile. I hoped I didn't need to find out.

The next order of business was to get some food into my stomach. As I made my way out of the Belmont, it occurred to me that I probably didn't need to sleep or eat. Like the cold, perhaps these too were mortal desires that my brain was continuing to cling to. I didn't mind the hunger part too much. I liked to eat.

I made my way out of the beat down section of town, keeping myself alert to any other Divines that may have been wandering Manhattan. It was almost three in the afternoon, and the city was in full swing. If it would be hard for me to pick them out in a crowd, the same could be said for my own exposure. I found a crowded deli to duck into to grab a bite to eat - Pastrami on rye, a pickle, a knish and a large coffee. I located a small empty table and sat down, picked up my sandwich and took a huge bite. I hadn't realized how hungry I was.

"Ah, pastrami. Did you know that pastrami was invented by the Ottoman Empire during the middle ages? It was even before my time."

I knew that voice. I looked up from my meal to see Dante in the chair across from me, a huge smile on his narrow face. He was still wearing the same suit, but now there was a single red rose pinned to his breast.

"Buongiorno Signore," he said, his mood jovial. "How was your first day back among the living?"

I dropped my sandwich.

"I'm still here," I said.

I felt... what? Anger, relief, frustration, sadness, joy? I had been waiting for Dante. Now that he was here, I wasn't sure I wanted him to be. I had no doubt he wouldn't think too highly about the relationship I had struck up with Josette.

"Yes, you are," he replied. He reached over and picked up my pickle, taking a bite out of the end. "Impressive on its own, given the circumstances. Was my gift helpful?"

I laughed out loud, attracting the attention of the people around me. "You could say that," I said. "Although I think paper might have been a little more durable." I told him about my run-in with Rebecca. He seemed amused.

"Come Signore," he said. "Let's go somewhere we can talk about more serious things." He reached over and put his hand on my shoulder, and we were back at the Belmont.

"Isn't that trick reserved for Mr. Ross?" I asked him. The quick trip had left me feeling a little lightheaded. "How did you know where I was staying anyway?"

"Mr. Ross' talents with transportation dwarf my own. I do have some abilities though, within a limited area of effect. As to your second question, I didn't," he said. "I just asked your subconscious to take us to a familiar place." He looked around. "You haven't figured out what to do with the blank card yet, have you?"

I had forgotten about the card. I dug it out of my pocket and looked at it, twirling it over in my fingers. I had an idea of what he was getting it.

"I've been a little busy trying not to have my face ripped off," I responded. "In any case, I'm done stealing other people's money."

I looked up at Dante. I don't think he heard me. He was consumed with deconstructing the apartment with his eyes, apparently not impressed by the accommodations.

"You don't like how I decorated the place?" I asked.

He turned on me, a look in his eyes that caused me to take a few steps back. An instant later it was gone, and he was smiling again.

"Not what I would have chosen," he said. "Now, why don't you tell me about the seraph."

Josette wasn't there, but I should have known that Dante would be able to sense her. It was nothing that he could have physically seen, but I knew there was an indelible presence of her hanging in the air. I had felt it the moment I had woken up, and it still sat in the apartment like a spring breeze. Oh well, no denying it.

"Just someone I met yesterday," I said. "The only one who didn't try to rip my face off. Well, she wanted to, but we came to an understanding."

Dante sat himself on the dilapidated sofa. "You came to an understanding with an angel? What kind of understanding?"

"Simple really," I said. "I kill some demons, she doesn't kill me."

He laughed at this. "As if she could," he said. "No Signore, it is not as simple as you say. The seraph Calmed you."

I didn't like the way he said it, and I didn't like the way it sounded. "Calmed?"

"Angels don't have dirty tricks," he said. "They don't lie, at least not well, and certainly not well enough to fool you. They won't stab you in the back or aim to outright deceive you. Instead they have the power to Calm. To put you at ease, and make you start talking about whatever they want to know."

I thought back to when we had sat together in the park. "Right, yeah, she did that to me. We came to the understanding after that. At first, she thought I was an angel, but she was suspicious, so she Calmed me."

He seemed surprised and puzzled. "She thought you were an angel?"

"Yup," I said. "I was in the Apple store up on Fifth Avenue, and she was in there with a friend. I noticed her, and I knew what she was right away, so I did my best to get out of there as fast as I could. It wasn't fast enough though, she spotted me and we left the store together. It was like she opened a port to my soul. I could hear her speaking to me, but she wasn't actually talking. She called me 'fellow'."

"Interesting. Angels rarely communicate with each other verbally, it's just safer for them that way. The fact that she was even able to establish a connection with you is incredible. This is not a trait that I believed diuscrucis possessed, and I am certain it was not in Charis's repertoire. You said that Rebecca mistook you for an angel also?"

I took a seat on the couch across from Dante. "Yeah. She said I smelled like an angel, but when she got up close she realized she was wrong. Here's the crazy part, I got marked as a demon by a couple of Touched. They would have killed me, but Rebecca showed up and stopped them."

"Why would she do that?" he asked.

His expression was pure confusion. His question was whispered, as if he was asking it of himself. I could tell he was fighting hard to make sense of the whole thing.

"She said she's done the math and realized that if Hell wins, vampires are going to become the new food source. She's not so sure she wants to play on the Devil's team anymore, because there isn't much of a future in it for her."

Dante didn't look convinced. "A vampire does not just change sides," he said. "To do so would make them a target for every demon on Earth. She may have helped you this once, but I would be wary of her true motives."

I hadn't thought about it, but it made sense. "Agreed," I said.

"Very good," he said. "Now, back to the seraph. You said you met her in Central Park, but she was in this apartment. She Calmed you in this apartment. I can feel the residual energy."

Calmed me here? I didn't think so. Sure, I could feel the energy too, but that was just *her*.

"Sorry Dante, but we were definitely in the park. We were attacked by a demon, a Great Were. We killed it together. She was injured, I brought her here and healed her wounds with some holy water."

I hadn't finished speaking when his expression darkened, his eyes turned black, and he rose to his feet. The next thing I knew, I was pinned against the wall by an invisible force that I couldn't break.

"You healed her," he shouted. "The seraphim are our enemies! How dare you!"

I tried to move, but it was an overwhelming effort just to gather the willpower to make the attempt. Every muscle in my body cried out in exhaustion, and even my eyes began to feel heavy. I could feel the evil soul inside me stirring, offering me the power to break free of these bounds and destroy the one who held me here. I could sense my growing anger, and the temptation that accompanied it. I remembered what Josette had told me. Not this time.

"What right do you have to judge me," I yelled back with all of the force I could muster. I doubted if it had come out as more than a whisper. "You dumped me here to fend for myself, the only thing you told me was that the balance had to be maintained. I don't know if you noticed, but the balance is totally out of whack."

As quickly as his anger had risen, it subsided. He lowered me to the floor and bowed his head.

"I am sorry, Signore," he said. "Your words are true. I have no right to judge you. Please forgive me."

He spoke with such honest regret, my own anger faded as well. I shook my arms out to make sure I was back to normal. Everything seemed to be functioning okay.

"It's all right," I said. "There's something else you should know. After I killed the demon, somehow I absorbed its soul."

Dante's smile returned. "You killed a Great Were, and you captured his soul? Fantastico!"

It was my turn to be confused. "Josette made it sound like it was a bad thing."

"Maybe for her," he replied. "Do not be afraid to make use of every tool at your disposal, Landon. The seraph will tell you that capturing souls this way is dangerous, but while you remain in control you can use this power to your advantage."

"What if I don't remain in control?" I asked.

"You have more power than you realize," he replied. "I think it will be very difficult for you to lose control so completely that the demon can subsume you."

Maybe not completely, but what horrible things would I do while I was under the influence? I wasn't so sure Dante was right about that one, his scruples seemed to be a little shaky when pitted against getting what he wanted. I decided that I would do my best to avoid absorbing any more souls, and to fight against the temptation to let the beast loose. I needed Josette to come back and teach me how to keep to that decision.

Josette. Dante said she had Calmed me in the apartment, before he had gotten all ape-crap angry on me. I knew she hadn't. I could clearly remember when she had, so I would have remembered if it had happened again. We had fought the vampires, and then come back to the apartment. She told me to get some rest, kissed my hand, and that was it. I had fallen asleep immedia... Oh, crap.

"She put me to sleep," I said to Dante.

"She Calmed you," Dante replied. "Putting you out is a more advanced form, but it is the same thing. A powerful seraph would be able to Calm you, and then press you for information while you slept."

She had played me like a game of Pac-man. She had made me think she was helping me, when in fact she just wanted information, but about what?

"What kind of information would she think I would have?" I asked Dante.

I felt my insides being ripped out, the anger and hurt of her betrayal sending chills through my body. I was too inexperienced, too naive. I had trusted her way too easily. I could feel my pulse quickening, the heat rising to my face.

"You are familiar with the Chalice, the Grail?" Dante asked. His words snapped my ricocheting mind back into focus.

"The one from the Last Supper?" I asked. "The one I was guarding?"

He nodded. "The same. It is the reason I came to see you today, the reason I am so thankful that you were delivered to me when you were. The demons have captured it, and plan to use it to complete their victory. You have to stop them."

Stop them. Yeah, right. Me. I couldn't even take out a messenger demon without help.

"Captured it?" I asked. "It wasn't exactly under guard. I mean, the demon who took it just waltzed right in to the Museum and plucked it right out of a bulletproof, tamper-proof case like it was made of fog."

"No, Signore," Dante said. "That was your experience, but not even close to the whole story. So that you will understand, let me first tell you the history of the Chalice. Do you recall what I told you about Jesus?"

I nodded. It hadn't been that long ago, though at times it felt like ages.

"Then the important part that you understand is that he was real," he said, "and he was the embodiment of God on Earth. From the moment he was born he knew when and how he would die, for it had been arranged by God in the hopes that his martyrdom would push the human race to a higher level of goodness. In some respects his plan was successful, for many mortals have done endless good deeds in His name. In other respects, it was a dismal failure. Corrupt kings under demonic influence used the name of God and the birthplace of His Son as an excuse for war and violence.

The final night of his life, Jesus took the Chalice and filled it with his blood, granting it to his disciples to imbue them with the diluted power of God. It was in this way that the first of the warrior angels were ordained, though they did not gain most of their power until after their death. The Chalice, having held the blood of God, also developed power of its own. For humans, it could grant eternal youth and rejuvenation."

"What about for the angels? Or the demons?" I asked. The story of the Holy Grail was nothing new to anybody. The fact that there was truth to the tale was the incredible part.

"Nobody knows how it affects the angels," Dante replied. "After the Last Supper, the Chalice was passed to a mortal warrior, a non-disciple who was loyal to Jesus. He was charged with protecting the secret of the Grail, and ensuring its safety for all eternity. Because of Judas, the secret did not stay that way among the demons for very long. The warrior spent many years in hiding, organizing a secret army known as the Knights Templar in order to help him guard it. The Templar Knights were granted a drink from the Chalice, and were armed by the angels with blessed weapons to assist in the battle against the demon hordes. For hundreds of years the Templars kept the Chalice safe.

The Industrial Revolution has not been kind to the Templars, or Heaven in general. With the growth of science and reasoned thinking came the dilution of the faithful, with more and more turning away from religion in return for logic. The Templars have become unable to maintain their number, and so their power has continued to diminish.

It was decided that the Chalice would be gifted to the Vatican and revealed to mankind so that it could be preserved in the open and guarded more easily. Once something has been brought to the human consciousness it becomes impossible to take away. The Grail became a part of the mortal world, and as such mortals as well as angels kept watch over it and protected it. The value of using the Chalice was minor compared to the harm that would befall Heaven should it be lost to the demons."

"It has been lost to the demons," I reminded him.

"Yes, Signore, it has," he said. "The Templars underestimated the power of the Demon Queen. In your mortal mind you may have thought the Chalice was unguarded. In fact three angels and a dozen Templars were in or around the Museum on the day you were killed, including the warrior who was given the Grail by Christ himself over two thousand years before. The most powerful mortals the world has ever known did battle with the Demon Queen in the basement of the museum. All were defeated."

I felt my breath get choked off, my terrified heart unwilling to draw in more oxygen. I thought back to my final living memory, to the woman who had taken the Chalice, and my life.

"The woman who stole the Chalice. She was the Demon Queen?" I asked. "As in, the wife of the Devil?"

"No," he said. "When I use the word Queen, I use it in a more hierarchical term of power. She is not wed to the Devil. Rather, she is the most powerful female demon waging war in the mortal realm."

"And you want me to stop her?" If I had been able to breathe, I probably would have laughed at the absurdity of the thought.

"You do not need to confront her head on to stop her," Dante said. "What you must do is recover the Chalice, and make sure it becomes lost for all time. Mr. Ross has told me that the demons are using it to create these."

Dante reached into the inner pocket of his blazer and produced a simple iron necklace with a liquid filled container hanging from it. The container looked like glass, or crystal. The fluid was a blackish, reddish color. It undulated and flowed inside its cage as if it had a life of its own. It looked familiar.

"They spill their blood into the Chalice and mix it with the blood of a mortal," he explained, "then trap it in a crystal which has been cursed by a powerful demon. Any demon who wears one becomes almost invincible."

I reached into my pocket and pulled out the necklace I had captured from the Great Were. Dante looked at it with surprise.

"It doesn't work if it isn't touching them," I told him.

"Where did you get that?" he asked.

"The Great Were had one," I said. "He let the seraph run him through so he could show her how it worked. I pulled it off his neck before I killed him."

Dante's face lit up with another of his familiar smiles. "Excellente! You have already discovered a weakness."

I wasn't as enthused. "It isn't much of a weakness. It was closer to dumb luck, really."

Dante was unswayed. "Maybe not a huge weakness, but any advantage will make this an easier task. Already demons are becoming bolder, attacking angels with a comfort level never before seen, and taking mortals for sacrifice in increasing numbers. If we do not stop them, Armageddon will happen sooner than we could ever want."

I wasn't feeling very confident about this, but what choice did I have? For better or worse I had agreed to be mankind's Champion. Going down fighting had to be better than toiling away in Purgatory for the rest of eternity.

"I could use some help," I said.

Dante held his hands in front of him. "My apologies, but I have none to offer beyond Mr. Ross' extraordinary ability to gather information. I had thought to teach you basic skills before sending you from Purgatory, but you have learned so much more in a single night than I could have believed. Survival will educate you far better and more quickly than I ever could."

I was being thrown to the werewolves. I don't know if Dante thought I stood a chance, but he seemed convinced that I did.

"So what do I do next?" I asked.

Dante rose from the couch and stood right in front of me, his face looking up at mine. His expression was grave.

"Survive, Signore. Survive and fight. Find out where these necklaces are being created. Find out where the Chalice is being kept. Retrieve it, and hide it from the demons, from the angels, from the humans. Let none know where it resides. Destroy these amulets and the demons that wear them. Above all, survive. I will be in touch when I have more information for you. Good luck Landon."

Without waiting for my reply, without giving me a chance to question him, to ask him about Charis, he vanished and I was alone. Maybe eternity in Purgatory wouldn't have been so bad after all.

Chapter 9

After Dante left, I made my way back down to the Deli, only to find my sandwich had already been trashed. Slightly annoyed, I bought another one and savored every bite. As I ate, I considered everything that Dante had said, and tried to decide what I should do next. I felt pressured to do as Dante had asked, but at the same time I knew that in my current state I was no match for anything much stronger than a Girl Scout. I had only defeated the vampires with a lot of help, and I wasn't feeling too good about letting the Were's soul take over again.

Despite Dante's opinion, nothing I had experienced the prior night had suggested that I would be able to regain control once I had passed it over. Add to that the fact that Josette had suckered me, and I was left feeling alone and powerless in the middle of a race to save mankind from being literally devoured by monsters. I had thought dying was the hard part. There was something funny in there somewhere, I was sure.

I took the amulet out of my pocket and took a closer look at it. To think that there was some vestige of the embodiment of

God trapped in that crystal. It was heady stuff and it kept me captivated for a while, watching the smoky liquid ebb and flow inside its prison.

Power. That was the lock and key to all of this. Without power, I couldn't hope to carry through with my assignment. Dante was so certain I had power. He had said that Josette couldn't hope to defeat me in a flat out fight. Now that was comedy. The Demon Queen seemed to have the most power. Thinking about her ripping through the angels and the Templars to get to the Chalice made me shiver with trepidation. If I was going to survive, I would have to figure out what my power was, how much of it I had, and how best to utilize it. Did David go through this same mental exercise before he had to go out to face Goliath?

I left the deli and headed back to the Belmont. I stopped at my room to grab the seraphim sword and demonic dagger, and carried them to the roof. Once there, I dropped into the pose Josette had taught me hours earlier. I ran through the limited exercises she had shown me with abandon, trying to free myself from the bonds of humanity that I knew I was clinging onto. In the last twenty four hours I had seen and done things that I knew were impossible as part of a normal human existence, but normalcy had been left far behind, and now I was part of something that rose above mortality, that lorded over it in a sickly sweet dance with one too many partners. I was the odd man out, and I would have to earn my place in line.

When I slipped on an icy patch and landed on my ass, I gave up on the swordplay. Maybe this was how the angels handled conflict, but it just wasn't working for me. I was born in an age of weapons of mass destruction, missile toting drones, and frickin' laser beams. I needed my own approach.

Embarrassed and angry for having fallen, I cast my gaze to a large piece of the building's frieze that had crumbled at some point over the last century. I thought first about the rain making exercise, and then changed my focus from condensing water vapor, to expanding the air trapped inside the cement. I felt the now familiar tug in my mind, and watched the chunk of wall burst outward as no more than powder. Now that's what I was talking about!

I got a little bit punch drunk on my newfound ability to pulverize rock, and I spent the better part of an hour blasting small chunks of stone out of the roof of the Belmont. As time wore on, I could feel my concentration improving, my control improving. I still failed to get results three out of every ten tries, but it was progress, and I was happy with it. I felt alive, and strong! Better than I had ever felt before.

I picked up the sword again and charged toward the metal door to the stairwell, racing forward and focusing my will along the blade, making it sharper, stronger. I took a nasty hack, and laughed as the blade ripped through the door, shredding it almost in half. Intoxicated, I threw a fist at the top half, and watched as it knocked the weakened door off its hinges and over the edge of the rooftop. A moment later I heard it crash onto the empty alley below. Power. It was raw, unchained, and somewhat uneven, but it was there, and it was mine.

I left the rooftop in ruins before I retreated back to my room. I didn't know how much my display of rock-smashing would help me in a real fight, but if nothing else I felt a little bit less like a piece of meat dangling from a large hook. With any luck I'd at least be able to make myself look formidable, even if I couldn't seal the deal.

I stripped off my clothes and hopped into the shower. I didn’t need it to stay clean or smell fresh, but I had always found the feeling of the water and the small space of the stall helped me focus my thoughts, and I had a lot to think about. First, there was the matter of the Chalice. I needed to find it, but I had no idea where to look, or even where to begin looking.

I was pretty sure that the demon Reyzl would have the intel I needed, but there was no way I was in any shape to confront a major power like that. I doubted I ever would be. Moving stuff around for a few seconds was a parlor trick compared to what I imagined a major demon was capable of.

No, I needed to start at the bottom, to find the lowest rung on the ladder that might be able to point me in the right direction, and to stay near the bottom of the barrel for as long as I could. Surprise was my only real advantage right now. I had used it to the fullest against the Great Were, and I needed to do the same here. I closed my eyes and let the water run down my body, listening to the sound of it as it dripped off my limbs and landed on the chipped and scratched porcelain below.

My second problem was a little more complicated. Josette. She would be back to see me at some point, I was sure of it. Whether it would be as a teacher or as an inquisitor, I just had no idea. She confused me in so many ways. She could be sweet, impulsive, playful, and light, and within an instant serious, introspective, and frightening.

She was good, and the goodness was beautiful. She had a sensitivity and empathy that I admired, and from the moment she had connected her soul to mine I had felt a bond to her that I couldn't understand or explain. I wanted to be her ally, her friend, her... I didn't know. I had thought that could have been possible, despite our differences in opinion. She seemed both open to it and against it at the same time. She had agreed to teach me even though it was against her laws. Then she had used my trust to try to wring information out of me. Information I didn't have.

What would I do when she returned? I could call her on her deception, and she would not be able to lie to me. That didn't mean she would be honest. I was learning the difference, and just knowing that there was one sucked. My other alternative was to say nothing, pretend I didn't know, and see what she did next. She hadn't gotten anything out of me, so maybe she would try again. If I were ready the next time I could catch her at it, but wouldn't I just end up right back where I was now? Either way my shot at friendship was lost, and that sucked too.

I turned off the flow of water and pushed all of the moisture off my body with a thought. I was getting pretty good at small pushes. As far as Josette was concerned, I would make a game-time decision based on whatever emotions bubbled up the next time I saw her. There was enough dishonesty going around to deny the truth from myself too. With respect to the Chalice, I had an idea on that one. It was a long shot, but long was better than none.

I finished dressing, altering my clothes into a simple black cotton collared shirt and a pair of destroyed blue jeans. Slipping back into the bedroom, I grabbed my iPad, hopped on the bed, tapped into the browser, and made my way back to SamChan. I may not be a Collector like Mr. Ross, but I did have at least one source to depend on for this type of otherwise insane information.

I found the thread from the guy with the vampire video on the third page. It had been posted a couple of days ago, and he swore up and down in his post that it was legit, that he had stumbled across two vamps fighting each other in an alley as he was heading home from work that night.

I recognized his screen name, 'Oblitrix'. He had been on the Chan for years, working different hacking schemes for groups like Anonymous. There were a couple of replies on his thread, and they were filled with derision and jokes about random drug testing and drug-free workplaces. I spent some time staring at the screen before I hit the personal message button. I needed to get a line on someone who might have info about the Chalice, and vampires fit my decision to stick to the bottom of the power ladder to a tee. Oblitrix knew where to find them, or at least had a general idea where they might be found. I briefly thought about tracking Rebecca down on Liberty Island, but I couldn't come up with any sane reason why she would help me with this. So, I started typing.

O - GCT, 104 11 21 0900

The message was short and cryptic, but I knew Oblitrix would be there. Getting a PM from a dead guy's account would be irresistible to a guy like him. With that taken care of, there was little else to do but wait until morning. I had about sixteen hours before the meeting, and I needed to take advantage of every minute. I propped myself up against the back of the bed and ran through the rain exercise three or four dozen times. False starts were one thing in this environment. Failure in a tight spot could mean my end.

As Dante had suggested, overexertion left me weary. I had continued my practice non-stop for almost three hours, alternating between making it rain and sending objects flying through the room. By the time my splitting headache and dead tired body demanded that I call it a night, I figured I was getting a ninety percent success rate on my efforts. During one attempt I had even managed to keep the sword, the dagger, and my socks rotating above the bed for about twelve seconds. Not too bad for a newbie.

My mind was too tired to focus, too frenetic to sleep. Restless, I picked up the iPad and made my way over to YouTube. In my tired, restless boredom, I decided to check out some videos on sword fighting and martial arts. My own ability thus far had proven to be pathetic at best, and at the very least maybe I could learn to not be a greater threat to myself than my opponent.

I spent the next couple of hours navigating the chain of clips from one to the next, my mind vaguely aware of what I was watching as it began to settle into a deeper state of rest. I wasn't sure I needed to sleep, but I closed my eyes anyway. At some point soon after, the iPad slipped from my hand and landed on the floor next to the bed.

I woke up around eight thirty. Whether or not I needed to sleep, I felt so much better for having done so. My body felt recharged, renewed, and full of energy. My mind was clear, sharp, and focused. I had a plan, I knew what needed to be done, and I was feeling good about doing it. For the first time since I had died, or maybe even for the first time since my soul gained its first spark of life, I felt like I was in control.

I hopped out of bed, grabbed the sword and dagger, and headed out the door. Punkmo was manning the front desk when I stepped purposefully past, his eyes bloodshot and droopy as he came down from his morning high. The look he gave me reminded me that I needed to disguise the sword. I glamoured it into an umbrella before anyone sober took notice.

It was a long walk from the Belmont to Grand Central Station, so I moved at a brisk pace. As I walked, I paid extra attention to the world around me; to the smell of coffee, donuts, and fried foods permeating the morning air, to the sounds of cars driving by, people talking, high heels on cement, cellphones, car horns, sirens, beggars asking for change... Every noise was a musical note in my mind, and as I paid more attention to it I began to recognize the tune, and then to anticipate it. This was my world, and in my Awakened state I could understand it in a way that exposed every beauty it possessed, and appreciate it for every nuance. To the untrained it would have seemed chaotic and disorganized, but in it I was beginning to see the balance as much as I could innately feel it. It was so much more complex than just good versus evil. It was in and of everything, and it was incredible.

Grand Central Station was a hub of activity, the famous main concourse thronged with people. They moved smoothly with and around one another, effortless in their negotiation of passage as they went about their daily lives. I spent a moment admiring the controlled chaos of the masses before heading straight for the lower concourse. I had told Oblitrix I would meet him near Track 104. He wouldn't know who he was looking for, and neither would I by sight, but I was hoping I would be able to pick him out based on his body language. He was sure to be on edge, filled with nervous, anxious anticipation. His heart would be racing, his breathing shallow, and his palms sweaty and cold. As I navigated the lower concourse towards Track 104, I paid close attention to all of the people moving through the station, watching the vibration of their bodies, listening to their heartbeats.

I found him sitting on a bench towards the outer fringe. His body was hunched forward, his head resting on his hands, his right foot tapping at a rabbit's pace and his eyes darting back and forth to watch every person as they angled by. He was African-American, with a wide nose, small ears, and a chiseled jaw. He was wearing a black caddy hat, a heavy wool pea coat, black paratrooper pants and combat boots. He also had a black nylon messenger bag draped over his chest with a huge 'O' embroidered on the center.

I stood behind him and watched for a minute, just to make sure I had my man. I also did a quick scan of the rest of the crowd to make sure neither of us had been followed. I was just about to go over and sit next to him when someone else from the crowd approached him. The new guy said something to him, and then Oblitrix stood up and held out his hand in greeting, a big smile growing on his face. So much for my private message.

The newcomer wasn't Divine, I was sure of it. That didn't mean he was innocent though. I watched the two exchange a few more words before Oblitrix motioned to his messenger bag. I didn't need to eavesdrop on the conversation to know what was being said. I didn't even need to try to spot the bad guys when they started closing in.

I looked around, taking note of how the crowded floor was thinning out as people subconsciously decided to take a different train, stop to grab a bite to eat, or otherwise move themselves away from the incoming demons. I avoided looking at them in hopes of staying off their radar for as long as possible. Instead, I started making my way past Oblitrix and the not-me, pretending that I was vacating the area.

I was six feet away from them when my fake looked up and caught my eye. His expression changed immediately, from a warm friendliness to a fearful animosity. His eyes shifted to glance at the demons coming toward us, trying to judge his odds of survival. They weren't good.

I reached out and grabbed Oblitrix by the collar of his pea coat, pulling him backwards with enough force to get his neck out of the way as a serrated dagger flashed by. Without hesitation, I lunged forward and stabbed the man with my umbrella-sword. The feeling of the blade sinking into his flesh was both sickening and satisfying, but I didn't have time to dwell on any of the emotions. I could feel the demons' eyes on me now, recognizing me as Divine. There were four in total, approaching from each end of the concourse. Not vampires. I knew that much by the feeling of fear that started encroaching on my crumbling bravado. Whatever they were, they were higher up the ladder than I had been looking to scrap with.

"What the?" It was all Oblitrix had managed to get out during the whole maneuver. I held him up to keep him from losing his feet, and then spun him to face me.

"Oblitrix, I presume," I said. "My name is Landon, and I need you to come with me right now or we're both going to be demon food."

I didn't give him a choice. The demons didn't give me a choice. There was one direction they didn't have covered, and that was down the steps into the train tunnels. I moved my grip to Oblitrix's arm and yanked him along. It was a bad idea to be moving further away from daylight, but I didn't see that I had a choice.

"Let me go man," he cried as I pulled him.

My grip was iron as we started descending, the demons quickly gaining ground. It was my fault he had come here, so I was responsible for him. I wasn't about to let him die without a fight.

"Trust me," I said. "You don't want me to let go."

He trusted me when they burst onto the stairs. They had shed their human skins for their natural forms. At least seven feet tall, with furry humanoid bodies and long, powerful limbs that ended in sharp claws. They reminded me of werewolves, but their heads didn't look canine at all. I could hear them growling and shrieking. I could hear their claws scraping along the cement. We needed to move faster, or they needed to move slower.

I focused my will on a couple of nearby garbage cans, sending them flying towards the monsters. They danced aside without slowing, the effort not preventing them from gaining ground.

"Down the tunnel," I told Oblitrix, letting go of his arm. "Keep running, don't look back. If a train comes, get out of the way."

He was too scared to argue. I let him go and turned to face the oncoming demons. There was no way I could take on all of them at once. I wasn't even sure if I could survive against just one. There was no time left to think, just react.

I held the blessed sword in front of me the way I had seen in the videos, trying to focus myself on the task at hand. I painted a picture of calm control as I watched the demons approach unabated, eight pairs of claws ready to rip me apart. I could hear Oblitrix hop down onto the sunken tracks behind me. I could hear his messenger bag slapping against his body while he ran.

The lead demon lunged forward, its body propelled toward me like an ugly rocket. I fought my flight reflex and held my ground, trying to keep my mind relaxed so that my subconscious sense of self-preservation could guide me. Time slowed down for me then, and I had a clear view of the oncoming demon. I could see the vector of its body towards mine, the angle of its limbs as it brought its claws to bear. I could smell the pheromones it was pushing off to enhance my sense of fear. I could taste the sickly sulfurous air that surrounded it, leaving a burnt iron residue on my tongue.

I saw its left arm flex and begin a movement intended to sever my head from my torso. I stood firm and stabbed forward with the sword, catching the demon under its collarbone. I combined its momentum with my own to deflect it away from me, sending it tumbling off the platform and onto the tracks. I could only hope that the wound was enough to be fatal.

The other three demons came in together, only a fraction of a second behind the first. Their howls were deafening as they sensed the kill. I put up the sword again, but I may as well have been holding a toothpick. I managed to block the first two attacks through either fast reflexes or dumb luck, but first one strike slipped through my defenses, and then another. Pain blossomed throughout my abdomen as their claws ripped flesh from bone and tore into my innards. I didn't know how much damage I could take, but with no way to stop the assault I had to assume they would just keep clawing until I stopped moving.

I dropped to the ground, my eyes losing focus as I struggled to put up some kind of a fight. In desperation I tried reaching out for the power of the Great Were, but even it had deserted me. For all my desire to fight for mankind, I was the guy throwing rocks at tanks.

I knew the demons were mangling my body. I could feel their claws digging into my flesh like it was just another piece of meat. I could hear their satisfied growls while they tore me apart, their bloodlust in full control. My vision was blurring, and I was starting to feel really warm. I didn't know what would happen to me or where I was going, but at least I knew I wouldn't be in any more pain. I welcomed the warmth with open arms, beckoning the end.

I was vaguely aware of the deafening pops that followed. I wouldn't have known anything had happened at all if the rending pain hadn't ceased, replaced with the warm, wet, stinky feeling of thick demon blood splattering down onto me and mixing with my own. My vision had fled, but I could hear the shrieks of pain as more pops followed. I tried to move, to get to my feet, but I had no feeling in my legs. I didn't even know if I still had legs. I could hear someone running up towards me, their breathing heavy.

"I don't know what's going on here, man," Oblitrix said between breaths. "But this is seriously crazy."

"You don't even know the half of it," I tried to say.

My mouth must have been in rough shape, because it came out as little more than a mumbled gurgle. Bullets, I realized. He had shot them. I needed to heal fast, or we were both screwed. I focused my will inward, forcing the impossible to happen even faster. My vision returned in a blink, and I could see Oblitrix leaning over me, a sheen of sweat on his forehead, a Desert Eagle in his hand, aimed in the direction of the demons.

I opened and closed my mouth to see that it was working, clenched and unclenched my fists and toes. He watched me with disgusted, frightened fascination.

"Those bullets aren't going to keep them down long," I said, jumping to my feet. I was surprised to see the demons still on the ground, hunched over on hands and knees.

"Silver," Oblitrix said. "I've been doing some digging since I made that video, figured I ought to come prepared. I wasn't expecting *this*. You looked like a mincemeat pie thirty seconds ago."

"I have a good health plan," I replied, bending down and picking up my sword.

I could see the silver had slowed them, but it wasn't going to stop them. I didn't waste any time, walking over to the first and bringing my blade down on its neck.

Sensing their fate, the remaining two demons reared up. I took a step back to defend myself, but needn't have bothered. Two more loud pops, two more silver bullet holes, and they were back on the ground. I stabbed both of them through the back, this time taking pleasure in the killing strokes. I began to turn to face Oblitrix when I noticed the black cloud forming around them.

"What the hell is that?" Oblitrix asked.

Their souls, I knew, but I didn't tell him. Josette had never told me how to keep them away, and now I could feel the darkness trying to find its way into my body. The cloud began swirling around me, rising up towards my face as its vortex increased velocity. I tried to close my mouth to it, but the black cloud began slipping into my nose and sliding down into me. I dropped to my knees and closed my eyes, focusing inward again to find the encroaching mass of demonic energy. It was going to overtake me, and there was nothing I could do to stop it.

"No," I said.

I was quiet and calm while I focused my will against the cloud as I hard as I knew how. I felt the tug and the feedback of the command blasting against my mind, imploding at the same time it exploded. The black cloud vaporized instantly, leaving me standing there shaking from the pushback. The pressure was so tight around my head that I thought it would burst, my vision went dark again, and I passed out.

Chapter 10

In the dream, I was back at the Statue of Liberty, standing on the small walkway that encircled the torch. I wasn't alone. His long black hair was tied back in a ponytail, his eyes covered by a pair of aviator shades. His expression was smug.

"Where were you two minutes ago?" I asked him. "I could have used you."

"You mean I could have used you," he replied. He smiled, revealing a mouth full of razor pointed teeth. "Sorry man, but I won't kill my own kind."

The whole thing was weird. I knew I was dreaming, or hallucinating, or something. It felt real enough. The air was cold and crisp, the wind whistling through the metal structure of the Statue. I could even hear tourists clanging up and down the steps nearby. At the same time, there was this otherness to it. Something was just off. I couldn't place it, but I could feel it. That, and the fact that the Great Were I had killed was here, laughing at me.

"I don't suppose you know what this is?" I asked him.

He seemed pretty comfortable with the situation. I felt surprisingly comfortable with him. I knew he couldn't harm me here.

"I can't believe you killed me and captured my soul," he said with a sigh. "This is you. Your subconscious, your REM state, whatever the hell you want to call it. Divine spend hundreds of years trying to get to this place. You don't even know what it is."

He started laughing again, louder and stronger.

"Why?" I asked.

He stopped laughing and looked at me. "What do you mean why?"

"Why do Divine spend years trying to get into their subconscious?" I repeated. It doesn't seem that great in here, present company included."

"Man, you don't know anything. This is the source of all of your power." He waved his hand around at the world. "You trapped me here with it, even though you had no idea what you were doing. I was trying to take your body for my own. You fought like crap, got me because I was too busy ogling that little white honey. I thought it would be easy. Let me just say, you're a blast to hang out with though. Those two girls were smokin'. And that angel... A little young for me, and her face is nothing to write home about, but damn she knew what to do with that sword of hers."

He was baiting me, and I knew it. With a thought, I pushed him back against the railing, shoving him back until he was teetering over it.

"I know what you're doing," I said.

He laughed again. "Do you? Look around, Landon. Look at the scope of your power. You have the whole world at your disposal. I'm trying to help you realize your true potential. We could have Reyzl licking your feet within an hour."

I hesitated. Just long enough for him to catch my weakness and seize on it.

"How many times have you been beaten up already?" he asked. "Aren't you getting sick of it? You have the power, and I know how to use it. We can co-exist, and you can have anything you desire." His face turned to a perverted sneer. "Like that angel of yours. Sexy little thing like that, I bet she knows quite a few tricks after seven hundred years."

I'd had enough. My moment of weakness was replaced with pure anger. I gave the equivalent of a flick with my mind, and the Great Were went flying off the torch. I watched him fall, getting no satisfaction when his body slammed into the ground below and dissolved.

His words reverberated through me. The whole world at my disposal. There was a seductiveness to the thought. Wasn't that the idea? If the demon couldn't overpower me physically, he was going to try to do it mentally. The fact that I was affected by his words at all was proof that no matter the scope of my power, I was only as strong as my will. I remembered Dante's last words to me. 'Survive and fight'. It was simple, straightforward, and easy to remember. Somehow I had been surviving. It was time to start fighting. I turned towards the torch, where the Great Were was perched once more.

"Ulnyx," I called. He raised his eyebrows in surprise at hearing his name. "I'll see you around."

I flipped him the bird, and woke myself up.

Chapter 11

I hadn't expected to find myself lying in a hospital bed. I wasn't even really human! There was nothing any doctor could do to help me. There was no one to help me except myself.

Oblitrix was sitting in a chair next to me, his feet up on the bed I was lying in, an iPad resting on his thighs. He didn't even notice that I was awake. I felt a draft, and grimaced. They had changed me into one of those lousy robes, and stuck an IV into my arm. I grabbed it and pulled it out, then morphed the robe into something more suitable. That got his attention.

"Hey man, you're awake," he said, dropping his feet and standing up.

"I've got to get out of here," I told him, tossing aside the blankets and sliding out of the bed.

He put his arms up to block me. "Hold on man, you can't just waltz out of here like that."

"Why not?" I asked.

He pointed at the window. "For one, NYPD is out there. They want to talk to you real bad."

I followed his finger. There was a pair of detectives hanging outside the room. They hadn't noticed me yet, and they wouldn't. I focused my will, altering the room to look undisturbed to anyone outside of it. I couldn't see the illusion, but the tug in my mind told me it had taken.

"What do they want to talk to me about?" I asked.

He looked at me like I was crazy. "You don't know?"

"Would I have asked if I did?" I replied. "I've been a little indisposed to keep up with current events."

He laughed. "True enough. I don't know what was happening to you man, but you caused an earthquake when you dropped. Took out two of the tunnels."

An earthquake? I had thought the pressure was internal. "Was anybody hurt?"

"No, " he said, "but the cops think it was a terrorist attack or something. They already questioned me. They just want to talk to you, see if you know or saw anything."

"Is that how I ended up here?" I didn't even know how long I had been out. By the fact that Oblitrix was still hanging around, it couldn't have been too long.

He nodded. "Yup. I didn't want to just leave you like that, especially after what I saw you do. I hung around and made sure nothing else from my nightmares popped up until the cops showed. Good thing I have a permit. I told them I didn't know what had happened, but I was trying to protect you."

I looked at Oblitrix and tilted my head. After what he had seen, he could have just kept running in the tunnel and left me to be destroyed. Not only had he come back, but he had stayed with me when I was most vulnerable.

"Thank you," I said. "You didn't have to come back."

He laughed again. "I don't care who or what you are, nobody deserves to get eaten by whatever those were. You're the one who sent me the PM, aren't you? The screen name looked familiar, but from what I hear that guy died like six months ago."

"Yeah, that was me," I admitted. "Death didn't work out so well." I held out my hand. "Landon Hamilton."

He didn't hesitate to grab my hand and give it a firm shake. "Obi-Wan Sampson," he said. "Most people just call me Obi."

"Obi-wan?"

He sighed. "Yeah. My folks were huge Star Wars fans, the classic trilogy anyway. I'm just glad they didn't name me Jar Jar."

"So am I," I said. "You're a crack shot with that hand cannon of yours."

"I did four years in the Corps," he said. "Two in the field, two behind a computer. I still work out every day, and hit the range at least once a week. Once a Marine, always a Marine. Semper Fi, you know."

"I'm impressed, and super glad to meet you," I said. "If you want to stick around, I'd love to chat some more, but right now I've got to get out of here before they try to come in."

He looked back at the detectives. "Alright man. I'll distract them so you can slip past. The elevator is down the hall to the..."

I went over to the window and flung it open.

"There's bound to be a Starbucks nearby," I said. "Meet me there."

I was on the third floor. Not too high to jump, so I did. I focused my will on the air below me as I fell, feeling it give to my demands. It became denser, heavier, slowing me down as though I were falling through mud. I landed almost gently and looked up to where Obi was hanging out the window. I gave him a thumbs up and headed down the street, thoroughly impressed with myself.

I changed my appearance and circled back around to the front of the hospital, getting out front just as Obi pushed his way through the large glass doors. I let him walk by, then tailed close behind him as he headed away from the building. It wasn't that I didn't trust him. Okay, it was that I didn't trust him. Divinity was making me paranoid, and I didn't have any confidence that his bravery wasn't one huge setup. I didn't see any downside to being extra cautious.

He rounded the corner ahead of me, and I followed a good twenty feet behind, mixed in with a few other pedestrians who were headed in the same general direction. When I turned the corner I could see the Starbucks sign dead ahead. What I didn't see was Obi.

I sensed the danger before I saw it, and reacted immediately. I ducked to the left to avoid a strong right hook, then reached out and twisted his other hand away before he could get a shot off with his gun. I pulled us both off to the side of the pavement to get clear of the bystanders, who hadn't even noticed the attack. I was going to drop my disguise, to show him it was me, but he had already relaxed his guard.

"What's up, Landon," he said. "Nice moves."

"What was that all about?" I asked him. "How did you know it was me?"

He dropped his gun back into the messenger bag. "I knew it was you when I left the hospital. You started tailing me, so I decided to jump you. Figured if you were hostile you would kill me, otherwise you'd trust me."

"You do know I'm throwing an illusion, a glamour?" I said. "You aren't supposed to recognize me."

He laughed. "Sorry man, I only see you. There's this weird haze around you, almost like looking through some foggy glass, but that's it. Hey, do you think you could tell me what all of this is about?"

I was hesitant to let him get involved. “Are you sure you want to know?”

“This is the most action I’ve had since Afghanistan,’ he replied. “Computers are fun toys, but nothing compared to an adrenaline high.”

“Come on,” I said, leading him towards the Starbucks. “I’ve got a craving for an Americano.”

I put us in the corner, out of earshot of all but the most adept listeners. Obi opened his bag and pulled out a manila folder, then sat down.

“Why don’t you tell me what you already know, and I’ll try to fill in the blanks,” I said.

He handed the folder over to me. I opened it up, and was greeted with a photo of two vampires, fangs and claws extended, looking as if they were about to tear each other apart.

“A still from the video,” he said. “I was walking home from work; I’m a backend developer for a startup. Anyway, I hear this commotion in the alley, and being the nosy-ass son of a bitch I am, I make my way down with my cellphone camera running. That’s what I saw.”

I flipped past the photo to a print out of a message board thread.

“What is this?” I asked.

"After I saw those guys go at it, I hit the internet in search of information about real vampires," he said. "What you saw on SamChan was just the tip of the iceberg, I didn't expect much from that collection of miscreants... no offense."

I couldn't help but smile. "None taken."

"Cool. So I started digging a bit more, hitting up some Tor sites, looking for a lead into illegal blood trade. I figured if these guys are real, they've got to eat. If they've got to eat, there's bound to be suppliers. That's my pay dirt."

I looked at the printout again. Everything was written in code.

"You cracked this?" I asked.

"Yeah man," he said. "That wasn't easy though. They're using a lexical encryption based on Romanian, circa six hundred A.D. Figures right? Anyway, it took me close to ten hours to find a reference to the language, another four to crack it. In a nutshell, it's a blood exchange. The most twisted market you could imagine - with a premium for two things."

He stopped talking and started tapping his fingers on the table.

"You're going to make me guess?" I asked.

He nodded. I thought about it for a couple of minutes while he waited.

"Angels, and young girls?"

He slapped his hand on the table. “Close; angels, and *virgin* young girls. It was the angel part that got me going. I mean, vampires and angels? So I followed the trail a little further.”

I flipped past all of the prints of Romanian cryptography, and my breath caught in my throat. She looked like she was looking right at the camera. Josette.

“You know her?” he asked me.

I knew my expression was giving me away.

“We’ve met,” I said.

“She’s an angel,” he said. “From what I can gather, she’s worth quite a bit of coin to capture alive. I’m guessing they think she’s the best of both worlds.”

She was an angel, and a virgin. In seven hundred years, had she never found love? Or was it forbidden for angels to get involved in those kinds of relationships. I hoped it was the latter. The thought of her spending all of those years alone saddened me.

“How did you find her?” I asked.

“The vampires are tracking her for a guy named Reyzl,” he replied. “They have all kinds of spotters trying to keep their eyes on her. She still manages to fall off their radar from time to time, but she always turns up again. When I took the pic, she was working at a soup kitchen down in Chelsea. You can see the entrance in the background. Anyway, the homeless I talked to seemed to know her, so I guess she works there pretty regularly."

I fought back a sudden bout of embarrassment. I had been under the impression that angels kept the balance by hunting demons. It had never occurred to me that they would take on such mundane tasks as manning the line at a shelter. Then there was Reyzl. He seemed to be involved in everything around here, and not in a good way. I took note of the sign on the building, 'Holy Trinity'. I should have guessed.

"What do you know about Reyzl?" I asked.

He shook his head. "Not much man. The vamps seem like they're afraid to even type his name."

He sat back and took a sip of his Quad Caramel Latte with Extra Caramel. If vampires ran on blood, I imagined Obi ran on sugar.

"Your turn," he said.

Until he said it, I had never considered how I would explain myself to a mortal. He knew what vampires were, and he knew angels existed, so that was a good start. I gulped my Americano and took a deep breath.

"So you have angels, and you have demons," I said. "And then you have me. I'm kind of a Divine mutt, the only one my kind."

I told him everything I knew, using much the same description that Dante had used with me. Obi was stoic through it all, not reacting to anything I said, but analyzing every word. When I was finished, he just sat there for a minute, then licked his lips and reached for his bag.

"Silver won't work on me," I told him.

He didn't say anything. I watched while he opened the messenger bag, pulled out the Desert Eagle, and handed it to me, butt first.

"Knights used to pledge their swords," he said. "I don't have a sword."

I didn't take it right away. I looked into his eyes. He looked back, unflinching. I could see the strength in him, the conviction. If I was going to champion mankind, he was going to squire, and nothing I said or did was going to change his mind. I reached out and took the offered handle.

"You're probably going to be dead within a week," I told him.

His laugh was loud. "You have a strange way of welcoming people, man."

He reached out and clapped me on the shoulder. I discreetly handed the gun back to him.

"So what's next?" he asked me.

I picked up the folder. "I need to find out what the demons know about the Chalice Jesus drank from at the Last Supper, the Holy Grail. They've begun using it to make themselves near invincible."

I had just told him that the Holy Grail was real. I might as well have told him his shoe was untied. He was all business.

"That's heavy stuff,' he said. "I think I can help you out there. There's a vampire named Merov. He's a big deal in that circle, one of the largest suppliers on the exchange. He's having a big party tonight at his penthouse. From what I gather, its his daughter's eighty fourth birthday."

That sounded promising. "You have an address?" I asked.

"I wouldn't have mentioned it if I didn't," he replied.

I swallowed the last of my Americano and stood up. "Let's go," I said. "I'd say we could stop by your place, but I'm going to venture to guess it's been trashed by now. Was there anything on your computer that might give them a clue you know about this party?"

"Unencrypted?" he asked, offended.

I smiled. "Right. Then we'll go back to my place. Maybe you could teach me to fight."

It was good to have a friend, for as long as he lasted. I had a feeling the lifespan of mortal Purgatorian sympathizers was pretty short.

Chapter 12

“Man, you need a serious upgrade.” Obi looked around my apartment. It was the third or fourth time he had commented on my lousy living conditions.

“It suits my needs,” I told him. “It’s not like I get social security or anything. I’ve got about three thousand dollars to last me the rest of eternity, or until a die, whichever comes first. I’ll take bets on which one it’ll be.”

“Come on man, I saw you. I don’t think anything can keep you down.”

“If I lose my head, I die. If I take enough damage, I could be thrown in a safe somewhere and buried for all time. I won’t die, but I’ll be trapped.”

I hadn’t thought about that scenario before. I had to fight back a wave of panic. With any luck the other players wouldn’t think about that one either.

Obi’s voice snapped me out of my macabre introspective. “So you said you wanted to learn to fight. How much do you know?”

"You saw me," I said. "How much do you think I know?"

"Good point. Lucky for you, I served as an assistant instructor for my squad while we were in Afghanistan. I'll whip you into shape in no time."

I wanted to go up to the roof, but Obi protested due to the cold. I had already forgotten that he wasn't immune to the elements. I led us over to the room across the hall instead, pushing the furniture out of the way so we would have some room to maneuver.

The second we had finished clearing the floor he started barking at me Marine style, ordering me to drop and give him fifty. Just to make a point, I pumped out two hundred, asked him to sit on me, and did one hundred more. It didn't take too much effort for me to make myself a little stronger, and I had already found that my physical endurance was pretty much limitless.

"Point made she-hulk," Obi said, hopping off of me. "I'll show you some mixed martial arts moves instead."

He had me stand next to him and mimic his movements. He was a natural teacher, his manner and pace easy to follow and understand. Within a couple of hours I was able to deflect his most aggressive advances. I wasn't as successful on offense, having to pull my punches so I wouldn't hurt him. He seemed pleased with the results though.

"Best grub I've trained," he told me. "Hit the shower private, the party starts in three hours, and you need to get uptown."

I took another shower, and then sat with Obi to go over the plan. It was pretty basic, but the best we could do with the limited information we had. I would go in alone, disguised as a vampire and hoping that nobody there could see through the glamour. I would talk up the guests a bit, using some of the code words Obi taught me so I could intelligently make reference to the trade. The goal would be to try to coerce the guests into talking, or otherwise overhear anything that could be related to the Chalice.

As an aside, I also intended to listen for any chatter regarding Josette. There was no way I was going to let her wind up as some rich vampire's tasty snack. Once I had gotten what I needed, or decided I had overstayed my welcome, I would duck back out and return to the Belmont to debrief General Kenobi.

At the same time that I was attending the soiree, Obi would be working the Internet some more, trying to land info about the Chalice. Now that he knew what he was up against, he knew well enough to stay on the move and hop hotspots.

"I wish I was feeling confident about this," I said to Obi.

The party started in half an hour, which was just enough time to be fashionably late. I hadn't vamped myself out yet, but I had changed my clothes into a super sharp black tuxedo with a Nehru jacket and gaudy diamond cufflinks. We decided I should go as a major player, and being able to look the part would help me integrate and get them talking.

Regardless, I was doing battle with the feeling of being over exposed. It didn't help that I had lost possession of the blessed sword back at Grand Central. What would happen to it now? Would some homeless guy just happen by and find himself in possession of an incredibly sharp and deadly demon-killing tool?

"I've been pulped three times already, and I won't have backup," I said.

Well, I guess I did have backup, if Ulnyx decided to make himself available. After the not-dream I had experienced I was feeling a little bit better about being able to control that bastard, but he knew I could control him too, which made his participation iffy.

"Don't worry about it, man," Obi said. "All you have to do is keep the disguise going, and you won't have any trouble. Just channel your inner James Bond."

Obi's overconfidence was a great counter to my apprehension. I walked over to the door and swung it open.

"Wish me luck," I said, trying to keep my nerves in check.

Obi laughed. "Nah. Good hunting!" He gave me a stiff salute as I shut the door behind me.

The party was taking place in the penthouse of a Trump property on the Upper East Side, a ritzy glitzy area where celebrity sightings were sure to be more common than vampire sightings. It was at the total end of the island from where I was starting, but the distance wasn't a problem. Obi had called a livery while I had showered, and a confused limo driver greeted me when I exited the Belmont.

"Are you okay?" I asked him as he pulled the back door of the stretch limo open for me.

This was costing ten percent of my stash, but Obi had insisted I needed to go all in to earn their trust. He had even gone so far as to plant some messages about 'Stefano Giovanni' across the online blood exchanges, hushed whispers of a reclusive trafficker who had decided at the last minute to fly in from Venice to attend the birthday bash. He was sure there were no other major players in Venice; it seemed vampires weren't big fans of water, and my ability to operate there would also gain me some respect.

The limo driver looked from me, to the Belmont, and then back. I had changed my appearance, going for more of a Brad Pitt, *Interview With a Vampire* look, complete with a set of small fangs that would only be apparent if I smiled fully.

"No sir," he said. He ushered me in and closed the door. "Frickin' drug dealers," I heard him mutter. "Just drive 'em up, drop 'em off, get the hell outta there."

The limo ride was short, but I took the opportunity to enjoy it. I hadn't been in a limo since my high school prom. Carly

Lane. The name made me shake my head and smile at the same time. I hadn't thought about her in years. I was her first crush, an awkward computer nerd who looked at women and saw only distraction. She had asked me to the Prom, and against my better judgment, I had accepted. It had never occurred to me then, but she had been really pretty. What would she say if she could see me now? The date hadn't gone so well, but we had stayed friends for the remainder of High School. I bet she was married and had a few kids. She always had been the motherly type.

The driver's voice snapped my out of my reminiscing. "Here you are sir," he said as the limo glided to a halt.

I turned my head to look out the window while I waited for him to come around and get the door. The building was huge, at least fifty stories or more, all glass and steel. It just oozed power and money. There was a doorman waiting by the huge revolving door, and just inside I could see about half a dozen vampires standing in a line. My heart leapt to my throat as the slide into panic started. If they were able to see through my glamour, I would be dead before I got across the street. I was beginning to regret my current course of action. The door opened.

I took one more deep breath and stepped out of the limo. I handed the driver the cash plus a generous tip.

"Thank you," I said.

He was halfway to the driver's seat before the 'you' made it out of my mouth. My senses were getting a little crazy with the number of Divine gathering in the building. I could feel the combined energy of the masses. It didn't help my nerves any.

I slipped through the revolving door, and was approached by the first vampire in the line. He was well-dressed, well kept, and well-built, equal parts class and muscle.

"I'm here for the Solen birthday party," I said, trying to stay calm even though my chest felt like it was about to give birth to something nasty. "My name is Stefano Giovanni."

The vampire took his time looking me over, but it was his nose I was worried about. I had done my best to mimic the smell that I associated with Rebecca, because she was the only good example I had of how a vampire should smell. I had toned down the floweriness of her perfume, but maintained the musky iron and mixed it with Drakkar.

I waited; internally tense enough to break a board, externally playing it cool. He completed his sniff test, took a step back and smiled, his fangs betraying him for the first time.

"Mr. Solen has directed me to cater to your every whim," he said. "He is very eager to speak with you regarding the Italian markets. This way, Mr. Giovanni."

He bowed and put out his arm to direct me to the elevator. I didn't look at him, or respond. I just started walking like the stuck up evil prick I was supposed to be.

We stepped into the elevator, and he hit the only button in it. Private. Impressive.

"What's your name?" I asked. My voice sounded normal to me, but I was projecting it to him with a soft Italian accent.

"Tarly, sir," he replied.

He waited for me to speak again. I decided against it, leaving him to deal with the awkward moment. The elevator had us up to the penthouse in no time.

Obi had warned me about what to expect at a vampire-organized event. Even so, it was a challenge to hide my reaction as the elevator doors slid open and Tarly and I stepped out into the apartment.

The living space was huge, bigger than anything I could have imagined. The elevator let out on a large balcony that overlooked the main living area, where I could see about a hundred guests had already gathered. To the right were the rest of the smaller rooms, to the left and front nothing but a wall of twenty-foot tall floor-to-ceiling windows that exposed an incredible view of the city. The balcony fed down into the party through a pair of matching marble staircases, which were lined with a menagerie of antiques that I was sure cost a fortune. The front corner by the windows held a more typical interior decoration, with a sofa and loveseat caddy cornered in front of a free standing fireplace, enabling their inhabitants to get the best view of the city below. Hanging from the ceiling over the furniture was a huge canvas banner that read 'Happy Birthday Reyka!'.

All of this was impressive, but not out of place for the rich. What gave the affair away as being oh-so-not-normal was the open area that had been created by removing a bunch of the ancillary furniture. Sitting in the middle of it was a huge classic roman fountain, but instead of spouting water it was circulating blood, tossing it up into the air and dribbling it over the sides into the main pool. The guests around it would dip a finger in from time to time to get a quick taste, then resume whatever conversation they were having. It was gross, but not completely stomach churning as long as you tried not to think of where the blood had come from.

That prize went to the fringe of the open area, near the southern wall of glass, where they had set up about half a dozen beds. On the beds were women, human women, unclothed, tied up, and drugged. They weren't alone on the beds, the guests were free to step right up and have a taste.

I was nearing the breaking point of my ability to contain my disgust, repulsion, and anger when Tarly stepped in front of me.

"Mr. Giovanni," he said.

I must have given him a look of death, because he stooped over and looked up at me like a beaten animal.

"I'm sorry sir, but Mr. Solen requested that I bring you over to him. If you'll follow me?"

Making a scene about the 'Fresh Fleshette', as Obi had told me the vamps called it, would have blown my disguise in about point oh one seconds. As much as it pained me to have to ignore it, failing to find the Chalice was going to cost a heck of a lot more.

"Lead the way," I said, maintaining the assertive posture that was causing Tarly to stoop like Quasimodo.

He straightened up, but not too much, and started walking down the southern staircase. Great, now I had to get even closer to it.

Closer would have been a bonus. As it turned out, Merov Solen was just finishing up with a taste of his own. There was nothing frightening or imposing about the vampire who was considered the most powerful in the Americas. He was small, maybe a couple of inches over five feet, with a bald head and a plentiful gut. His eyes were large and blue, his clothes a simple pair of corduroys and a plaid button-down shirt that made him conspicuously out of place amidst the rest of the partygoers in their black ties and gowns.

When he saw me approaching, he gave me a car salesman smile, and then licked away a bit of blood that had coagulated in the corner of his mouth. I glanced over at the girl on the bed. At least she had no idea where she was or what was happening to her. If I had a chance to get her out, I would. If not, I would avenge her somehow.

"Care for a small bite?" he asked. "There's nothing quite like a virgin to get the old heart pumping again, is there?"

I bit my tongue, almost hard enough to get a taste of my own blood. "Personally, I prefer pure. I find the alterations caused by external agents unpalatable."

Merov smiled and reached his arm up to put it around my shoulder. "A demon of exquisite taste and standards. I respect that. Between you and me, I wouldn't have even bothered with the drugs, but this is my daughter's birthday party and she's going to be mad enough at me for providing the Fresh Fleshette at all. Sometimes I don't know if she's really mine, the way she carries on about drinking human blood. We're vampires for Hell's sake!"

A vampiress after my own heart. I felt an instant unknown kinship with Merov's daughter. We were both in a vast minority after all.

"Is she here?" I asked him. "I'm most interested in learning more about her ideas for survival without our primary food source."

He laughed. "Do you have any idea how much of my money she's sunk into researching vampire physiology, trying to figure out exactly what's in human blood that we need to survive? She's even had me try some of her sample synthetics.

You could live on it, but it tastes like sewage. And that's ignoring the fact that such a thing would put me out of business. Can you believe I'm financing my own destruction?"

He started leading me through the throng, acknowledging all of the guests who noticed him. When they saw him coming, they would turn, fall to one knee, and bow their head.

"Besides," he continued, "humans are meant to be cattle to us. We're superior in every way, am I right?"

I wanted to crush his melon head between my hands. "Right," I said instead.

"Anyway, she hasn't shown up yet. She doesn't know about the party, so I'm hopeful that she'll respect her father's wishes for once. She's a handful, but she's my only child and I love her as much as my cold heart will allow."

He was taking me past the gathering, towards the more private living spaces on the northern end of the apartment.

"I wouldn't know," I said. "I have never had a desire for offspring."

He nodded at the two burly guards as he brought me past them and into a long hallway. Looking at them as I passed, I realized they weren't vampires. I felt a small stirring in my soul. Weres.

"I didn't either," Merov said. "Reyka's mother was a Succubus. She tricked me into it. At first, I was so angry I almost had her killed. Then, I decided to wait until my little girl was born. I was curious about what kind of demon the union would produce. After I saw her, I claimed her as my own, and removed her mother's head myself. I think that's where she gets her soft spot for humans. Her mother always had a thing for them. She said they were most creative."

Merov stopped at a set of double-doors near the end of the long hallway, then fumbled around in his pants pockets, looking for the keys.

"Anyway, enough about my daughter. If you'd like I can introduce you when she arrives. What I'd really like to speak with you about is my interest in working out a trade agreement. I have a number of parties interested in getting their fangs on a good European source. My servants have told me you have quite a reputation, and that you are a mystery to most."

"I try to keep a low profile," I agreed. "The element of surprise can be quite powerful."

He finally found what he was looking for, a small coin that he pressed against a flat panel attached to one of the doors. It beeped, and the door unlocked.

"That's how I came to power here," he said. "This apartment used to belong to another, before I claimed it and threw him from the roof. But not before I took this."

He held up the small coin. It wasn't a coin after all, but a round piece of glass with the edge of a finger nestled inside. He needed the prior inhabitant's fingerprint to get into the room.

He was about to push the door open when one of the were guards stepped up to us. "Pardon me sirs," he said. He sounded like he was chewing on gravel. "Mr. Solen, your daughter has arrived."

Merov sighed. "Perfect timing as usual," he said, turning to me. "We will talk again later, after the party."

It wasn't a suggestion, but a command. He didn't wait for me to react. He turned and started walking back towards the elevators, leaving me standing there with the were. He ushered me back to the party.

When I stepped back out into the main reception area I looked up to try to catch a glimpse of Merov's daughter Reyka. I could see Merov making his way up the steps, but the angle was no good to see more than a few feet past the landing. Oh well, I could wait. Merov had said he would introduce us. I moved into the crowd, focusing my attention on the conversations swirling around me.

"It's just ridiculous," one of the vampires was saying to a group of five or six. "The market is just flooded with poor quality. Every vampire who has ever hunted is trying to start their own exchange service, and they think that we can't tell the difference between a debutante and a prostitute."

"Give me an angel any day," his companion said. She looked like she was fifty or sixty years old, but solid as a rock. "I still remember the last time I had an angel. It cost me a fortune, but it was so worth it."

"I heard the Masters have a new weapon in the war," said a third. This one got my attention. "Some kind of amulet that makes the wearer completely indestructible."

The others expressed their shock and awe. "Where did they get it from?" asked the older vampire woman.

I didn't get to hear the response. An immediate hush fell over the whole crowd, and they turned as one to face the landing. I was the odd man out, not catching on to whatever invisible signal had been sent. I turned to look just as they all shouted, "Surprise!"

It sure was a surprise. Reyka was Rebecca.

She was stunning in a perfect little black dress and black pumps, her long black hair piled up on top of her head. The contrast of all of the black against her white skin accentuated everything about her perfect form, and it almost drove me to the point of distraction. I could tell by her reaction that she was less than pleased with the surprise. Not that any of the other attendees would have noticed, because she was an expert at faking the enthusiasm. I knew she was lying though, as she laughed and gave her father a big hug.

He turned her and faced her back out to the gathering below, and they applauded her. Stealing glances, I saw the feeling was mutual. The crowd wasn't cheering for Rebecca. They were cheering because Merov expected them to cheer. To them, Rebecca was every bit the outcast she had explained herself to be. I could guess why she had given me an alternate name.

After a satisfactory length of applause, Merov raised his hand to quiet the gathering. Once he had achieved silence, he took Rebecca by the hands and spoke to her loudly enough for everyone to hear.

"My dearest daughter," he said. "Every year as this day comes I am so very grateful that you were brought into my world. You're smile is the blood on which I thrive."

Merov motioned with his head, and Tarly stepped over, holding a small gilded box. Merov let go of his daughter's hands and took the box from the servant, holding it out to her and opening it. I couldn't see the contents, so I watched her reaction instead - surprise, confusion, and a hint of disgust? Those were her real feelings. To her father, she showed only joy.

Merov reached into the box with one hand and withdrew a long silver necklace, at the end of which hung a crystal. It looked red from the distance, but I knew the crystal was clear. The red came from the blood trapped inside. Just for confirmation, I reached into my tuxedo pocket and withdrew the business end of the necklace I had taken from Ulnyx. It was a near perfect match.

"May you always stay safe from harm," he said as he placed it over her head. "Happy birthday dear."

The applause started up again and I could almost feel Rebecca cringing at the pomp of it all. She turned and waved at the crowd, holding up the crystal for them all to get a better look at her gift. That was when I felt her eyes meet mine, and my heart fell out of my chest. She recognized me.

I had an option to either be bold or submissive. I went for bold, keeping my eyes locked on hers, letting them tell her that I knew that she knew it was me. I saw a slight smile crease the corner of her lip, so I winked at her. She winked back, then turned and gave her father a big hug. They talked privately for a minute, and then started down the steps. On the way, Rebecca not-too-subtly pointed at me and asked him who I was. I gave them my best bow.

"Stefan," Merov said as he reached the bottom of the stairs, Rebecca on his arm. "I'd like you to meet my daughter, Reyka."

Rebecca unhooked herself and held her hand forward. I dropped to my knee and kissed it, dizzied by the smell of her.

"A pleasure," I said as I rose back to somewhat shaky feet. She was smiling, a beautiful, honest smile. She really was happy to see me.

"Sir Giovanni," she said with a hint of playfulness. "You are too kind."

"Nonsense," Merov said. "You are always a pleasure my dear. If you don't mind, I have some other people I need to speak with. Stefan, take good care of my daughter." Again with the command.

"As you wish, Sir Solen," I replied. Merov leaned up to kiss Rebecca on the cheek, and then wandered off to speak with some of the other guests. "What's with that?" I whispered to her as soon as he was out of range.

She leaned in close so we could speak without being overheard. Her proximity was intoxicating. Half-succubus, I remembered. "He's trying to Command you," she said. "He doesn't know you're resistant to demonic possession."

There went the half-succubus excuse. She was giving me heart palpitations on her own merit. It had to be the perfume.

"What are you doing here?" she asked. "Do you know what will happen if anyone figures out who or what you are?"

"Your necklace," I said.

She looked down at it. "What about it?"

"That's what I'm doing here. I'd tell you more, but you aren't on my side. Needless to say, it's worth the risk to me. Finding you here is an unexpected bonus."

I hadn't intended to say the last part out loud, but it found its way through my lips of its own accord. Rebecca's face flushed.

"Your father was very eager to have us meet," I said, loud enough for those nearby to hear. I didn't want anyone to suspect we already knew one another.

"My father is trying to find me a suitable mate," she said. There went my heart again, right into my throat. "He knows none of the meat around here can control me."

"Nor should they seek to," I told her. "He was telling me of the research you are conducting. Perhaps these lesser nosferatu find the idea uninspired, but I think it is a fascinating endeavor." I could tell she was trying not to laugh at my faux snobbishness.

She sighed a sigh that could launch a thousand ships. "You have no idea how refreshing it is to speak to someone with vision, Sir Giovanni."

I could feel the sets of eyes on me, trying to figure out who the fruitcake that thought not killing humans for food was. Our conversation was momentarily interrupted when the elevator opened again and a human band rushed out, set up their instruments on the landing, and began playing.

"I hate when he does that," she said to me. I assumed Merov had Commanded the band to come and play, and they had literally jumped at the opportunity.

"Shall we Miss Solen?" I asked, holding out my arm to lead her to where a makeshift dance floor was opening around the fountain.

She reached out and took it, the warmth of her touch sending a hot shiver down my entire arm. My prom date with Carly hadn't been a total waste.

I don't know what the song was, or even if there was music. When Rebecca looked at me, all I could see was her face. When she spoke, all I could hear was her voice. She hadn't affected me like this the last time we met, but maybe I had been too afraid to take full notice of her. We moved with such fluid grace it was like we were destined to be dance partners. Her closeness felt so natural, so perfect.

"How did you know who I was as soon as you saw me?" I asked her. The dance had afforded us the opportunity to get super close, and the music aided in drowning out any possibility of being overheard.

"Your glamour doesn't work on me," she replied. "Didn't the Outcast tell you not all demons could be tricked?"

"Because of your mother? I seem to be doing okay with the rest of the room."

"My father told you about her?" She seemed surprised. "He must like you."

I spun her around and expertly regained the step, leading her forward without hesitation. "He likes who he thinks I am, a big shot Lord from Venice. You know what he did to your mother?"

I felt her grip tighten on me, threatening to break my skin. "I know," she said, the anger obvious in her voice. "He's never tried to keep it a secret. He's quite proud of himself. Once a succubus has you, it's very difficult to escape."

"And..."

"And what? He's my father. I am obligated to either obey, or overthrow. There is no middle ground."

"Overthrow?" I knew what the word meant. I knew what it sounded like. It was just weird to hear someone say it about their family.

Rebecca's iron grip relaxed. "A vampire can rightfully seize control of their house by disposing of the patriarch. It is the normal means by which we rise and fall from power. Until that time, we are bound by our honor to show respect, even to those we despise. I am powerful for a vampire because of my mixed heritage, but I am not strong enough to defeat Merov Solen, and so I've had to endure his story of how he murdered my mother for much of my life."

"He seems to care for you," I said. At least he had claimed he did.

"In his own way," she admitted. "He has provided me with everything I have ever asked for, anything I could ever want. But there are strings. Always strings."

I could see the sadness in her eyes, and I wanted nothing more than to be able to help her. "I'm sorry," I whispered.

She gave me a look of strange fascination, and then she kissed me.

It was a short, soft kiss, but it sent a wave of energy rolling from my head all the way down to my toes. I could feel the tips of her fangs brush up against my lip, the sharp edges threatening to puncture the skin. I could taste the cold moisture of her mouth, blood and iron and lipstick. My entire body turned to jello.

"Thank you," she said in a hoarse whisper. She pulled back and helped me resume the dance. My rubbery legs fought to comply.

We finished out the song in silence, our hands and eyes staying locked together. My mission. I hadn't come here to flirt with the birthday girl, regardless of how much I was enjoying it. I was here to get information about the source of the very thing that Merov had gifted to his daughter. It was only logical to think that Merov knew the origin. My mind went back to the room with the fingerprint lock. I was willing to bet anything that the answers I sought could be found in that room. The real question was how in the world was I going to get inside? The answer - I wasn't; at least not tonight. I needed to beat a hasty retreat while the going was still good.

"Thank you for the dance, Lady Solen," I said to Rebecca in my Sir Giovanni voice while letting go of her hands. "If you'll excuse me, I need to go downstairs to make a phone call. I would be honored if you would offer me the opportunity to speak with you further about your scientific achievements. I believe they are most fascinating."

Rebecca smiled. "Perhaps we can continue the conversation after you complete your call," she said. "I can escort you down to the lobby."

"You are very kind," I replied, holding out my arm for her again.

She wrapped her own arm in it and started walking me towards the stairs as the band began playing another tune. I glanced around the crowd looking for Merov, finding him back at the Fresh Fleshette. He noticed me with Rebecca on my arm and smiled his approval. I could imagine what he'd be thinking if he knew what I was intending to do.

"Leaving so soon?" Rebecca whispered to me as we ascended the stairs to the elevator. "You couldn't possibly have gotten what you were looking for from me."

"I got something better from you," I replied, causing her another round of embarrassment. "What I was looking for, I got from your father, although he doesn't know it yet."

We reached the top of the stairs and stepped out onto the landing. It was clear except for the band and another pair of weres who were guarding the elevator. I had almost made it out without a negative incident.

"Sir Giovanni needs to go make a call," Rebecca told the guards. "I'm going to escort him down."

The were on the left held up his hand. "Just one minute Lady Solen. The elevator is on its way up. You'll never believe who decided to come to your party."

I looked at Rebecca. She shrugged her shoulders. "Who is it?" she asked.

The timing was impeccable. The elevator dinged, the door slid open, and out of it stepped pure evil.

Reyzl. I knew it was him the moment the elevator doors finished opening. He was resplendent in crisp, fitted tails, complete with top hat, gloves, cane, and fur lined cape. He was dark skinned, Indian maybe, tall and bony with boyish good looks. The kicker was the eyes, huge solid black orbs that absorbed your soul, stole your will, and reflected you back as no more than a puppet on a string. They were empty, expressionless eyes, creepy and powerful and impossible to penetrate. He radiated total domination in the form of an unfeeling coldness that left no question that was the superior. It was the power of pure hate, greed, and evil resting just below the surface of the human facade he had wrapped himself up in for the occasion. It was my first glimpse at what a true demon was, and the hopelessness that followed was almost enough to crush my soul right then and there.

He knew me too, or at least he knew who I wasn't. He was emotionless as he stepped off the elevator and looked at me for the first time. I saw nothing in his eyes, but his lip curled at the edge in a rough snarl. He lifted the hand with the cane towards me, and every muscle in my body froze stiff, as if I had been encased in ice.

"Diuscrucis," he said with a perfect, flat calm, as if he had been expecting the encounter.

I struggled against myself, trying to will my body into motion. I could feel the tug in my mind, could feel my power butting up against his. It was no contest. "This is going to be quite an entertaining night after all, isn't it," he said to no one in particular. "Merov," he called out.

I continued fighting the invisible bonds, even though I knew I wasn't strong enough to break them. Rebecca had backed away from me towards Reyzl when he had called me out. I didn't blame her for choosing his side. I was a mouse with my tail firmly caught. I couldn't turn my head to look, but I could hear Merov Solen running up the steps to answer to his master.

"My Lord Reyzl," Merov said, reaching the landing and dropping to his knee.

Reyzl didn't even look at him. He just raised his cane and motioned towards the guests below. Merov got back to his feet and went to the edge of the platform.

"Ladies and gentlemen," he cried out to the assembly. The band stopped playing and the quiet din of so many conversations all hushed at once. "All hail the power and glory of Lord Reyzl the Dominator," he said, turning and dropping to his knee again.

Everyone else followed suit, including Rebecca, who looked at me as she did so, her eyes apologetic. I would have told her I understood, that it was okay, but I was the one still standing, stiff as a board and one hundred percent incapacitated.

Reyzl motioned for Merov to stand, which was the queue for the rest of the congregation to follow. They stood motionless, waiting for their master's command. "Now Merov, will you please explain to me how you allowed a diuscrucis into your home unchallenged."

Merov turned to look at me. "Sir Giovanni?" he asked. "I... I'm sorry my Lord. I do not understand."

"Do you question me?" Reyzl asked, his voice still calm and emotionless.

Merov's face turned bright red. "No, no my Lord," he replied, bowing down to the demon. "I cannot see what you see. I see only a vampire. He told me his name was Stefan Giovanni, from Venice."

I noticed the minutest change in Reyzl's expression. It was as if his body had attempted to feel mirth, but it had been crushed in an instant.

"Of course," he said. "Reyka, my dear. Tell me, what do you see?"

She didn't hesitate, and I understood why not. "He is a diuscrucis, my lord. His name is Landon. I have been befriending him, in order to learn his secrets, to learn what the Outcast and his servant are plotting."

As she spoke, her pale blue eyes were replaced with the same cold black orbs that I had seen the first time we met. They were expressionless eyes, used to hide from me. I had expected her to identify what I was, but I hadn't been expecting her complete betrayal. If I could have moved, I would have kicked myself for being so stupid. She didn't need to possess me with the power of a succubus. Her natural beauty had been more than enough to seduce me into trusting her.

Reyzl fixed his attention back on me. The only way I knew it was because he said my name. "Landon. I'm going to ask you a question. You'll need to be able to speak to answer it." I felt my head regain mobility.

It was tempting to say something stupid and pointless, but it would have looked panicked and weak. I was both, but I wasn't about to let him have the satisfaction of forcing it out of me. I said nothing, waiting for his question.

"No doubt the Outcast and his Collector have sent you on this fool's errand. Tell me, are they aware of the Chalice and the work we have being doing with it?"

He stepped closer to me as he spoke, his mere presence overpowering my senses. He was Commanding me, I knew, though he was much more subtle about it than Merov had been. Worse, it was a struggle to resist compliance.

"No," I said. "I was here to find out about the Exchange. To find a way to shut it down." I figured I'd try, but I had no doubt he would be able to see right through the lie.

"Reyka, is he telling the truth?" he asked.

"He wouldn't tell me what his goal in being here was, my Lord," she told him.

At least I had done something right, not telling her everything. He seemed to be going for the lie.

"No matter," he said. "No harm has been done. Goodbye, Landon."

He showed no outward sign of effort in causing every single nerve in my body to feel as though it were exploding at once. The agony of the event was indescribable, like a paper cut on every single cell that made up my living flesh. As each cut was made my body would heal in time to be cut again, multiplying the sensory pain a hundredfold. I would have passed out, would have welcomed it in fact, but my Divine being wouldn't allow it. I experienced a hundred lifetimes of pain each instant, all the while knowing it was just a prelude to my final fate.

I kept my eyes as focused as I could on Reyzl as he stepped forward, lifting the cane and pulling from its base with his free hand. The cane doubled as a sword, a cursed blade that would put me out of my misery. The demon's expression didn't change the entire time. It was lifeless, soulless. Not even my tortured pain was able to cause any sort of reaction. The complete ambivalence was the most frightening thing of all.

Before he could finish me off, the entire world erupted into a mess of chaos and frenzy. Reyzl's perfect ensemble was ruined when a clean silver blade burst from his heart, the blessed runes etched on its surface glowing red with heat. I felt the pain stop, felt my limbs regain their flexibility. I stumbled and fought to stay on my feet.

I heard Merov shouting his daughter's name, and then I saw her charging me, her eyes still black, her fangs bared. I couldn't recover fast enough to defend myself. She slammed into me, lifting me over her shoulder. With one motion she planted her foot on the top of the railing and carried us both off of the landing and down into the waiting crowd below.

We hit the ground hard, the momentum tossing me away from her. I had gone from bad to just as bad, because now I was lying in the middle of over a hundred angry vampires.

I leapt to my feet, getting into position to defend myself the way Obi had shown me earlier. Rebecca had regained her footing as well, coming at me from my left. I turned to defend myself from her when I saw a brown shape hurtling down from the landing above. She crouched low and kicked up with her foot, making a solid connection with the incoming missile, sending it careening off into the crowd. I stood there dumbstruck. The missile had been Merov.

"Move it, worm," she said, reaching out and grabbing my arm. "I'm trying to save your life."

The pain of her grip snapped me out of it, and my brain did the math. She had stabbed Reyzl from behind with a blessed dagger. Where she had gotten it, I had no idea, but she had saved my life for the moment at least. Her betrayal had been a ruse. She had chosen a side, and it was mine. The sum of that equation was the hardest kick in the ass I could have imagined.

I looked up at the landing, where Reyzl was working to get the dagger out of his chest. I was going to assume if Ulnyx had possessed an amulet, his boss would have one too. That meant we had about twenty seconds to find a way out of this mess, maybe less. The guests had overcome their surprise, and were turning towards us, their eyes going black, their fingernails and fangs elongating. I looked around the room in search of something, anything I could use. My eyes settled on the fountain of blood.

Blood, water, they weren't that different, and I had practiced making it rain for hours. I reached out and focused my will, pulling the fluid from the fountain and yanking it over to where Rebecca and I were standing. It splashed through the crowd in its haste to arrive, then circled around and spread over us like a plasma cocoon.

"I don't see how this is going to help," Rebecca said in response to my activity.

The blood was spinning around us, maintaining the form. I had turned water vapor into water. Now I took liquid blood and dried it into a solid.

"This is just part one," I said. Part two was going to be the hard part, and I didn't know if I would be able to pull it off. "Keep them off me if they get through."

I closed my eyes, picturing the twenty-foot walls of glass that occupied the outer corners of the penthouse. I focused my will on them, demanding that they lose their cohesion, that the crystalline structure of the glass break down at a vastly accelerated pace. I could hear the claws scraping against the wall of blood. I could hear Merov shouting from outside, cursing Rebecca for her betrayal. I didn't dare open my eyes for fear of losing my focus. I pushed again, as hard as I ever had before.

There was no build up, no warning. I could hear the groaning, cracking, and then the shattering as the glass succumbed to my will. One moment the windows were whole and perfect, the next they were imploding in a million fragments. The cries of pain from outside the blood sarcophagus were deafening. Nothing inside the apartment was able to avoid being pelted with shards of glass. Nothing except for Rebecca and I, encased in a protective shell. It wouldn't be enough to kill any of the vampires, but with any luck it would slow them down long enough for us to escape.

"Part three," I cried, opening my eyes and turning the blood barrier back to liquid.

It splashed onto the floor, and the true chaos of what I had created was revealed. All around us the gathered vampires writhed in pain on the floor, each having suffered at least a hundred cuts and piercings. They were healing already, but the pure volume of the damage was keeping their attention off of us. I took a quick look back towards Reyzl. As one of the few bodies on the upper floor he had been pin cushioned by the incoming glass. He was healing faster than the others, and I could tell by the position of his head that he was watching me when I took Rebecca by the hand and started to run towards the now open windows.

"Are you out of your mind," Rebecca shouted at me as we approached the exposed Manhattan skyline, a good fifty stories up. I just might be.

I pulled her in close to me and pushed off with my legs as hard as I could, putting us airborne even before we had reached the edge. I didn't know if I would be able to go through with it once I could see the drop, so I didn't give myself the chance. The floor of the penthouse disappeared, and then we were flying high over the quiet city street below. I took a deep breath and held it as my stomach lurched. Our flight was over, and now we were falling.

Rebecca's grip was painful as we plummeted towards the concrete under us. I had about seven seconds to slow us down enough to both survive the impact and heal before any of the demons above regrouped and came down in the elevator. I could only hope Reyzl wouldn't follow us in the express.

I forced my will on the air around us, demanding it to be denser, thicker, heavier, and to provide a greater level of friction and resistance in order to slow our fall. I could feel it responding around us, feel the pressure building and thickening. Not enough. The ground was still approaching at a breakneck pace.

I demanded it to compress even more, the pressure threatening to pop us from the inside. Rebecca's eyelids were raised in fear, though her black eyes told me nothing. I was going to say something comforting, but there was no time. I rolled myself so I was positioned under her just before we hit the ground.

The second we made contact with the earth I let go of our airbag, the release of the compressed air causing a small explosion that shattered the windows of the buildings around us and flipped over a couple of parked cars. We hit hard, but not too hard, and I knew when I felt my back shatter that the damage wouldn't be bad enough to prevent us from moving soon.

I still held Rebecca on top of me, clutching her body against mine. I had broken her fall, but she hadn't escaped unscathed. Her legs had been askew from my own, and her kneecaps had taken the same force as my back. She was alive and alert though, her eyes open and back to their perfect pale blue. Her face was twisted in pain.

"Are you okay?" I asked her.

"Nothing that won't heal," she said through her grimace, "But I can't do it as quickly as you."

I could feel my body was already mending. I maintained my grip on her as I pushed myself to my feet, lifting her up and over my shoulder. "Then allow me, Miss Solen," I said. Direction didn't matter, as long as it was away.

We had gone up about two blocks when we heard the roar of the first demons out onto the street.

"Put me down, Landon," Rebecca said.

I lowered her to the ground, being careful not to put too much stress on her knees. She pointed to a manhole cover near the end of the street. The sewer? Maybe I could turn off my sense of smell.

"We won't be able to lose them down there," she said, "but it will give us a better defensive position." She didn't wait for me to argue. She kicked off her heels and ran down the street. I followed behind her. She pulled the manhole cover off and began descending into the darkness.

It was pitch black underground, but I knew by now that it didn't have to be. I adjusted my eyes to be able to pierce the darkness, being met with stone walls and a six inch deep stream of who-knows-what. The smell was horrible, but not unbearable. I moved to put the cover back over the manhole, but Rebecca pulled me away.

"No time," she said, pulling me behind her.

We heard the splash when the weres hit the sewer. There wasn't enough room for them to maintain their demonic forms down here, something I hadn't considered but Rebecca must have. We could hear their footfalls as they chased behind us, moving just as fast as we were.

"We need to take them out, or they'll just catch us when we try to climb up," Rebecca said, coming to a stop and turning around. She reached over her shoulder and pulled another dagger from a sheathe hidden on her back.

"You can't kill them with that," I pointed out. The dagger was cursed.

"No," she agreed. "I'll slow them down, you stop them."

I didn't have a blessed weapon either. "How?" I asked. "I'm unarmed."

She smiled. "Landon, you're a diuscrucis. You're always armed. Be creative."

Her eyes turned black again as she morphed into killer-vampiress mode and dashed forward towards the oncoming weres. I could see that she intended to hit them when they turned the corner. Be creative, right. I heard a grunt of pain as the battle was joined, Rebecca's element of surprise giving her a clear advantage. Be creative. I looked down at the sewage running past my legs. It was my turn to smile.

When I reached the corner where Rebecca had vanished, she was having her way with the weres, her dagger lashing out like an angry viper to add to an ever growing number of cuts while they struggled to make contact with their own weapons. I recognized them as the two that had been guarding the elevator when Reyzl had made his entrance. It made sense that they would be the first ones down.

"Whenever you're ready," Rebecca said, ducking under a strike and stabbing one of the weres in the chest.

I focused my will on the sewage at my feet, finding a pair of splintered boards and pulling them out of the flotsam. I held them aloft, moving them back behind my head and down the tunnel as far as I could. I didn't want to take any chances that I wouldn't get enough momentum.

"Down," I yelled, pushing the huge splinters forward with all of the force I could manage. I could feel I was reaching the limits of my strength, and my head was enveloped in pain as I sent the missiles hurtling towards the fray.

Rebecca danced out of the path of the makeshift spears just in time. The weres weren't so lucky. They had just enough time to identify the threat before they were skewered, the twin wooden stakes piercing all the way through their chests, hearts, and backs. They both emitted an ear-splitting howl and toppled forward into the muck. I leaned up against the side of the sewer. My head was on fire, and I was having trouble seeing straight.

Rebecca pounced on the prone weres and used the cursed dagger to remove their heads, then hurried over to where I was leaning.

"Too much," I told her. "I need to rest."

"Don't get too embarrassed," she said.

Before I could ask her what she meant, she had me over her shoulder, carrying me through the sewer like a child. I wanted to protest, but I was just too weak. I let her be my legs without complaint.

Chapter 13

She put me down once we had neared the end of the sewer tunnel, which opened up into a larger area where multiple flows met and continued on in a single stream. We could hear voices through the large tunnel up ahead, a cacophony of sound that suggested more than just a wayward vagrant.

"Thanks for the ride," I said, the ground still a little shaky under me.

"You're welcome," she replied. "Can you walk?"

My head was still throbbing, but I could hold myself up. "Yeah, but I really need to rest for a while. I've never done anything like that before."

"The glass was impressive, but lets try not to have to jump like that again," she said. "There are humans up ahead, a squatter settlement I believe. We can rest there."

"What about Reyzl?"

"He won't give chase, and Merov's people will turn back once they see the headless henchmen. We've won for tonight. Reyzl is nothing if not patient."

"So he knows he can take me out pretty much any time, and isn't concerned?"

She giggled. "Something like that."

"I don't know why you decided to help me, but I'm glad you did," I told her, looking into her eyes. She dug her fangs into her bottom lip and gave me a sheepish smile.

"Just something about you I guess," she replied. "Come on."

We didn't have to walk too far down the larger adjoining sewer tunnel before it opened up into a much larger room. My guess was that it had been a pumping station many, many years ago.

There was a massive hunk of machinery resting just off to the side of the river of sewage, with old brass pipes jutting out and down into the muck. A shantytown had sprung up around it, home to at least three hundred people and complete with electricity and lighting provided by a hack on the pump's former connection to the grid. They even had clean water that they were leeching from a pipe that must have once been used to cool the giant beast.

The town itself was a loose grid of tents, tarps, and cardboard boxes molded together into workable living spaces for the homeless who resided here. They were going about their lives oblivious to the strangers in their midst, collecting water from the open pipe to cook their food on propane heaters, or to clean their clothes in makeshift washtubs. What did they have to fear, since they had nothing to lose?

I leaned on Rebecca while we walked, thankful to have her shoulder to keep me from falling over. I could only imagine being one of the vagrants seeing us go by, me in my torn up tuxedo that I was too weak to fix, Rebecca in her ragged black dress. We must have looked as if we had just stepped out of an explosion, fitting because we sort of had.

We split the center of the encampment, looking for a place to sit and rest for a while. The people around us did their best to pretend we didn't exist, even going so far as to turn away when we approached. It was ironic to me that the homeless were shunning us. Were they doing it to show us how others made them feel? I looked at Rebecca, who seemed unfazed by the community's reaction. Was she used to it, or did she just not care?

"I see you demon. I welcome you." The voice came from behind.

Rebecca and I turned as one to see who had called her out. A girl. A small girl, no more than ten years old, with a thin, frail frame, and shoulder length reddish blonde hair. She was wearing sneakers with a simple flowered dress; both surprisingly clean considering the amount of grime that covered everything else down here. That wasn't the most amazing thing about her though. Her eye sockets were barren, the skin sinking into them. She was blind. Blind, and Divine. I don't know why neither of us had known she was near. The feeling I got from her was different, unique. She was not a demon, or an angel.

"Do you address me child?" Rebecca asked. If she was surprised that a blind girl could see her, she didn't show it.

The girl stepped forward, stopping a few feet away. She definitely knew right where we were standing.

"I address both of you," she replied. She turned her head towards me. "Welcome, brother. My name is Sarah. Come sit with me. I can see that you are tired."

The other people around us had ignored the exchange, and they hurried to move out of the way of the little girl leading us towards the center of the encampment. There was an old man resting there, in front of a larger nylon tent. He looked more like your stereotypical vagrant, with a long white beard and layers of jackets and sweaters covering a rail thin body. He looked up at us when we passed, but said nothing.

The inside of the tent was sparsely decorated, a thin air mattress in the corner, a small shelf with a few random books on it, and a stack of boxed and canned food and drink. The center of the tent had a bunch of old blankets and rugs piled on top of it, creating a somewhat comfortable cushioning to sit on. Sarah beckoned us to do so, taking position right in front of us, close enough to touch.

"Welcome to my home," she said. "Please find peace and shelter here."

"Thank you," I said. The whole thing seemed surreal, and in my exhausted state I wasn't positive it was happening. "Who are you?"

"I am Sarah," the girl replied, laughing. "The question you should be asking is, why are you. Why are you, Landon?"

I was taken off guard by the question, and the fact that Sarah knew my name. How did she know? How could she see me? Why am I? It was something I hadn't ever thought about. Even after dying and being returned to this world, I had never considered why I existed, why I had come back. I had agreed to it because I felt I had to, but why? It was so easy to ask, so hard to answer. "I don't know," I admitted. "Why are you?"

She smiled. "Few of us know why," she said. "Yet without knowing why we are, how can we ever know who we are? That is the secret to control, to power. The demons use it. The angels use it. They don't want you to think about it. You don't need to know to be Awake. You just need to question. Everyone here questions."

The homeless people outside. All of them could see what we were. "Is that why they turn away?"

"There are three, brother, always three. One, those who do not know they are being controlled, who live their happy oblivious lives. Two, those who know and accept control in exchange for something else. Three, those who know and reject control, who always ask why and become outcasts to society. See them, for they are the true casualties. They are caught in the war, and cannot fight. They see the war, and cannot end it. They lose their families, their jobs, their homes, because they question why. The Sleeping call them crazy, because they do not accept."

"I don't want to control them," I said. "I want to help them."

Sarah nodded. "Yes. I know that you believe it brother, but you are young."

"Why do you call me brother?"

"That is part of who you are," she replied, "but just a part. You will need to learn why before you can be whole."

"You are a half breed," Rebecca said, her voice and expression filled with excitement. "A first generation offspring of an angel and a demon, a true living diuscrucis. Such a thing was thought to have ended thousands of years ago." She turned to face me. "A direct offspring of such a union has command of much of the power you do," she explained. "But in order for a demon and an angel to pair, they must bind their child to this world such that the soul is conceived inside a mortal shell. Thus bound, she is limited by the fragility of mortality."

"What about when she dies?" I asked.

"I will have the same fate as all mortals," Sarah said. "I will be judged by my actions as all others are."

"If she is to return to this world in any form, her power will fully develop. That is the reason that such unions are forbidden."

"It is doubtful that I will ever be allowed to return," Sarah said.

The flap of the tent drew back and the old man stepped inside. He looked at us, then at Sarah. She patted the floor next to her, and he went to sit by her side.

"I should never have been," she said. "But there is no greater temptation to true evil than the forbidden. My father is a demon of great strength. He captured my mother, locked her up as his prisoner, drugged her and took her purity."

She spoke of such horror without emotion; her eyeless face a mask. "He impregnated her because he wanted to see a half breed for himself. When I was born, he murdered her in the delivery bed, and took my eyes so that I might never know who he was. For six months he had me raised as his own, to see if a diuscrucis could be made pure evil. He didn't know I could see him, could feel his heart that he had worked so hard to cloak in darkness. He would have destroyed me if he had discovered that I could see the Divine without my eyes, and know them even without knowing their exact form.

She motioned to the old man sitting next to her. "Izak was my mother's jailer, and he spent much time with her. He secretly fell in love with her, and then with me. He discovered first that I could See, and so he stole me from under my father's nose and has hidden me ever since. He is the one who has taught me of our kind."

"And your father?" I asked. I could make a guess who would do such a thing.

"I do not know," she replied. "It is not the demon Reyzl as you think, brother. Izak will not tell me his name, but he assures me that is not so."

It was a little creepy how she knew what I was thinking. I turned to Izak. "Why won't you tell her?" I asked. "You claim to love her."

Izak looked at me and said nothing. I was beginning to get angry when Sarah raised her hand between Izak and I.

"Hold your anger. Izak seeks to protect me from him. Even thinking his name could reveal me, and I am not yet ready to confront him."

"How did you wind up down here?" Rebecca asked. Sarah's story had brought tears to her eyes, which she now wiped away with the back of her hand.

"After Izak took me away from my father, we travelled for many months. He taught me of the world, of its beauty, and of how to see it without my eyes. I was in wonder of it all, and still am. In time we came to this place, hidden from the rest of the world, so that he could teach me of my power. Nobody lived here then, it was just Izak and I. I found that I could See not just the Divine, but also the Awake. Those who could see me, I could See back. I felt their anger, their pain, and their hopelessness. We began to bring them here, to give them a community."

"Aren't you afraid your father will find you?" I asked.

She shook her head. "None of these people will betray me. I can not give them their former lives back, but I have helped them make new ones down here, with others who understand."

She turned her head towards me, and this time I could feel her entering my thoughts. I was still tired, still weak. I pushed her out with as little force as I could manage, for fear I would not be able to stay conscious with any greater effort. She did not resist, instead she giggled out loud.

"I am glad to have found you, brother," she said. "Rest now demons. Find peace and shelter here."

I had so many questions, so much more I wanted to know. I didn't get to ask them, because she had both Calmed and Commanded me. I knew now how to recognize each, and I panicked at the thought of what she would do once I was out. I fought against her power, but I was too tired, too weak.

"Do not fear," she said to me, right before the world went dark.

Chapter 14

I was only out for a few seconds. When I woke, I was sitting on my bed at the Belmont, naked and coated in a sheen of sweat. Ulnyx was sitting across from me, behind a piano, his fingers tickling the ivories. When he saw me, he started laughing.

"Be quiet, Ulnyx," a familiar voice said.

The demon quieted and placed his hands in his lap. I looked over to the door. Sarah was standing there, looking the same as she had before she put me to sleep, except... different. It was her eyes. They were whole in this place, an incredible reddish gold that shimmered and danced like Josette's.

"I'm sorry, brother," she said to me. "You were weak, and you will need to be strong to carry on with your purpose."

"How can you be here?" I asked her, clothing myself in a simple black t-shirt and sweats before she could see me.

"You invited me," she replied.

"How?"

Sarah giggled again. "You called to me, and I came. There is so much you still have so little control over. Like him." She jerked her head towards Ulnyx. "You have trapped his soul, yet he refuses to do your bidding when it does not suit him."

"I can't make him," I said.

"No? Ulnyx, stand up," she Commanded. He kicked out the piano bench and stood. "This is your Source brother. If you cannot rule here, you will continue to fail."

Continue to fail? I looked at the Were. His expression was contained, a mixture of surprise and anger. The way he had jumped at her Command. This was my dream, my world, and yet she had more power in it then I did. The thought drove me to anger.

"How do I learn control, when there is no one to teach me?" I asked, my voice almost a snarl.

"You do not need to learn, all you must do is ask why. Why are you?" She hadn't reacted at all to my outburst. She remained calm, unaffected.

"I don't know," I said. Why were any of us? According to Dante, we were just pieces in a puzzle that did not fit, figures in a game with no end.

"The game cannot continue if you do not play." Sarah hopped over to me and looked up into my eyes. "Why are you?" she asked again.

I looked from Ulnyx, to her, and back. Continue to fail... His static posture was a representation of every failure I had experienced since Mr. Ross had left me on Lady Liberty. Yeah, I was still alive, but I had remained that way because of dumb luck. Every scrape I had been in had resulted in somebody intervening to save my sorry ass. Even now Sarah was here, showing me how powerless I truly was. Ulnyx had been right. I was pathetic.

"I don't know," I growled, the feeling of hopelessness spreading from the inside out.

"This world is your Source, brother," Sarah said, maintaining her perfect calm. "Its oceans are boundless, its mountains endless. Would you be a flea, or a titan? Why are you?"

"I don't know. How did you find me?" I was losing control of myself. Every word she spoke increased my anger, my frustration, and my despair.

"I didn't find you," she said. "You found me."

It was yet another statement that made no sense. I hadn't been looking for her. How could I have been looking for her? "I wasn't looking for you," I yelled.

"And yet you found me. Why were you looking?" she asked, calm, emotionless, serene. I couldn't take it anymore.

"I wasn't," I shouted, willing her out of my mind. She cried out in pain and was gone. The anger did not subside as easily. I could feel it permeating the entire world around me, staining everything with its pallid darkness. I turned to Ulnyx.

"You! Where the hell were you when I needed you?"

The Great Were looked at me, but didn't make a sound. I walked over to him and lifted him into the air by the throat. He didn't react.

"Why am I?" I asked, shaking him. "Why am I?"

His lips split in a mocking grin. Even in my fury, I could not make him obey.

I held him aloft, my fingers sinking deeper and deeper into his throat. Everything around me was black, the room quivering and oozing as I stained my Source with my anger, my evil intent. It was more than just Ulnyx. I wanted to destroy, to ruin, to end. Why had I been chosen to be reborn, when all I could accomplish was failure?

The Belmont crumbled away, and I found myself standing in a wasteland, a world desiccated by my will. The realization was a ten-ton anvil, stealing all of the anger from my soul and slamming me over the head into an instant state of calm. I dropped the Were and took a step back. All at once, the world reversed itself, snapping back to its original state.

Why was I? It was such a simple question with such an elusive, simple answer. The question was a trick, a misdirection, and a lie. It didn't matter why I was. Asking the question was more important than answering it, the point was that I made the effort to know and understand. To recognize who I was, and what I could become.

Sarah had brought me to anger to show me. No, I had brought Sarah here to show myself. I was of good, and of evil, and my power was a strange concoction of both. How could I hope to truly control any of it if I refused to accept equal parts? Everything rotated in balance, and I was no exception.

As I resolved the truth within myself, I could feel the power wash over me, a wave of energy that soaked into me like water, like blood. It came from nowhere, and everywhere. It had not been created, but released. It was my Source, it ran from my soul, and for better or worse, it was answering my call.

I looked over at Ulnyx, still kneeling on the floor, still wearing his crap-eating grin.

"Get up," I said.

I could feel the charge in the air, as if it had just been ionized by a lightning strike. The smile faded from his face.

"Get up," I repeated, my voice calm.

He didn't look like he wanted to, but he rose to his feet.

"If I call on your power, you will provide it," I told him.

His eyes burned with hatred, but he nodded.

What had I been looking for? Understanding - of myself foremost. Who better to help me understand than one who lived as I had died? It seemed crazy to think that I could have intended to wind up down in the sewers, taking a direct path to what was the world's only directly descended half-angel, half-demon. It seemed insane that in the entire world she was in the same city, always so close by. Yet so many things could have happened to me. So many choices made that could have brought me somewhere else, led me in another direction, or pulled me off this course.

Maybe what seemed crazy wasn't so crazy after all. Could I say for sure that I hadn't been looking for her, that my soul hadn't brought me here? Dante had said that in order to come into my full power, I had to let go of what I knew as a human and accept what I had become. My Source was a reflection of the world and my place in it. I would create, destroy, love, hate, and most of all survive, because my Source, my soul demanded balance. It was why I was. The question may have been a trick, but that didn't mean it had no answer.

Chapter 15

I woke with a start, my eyes flicking open to look at the apex of the tent above me. I felt something pressing into my shoulder, turned my head, and found Sarah there, her head resting on my arm and her body curled into a tight little ball. I remembered what I had done to her in my Source and felt a sudden wave of guilt wash over me. I reached over with my other hand and stroked her head.

"I'm sorry," I whispered. She was asleep.

"Landon." I turned my head to the other side. Rebecca had snuck up on me, and was leaning over me with her hand on my other shoulder. How did she do that? "Are you okay?"

It was a good question. I took a deep breath, turned my attention inward on myself. I felt good, really good. I was ready to accept myself in equal parts. Not all good, not all bad. Just me.

"Yeah," I replied. I looked back at Sarah, "How long?"

"Two days. Sarah hasn't left your side the entire time, but I think she's been having some pretty rough dreams. She was crying in her sleep." I looked back to Rebecca and noticed she had changed. She was wearing a pair of camouflage cargo pants and a tight black thermal henley. Her hair was tied back into a single ponytail. She looked like she was ready for war.

"We need to go," I said.

Rebecca smiled, showing off her fangs, and moved around to help me untangle myself from Sarah. Before she could touch her, the girl woke up.

"Landon," she said, her voice so much smaller and childish than I had remembered it. She pushed herself into a kneeling position next to me. "You are leaving."

"I have to go," I told her.

"Stay," she Commanded. I could feel the power of her word and her mind pulling at my will.

"No," I said, both with my mouth and in my mind. I had thought my rejection would upset her, but she smiled.

"You must continue your journey," she said. "You have found what you were looking for, and for that I am glad. Do not feel sorry for the way you handled me, it was what you needed to do." She had known what I was thinking, and pre-empted my second apology. "I will be thinking of you, brother, and wishing the best for you."

I wasn't ready to just leave her like that. "Sarah, Rebecca told me you were having dreams."

She stiffened up, the change in her demeanor almost imperceptible. “Sometimes I dream of what came before Izak saved me,” she lied. “I am thankful to have a brother to protect me. When you can, I hope you will return to visit.”

Protect her? From her father? Understanding myself was one thing. Defending anybody from a major demon was something totally different. I wasn’t about to argue that with her though.

“I will,” I said. I sat up, leaned forward and wrapped her in a tight hug. “Thank you.” I had found what I had been looking for, but it wouldn’t have been possible without her help.

I released her from the embrace and got to my feet, then reached out and took Rebecca’s hand, surprising her with my boldness.

“We’ve got work to do,” I told her.

As we headed out the door of the tent, I noticed Izak sitting motionless in the corner near the food stores, just watching. I gave him a small wave that he didn’t return, and then we were gone.

The inhabitants of the small community paid us no more attention on the way out as they had on the way in, turning away as we neared and staying occupied until we had passed. We slipped out of the sewer through a small access tunnel further south, catching up as we followed it towards our hopeful exodus from the underground.

"I hope you don't mind," Rebecca said as we walked. "I picked your pocket and stole some money so I could get some new clothes."

"You got one of the Awake to sell you those?" I motioned to the militant outfit. "You look like you're ready to join the Army. I wouldn't call it stealing, since I would have given it to you."

"I had to give the money to Izak. This is what he brought back for me."

"He spoke to you?"

"No. I told him what I needed, he held out his hand, I gave him some money, and he brought this back. Its better than that beat up dress."

I took a look at myself. I hadn't been strong enough to fix myself up earlier, and hadn't thought of it before now. I was still wearing the penguin suit, as shredded and bloodied as it was. I pushed, and watched it change into a matching outfit.

"It's fitting I guess," I said. "Our own little army."

"Two against infinity," she said with a humorless laugh.

"Three," I replied.

I hadn't thought about Obi until now. I wondered if he knew what had happened. I could imagine the word had hit the forums, and he was no doubt keeping a sharp lookout for any reported sightings of either of us. It was strange to have so much faith in him, despite our short acquaintance. I told Rebecca about how we had met, and then since she had thrown her entire life away to save me, I told her about everything else too, from Ulnyx, to the Demon Queen, to the Chalice. I got the feeling she was a little jealous when I told her about Josette, but she didn't say anything to confirm my theory.

"So what about you?" I asked her.

We had stopped below a manhole, finishing our conversation before climbing back into the world above. We stood facing one another, close enough that her sweet scent kept wafting across my senses.

"What about me?"

"You told me that you were obligated to obey your father, but you helped me anyway."

"I told you that we had a choice to obey, or to challenge."

"I thought you couldn't defeat your father."

She looked down at the ground. "I can't," she said.

I reached out and put my hand under her chin, lifting her face. "Rebecca." Tears ran from her eyes as she looked at me. 'Why would you do that?"

"Like I said, there's just something about you." She was lying.

"You can't lie to me Rebecca," I said, wiping away some of the tears with my thumb.

She took my hand in hers, squeezed it, and pushed it away. "No, I suppose I can't," she replied. "That doesn't mean I have to tell you anything, and you don't have the power to Command."

Wait a second. "I don't?"

"Sarah does, because she's first-generation," she explained. "You don't have any direct control over the Divine, because you aren't a direct descendent. You may be able to control the Were, but that's because you've already captured his soul."

"Oh." Not that I would have used it on her, except maybe to prevent her from throwing her life away for me. "How long?"

"I already sent him the challenge while you were asleep," she said. "Tomorrow night at the Statue."

I could feel the growing lump in my throat. It seemed like I was destined not to have many friends for very long.

"What can I do to help?" I asked.

She wiped the rest of the tears away herself. "I don't think there's anything you can do."

I had an idea. "Hold on... what about the amulet? He can't hurt you if you're wearing it."

"Landon, you're sweet. I can't use the amulet. It would be cheating. If I gave up my honor, I would be no better than any other demon. I don't believe we have to operate that way to survive, and if you look at the situation my kind is in, it's the change that I'm fighting for so we can thrive as we deserve. We have a physical and mental superiority to humans, we have a numerical superiority to most other Divine, but we're relegated to slinking about at night, hiding from daylight, and using the majority of our strength figuring out where and how to get our next meal. For as much as I dislike feeding on humans, I have still done it, and will again if it means their life or mine. With my research cut off, that seems more and more likely." She reached up and took hold of the ladder. "If I can defeat Merov, I will earn access to everything he has. It will all become mine, and I can continue my work. It's a long shot, but the risk is worth it to me."

"What about Reyzl?" I asked.

"You're going to take care of Reyzl," she said. She winked at me, and climbed the ladder, pushing the cover aside with ease.

Take care of Reyzl. Right. I reached inward and touched on Ulnyx's soul. I could feel the power respond to my mental tap. Maybe with the Great Were's help I would stand a chance.

We exited the sewer onto an empty street. It took me a minute to get my bearings, but we weren't too far from the Belmont. It was midday, and the sun was out. I pulled Rebecca into the shadows.

"Can you manage?" I asked.

She reached under her henley and pulled out the amulet. "As long as this thing works, I should be fine," she said. She stepped tentatively out into the sunlight. She squinted her eyes, and moved back into the cover of the building. "It's not working," she said. What?

I reached into my pocket and pulled out the necklace I had claimed from Ulnyx. I knew this one worked, I had seen it do its thing. I swapped it with hers. “Try this.”

She stepped out into the sunlight again, and then retreated. “No good,” she told me.

“I don’t get it,” I said. “I saw Ulnyx use that one to heal. I know it works.” She handed the amulet back to me, and I looked at it in disgust.

“Maybe they don’t work on vampires,” she suggested. “Let’s just try to stay in the shade.”

Dante hadn’t said anything about there being exceptions to the amulet’s usefulness. There had to be something else going on, something we didn’t know about. If he came calling again, maybe he would have the answer.

We covered the last few blocks by sticking to the darkness and running across the open sunlight when necessary. Punkmo’s eyes bugged out of his head when I held the door for Rebecca to let her into the Hotel. I could feel him ogling her until we had passed the front desk and started up the stairs.

“You must get that all the time,” I said to her. “Not that I blame him, you are beautiful.”

She smiled, her pale face adding just a hint of redness. “I’m used to it from mortals, it comes with the territory. It means more coming from you.”

"Consider yourself flattered," I replied, stopping and turning to face her. "I thought so the first time I saw you, after you threw me onto the floor of the closet. Of course, I was scared witless of you at the same time, so it was kind of a unique situation. Still..."

I didn't get to finish talking, because she wrapped her arms around me and put her lips to mine. I didn't get to kiss her either, because at that moment the stairwell door above us slammed open, and Obi came tumbling out. Following right behind him was a demon. It twisted in the air, using its thick leathery wings to balance itself while it planted its claws on the opposite wall to spring downwards towards him. It shrieked through a short, fang-filled snout.

I felt Rebecca tensing to move, and I held out my hand. "I've got this one," I said.

I focused my will and sprang forward, launching up the steps like a rocket, the momentum carrying me over Obi as he turned onto his back with the Desert Eagle raised above his chest. I heard the gunfire, and felt the bullet rip through my leg, but I didn't pay it any mind. I reached out with my hand and caught the demon's bald head, slamming the creature down onto the steps, its skull shattering beneath the force. Before it could recover, I twisted and pulled, ripping its head off.

Once it was dead, I recognized the pain the bullet had caused. I looked down at my leg, watching it knit back together, the process slowed by the silver. Then I looked at Obi. He was still sprawled out on the steps, his forehead covered in sweat and his breathing ragged. He gawked at me with huge, relieved eyes.

"Holy crap man, sorry about the leg," he said. "You picked the right time to show up though. There are two more incoming. I shot them in the head but these assholes don't stay down long."

"How did they find you?" I asked.

He started pulling himself to his feet. "You got me, man. Maybe triangulated the Wi-Fi access points? I thought I had done enough variance, but maybe they have some giant brain demons or something."

"There are no giant brain demons," Rebecca said, reaching down lifting the muscular ex-marine to a standing position. "The Cthulhu are incredibly intelligent, but they don't get involved outside of their own affairs." She smiled, showing Obi her fangs.

He had been giving her the oh-my-god-you're-so-hot stare before she smiled. The effect was like breaking a spell. I'm sure mortals would see a perfect set of pearly whites, until they were being drained at least. I could see his throat move as he swallowed his heart and backed up a few steps.

"What the," he cried. He started raising the Desert Eagle, but I put my hand over it.

"Obi, this is Rebecca. Rebecca, Obi-Wan. She's on our side," I told him.

Rebecca scrunched her face. "Obi-Wan? Like Star Wars?"

He rolled his eyes and shook his head. "Man, even vampires make fun of me. My parents," he said.

I cleared my throat to interrupt them. I could feel the shifting heat of a Hellish mass pressing down on my soul. "Now that the introductions are out of the way, we need to move. Those two you shot either brought friends or called for backup."

"If you can get to your room, I went back to Grand Central yesterday and got your sword. It was sitting on the tracks." He looked over at the half-dissolved headless demon. "Not that you seem to need it."

"I could use it," Rebecca said. "I don't have the strength to rip skulls off spines."

I could feel the demons getting closer. "Okay," I said. "Obi, stay back and cover us. Try not to shoot me again."

Rebecca and I hopped up the steps and out into the hallway.

"Do you know what those things are?" I asked.

She nodded. "Standard grunts. Reyzl makes them. They're all brawn, no brains. They can survive for short times in the daylight, but they're especially vulnerable to water. Make sure to mind your neck, they can remove your head with one finger."

She reached down and pulled her dagger from her boot, never breaking stride. Obi stayed ten feet behind, his Eagle aimed between us. I didn't doubt he was an excellent shot, but I hoped that if he did miss, he would miss to the right. I could take the silver bullet, Rebecca couldn't.

"He makes them?" I asked. "Get ready."

The demons came rushing around the corner, spittle flying from their fangs as they changed direction. They had two more holes in their skulls before Rebecca and I could even move. I grabbed each by the head and twisted, becoming more comfortable with the sickening crack each time I caused it. I looked back at Obi, who just shrugged.

"How many bullets do you have?" I asked him. Silver wasn't cheap and making bullets from it couldn't have been easy.

"About fifty," he said.

"Hold your fire unless it looks like we're in trouble. I have a feeling we'll need those later." We reached the corner and I pointed to the room down the hall. "My room is down there. Grab the sword so we can get out of here."

I reached out and felt for the demons. They were coming down the stairwell. I heard breaking glass. They were coming in from the windows too. Rebecca took off for my room at a sprint. I turned around to see a grunt bearing down on Obi from behind. He didn't know it was coming.

"Obi," I shouted. I couldn't reach him in time. Desperate, I focused on the floor right behind him, pulling the nails from the wood and sending them hurtling into the demon. It stumbled backwards as a hundred tiny spears checkered its chest. Obi stopped next to me and looked to see what I had done.

"Nice," he said.

The demon recovered in a hurry and began rushing towards us again. I hoped I was as fast a learner as Obi had said I was.

It arrived as a mass of swinging claws, strong, powerful muscles driving me backwards while I tried to find a way to maneuver around them. I felt the heat of a wound to my shoulder and another to my leg, but it was nothing that wouldn't heal. It snapped and growled, trying to get to my face with its teeth. I ducked in close enough to smell stale, hot breath, then slipped around behind it, reached around its neck and twisted my arms, hearing its spine shatter. I was going to remove its head, but three more grunts had filed out into the hallway.

Obi downed one of them, but couldn't get a shot off on the other two. I grabbed him and pushed him to the ground to get him out of the way of a set of claws, then took hold of the monstrous arm and broke it at the elbow. The move would buy us seconds at most.

I heard the snarl of the second demon, and then smiled when a blessed sword severed its head from behind.

"This way," I said, motioning to the nearest room. "We can take the fire escape to the ground."

Rebecca took a moment to stab the other two grunts, and then followed us into the empty room. I blew out the glass with a thought.

"This is going from bad to worse," I said. I could feel the gathered mass of evil growing, their power pushing in on me. It felt like the Belmont was on fire. "I think they're trying to surround us."

The building shook from the force of so many monsters moving through the old structure, all converging on our location. Reyzl was using more force than I had expected. I leaned out through the window and looked down. There were more grunts waiting in the alley, covering the exit. I looked up. The roof was clear.

"Up," I said.

"Up?" Obi asked. "Are you crazy, man?"

I pushed him out onto the fire escape. "Go up sergeant," I shouted back. He started climbing. "Rebecca, go."

"You first," she said.

I shook my head. "Someone needs to cover our escape."

Rebecca smiled and winked at me. "Escape? You're leading us further *into* them. Now go!"

I started climbing, hearing the sword thunking into flesh behind me. I doubted the roof was the safest place to be either, but it was open, and I wanted the breathing room. I caught up to Obi, and we dropped over the side of the building onto the roof together. There were already six grunts waiting for us, and three more came up behind Rebecca when she joined us a few seconds later. They didn't attack right away, choosing instead to surround us. I assumed they were waiting for greater numbers, knowing they had us trapped.

"Now what?" Obi asked, spinning in a circle to keep an eye on all of the demons.

More of the grunts were reaching the rooftop every second, and three weres came up from the stairwell, joining the throng. They cut their way through the hissing demons, coming to a stop in front of me. The largest of them took two more steps forward and spoke.

"Diuscrucis," the were said. "Master Reyzl demands to meet with you. Come with us, and we'll let your companions go." I didn't need any special power to know he was lying.

"Landon," Rebecca said, sounding worried, and looking ashen in the sun, "tell me you have a plan. I can't stay out here like this for long."

"I have a plan," I replied. Okay, I didn't have a solid plan, but I had one idea. I closed my eyes and reached inward, calling out for Ulnyx. I could feel the Great Were's strength forming in the base of my spine. This time, I could drink from it and stay in control. The power was his, but my mind was my own.

I smiled at the were, my mouth growing, elongating, and filling with razor sharp teeth. I could feel the rest of my body changing as well, shifting form into the monstrosity of skin, muscle, and bone that was Ulnyx's morphed form. I lifted my middle finger and aimed it at the demon, then used it to beckon them towards us. The weres hesitated, torn between the risk of death at my hands or Reyzl's. There was no doubt he wouldn't be pleased if they returned without some piece of me. The grunts weren't smart enough to know any better, and they rushed to close the circle.

I dropped down to all fours and launched myself at the demons; claws ripping and tearing, powerful muscles tossing them aside like matchsticks. There were at least fifty of them squeezing in on us. I grabbed one of the grunts and threw it back at the frightened weres. They moved aside and it disappeared down the open stairwell. While I was watching its path, I noticed the water tower behind the door.

I raked my claws through three more grunts, and then paused to focus on the tower. Even with Ulnyx's massive strength there were just too many of the creatures to deal with this way. I might be able to kill them all in this powerful form, but not without risking Rebecca and Obi.

I let loose a massive roar, feeling the tug in my mind and demanding the water in the tower to set itself free and join me on the roof. I pulled at it, forcing it through the wooden planks that contained it, causing it to geyser out through the weakest seam. The grunts had been frozen by the roar, and now they cried out in agony as the water splashed downward from the sky, soaking everything on the rooftop.

"Damn that's cold," Obi cried. I swung my head around to check on him, and he stumbled backwards, away from my gaze.

Rebecca wrapped an arm around him to steady him and winked at me. She looked like crap, the sunlight and the water taking their toll. The grunts behind them were dancing across the rooftop, desperate to shake the water from their bodies. Their skin puckered and oozed, their life force seeping out from everywhere. Many had already dropped lifeless to the ground, and I was sure the rest would follow.

I heard claws on the blacktop and turned back around in time to see the three weres had made up their minds. They had morphed into their demon forms and were charging towards me, teeth bared. I let out another roar and shot forward to meet them. Blood blossomed from them and I heard the echoes of gunfire in the sky. The weres stumbled and rolled, coming to a rest right under my feet. I brought up a massive foot and slammed it down on one skull, then another. The third were, the leader, I let live.

I had felt Ulnyx in my mind, his presence a pressure in my skull as he sought for a way to overpower me. I pushed back against him now, kicking him back down into my soul, dismissing his power as if flipping off a light switch. My body began changing, shrinking, returning to my human form. My clothes were rags hanging from my neck and I pulled them back into shape, then reached down and lifted the still stunned were to his feet. I grabbed his face and brought it in line with mine.

"Tell Reyzl I'm coming for him," I said.

I would have sent him on his way, but Rebecca had other ideas. Without a word, she stepped up next to me and ran him through on the blessed sword.

"Send that message and Reyzl will come for you himself," she said to me. "You may control the Great Were, but his power can still pollute you."

I knew she was right. I could still feel my adrenaline pumping from the experience of being the terrifying killing machine. He might not have been able to overtake me, but the promise of his power was an intoxicating temptation that I would be at risk of accepting every time I called on it, opening the door to the Great Were's dominion. Everything had its price, and I would have to reconsider the cost before calling on Ulnyx again.

Rebecca looked awful, her skin a translucent white, her hair dull and greying. The water had done its damage, drying her out to the point that bits of her skin flaked off with every movement she made.

"Let's get you out of here," I said.

"That was so awesome," Obi said, walking up behind us. "You guys kick complete ass."

Rebecca gave him a weak smile. "You were pretty good yourself, for a mortal," she told him. He laughed off his adrenaline as we headed for the stairs.

"So what's next?" Obi asked when we reached the ground floor. Punkmo was hunched down behind the front desk, on the phone with the Police.

"That's right, gunshots," he was saying. "Drug dealers? I don't know, could be a gang too, who gives a crap. Are you going to send a car or what?" He didn't look up as we walked past.

"We need to get Rebecca someplace dark so she can rest for awhile, " I said. "And you and I need to talk."

Just being out of the sun had already returned some of the opacity to the vampiress' skin, and her hair was darkening by the moment. Even so, she still looked dry and sick. Dry and sick and stunning. We left the Belmont and headed uptown. I kept us to the shadows as we walked, only crossing the sun's direct path when the limited cloud cover would obscure it.

"Why attack during the day?" I asked Rebecca.

"It was a calculated risk," she replied. "Reyzl was hoping to catch you off-guard, maybe while you slept. He underestimated you."

Him and me both. I had returned from my Source with a new sense of self, but I hadn't expected the change to be so dramatic. Even after pulling down the water tower, I still felt like I had plenty in reserve. It had taken a fair share of missteps, but I was coming into my own.

"Where are we going anyway?" Rebecca asked.

"I'm upgrading our accommodations," I said.

Chapter 16

"Man, I've always wanted to stay here," Obi said as I pushed open the door to Room 1601 of the Waldorf=Astoria Hotel.

I had too, which is why I had decided to use the blank card Dante had given me to create a simulacrum of one of my mother's credit cards. They had put the card on file at the front desk, but I had paid for the room with my remaining cash. After all, it wasn't stealing if nothing got charged to it, right?

The suite itself was as magnificent as I had always imagined it would be, the large living area home to a fancy nineteenth century sofa and loveseat, some expensive looking ornate wood furniture and a big flat screen television. The bedroom was just as large, fitting a huge dresser and a king size bed covered in finery. The marble bathroom rounded out the opulence, and it was easy to picture myself as someone important like a movie star, or royalty. I laughed at the irony.

"What's funny?" Rebecca asked. We were standing in the bedroom together, having left Obi watching television on the other side of the door.

"I was just thinking about being someone important like an actor," I said. I looked at her. The daytime stroll hadn't done her any favors. No amount of damage could undo her nascent beauty, but she looked ragged and tired. "How are you feeling?"

She was tentative in her reply. "I have a small problem," she said.

I looked over to the windows. There was a fair amount of light coming in, but I hadn't pulled the heavy drapes closed yet.

"Not dark enough?" I asked.

She smiled, but it wasn't a positive smile. She looked anxious and uncomfortable. "Between the sun and the water, and I haven't been home in almost three days," she looked down at the floor, embarrassed. "I'm hungry."

I felt like an idiot. I had forgotten about her dietary needs. Maybe the thought of her dining should have turned my stomach, but I had seen so much worse in the last twenty-four hours. Besides, I needed her far more than the world needed another pimp or gangbanger. I went over to the windows and pulled the drapes closed, making sure it was nice and dark.

"Just lay down for awhile," I told her. "I'll be back as soon as I can." I leaned in to kiss her on the cheek. It was colder than usual. "It shouldn't take me too long to find somebody the world won't miss."

She lifted her head. There were tears in her perfect blue eyes. "You're sweet, but there isn't enough time," she said. "I've taken too much of a beating the last few days. You're not exactly Gandhi you know."

"Okay, how about if I grab the bellhop?" It was intended as a joke, but the blunt truth was that if it came down to it I would have if she had asked. What she did ask for was easier to live with, but harder to acquiesce to.

"Landon, I don't want to ask you to do this but... you're a diuscrucis. Whatever I took, you'd regenerate." Her eyes pleaded with me.

"You said my blood could be poison to you," I reminded her. I wanted to help her, but the idea of anybody sucking up my life force was giving me the creepy crawlies.

"I have to risk it," she said. "I don't want you to kill an innocent person because of me. "

I took a few steps back from her. "Just give me a second," I said.

I had already been shot, stabbed, torn apart, and fallen from the fifty-something-ith story of a skyscraper. It was just the concept of it that was frightening me. I had seen enough vampire movies to be influenced, and I was being stupid. The only one who could be harmed was Rebecca, and she was as good as gone if I didn't agree to it. Seeing her standing there, her skin dry, her hair dull, her eyes wet with tears, there was no way I wouldn't do it.

I rushed forward, wrapped her up in my arms, pulled her head into my neck and closed my eyes. I felt the warmth of her breath on my skin, and then the soft touch of her incisors as she bit into me.

I had expected it to hurt, but it didn't cause any pain at all. The feeling was more of a euphoria, a strange emotional high. I could feel her mouth moving against my neck, and I could feel my body reacting as if we were engaged in more intimate activity. My heart was racing, my eyes blurred, and a million colors swam and danced in front of me, distracting me from the act.

All too soon, it was done. She pulled away from me, holding me up as I came off of the vampiric high and was left breathless and weak. Rebecca put me down on the bed, and then lay down on her side facing me. I stared at the ceiling for a few minutes while my body began to regenerate.

"Thank you," she said. She reached over and stroked my hair. "You don't know how much it means to me that you did this."

I turned my head. She looked healthy, radiant even. Her eyes were a cold blue fire, her lips redder and fuller, her skin smooth, silky, and shimmering as though she were covered in glitter. I had never seen anything like it. No human could ever hope to be as amazingly attractive.

"Chocolate or garlic?" I asked her.

She ran her tongue along her lips, tasting whatever leftovers remained there. "Better than chocolate," she replied. "I've never felt like this before."

"Me neither." I closed my eyes and took a deep breath. My entire body was warm and tingling. With my eyes closed, I could still see residual ribbons of color like an aurora borealis in my brain.

"Are you okay?"

"I'll be fine," I said. "I just need a few minutes to recover. Did you get enough?"

"Right now I feel like I'll never need to feed again. If word got out about the potency of your blood, you'd have every vampire on the planet hunting you down for a taste."

"You mean I don't already?"

She laughed. "Good point."

She slid closer to me and put her head on my shoulder and her arm over my chest. I reached around and held her to me. Such a simple closeness, but it felt so perfect. We sat together for a while, just enjoying the moment of quiet. When I heard Rebecca's breathing deepen, I carefully extracted myself and snuck out of the bedroom.

Obi was stretched out on the sofa, still watching television. When I slipped into the room, he sat up and turned it off.

"I was worried you weren't going to make it out of there," he said with a laugh.

I reached up and ran my hand over my neck. The bite marks had already healed over. “We’re just friends,” I told him.

Weren’t we? I hadn’t had time to give it much thought. She was beautiful, and I was attracted to her, but it was a lot more complicated than that, her impending death match with her father not withstanding.

“It’s none of my business anyway,” he said, sitting up and turning of the TV. “The Exchange is a mess because of you,” he continued. “After your little event at the soiree, most of the biggest dealers have gone to ground. They know we’ve been eavesdropping, and they’re afraid of becoming your next target.”

“They thought I was there to take down Merov?” I asked. That was better than I could have hoped for. We didn’t need word getting back to the Demon Queen that I was after the Chalice.

“Yup, but there’s more.” His smile was huge. “They think the only reason anybody got out alive was because Reyzl showed up. They’re scared bloodless of you. Hell, after what I saw today, so am I.”

I hadn’t thought about the positive effect I could have had if I had gone after the vampires. Dante had given me a goal, but maybe there were other opportunities that I wasn’t considering.

"So the Exchange isn't producing much info anymore," I said. "Tell me you found another source."

"Who knew that demons were so into computers?" he said. "There's another site, it's a Freenet image board. They upload pics with the messages encrypted in the byte code. Nasty stuff. Nothing you'd ever want to have to look at." His smile faded and he looked distracted. "But yeah, anyway I had some samples on the iPad, but they took it. I didn't get a chance to crack the encryption."

"It's okay if you don't want to go any deeper into that stuff," I said. I was already sorry for whatever it was he had seen.

"Don't sweat it man. I want to crack that code so we can find those assholes and I can watch you rip their twisted heads off."

"I have another task for you, if you're up to it. It's something a little more clandestine. Merov's apartment."

"What about it?" he asked.

"We need to get back in, and we need to break into his office. It's got some kind of fingerprint security system, but it's not his fingerprint. He keeps a sliver of the prior owner's finger in a case so he can get by. I think our lead on the Chalice is somewhere in that room. "

"Man, you had to swan dive fifty stories to get out of there, and now you want to go back *in*?" He shook his head. "Wait a second. You said we."

“I need you to come with. If Merov has a computer, and I’m sure he does, you’re going to need to be there to hack it.”

Obi tapped his fingers on the coffee table while he thought about it. “So, you need me to try to figure out what kind of security he’s using, come up with a way to circumvent it, and then hack his computer. Is that about right?”

“A blueprint of the building might come in handy too,” I said. “I can’t take you out the window.”

“I’m starting to rethink my pledge of service,” he said.

“Sorry Obi, you can’t unbend the knee.”

Obi stood up and headed for the door, grabbing his gun on the way by and tucking it into the back of his jeans. “I’ll be at the library, doing some research,” he said. He motioned towards the bedroom door with his head. “Try not to have too much fun while I’m gone.”

He laughed when my face reddened, and left before I could stammer on about how it wasn’t like that, we were just friends, and we had business to take care of. Just thinking about the vampire girl sleeping in the bed on the other side of the door drove me to distraction. I had something else I wanted to take care of, so I scribbled out a quick note to Rebecca and slid it under the door.

Chapter 17

The sun was sinking towards the horizon when I pushed through the revolving doors of the Waldorf and stepped out into the street. The city around me was bustling with life, the organized chaos of humanity a comforting sight to my changing eyes. Before, I had seen myself as one of them who had been picked up and carried into something much bigger than I could have ever imagined. After my experience in my Source, I didn't feel as human anymore. I had grown, evolved into something... better?

I hoped so, but it wasn't without its price. Watching people scurrying through the streets on their way here or there without a thought in their mind about what was happening out of their sight, they seemed so small and insignificant. My compassion was the one thing I least wanted to lose, because I knew there was nothing balanced in a total lack of feeling, and so I drank in the sight, took a moment to appreciate it, and continued on.

Dusk was creeping in by the time I finished the mile and a half walk down to the Garment District and came to a stop in front of the Holy Trinity Soup Kitchen, a small storefront at the bottom of an office building that looked more like a former deli than a food bank. I don't know what had driven me there at this time of day, and I should have known that Josette wouldn't be there, the place had closed three hours ago. Even so, I could feel her presence in the air around me, much like I had at the Belmont the day after her visit, and I found a certain peace and comfort in it. She was spending her mornings doing good in one of the simplest ways possible, and while I wouldn't have thought much of it while I had been alive, I was coming to appreciate such simplicity now.

"Hey buddy, any spare change?"

I had been lost in thought, so the vagrant's hoarse voice startled me. He was standing on my right, dressed in an assortment of sweaters and jackets, his head wound up in three or four different hats. He was clean-shaven, young, and round enough that I didn't doubt he spent the money he begged for feeding himself.

"Sure," I replied, reaching into my pocket and pulling out one of my last twenties. .

"Thank you sir," he said as I handed it to him. "Thank you so much." He turned to leave, but I stopped him.

"You don't happen to know a girl who volunteers here, she's about fourteen or so? Her name is Josette."

The homeless man got all doe-eyed at the name. "Everybody around here knows Josie," he said. "She's the sweetest little thing. She likes to do magic tricks for us to cheer us up. She's not in trouble or anything, is she?"

"No," I said. Not any more than usual I'd imagine. "But if you see her, can you tell her that Landon was looking for her. She knows who I am."

"Sure, buddy," he replied. "Have a good night."

"You too."

I watched him wander off into the night, then spun around to begin the walk back up to the Waldorf. With any luck, Obi would have gotten what he needed before the evening wore on too long, and Rebecca would be as good as new after her nap. There was no part of me that was thinking my planned break-in of Merov's apartment was going to be easy or straightforward, and I wanted to be as prepared as possible.

I was headed away from the soup kitchen when a flash of light from the rooftop caught my attention. I looked up and caught just the faintest recognition of someone Divine moving away from me. Josette? Had she been watching me the whole time, or had she just happened to stop by?

Assuming it was her, I wasn't going to just let her go. I did know why I had come to see her. It was because I wasn't sure what was going to happen over the next few days, and I wanted a chance to talk to her one last time. If it wasn't her, maybe they could tell me where she went at sundown. I started running.

My pace was intense, but I handled it with ease, my legs pumping hard to keep me moving on the ground faster than the angel was crossing the air. I kept my eyes focused on the path in front of me while keeping my senses trained on them. The pedestrian traffic was a blur around me as something in their subconscious told the crowd to part and let me through. To my amazement, even as I dissected busy intersections there was never a car crossing at the same time I was.

The chase continued for a few more blocks before the angel came to a stop. I slowed to a walk as I got closer, taking in my surroundings and ensuring they were alone. Satisfied, I glanced up to the rooftop where I knew the angel was waiting for me. Why they had chosen Macy's, *the* Macy's, I had no idea.

I changed my appearance before I made my way into the crowded department store, going for a more conservative businessman look with a long wool trench coat, Armani suit, and Italian leather shoes. To the shoppers around me, I was just another guy who had decided to do his Christmas shopping after work. I headed straight for the perimeter in search of a way onto the roof. I could sense the angel was stationary, waiting for me to arrive. I wished I knew how

Josette had made that call to my soul so I could get in touch with whoever was up there with a little less effort.

I made my way towards the rear of the store, following the flow of employees as they moved from the storerooms back out onto the floor. There had to be a service elevator back there somewhere, or at the very least a stairwell that would lead to the top of the building. I slipped in behind a pair of Santa's elves that stepped out of the back pointing and giggling at each other, and then circuited the area until I found the maintenance stairs. Locked. I took the knob in my hand and focused, twisting the handle until I felt the whole mechanism crumble under the pressure.

"It took you long enough," the angel said when I stepped through the doorway and out onto the rooftop. I knew in an instant that it wasn't Josette. She was older, taller, and way prettier, with long golden locks, a golden complexion and a dancer's body. She was wearing a fitted leopard print raincoat and funky red plastic boots over a simple blouse and pants. It was a weird look, but somehow it worked.

"Do I know you?" I asked, stepping towards her. I hadn't bothered to bring a weapon with me. When would I learn?

"You do not," Boots replied. "But I know you, diuscrucis. We have been looking for you." We? I hadn't felt any other Divine nearby.

They came from the sky, swooping down on pairs of great white feathered wings and landing on the rooftop without a sound. Three more angels, each of them dressed in something like a toga, draped around their bodies to give freedom to their wings. When they landed the wings tucked in behind them, compressing more than I would have thought possible so that they were almost invisible on their backs. Did Josette have wings? I hadn't noticed them.

I tried to stay calm and confident. If all angels could fight half as well as Josette, I didn't stand a chance. I could feel Ulnyx stirring within me. Now this was a fight he would be glad to join.

"How did you know where to find me?" I asked.

"Josette Confessed," she said, as though that would explain it for me. The other three angels had taken position around me, putting me in the middle of a very holy box.

"Confessed?" I asked.

She didn't respond. Instead, she reached into her raincoat and produced a manila envelope, which she tossed at my feet. I bent down and picked it up, unclasping it and turning it over to let out a small stack of printed images. Ulnyx. My room at the Belmont. The vampires. As I flipped through them, I realized that they had somehow extracted the pictures from Josette's brain. Had she done this of her own volition, or had they forced her?

"We know that she Calmed you," Boots said, after waiting for me to flip through all of the images. "She should have done an extraction. It would have been a misguided action, but it could have explained why she had helped you to that point. Instead, she just left. We knew you would come looking for her at some point, so we've been watching the area."

She left? I fought to contain myself with the news. She hadn't been using me as Dante had suggested. She had been honest with me.

"Where is she?" I asked, now fearing for what Confession meant. What had they done to her once they had uncovered her memories?

"That is none of your concern diuscrucis," Boots said. "What you should be worried about is yourself. We know you have one of the amulets. What do you know about the Chalice?"

So that's what this was about. They wanted the information that Josette hadn't tried to take. They didn't know I hadn't known anything about it at the time, which in a way was kind of funny, but also kind of sad. They were blaming Josette for not getting intel that she couldn't have gotten. Of course, I knew what they were after now, and I had a lead on where to find it. Maybe they could make themselves useful.

"I'll tell you what," I said. "You show up back here in an hour with Josette and agree to help me, and we can take care of the Chalice together."

There was no hesitation, no consideration.

"No," she replied. "Our laws are not to be bartered. Whether you tell us what you know or not, we will still destroy you."

I saw the swords appear in the hands of the other angels. It was time to plan my escape.

"It will hurt less if you talk," Boots said.

Why was it that it always came down to tired clichés? I flicked my eyes around the rooftop, hoping to find something to distract them. My greatest weapon was that I was an unknown quantity. They had to know I could call on Ulnyx, which I guessed was why they had come as a group, but they might not know what other tricks I could pull out of my sleeve. Or maybe they did know; the roof was sorely lacking in spare projectiles.

"Your laws are the reason you're losing," I said, refusing to let them see me sweat. "You think you can manage on your own, but it's pretty obvious that you can't, and the only one of you smart enough to see it ended up in your doghouse."

"What would a diuscrucis know of laws, rules, or righteousness," Boots hissed. "The power of the Lord guarantees our victory. Those of true faith know it to be so."

I could see by her eyes she was giving commands to the other angels. They were playing it cautious.

"Now," she said, "tell us what you know or raise your blade, but do not continue standing there like a coward."

I stood there like a coward. I remembered when Josette and I were in the park.

"You can't attack me if I don't defend myself, can you?" I asked. "It's against your rules." A demon would never hesitate to attack an angel, or defend themselves from one, so they never had a problem there.

"Defend yourself," Boots shouted, growing frustrated.

"No," I replied.

I turned away from her so that I was facing the stairwell back down into the store. One of the angels was standing between it and me, a tall muscular male with dark hair and a trimmed beard. I started walking away from them, moving to step around him when I got close enough.

Boots cried out in anger. "Do you know what we do to traitors," she yelled. "How we make them Confess?"

I stopped walking and ever so slowly turned back around. Her face was a twisted mess of rage, her golden eyes blazing with hate. I knew what she was trying to do. She couldn't lie, so she was making implications, hoping I would read malice and evil behind them. What I saw instead was desperation. I didn't blame her for that, the demons had the upper hand and that had to be eating away at her soul. I resumed my walk towards the stairs, but Beard stepped in front of me.

"We cannot fight you if you will not fight back," he said. "That doesn't mean we have to let you leave."

I looked up at him. I could feel Ulnyx all but begging me to let him out. The door was just a few feet away. I could be through it before they could stop me. All I had to do was get Beard to move over. We stood staring at each other for what seemed like an eternity. Then I stabbed him.

The single claw that had been my right middle finger pierced the angel's heart, causing him to crumple to the ground. I had taken just enough from Ulnyx to create it, and could almost hear the demon in my mind, laughing at the results. I shut him off before he could get me into any more trouble, and then looked up to the stairwell door. It would be so easy to get away, but where would I go that they couldn't find me? It wasn't like I could just skip town.

I picked up Beard's sword and once more turned to face Boots, unsure about what I was doing, but doing it anyway.

"You want to fight?" I asked.

Boots broke out her best supermodel smile and raised her sword up over her head. She seemed to float towards me, her feet leaving the ground and not touching back down until she was right on top of me. The other two angels had started moving too, and without a word, all three converged, their movements synchronized.

The sword I was holding was pretty much useless against them, and it wasn't like I knew what to do with it anyway. I had one idea, one somewhat twisted, desperate, crazy idea, and I had about three seconds to make it happen.

I focused my will hard on the sword, demanding that it lose its adhesion, its rigidity, and its molecular attraction. The weapon shattered in my hand much as the windows of Merov's apartment had. I held the pieces, twirling them around me as with as much velocity as I could manage. I could see the angels coming at me out of the corners of my eyes, could feel the rush of the air they were pushing toward me as they moved in, confident of their odds. They watched my maneuver with a measure of surprise, but didn't even slow their attack. I took a deep breath, closed my eyes, and focused again.

Peppering them with shrapnel would be a minor diversion at best, and wouldn't get me more than a few strides head start down the stairs. Instead, I sent the hundred or so slivers of metal hurtling forward on a different trajectory, one that put me right in their path. The pain of the steel passing through me was almost unbearable, but I convinced myself to stay lucent.

The angels cried out in pain as one, the shards exiting my body and entering theirs, coated in my blood. Josette had said all a demon needed to do to harm a seraph was to break the skin. Being half, I was betting my plasma wouldn't be too healthy lodged deep inside of them. It didn't matter if I were wrong. I wasn't going to survive this fight any other way.

It wasn't enough to stop their initial attack. The three blades all came down towards me at once, but the momentum had been broken, and I dropped and rolled backwards just fast enough to avoid the strikes. Their swords clanged and sparked against the rooftop. They turned towards me as one, ready for round two. My own body was wracked with pain, and I didn't know if I had the strength to dodge another three-pronged attack. That was when I noticed the lines.

"What have you done," Boots cried, a growing spider web of poisoned black veins climbing its way up her neck towards her face. She dropped her sword, her hand no longer strong enough to hold it. The other two angels weren't faring any better, their own blades clattering to the ground as they fell to their knees.

In that moment, I felt nothing but guilt. Good was struggling enough as it was, and here I was destroying four of its warriors. I hadn't wanted to, but what choice did I have? Maybe I should have run and taken my chances that they would have found me. It didn't matter. It was too late to second guess.

Tears fell from my eyes as the poison continued to spread and their skin turned black. It was one thing to kill a demon, a creature that existed to create chaos, fear, and pain. It was another to destroy an angel, a being that worked to save lives, care for the sick, and empower the meek.

"I'm sorry," I said.

Boots toppled to the ground in front of me. When her body fell to dust, I began to cry in earnest.

I sat on the rooftop for almost an hour, my body healing but my mind feeling as though it would be forever scarred by the vision of the dying seraphs. This was what I had agreed to do. It was what war was about. Raw, violent, and painful, filled with impossible choices, and unwinnable situations. I should have never gone to see Josette. I should have stayed with Rebecca, curled up on the bed with her, keeping her company while she slept.

To make it worse, I knew Josette hadn't betrayed me as I had thought, and that something had happened to her as a result. I didn't know where she was, or if she was okay. When this was over, if I lived, I would find her and tell her I was sorry for doubting her.

Chapter 18

Rebecca and Obi were sitting on the couch together watching *Buffy the Vampire Slayer* when I returned. Rebecca was in the middle of explaining how people couldn't be turned into vampires by being bitten when I pushed open the door to the room and stepped inside.

"Landon?" Rebecca asked, her voice concerned. Obi turned off the television and got to his feet.

"Are you okay?" he asked.

I shook my head and walked over to them, then dropped the three blessed swords I had collected onto the coffee table. I didn't care that they chipped the wood and cracked the glass.

"What happened?" Rebecca glided to her feet and came over to me, reaching out and taking my hand in hers. She led me over to the sofa and eased me down onto it.

"I went to find Josette," I said. "Just to talk. I found someone else instead." I motioned towards the swords. "I didn't want to kill them. They wouldn't let me walk away."

"Touched?" Rebecca asked. She used her other hand to rub my back. It wasn't helping, but I appreciated the gesture.

"Angels," I replied.

She froze in shock. "Three of them?"

"Four," I said, then told them the entire story. They listened intently, though Obi blanched when I described how the angels had died.

"There was nothing you could have done, man," Obi said. "They decided they wouldn't let you walk, they paid the price for it. I don't like the idea of killing the good guys either, but you're a lot more important to mankind than they are."

"The servants of good are stubborn beyond reason." Rebecca agreed. "How many do they need to lose before they realize they can't fight on their own?"

"At least four," I replied. I wasn't looking to be cheered up, or have my actions justified. All I wanted was to just get it off my chest. Their words didn't comfort me, but I did find myself growing angrier at the situation. I took a deep breath and put it from my mind. Whatever feelings were being generated by the experience, they had to wait. I turned to Rebecca.

"How are you feeling?" I asked. She looked great, but I wanted to be sure.

"Ready to go," she said. "To be honest, I don't think I've ever felt better."

I couldn't help but smile. She returned a demure smile of her own. "Obi?"

He noticed the moment and stifled a laugh. "I got as much as I could."

"Tell me."

Obi got up and went over to his bag, flopping it open and pulling out a new stack of printed papers. He moved the swords off the coffee table with surgical delicacy and spread the papers out on the surface.

"It was a bitch to get this thing printed," he said of the architectural drawings of the building Merov called home.

"Wait a second," Rebecca said, recognizing the layout. "What is it you're planning?" She took her hand from my back and moved to get a closer look at the prints.

"Your father has a room that can only be opened by fingerprint. A very specific fingerprint," I said.

"It's his office," she said. "The fingerprint belonged to Trevan Solen, my grandfather. He built the room to prevent anyone from being able to enter, including the Divine. The fingerprint only disables the electromagnetic lock on the door. There are other defenses inside that require spoken passphrases to shut down. Do you think that Merov knows where the Chalice is?"

"I'm not sure. I know he's enough of an influence that Reyzl showed up at his... well, your party, and that he gave you an amulet. I'm pretty sure Reyzl knows where the Chalice is, but I'm guessing that he'll never give it up, and I'm not too keen on going head to head with him again right now anyway. Oh, I never did ask you, why was Reyzl at your party?"

It didn't seem possible that she could have become paler than she already was, but Rebecca's alabaster complexion turned almost all white.

"Merov's been trying for years to get in Reyzl's good graces," she said. "As a major demon he has the power to lift him to archvampire, which would put him in charge of all of the families in North America, provided he could defeat the current archvampire in combat. The demon is... intrigued with me."

"Intrigued as in...."

She didn't want to say it, but after a long awkward pause, she did. "He wants to dissect my brain, to understand why I am 'so sentimental towards my food', as he puts it. Then he wants to see if he can reprogram me to be less sympathetic. Then he wants to take me as his concubine. At least, that's how Merov described it. I doubt it would be as clinical as that."

I took a deep breath and swallowed the lump that had grown in my throat. For as much as I had been hoping to avoid a direct confrontation with Reyzl, everything I learned about him made it sound more and more inevitable. Would my anger be enough to overpower him? In that moment, I was dying to find out.

"I see," I said, trying to be calm. "Another good reason to come over to my side."

I guess I could have been angry she had chosen me because she was stuck between a rock and a hard place, but she had already proven too valuable to care too much about the circumstances. The fact that I was developing a more-than-friends kind of crush on her didn't hurt either. It was all Obi's fault for putting the thought into my head.

"It wasn't like that," Rebecca said, her eyes locking onto mine. "Landon, I didn't help you just to get away from Reyzl." She wasn't lying.

I put my hand on her face and looked into her eyes. "I know," I said. "Don't worry about it. I just can't believe your own father would sell you out like that."

She reached up and put her hand over mine. "He is nosferatu; a minor demon, but still a demon. There is nothing that comes ahead of gaining power and favor. Family is either a bargaining chip, or a liability. Nothing more."

"Cough cough," Obi said, interrupting our moment. "I hate to get in the middle of the Princess Bride, but um... yeah?"

I took my hand away and looked down at the prints. "I don't suppose you know what the passphrases are?" I asked Rebecca. Her laugh was enough of an answer. "Then let's just hope he didn't design his traps to stop a diuscrucis. Obi, tell me what I'm looking at."

The former marine pointed at the schematic. "Okay, the normal human entry points are here." The elevator. "Here." A stairwell. "And here." He pointed to another area that looked like it should have been a solid wall. "That one, I had to dig deep to find. I'm sure you know this Rebecca, but the building was constructed by Alpha Industries, a huge contracting firm owned very indirectly by the Solen family."

"Your human mob does a lot of garbage collecting," she said. 'Vampires tend to prefer architecture."

"It's a hidden escape route," Obi continued. "An elevator shaft with a small stairwell that wraps around it. I found one reference to it in the first draft of the blueprints, which I had to hack into Alpha's servers to get. Don't ask me how," he said, cutting me off before I could. "Anyway, it doesn't go to ground level, it goes deeper. Much deeper; it's below the sewer and subway systems."

"Where does it lead?" I asked.

"I don't know," Obi answered. "I was hoping your girlfriend could tell us." Rebecca and I both flushed. "Man, you guys are like a pair of grade schoolers."

Rebecca ignored his jab. "It most likely leads to an escape tunnel. It's a standard defense against demons."

I was confused. "Demons? Not angels?"

"Okay, I can see you're still missing a little from basic training," she said. "Think about how many demons there are, and how many angels there are."

I had no idea what the numbers looked like, but now that she mentioned it, demons did seem to be a lot more prevalent.

"So how does one defeat an enemy force that has ten to twenty times more combatants?" she asked. "In the case of demons, most times you don't have to. If we didn't spend so much time fighting amongst ourselves, we could have laid waste to this world years ago. The angel's favorite tactic is to turn demons on each other."

Pure genius. It explained how the seraphim had managed to hold the tide as long as they had, when as Josette had said few enough were willing to abandon Heaven for the real Holy War.

"So that's our emergency exit too," I said. "The tunnel will funnel any defenders from being able to gang up on us. It should be a cakewalk for the three of us to hold them back down there and make an organized retreat."

"Agreed," Rebecca said.

Obi didn't look too comfortable with the idea, but he nodded. "What about going in?" he asked.

"Tell me if there's any reason we shouldn't just use the front door, " I said.

There were the were guards, but I was pretty confident I could get us past them again. There was no way they would expect me to try to go into the building a second time, so they'd never suspect anyone they recognized.

"None that I can think of," Obi replied.

"Rebecca?"

"If we're discovered, it won't matter much where we are - we'll have to fight them off either way. The front door is as good as anything else."

"Okay, then we'll go in through the lobby. Play it straight, take the stairs."

"The stairs," Obi said. "Man, that's fifty stories."

I looked at him. "Weren't you a Marine?"

"I'm a former Marine. I haven't done that kind of hike in two years."

"I'll help you if you're too weak to make it," Rebecca said.

That was just what Obi needed to hear. "I've got it," he said.

I turned to Rebecca. "Do you have any idea what kind of entourage your father has? Or if he'll be there?"

She shrugged. "I have no idea. I've never lived in the apartment with him, and before the party we hadn't spoken in at least four months. Since he told me about the deal he was trying to make with Reyzl."

I cringed at her mention of the deal, my anger bubbling back up. "Then I guess we'll see what's what when we get there. Now, how do we handle the lock?"

Obi picked up the prints of the apartment building and exchanged it for some diagrams of the security system.

"It may not be this one," he said. "The records listed the manufacturer, not the exact model, but I bet most of them are the same. It's an electromagnetic fingerprint lock, five thousand pounds of pressure, powered by the electricity in the building when it's working, a backup battery when it isn't." He looked at me. "I was thinking maybe you could short out the power and disrupt the battery somehow. Otherwise, we'll need to remove the faceplate and wire it up to a laptop to hack the software that runs it. I could do it, except I don't have tools or a laptop."

I reached into my pocket and took out the remaining cash. I had sixty dollars left. "I don't think this will cover it," I said.

"All my funds were cut off," Rebecca said. We both looked at Obi.

"Fine," he said after thirty seconds of being stared down. "I'll put it on my card, but you owe me."

"Thanks Obi," I said. "So Plan A is for me to try to short the system somehow. I haven't tried to control electricity yet, so that scares me. I don't want to end up frying myself or either one of you." I looked at Obi. "Especially you, Rebecca will heal."

"I'd rather not," Rebecca said. "We don't recover very quickly from burns, and pardon the bad pun, but it hurts like Hell."

"Right. Plan B is for Obi to hack the software to disable the lock. I won't spend a lot of time on Plan A, so be lets be ready for B as soon as we get in. Also, if we end up in a fight, Plan A is out the window because I'll be busy covering you. We'll do our best to go in and out through the main entrance. I'll try to keep us disguised, but if we end up in a scrape we'll exit through the emergency hatch. Even if they follow we can defend ourselves better in the smaller space. If you don't like the plan, speak up now." I waited a minute for either of them to object. They didn't. "Okay, we'll hit up an electronics shop first for the laptop and any other equipment, then we'll head straight over. Saddle up, move out, game on."

I put my hand out over the table. Obi didn't hesitate to throw his hand in, but Rebecca was confused by the gesture.

"Just put your hand in," Obi told her, laughing. She did.

"Break on three," I said. "One... Two... Three..."

"Break," Obi and I shouted. Rebecca didn't know what to do, but she found it amusing all the same. It was corny, but better to go in loose.

Chapter 19

"You guys ready?" I asked.

We were standing on the corner opposite the apartment building, after having visited a nearby pawnshop to pick up the tools we needed for Obi to hack the lock. An older laptop, a lock pick set, a magnetic screwdriver and a bunch of bits, a circuit board, and some wires that I didn't recognize but Obi claimed would do the job.

Rebecca had brought two of the angels' swords with her, and I was carrying the other one - Boot's sword. When I had taken a closer look at it I had found it was different than the others. It was a little bit shorter and lighter, and had a few extra characters engraved into it. I didn't know what they meant or if they gave it any special powers, but I figured the size difference might make it easier for me to stab something that wasn't myself.

"I'm ready," Rebecca said.

She had created a makeshift sling out of a few belts she had picked out at the pawnshop to hold the blades over her back. I could imagine what the clerk would have thought if he had been able to see her true nature. A pale, raven haired, ice-blue eyed, glittering vampire-slash-succubus beauty in paramilitary garb toting two super badass looking samurai swords. Instead, he had seen a girl-next-door type with a pair of golf clubs that she was looking to pawn. The clerk had offered her ten bucks; she had refused.

I looked at Obi, who gave me the thumbs up. He had traded in the messenger bag for a backpack, and was wearing the Desert Eagle tucked into the back of his pants, hidden by his shirt.

"Okay, once we get a visual we'll move in," I said.

Obi had the idea to wait for three people to leave the building, and then go in disguised as them. It was a great idea, but I wasn't sure I could pull it off. A couple was the first to exit, two Turned humans dressed in their finery, headed off to some other well-to-do event elsewhere in the city. I paid close attention to them from a distance as they walked down the street. I didn't need to get every detail right, but the closer the better.

A third Turned male exited the building a couple of minutes later. I took a deep breath and focused; changing reality around us so that we took on the visage of the three people I had seen. It was a little troubling that they had all been evil, but I guess it made sense that Merov would keep his allies close at hand.

"You two go in first as the couple," I said. "I'll be right behind you."

Obi and Rebecca started forward, crossing the street and walking towards the building. I started half a minute later, keeping the same pace so we wouldn't look like we were together. I bit back a smile when they made it in past the doorman without a second glance. I wasn't so lucky.

"Mr. Taylor," the doorman said as I approached. "Back so soon?"

"Yeah," I replied. "I forgot my wallet." I patted my pocket for emphasis.

"Have a good evening sir."

I didn't answer him. I doubted a Turned would be that polite. I caught up to Obi and Rebecca in the lobby near the elevators. We had made it into the building, now we just had to ascend. I motioned to the stairwell off to the right. I would go in first, and they would follow one at a time over the next three minutes.

Getting to the stairs unseen proved to be a simple task, and we were formed up together six minutes later.

"Now comes the hard part," Obi said as we started to climb. Rebecca had offered to carry his pack for him, an offer which he had impolitely refused while she laughed.

I took us almost half an hour to reach the fiftieth floor. As expected, the door into the penthouse was both locked and alarmed.

"Just give me a minute," Obi said, opening his pack and digging out the lock pick set and a magnet. "I'll unlock the door, then use this magnet to loop the signal back on itself so the alarm doesn't know it should be going off." A minute later, he was done, and we were in.

"You're my own personal MacGyver," I said.

We slipped through the quieted doorway and into Merov's penthouse. We were in the kitchen, a large commercial grade menagerie of stainless steel and tile. I didn't want to imagine what kind of meat had passed through this room, or how it had been prepared. Drained and discarded was my best-case scenario, but the Fresh Fleshette had proven it wasn't as simple as all that. We were in luck. The place was deserted.

I recalled the schematics in my mind. The kitchen led out into the main service area, where there would be a big freezer, storage closet, and a couple of other rooms that hadn't been labeled. I focused on my senses, but I didn't pick anything up. As near as I could tell, the entire apartment was deserted. I hadn't sensed those angels either. Were they able to disguise themselves, or was it just the distance that had messed with my head? I wasn't about to take chances.

We moved out of the kitchen and into the main service hallway. The entrance to the penthouse proper was thirty feet forward, with a freezer and three more doors symmetrically placed on either side. I heard the crying as we neared the end of the hallway.

"Do you hear that?" I asked Rebecca.

The sobs were barely audible even in the silence, and seemed to be coming from the last door on the left. Rebecca cocked her head to the side and listened.

"Yes," she said after a few seconds. "Stay focused on our task." She didn't need me to say anything to know I would look to help whomever was in there.

I put my ear up against the door. Someone in there was crying, most likely another victim, waiting to be consumed. My actions the other night had killed the women Merov had put out as hors devours, I wasn't about to let another one die to this asshole.

"We get her out before we leave," I whispered. There was nothing in my expression or tone that left it open to argument.

The doors to the service hallway were actually a hidden part of the wall that slid outward from the center so as not to obstruct the space. We were fortunate that they were well maintained and didn't make a sound when we opened them. Or maybe we weren't so fortunate. The scene behind the door wasn't worth the price of admission.

It looked as though the entire apartment had been abandoned since the party. The blood fountain still sat in the center of the main open area, though there was no blood remaining in it. The band's instruments were resting at the top of the landing. Even what was left of the 'Happy Birthday' banner remained hanging above the living room. What caught my attention though were the beds, stained with the blood of the victims that I had killed, and the windows.

The huge windows that I had brought in on the party had been repaired. They looked like stained glass, with the millions of shards haphazardly mashed together in no discernible pattern, held together by dried blood, bones, and skin. It was a gruesome paste of death, conceived to restore the mirrored glass and prevent the sunlight from piercing the penthouse. The sight made it hard to think, and the smell made it hard to stay upright. It was impossible for Obi, and he doubled over, fighting to keep himself from vomiting.

I was about to step into the room, eager to get this over with and get out of this freakish nightmare, when Rebecca grabbed my arm and pointed up at the stairway leading to the landing. I followed her arm until it led me to a stone figure, a four-foot tall gargoyle. There were six of them on each side of the landing.

"Real?" I asked her. She nodded. "I thought gargoyles were good? They're on a lot of churches."

"A trick," Rebecca said. "Church architects used to put them there to fool demons into thinking they already had the building covered. They can't be sensed unless they're animated. I didn't think Merov had access to them. Gargoyles are incredibly hard to control."

"Not Merov then," I said. "Does anyone else have a bad feeling about this?"

"A trap?" Rebecca asked.

"Maybe; or maybe an educated guess. Let's just try to be quiet."

Of course Obi chose that moment to lose the battle against his delicate sensibilities, and the contents of his stomach came spilling out onto the floor. I don't know if it was the noise or the smell, but twenty-four small yellow eyes snapped open at once, and twelve monstrous heads turned our way.

"Crap," Obi said, seeing the fruits of his labor. He reached behind his back to grab the Eagle.

"Don't," Rebecca hissed at him. She unslung her blades. "Gargoyles are immune to silver, and the bullets will just bounce off them anyway."

Obi sighed. "What should I do then, make myself look really big?"

I motioned towards the living area. "Head that way, make a right at the first hallway. Down to the end on the left, start working on the door. Go!"

Obi broke into a run. The gargoyles were unballing themselves and stretching, their hard grey skin cracking as they shifted. With a soft hiss, the lead gargoyle launched into the air and unfurled its wings. It made a beeline straight for Obi while the rest of the demons headed our way.

"Anything they aren't immune to?" I asked Rebecca. I had to keep them away from Obi, so I didn't wait for her to answer before chasing after the ex-Marine.

"You're carrying it," she shouted. I turned my head to look at her while she set herself for the onslaught. Carrying it? I had forgotten about Boots' sword. It figured they were going to make me use it.

Rebecca had made me a sling also, and I stumbled when I reached back to retrieve the blade. The lead gargoyle had flown upward in order to come down on Obi from a higher angle. I launched myself forward, desperate to reach him before it did.

The demon swooped, not a single note of sound escaping from it as it dove down.

"Obi," I screamed, diving towards him with my shoulder forward.

I hit him hard, sending him sprawling, but saving him from the gargoyle that slammed off-center into my back instead. The force and momentum pushed me to ground, and sent the gargoyle caroming off into the wall. We both recovered while Obi regained his senses and resumed his run for the office.

I crouched down and held the sword out in front of me. The gargoyle climbed back to its clawed feet. Outstretched, it was eight feet of rippling muscle. It mimicked my crouch, cautious in its approach.

I used the opportunity to glance over at Rebecca. She had her back against the wall, and was squaring off against three of the demons. Her fangs were bared and elongated, her eyes clouded over to their lifeless black. I checked on the other gargoyles. They were headed this way.

The first gargoyle got tired of waiting on me and lunged. I dodged its swipe, and then danced out of the way of a second blow. One more swing and miss, and I flicked the blessed sword up and under its chin, feeling almost no resistance from the blade opening a long cut in its neck. The creature howled in pain and backed away, replaced by the reinforcements. I looked down the room for Obi, but he had at least managed to get out of the action and with any luck was in the process of disarming the door.

Three to one were bad odds against a demon that was impervious to almost everything. I focused my will inward; pushing myself to be stronger, faster, and tougher than any human could ever hope to be. I was almost decapitated when my first effort failed, my skill at bending the universe still not a surety. The attack put a deep gash into my neck and sent me skidding across the floor, the gargoyles trailing right behind. It hurt, and the sensation of having my head hanging from my spine was weird and creepy.

I focused again, rewarded for my persistence with the results I had been looking for. I healed in no time, and grabbed the first gargoyle that tried to jump on me and threw it away. I could hear it go smashing through the living room, but I didn't know how much damage I had inflicted. It didn't matter, because I had more demons incoming. I pushed off on the ground with my free hand, the augmented strength sending me high into the air. Everything around me looked like it was in slow motion, and I felt as though I had all day to make whatever maneuvers I needed on the way down.

I lashed out with my foot at one gargoyle, launching it backwards to land on the floor stunned a dozen feet away, whipped around with the sword on two more, hit the ground, crouched under an attempted grab, then propelled myself into the fourth blade-first. I landed on its chest and it slid across the floor, impaled. When I looked up, Rebecca was standing over me, her mouth wide in an impressed grin.

"Having fun yet?" she asked.

To be honest, I was.

There were five gargoyles left, and Rebecca and I tore into them with an unmatched fury. She was a blur of steel, legs, and hair, leaping into the air, kicking the gargoyle's claws aside and depositing one of the blades deep into its skull.

I used Boots' sword to remove a claw, then a leg, leaving a howling monster for Rebecca to finish off while I stabbed the third in the heart. The remaining two decided it was time to flee, but Rebecca threw a blade into one of the gargoyle's backs, then pounced onto the other one, hissing as she reached around and cut its throat. She was wiping the weapon clean on its skin before it hit the ground.

"I didn't know you could fight like that," I said to her after she retrieved the other sword and rendezvoused with me. She leaned in and kissed my cheek.

"Me neither," she said. "Your blood is amazing." Her eyes changed back to their beautiful blue, and the look she gave me melted my brain.

"I think we better check on Obi," I said, trying to catch my breath. We made our way to where the former Marine was working the electromagnetic lock.

"Man, I don't know if I can hotwire this thing," he said when we got to him. "This isn't the standard software package, it's been seriously customized."

"The gargoyles may not have gotten away, but its a good bet they sent an alarm out when they woke," Rebecca said. "I don't think we have a lot of time."

"It looks like Plan A is the new Plan B," I said. "Both of you back away from the door."

Once they had moved, I stood in front of the door and focused, trying to force the lock to disengage. It was a futile effort. I tried to short out the electrical connection, and was rewarded with a whole bucket of nothing. We were running out of time, and we weren't getting anywhere.

"Obi," I said. "Go back to the service area and let out whoever is trapped in there. Bring them back here, they aren't safe on their own."

"I don't think that's a good idea, man," Obi said.

"Do it," I shouted.

Obi's expression said 'screw you', but he followed the order. I looked at the door again. There had to be some way through. I crouched down and lifted the fingerprint sensor so I could look at it. If Rebecca's grandfather had ever touched the surface, maybe I could get his print. I stood up again.

"Open your mouth," I said to Rebecca.

"What?"

"Just open your mouth."

She did, and I took my thumb and ran it up along her fang, slicing it open. She licked at the blood that dripped onto her lips while I crouched back down and pressed it to the sensor. I focused on it, using it like a detective would use chalk. It was our lucky day, because a defined print assembled itself in my blood. I focused again to thicken and solidify it, creating enough light resistance to fool the system. The door clicked and swung open a few inches. We were in!

"Nice trick."

I knew that voice. Rebecca and I both turned our heads to see Merov standing at the end of the hallway with two burly weres. One was restraining Obi. The other one was holding the girl I assumed was Merov's prisoner. She was young, a little chubby, wearing a grey wool sweater and a pair of jeans. Her face was ordinary; her eyes brown and glazed from tears. She was still whimpering. I had been too distracted with the lock to notice them coming.

"Wait until you see my next one," I replied. It seemed like as good a time as any for a smartass remark. Merov was unfazed.

"Reyzl was sure you'd be back. I told him there was no way, but I guess that's why he's the Boss. I'm surprised you brought a human with you though. He's not even Touched! And he was trying to make off with my virgin! By the way, it's good to see you again my dear." Malicious was too soft a word for the smile he gave his daughter.

I held up my hands. "Okay, you've got us," I said. "Now what."

He laughed. "As if it would be that easy to capture you. I didn't rise this far by being stupid diuscrucis." He raised his hands and gestured for his goons to release their prisoners.

Both Obi and the girl stumbled down the hallway. "I know if it came down to it, you'd just kill them to get to me," he said.

I would never have told Obi, but the vampire was right.

"So what is it you want?" I asked. When they reached us, the girl put her arms around Obi and continued to shake.

"A deal of course," he replied.

"Landon," Rebecca said. "Be careful making deals with demons."

"Of course. Name it," I said.

He walked forward, unconcerned for his safety. I doubted he was as vulnerable as he appeared. "My sweet daughter owes me a dance," he said, looking right at her. "If she wins, I'll be dead, and she'll be in control of the family. You can get whatever information you want, no tricks needed." He stopped right in front of me. "If I win, you'll kill Reyzl for me. Once he's dead, you'll leave me to control the Northeast, and take your nasty business elsewhere."

There was something amusing about him calling my work nasty. I wasn't the one torturing young virgins before drinking their blood.

"Landon, don't," Rebecca said. "Remember what I told you."

Merov laughed. "Did she tell you she can't beat me?" he asked. "Ironic that it should come down to a question of faith. Do you have faith in my daughter, even when she doesn't have it in herself?"

I looked at Rebecca. She was frightened. "What if I just kill you where you stand?" I asked him.

"You won't," he said.

"Because..."

He smiled again. "Because then she gets nothing. You know where she stands. Now imagine having our family capitulating to her orders; three thousand nosferatu following her lead."

He was willing to do the deal because he was confident. He had no doubt in his mind that he could kill his daughter, and this was his big chance to get rid of Reyzl, get rid of me, and put himself into greater power. Rebecca had said Reyzl could make him an archvampire, but why settle for that when you could aim even higher? I glanced between Merov and Rebecca - the confident father and his frightened child. It was an offer I couldn't refuse.

"You have a deal," I said.

"Landon, no," Rebecca cried. It was too late, and she knew it.

"You have five minutes," Merov said. "I'll be waiting in the living room." He turned and left, his heavies following close behind.

"What did you just do," Rebecca hissed once Merov was out of range.

I took hold of her shoulders and lowered my head so she could see into my eyes. "I doubled-down on your bet," I told her. "Like you said, it's a risk, but it's one both of us need to take."

Her angry expression softened. She slumped forward into my arms. "I'll do my best. If I lose... I'm sorry."

I held her for a minute before easing her out of the embrace. My heart was thudding in my chest, my body feeling an unnatural chill. It wasn't the temperature that was making me so cold. I was finding the thought of Merov winning more frightening than anything I had experienced. Merov winning meant Rebecca would be gone.

"You won't lose," I said. "You can't. You're running on premium."

It was a joke that ended up feeling lame to say, but the statement perked her up. She straightened her posture, licked her lips, and then smiled. "I hadn't even considered that. I'm going to wipe the floor with that asshole."

"Can somebody tell me what's going on here?" Merov's prisoner had stopped whimpering long enough to speak. She was still holding onto Obi's arm like it was the only thing keeping her sane.

"I'm sorry," I said to her. "It's better for you if you don't know. What's your name?"

"Cathy."

"Cathy, I'm going to get you out of here unharmed, okay?"

She didn't look convinced, but she nodded. "Okay."

“Good. Don’t worry about anything. Rebecca, can you?”

Rebecca stepped over to Cathy and took her face in her hand. “You’re so pretty,” Cathy said.

“Thank you Cathy,” Rebecca replied. “Now go to sleep.”

She received the Command as though she had been hypnotized, her eyes rolling back in her head and her entire body going limp. Obi caught her on the way down, easing her fall.

“Time to go kill my father,” Rebecca said.

“Rebecca.” I reached out and grabbed her by the arm as she started to storm away.

It was all I had time to say, because then her lips were locked onto mine, and she was kissing me like it would be her last chance. Every sense of everything else in the universe faded away. I absorbed every ounce of emotion that she poured into the kiss, amplifying and returning it mixed with every feeling she had created within me since we had met. It was deep, meaningful, and passionate, a hello and a goodbye both. When she pulled away from me, it was all I could do to stay balanced.

“Much better than chocolate,” she repeated.

“Break a leg,” I said, trying to catch my breath.

“I’ll break a lot more than that.”

Obi and I followed behind her as she resumed her angry march towards her destiny. Reaching the main living space, I saw that Merov had stripped down to a white t-shirt and a pair of black sweats. I had thought the vampire was stocky, but his body was well muscled. It was his powerful barrel chest that had made him appear fat. He looked like he could pulverize his child without effort.

"I'm sorry to have to do this to you my dear," he said when he noticed Rebecca approaching.

She didn't waste time with formality. Instead she kicked off her shoes, opened her mouth and hissed a challenge, her body shifting back into attack mode. This time she did a complete transformation, her fingers and toes elongating into deadly claws. She was on Merov in an instant, catching him off guard and leaving a deep gash in his cheek before he could react. He bellowed and shifted himself, showing us why he was the head of the family.

Where Rebecca could grow longer fangs and claws, Merov's entire body changed. He grew at least six feet, his muscle expanding his skin so much it looked like it was going to tear, his face taking on a non-humanoid look as all of his teeth grew and pushed against his mouth. He was more beast than man, a monster in civilized clothing.

He caught Rebecca's fist when she tried to dig into his chest, twisted her arm and threw her across the floor. "Come now dear, you can do better than that," he said, his voice so deep it was hard to understand.

Rebecca got back to her feet and approached again, more cautious after the last hit. She looked miniscule framed against her father's insane mass of power.

"I've hated you my entire life," she told him. "I can't wait to watch you die."

She danced forward, dodged a heavy punch, and raked her claws across his chest. It was so thick it didn't even break through the skin, and she was rewarded by a backhanded blow to the head that sent her tumbling away. He was toying with her.

"You know how I hate to disappoint you," he said. "But I'm afraid I'll have to make you wait a while longer."

He dashed forward with a speed that should have been impossible for his size, then raised his foot to stomp his daughter. I cringed as the huge claw came down on her. Somehow she was able to get her feet under her, and she caught the foot in her hands and shoved. Off balance, Merov crashed backwards onto the ground.

Rebecca didn't hesitate, leaping into the air and leading with her feet. She managed to dig a little deeper into his chest when she hit, but he lashed out and sent her flying off him again, then got back up. Rebecca recovered, landing upright and pressing the attack. She angled back and forth, trying to keep Merov off balance. She had no chance against him on strength, but she was still quicker and more agile.

"I didn't think you'd be this much fun," Merov said with a laugh.

Rebecca responded with a flurry of blows that her father either blocked or absorbed with his massive bulk. The wounds she was inflicting were adding up, but they seemed like no more than paper cuts across the massive expansive of his body. The wave left her winded and off-balance, and Merov didn't waste the opening, grabbing her by the throat and lifting her well off the ground.

"Goodbye dear," he said, turning his head so he could leer at me while he finished the fight.

I assume he had been planning to pop her head right off like a cork. He didn't get the chance. With a blinding speed that I almost couldn't follow, Rebecca kicked her legs up and wrapped them around his arm, then twisted her hips. The crack of his limb breaking was painfully loud, and he dropped her and cried out as it fell limp. She landed on her feet and moved in again, grabbing his other arm and snapping it at the elbow before he could react. He lashed out with his foot, but she sidestepped it and brought her own kick down on his kneecap, shattering those bones as well.

Unable to support the massive weight, Merov sank to his knees, his eyes filled with rage, fury, and pride? Rebecca saw it too, and she stopped her assault.

"You've grown so much," the vampire said to his daughter. "I didn't think you had it in you."

She had fooled him into thinking she was spent, and he would pay with his life.

"You've never thought much of me," she said to him.

"No," he admitted. "That's because your mother was such a filthy whore."

Without another word, she reached out and grabbed his head, breaking his neck before he could say anything else. She stood motionless, watching his lifeless body topple to the ground, her black eyes a mask to whatever emotions were playing across her mind. A moment later, black fog began rising out of Merov's mouth. I started moving towards her, to warn her of the danger, but she closed her eyes and opened her mouth to receive it. What was she doing?

I had never seen the process from the outside. The cloud transferred from father to daughter in a steady stream of ashen smoke that twisted and curled around her. Once it was finished, she bowed her head to the disintegrating carcass and turned to the two weres who had waited on the sidelines.

"You have borne witness," she said to them.

"Yes, mistress," they agreed.

"Go wait in the lobby," she commanded.

"Yes, mistress," they said in unison. They headed off towards the elevator. Rebecca looked at me, the black of her eyes fading away to reveal oceans of blue. She looked the same, but different, more regal. I gave her a concerned smile. She came over.

"Man, that was unreal," Obi said from behind me. "I couldn't even see her she was moving so fast."

"That was incredible," I told her. She threw her arms around my neck and pulled me down to her, kissing me as with the same force as she had the last time.

"I have you to thank," she said once we had broken our embrace. "I've never felt so strong."

"Merov's soul?" I asked.

"It is part of the rights of ascension. The defeated surrenders their power to the victor, along with their knowledge."

"Do you mean you can turn into a ten-foot tall Rebecca now?" I asked.

"Come on, worm," she replied. "My power doesn't manifest the same way, since I'm only half-nosferatu. For Merov, it was strength. For me, it's speed. I also inherited a measure of his memories. I know the passphrases to get into his office."

Excited didn't even scratch the surface of what that statement made me feel. "I hate to be a bother," I said, "but would you mind?"

Rebecca laughed. "I don't mind, but we don't have time." Her attitude turned serious. "I have a lot more to tell you, but we have to go. Your friend Josette is in trouble."

"Trouble?" I asked. I didn't even know where Josette was.

"The demons are making a move tonight," she said. "Merov had just left to participate when the gargoyles alerted him to our break in. They're going after an angel sanctuary, and all of the major players have amulets."

"The amulets don't work," I said.

"They do, but there's a catch," Rebecca said. "The demon who controls the Chalice can manipulate the power of the crystals. If they lose one, or one is taken, they can shut it down."

"Like a remote kill switch?" Obi asked, moving in to join the conversation.

"Exactly."

"How do you know Josette is at this sanctuary?" I asked. I didn't even know what an angel sanctuary was.

"Reyzl promised her to Merov in exchange for his participation. She's there, and she's in trouble. I know she's your friend, so if you want any hope of saving her we have to go now."

It wasn't like there was a decision to be made. "Where to?" I asked.

"The Catskills," Rebecca said.

"Whoa," Obi said. "Catskills? Like the mountains?"

Rebecca looked at him as if he had two heads. "Yes. There is a Monastery there that serves as a seraphim sanctuary. The demons have known about it for some time, but they didn't believe they could win a battle on the angel's home turf. The Grail has changed that."

I knew what Obi was getting at. "Rebecca, we don't have any way to get to the Catskills."

She gave me a big smile. "We do now," she said.

Chapter 20

The battle started before we even got down into the parking garage of the building, when I told Obi I needed him to stay with Cathy and take her home once she woke up. His protests were loud, angry, and laced with profanity. They were also ineffective. We had no idea what we would be walking into, and as tough as the former Marine had proven to be, he was still human. He would have been little more than a red-shirt out there, even more so once he had finished off his remaining forty something rounds. He gave up when Rebecca threatened to Command him. At least this way he could pretend it was his choice, he had said.

Merov's... no, Rebecca's private elevator led down into a secluded area of the garage, complete with its own attendants. They stood at attention when the doors opened, not even questioning Rebecca's newfound authority. She led me out into a sea of luxurious excess.

There were at least thirty cars here, all of them washed, waxed, and primed for driving. They varied in size and shape, but I imagined none of them cost less than a hundred grand. They sat arranged by type in two rows on either side of the main aisle, sports cars, sport utility vehicles, sedans, and even a few that I couldn't classify. Growing up in a city, I had never been a big car guy, but even the little bit I knew was enough to be impressed.

"We'll take the Rolls," Rebecca said to one of the attendants, an older vampire with long greying hair.

"Yes, mistress," he said, dashing off to get the car.

"It's not the fastest thing in here, but its armor plated," she said.

I had a feeling we were going to need the protection. "How do they just know you're the boss?" I asked her. I could hear the heavy growl of the car's engine coming to life, and then I saw the headlights flick on.

"The transfer," she replied. "They can feel the shift the same way you did. They just understand it better."

"Have I told you how awesome I think you are," I said to her.

The car rumbled up to where we were standing and the attendant popped out. He held the driver's side door while the other one opened the passenger side.

"We'll settle that later," she said to me with a wink and a grin.

I wasn't one hundred percent sure what she meant, but it didn't sound bad. She tossed the blessed swords in the back seat and sank in behind the wheel while I circled around and hopped in on the other side, putting Boots' weapon with the others. The attendants slammed the doors shut, and with a slight squeal of tires and roar from the engine we were off.

"What time is it starting?" I asked when we pulled out of the parking garage and onto the street. It was almost ten o'clock, which made the otherwise insane Manhattan traffic almost bearable.

"I don't know," she replied. "It can't be too soon, or Merov would never have made it in time. I'm going to guess around one or two. It's a three hour drive."

I looked over at her, admiring the shape of her face in profile, her expression purposeful as she drove. I respected her for her strength and resolve, and for being so unequivocally willing to do this for an angel, her kind's mortal enemies, just because she knew it was important to me. What the beautiful creature driving the car saw in me, I had no idea, but for some reason she wanted to be with me, to be on my side. It was insane, but despite everything I was happier in that moment than I had ever been before.

"You should rest," she said. She snaked around the slower moving traffic with practiced ease. "I think we're going to need everything you've got."

The truth was, I felt good. "What about you?" I asked. "I've never driven before, but once we get out onto the open road I'm sure I can figure it out."

One eye pivoted to look at me, and she laughed. "We'll be dead before we get there," she said. "I'm fine. Between your blood and the transfer, I don't think I'll need to rest for a while."

We rode in comfortable silence, the interior of the car impervious to outside noise. There was so much I wanted to ask her, about the transfer, about demons, about Reyzl. I couldn't bring myself to do it. The moment of peaceful companionship was just too appealing. I kept my eyes out the window, watching all of the people who turned their heads to stare, who tried to see through the vehicle's tinted glass. What would they think if they saw us as we were, a vampiress and the bastard son of the universe? An image of pitchforks was the first thing that came to mind.

It took us about half an hour to get out of Manhattan and onto the George Washington bridge. I could sense Rebecca tense up when the car eased out over the open expanse of water, then relax after we crossed it. She breathed out a deep sigh on the other side.

"What's it like?" she asked me then.

"What's what like?"

"To be a human. To be so inferior and weak."

I couldn't help but smile. "Thanks Becca," I said. Her head snapped to the right so she could look at me. "You don't like being called Becca, do you?"

She tilted her head ever a tiny bit, smiled, then put her eyes back on the road. "It's not that. I've never had anyone refer to me like that before. Like a friend."

"I am your friend," I told her. "It must be hard to have been ostracized by your people for thinking different. For trying to help them see the bigger picture."

She stared straight ahead. "It has been lonely," she admitted. "I never thought that I would achieve much more than being Merov's laughable daughter, or Reyzl's toy. Even the scientists who were working on the synthetic... I know they thought the project was an eccentric waste."

"Now you're the boss though," I said. "That has to count for something."

Rebecca sighed again. "I wish it were that simple. The family will follow me because it's our way, but I expect that I'll be challenged quite often, at least in the beginning. At least until they see that I'm not someone to be taken lightly."

I reached over and squeezed her shoulder. "Nobody will take you lightly. Merov was a serious monster, and you destroyed him." She didn't look too sure. "Anyway, I'll be with you."

The engine roared as she accelerated past an eighteen-wheeler, flipping off the driver on the way past. "Asshole," she shouted into the cabin.

I doubted the sound would be able to penetrate the armored walls, but the simple normalcy of the gesture made me laugh.

"Being human isn't much different than that," I said. "You just do your best to have some fun, stay sane, not be lonely, and navigate around all the assholes. "

She was thoughtful for a minute, as if I had said something profound. "What about your family?" she asked. "Do you miss them?"

It occurred to me then that I hadn't thought much about my family since returning from Purgatory. My mind wandered back to my mother, sitting in the kitchen reading a trashy romance novel and drinking tea. She had been a good enough mother, there for me when I needed her, a decent moral guide. It hadn't been her fault I thought I was smarter than I was. She had supported me as best she could during the trial and my incarceration.

My father? He was there some of the time, gone the rest. He had popped back in and out of our lives a few times over the years, usually to have someplace to be when he couldn't think of anywhere else. I didn't know if he was even still alive. I had some extended family too, but I didn't know any of them that well. It had just been my mother and I, and even so I wouldn't say that I felt close to her.

"No," I said after a long pause. "My mother is super religious. No offense, but I don't think she'd approve of my choice of friends."

We continued talking for the rest of the drive. It was simple, easy talk about everything and nothing. I learned about how she was raised, her first taste of fresh blood, how she came to be appalled by the way Merov killed humans so casually for food. I told her about my mortal childhood, my love of technology, my first kiss, the sadness I had felt when my dog Whisper had been hit by a car when I was nine years old. We were new friends and old friends at the same time, keeping each other good company while we drove through the night towards an uncertain future. I took comfort in knowing that there was nobody else I would rather have headed towards oblivion with, and that if oblivion did come at least I wouldn't end alone.

Chapter 21

I was looking out of the window, listening to Rebecca tell me about how she had come to live at the Statue of Liberty and marveling at the snowy landscape of the Catskill mountains when the darkness of the night was pierced by a blinding beam of white light off in the distance, shooting straight up into the sky. At the same instant I felt a distinct unease in my gut, my soul reverberating in alarm.

"Do you see that?" I asked Rebecca.

She stopped talking and looked around. "I don't see anything," she replied.

"It's started," I told her. "There's a light shining out that way." I pointed into the woods. "If you can't see it, it's for angel eyes only, I guess."

"How far?"

"Five miles at least, maybe ten," I replied.

We had been slowed by the snow, which was at least three inches deep and counting. While it had provided for a beautiful visual distraction, it was costing us now.

"Can you go any faster?" I asked.

She put her foot down on the accelerator. I could hear the wheels spinning, fighting to find traction.

"Not if you want to stay on the road," she said.

"Then let's hope they can hold out," I said.

Twenty minutes had passed by the time we reached a small, unpaved roadway marked by a small wooden sign that read 'St. Francis Monastery'. I had kept my eyes on the beacon the entire time, and now I could see it down the road.

"That's the place," I said. "Turn here."

Rebecca complied, putting us on a straight track towards the fight. There was still at least two or three miles left to travel through the snow covered woods, and the weather was getting worse. The snow was falling in such volume that we couldn't see the road five feet in front of us. I focused on the light ahead and reached out with my senses, only to be crushed from the weight of so many demons concentrated in such a small area. We weren't far away, but we would have to go in blind in every sense of the word.

"We're close," I told Rebecca, my head still pounding from the effort. There was a thump and a cry as we slammed into something dark that had been standing in the road.

"Scratch that, we're here," I said. A moment later, another thump, this one on the roof.

"I think we've been spotted," she said. A batlike head peered down at me from the passenger side window. A clawed fist tried to punch through the glass, but the armor was too tough for it. I heard another thump, then another, as more demons spotted the car and leaped onto it.

"How do they know we're not on their side?" I asked, trying to keep my voice somewhat calm.

"I don't think they care," Rebecca replied. "Now what?"

"Just keep driving," I said. "We need to get to wherever the angels are."

The demons on the car were pounding on the roof, on the windows. Another one landed on the hood, looking in at us and hissing. It reminded me of Reyzl's messenger, but bigger.

"Scouts," Rebecca said. "Their job would have been to gather info on the location, then back up when the stronger demons arrived. If Reyzl isn't here, one of his lackeys will be. He'll be Commanding them, and holding open the Rift."

"Rift? Is that what it sounds like?"

"Yes. It's a passageway to and from Hell. Get off!" She cursed as two more demons slammed into the side of the car, almost sending us into spin. "There are hundreds of types of demons. Most are big, ugly, mean, and dumb, like the grunts at the Belmont. The higher order demons create them to fight, but they can't organize without being Commanded, and they don't have the power to travel a Rift on their own. You'll find some strays once in awhile, but for the most part they remain in Hell."

It was a weird time to be having this conversation, but she wouldn't have been telling me this stuff if it weren't important. The outer shell of the car was a cacophony of hammer blows as the smaller demons tried to break through. I could see the beacon clearly now, a laser thread of light that reached up into eternity. We were almost there.

"So what about the weres, and the nosferatu, or Reyzl for that matter?" I asked her. "You reproduce like mortals, have families, loyalties, the whole deal."

Rebecca's face was a mask of concentration, fighting to keep the car under control. I was impressed with her ability to multi-task.

"God created man," she said. "When he gave Hell to the Devil, the Devil wanted to one up him, and to thwart his designs. He started creating his own vision of mankind, one that was not so... constrained. His early efforts were fruitless, after all he's not God, but in time he found limited success. The problem was that his creations still required God's original touch of life, and so the demons such as nosferatu required human blood to survive. Our story has grown and evolved much the same as man. We have lived secretly in parallel and worked to claim for our own whatever God and man has built. No demon can stay here indefinitely without feeding on a human, or feeding on a demon that has fed on a human. We all need God's seed to survive."

"Or some badass technology," I said. "Synthetic blood to replace the touch of God?"

"Stem cells," she said. "Even the synthetic uses human blood, we just manufacture it ourselves. One day maybe we'll be able to make it fast enough we won't need any synthetic materials, but that day is a long way off."

We were within a mile of our destination, and the number of demons assaulting the car was reaching ridiculousness. How Rebecca was managing to keep the vehicle under control with so many of the things pounding against it was a feat beyond understanding. Finally, she skidded the car to a stop.

"We're close enough," she growled. The angel light was burning up the sky now, and I could tell that it was originating from the center of a large stone building. Even with the illumination from the light visibility still sucked, the snowfall creating a whiteout across the entire area.

Rebecca reached behind the seat and grabbed the swords. She handed me mine with a smile, and then her eyes clouded over and the smile grew longer and more frightening. The car began to rock. The demons covering it were able to get a better purchase now that it wasn't moving. She reached for the door handle.

"Hold on," I said. "How much do you like this car?"

"I can get another," she replied.

"Just what I wanted to hear," I told her. "The air's going to get a little weird in here."

I looked down at my feet and focused my will, pulling cold air in through the ventilation system, packing it into the cabin and compressing it. I could feel the pressure building as I did so, pushing in on us and making it hard to breathe. The demons continued to rock the car, and a claw managed to sneak in through the seam of the driver's side door.

My head was a melon ready to explode from the intense pressure. Rebecca was moaning, unable to handle the discomfort any longer. The inhale complete, I pushed out the exhale, forcing the air to expand around us.

The air exited at supersonic speed, ripping apart the Rolls Royce and sending its pieces exploding outward. The demons that had been assaulting the car were shredded by the power of the blast, their bodies pulled apart by the decompressing air and fragments of steel. In the distance, I could hear more cries of pain as the bullets found other soft flesh to dig into. The frame of the car was all that remained, with us sitting in the center.

If Rebecca was impressed, she didn't show it. She was all business. "The Commander will be near the center of the assault, ringed with the strongest of the demons," she said. "Unless he brought a second, killing him will cause the less intelligent to lose cohesiveness and start fighting with one another."

"Got it. Are you ready?" I asked.

She responded with a wink, and then disappeared into the snow. I didn't waste any time following after her.

"This way," she said, leading me at a slight angle away from the light. "I can smell them. The main force is already inside."

We ran about a thousand feet, passing pieces of the Rolls and disintegrating parts of demons. The snow was well packed here, trampled by hundreds of claws. I could hear the sound of steel, the roar of monsters. A fourteen foot mass of muscle appeared out of nowhere, throwing a huge ham fist right at me. I dove to the side and rolled to my feet just in time to see Rebecca leap upwards and decapitate it with one smooth stroke. The somewhat humanoid head landed at my feet, its patchy black hair matted with blood.

"Trolls," she said, kicking the head away. "They're too big to go inside."

"I'm glad you aren't," I told her. We went another hundred feet or so before we came across the first dead angel.

He had long blonde hair, delicate features, and a smooth, boyish face. He was lying in blood soaked snow, one wing torn from his body, his skin marbleized by the black demon poison that had felled him. He wore a pair of white linen pants, his chest and feet bare. He had died recently enough that he hadn't yet turned to dust, and his blood steamed against the cold snow. I stood there smoldering until Rebecca pulled me away.

"Come on, Landon," she said. "There are still some that we can save."

And plenty of demons left to kill. As if on cue, another troll charged in through the veil of snow. Before Rebecca could react, I leapt forward at the creature, digging my sword deep into its chest and using it as a springboard to bounce away. It all happened too fast for the demon to follow, and it stopped and grabbed at its wound with a look of confusion before toppling to the ground.

"Lead on," I said.

Our pace slowed as we moved in closer to the Monastery, the entire grounds heavy with demons. 'Fodder', Rebecca had called them. They were weak demons whose role was to harass and distract the defenders while trying to overwhelm them with their numbers and get in a lucky hit that would break the skin and allow entry to their poison. They were simple humanoid creatures, five feet tall, skeletal frames with clawed hands and feet, and skin that lay taut against sinewy muscle and bone. It was like they had taken a human being, flayed it, and shrink-wrapped it with a new skin.

There were hundreds of them still wandering about outside in search of more enemies to attack. They hooted when they saw us coming, bringing even more of their brethren to the scene. They dropped like flies. Even with my non-existent skill at swordplay they were too slow to be a threat to us.

"Landon, behind you," Rebecca shouted. I didn't turn to look, but instead bent my knees and launched myself into the air, shooting up and over the troll's fist as it smashed into the ground where I had been standing. It was becoming a favorite tactic of mine since I had tried it with the gargoyles. It allowed me to both evade attack and also get a better perspective on the attacker and my surroundings.

The troll looked at me as I reached the apex of my ascent, pulling back his fist and throwing it upwards. He was faster than the others had been, and I scrambled to get my sword up in time to block the incoming ball of demonic muscle. He didn't hit me dead on, but even so the impact sent me flying.

I crashed on the ground twenty feet away, just in time to see Rebecca decapitate the troll while it was trying to gauge my descent. I jumped to my feet to sidestep a clumsy lunge by a fodder demon and plant my sword in its back, then drop under another blow and bring the blade back around and through the head of the second demon. I had dispatched six more by the time Rebecca got over to me.

"How much further?" I asked her. I could hear more demons heading our way, the shaking ground a cue that it wasn't just more fodder. "We're losing too much time out here."

Rebecca didn't seem to mind all the fighting. In fact she looked radiant in her adrenaline stoked attack mode. The melting snow had caused her hair to stick to her face in an alluring way, and her well-worn henley was clinging to the outline of her form.

"Agreed," she said. "We need to get inside."

We hurried the rest of the way to the Monastery, slowing only when the chasing demons caught up to us. The trolls were the most difficult, their size allowing them to outrun the fodder, but we were fortunate that there was no strategy to their attack, and no cooperation. For all of their brute power, we were just flat out superior.

The Monastery entrance was a plain human-sized wooden door affixed to the center of a long, high stone wall that comprised the south side of the building. According to Rebecca's inherited memory, it had been constructed in the nineteen fifties to resemble a fourteenth century monastic retreat, complete with a total absence of windows and no electricity, and therefore lots and lots of candles. The idea was that this type of environment would keep the monks focused on God and prayer because there was nothing else to look at or do. What she hadn't known was why the angels were using it, since they tended to prefer wide, open spaces to small, dark containment; the precise environment that most demons preferred.

The door had already been torn apart, and it lay on the ground ten feet away. Scattered around the entrance were the remains of a bloody and violent battle, with a large number of half-decayed fodder and trolls littering the area along with at least three or four angels. Since the Divine lost their physical manifestations so soon after being destroyed, I was judging the outcome based on how many blessed swords I found discarded.

"The monks were Touched warriors," Rebecca reminded me when I commented on my system.

"Their bodies would still be here," I countered. I knew she was trying to help alleviate my concern for Josette, and I appreciated it, but I was going to worry until we found her.

"Not if the demons took them off to consume them," Rebecca said. I hadn't thought about that outcome, and it did give me a little bit of macabre peace. "We'll be safe from the outer demons once we're inside. They would have entered already if they hadn't been Commanded not to."

We came across some of the monks on the other side of the door, in a small foyer that had contained some kind of mechanism with seraph-scripted spikes. The spikes were covered in blood, but the apparatus that had held them was smashed to pieces, leaving them scattered among the casualties - three Touched monks who had been assigned to work the trap, and a number of decayed fodder corpses. A heavy stone door had lain on the other side of the room, but the intruders had managed to obliterate it. Beyond the door, the hallway split in three directions.

"Which way?" I asked Rebecca.

The inside of the building was almost silent. The scrape of claws and the occasional echoed howl were the only indication that there was anything in here at all. There was no sound of battle, no hint of angels fighting demons, and that was bad. Were we too late? Had the battle already been lost?

"They split off," she replied. "They're here to kill everything they find."

Which way then? I hated to split up, but we didn't have a choice. "Okay, take the left, I'll go straight, and let's hope the right corridor is a dud."

"Landon," Rebecca said, reaching out and grabbing my arm. "We can't. Even with the transfer, I'm not powerful enough to take on a major demon on my own. I'm not sure you are either."

She had a point. I had seen her do so much damage with so little effort I had forgotten that there were demons out there that could eat us for breakfast. "You're right. We'll go to the left."

The corridor was dark, lit by candles that sat in plain iron sconces along the walls. There was a small door every ten feet or so which led into simple eight foot by eight foot rooms that reminded me of prison cells, outfitted with just a small bed and a toilet. The doors had been torn off every single one of the rooms we passed. Some were empty, but the others... the others were a gruesome scene of blood splattered walls, decaying demons, and half-eaten corpses. When we came upon demons that were still feeding, we destroyed them and moved on.

We continued down the hallway. A rhythmic thumping sound began reverberating through the walls. It was a steady pounding, every four or five seconds, a huge THUMP that shook mortar from the stone construction. There was no other sound now, wherever the demons were they no longer seemed to be on the move. We hadn't seen evidence of angels in any of the rooms, which was a good thing. We didn't know where they were though, and that was a bad thing.

"They must have locked themselves in the chapel," Rebecca said after considering the banging. "We may be out of time." I started running, and she followed.

My pace was reckless, but in the moment I didn't care. The balance of power was already in Hell's favor, and every angel that died gave them a stronger foothold. I hadn't helped the cause any earlier, and that drove me even harder to want to ensure that no more seraphs were destroyed. We happened along a few demon stragglers as we ran, and I tore through them without slowing, Rebecca staying close behind.

The split corridors seemed to reconnect at the back end of the Monastery, then turn inward to the central part of the building. Following the layout brought us to one more heavy doorframe that had lost its thick wooden door, and beyond it a dining hall. It was here that the demons remained, pounding at a gigantic, ornately decorated door that was covered top to bottom in seraphim writing.

"Now what?" I whispered to Rebecca.

We had taken position outside the dining room, peeking in from the doorway. There were at least a hundred demons gathered inside - a whole bunch of fodder, a handful of weres, a couple of dog-like creatures I hadn't seen before, four female demons that Rebecca whispered were harpies, and the main power players, seven fallen angels.

The angels were the ones pounding the door, standing in a circle with their arms held up and wings spread, a blue flame dancing in the center of a pentagram they had scratched into the stone floor. The flame would grow and congeal, and a ball of energy would launch out and slam against the barrier, rocking it back and forth. A return flash of lightning-like defensive energy would lash into the angels, burning and tearing at their bodies, which would heal before the next attack and counterattack. Each of them was wearing an amulet around their neck, negating the effectiveness of the angels' last line of defense.

"Do you see the angel closest to the door, the one with the short black hair?" Rebecca asked.

I looked to the figure she had described. Like the others, he was shirtless, wearing only a pair of cloth pants cinched by a simple rope belt. His entire upper body was covered in ragged tattooed sigils, and his wings had been dyed black with red at the tips that made them look like they were dripping blood.

"That's Lazar," she said. "He'll be Commanding the fodder and the hounds. If we can take him out we may be able to cause enough confusion to disable the other angels before they can recover."

"That's the plan?" I asked. "Why don't I just tap dance in there naked? That would be an easier distraction."

Rebecca bared her fangs in a twisted smile. "And a much more attractive one," she replied. "But I think the only demon that would be distracted is me."

I was able to be embarrassed despite our predicament. I could feel my face turn red. The hallway shook as another blast of energy slammed into the doorway. I looked over at it and noticed there was a small crack beginning to form in the upper left corner. We were running out of time.

I looked back at Rebecca, who was waiting for me to tell her what to do. Her face was fearsome beauty, framed to perfection by the flickering candles behind her. The flickering candles.

"Do fallen angels hate fire as much as heavenly ones?" I asked.

"Hell isn't all fire and brimstone," she said. "Of course they do."

It was the most ambitious demand I had ever made, and Dante's words were in my mind as I focused. "Bending the universe too much can have catastrophic consequences," he had written. I didn't know if I had the power to do this, but I was out of time and feeling desperate. I put my arm around Rebecca and whispered into her ear. "Hold on tight, and don't move."

The sound was something like a jet-propelled freight train; an oncoming wave of destruction and power that shook the Monastery with such force that I feared it might collapse. It started with a low rumble at the entrance to the structure, but built momentum in no time as I pulled and pulled on the air and the heat, bringing them to me in a gigantic combustible package.

The demons heard it coming too, but they didn't understand they were under attack, and couldn't understand how. They raised their heads to listen but stayed gathered in the dining hall while the fallen angels continued their assault.

They screamed in surprise when the flood of pure flame exploded into the room, filling it in moments with searing heat. The summoned demons were immune, but the weres were vaporized in an instant, and the angels cried out in pain and dropped their own attack while their flesh burned and healed and burned again.

I held Rebecca close to me in a bubble of air that I was holding the flood of flame away from. "Wait here," I told her. "You'll die if you go out there."

She hadn't realized what I planned to do, and her eyes shifted back to blue and begged me not to do it. "Landon, you can't survive. You won't heal fast enough," she said.

"Maybe, maybe not. If I do nothing I'm guaranteed to fail." I kissed her on the cheek, let go, and stepped out into the fire.

The pain was intense. My skin started burning and my clothes combusted away to dust in an instant. I pushed my body to heal faster, creating a constant battle of burn and cleanse on my own flesh. My eyes were burning blind, so I had to rely on my senses to see where my enemies were.

I would hit Lazar first, and then the other angels. My hand had melted to the handle of my sword, making it an almost cyborg-like extension. I broke into a run, dashing through the flames, my mind a volatile mixture of pain, calm, chaos, desperation, love, and anger.

I demanded my eyes to heal as I approached the angels, opening them just in time to see Lazar standing in front of me, his body flaming like a Burning Man, fear registering on his face to see me coming at him. He had no time to move before his head was severed clean from his body, the amulet slipping off his neck when the carcass tumbled to the ground. I was standing right in front of the angels' door now, and I spun around, took a deep breath, and dropped the firestorm, the recession sucking all of the oxygen from the room.

My face was a twisted wreck of pain and glory. I shattered Boot's sword into six deadly shards and sent them darting forward through the six angels' crystal amulets, through the six angels' necks. The blood of the Grail lost, their demon-turned bodies couldn't recover from the damage of the blades.

I slumped to the ground, the world around me turning fuzzy. I struggled to stay awake, noticing a female shape moving towards me, vaguely understanding that it wasn't Rebecca, and that I should defend myself. How could I defend myself? I had destroyed my sword. I had liked that sword too.

A clawed hand raked across my cheek, sending me flopping to the floor. The harpy jumped on me, her white fangs a stark contrast against ebony skin. She had a knife in her other hand. I should get her off me. I should do something.

There was an angry hiss, and then her head rolled forward and landed behind me, her body kicked away before it could cover me in blood. Rebecca stood above me, her expression worried despite her empty black eyes. I heard a growl, and then she fell backwards, a huge mass of muscle pouncing on her.

Focus. How could I focus? Everything was moving like mud. Like lightning. My eyes wouldn't stay straight. My head hurt. Rebecca needed me. I struggled to push myself to a sitting position. Rebecca was wrestling with the hellhound, its jaws snapping at her face, her arms at full extension to hold it back. More demons were coming, more of the harpies, and another hound. I knew there was another hound.

The angels' massive door began to open, sending a spreading ray of light into the room. I was still lying right in front of it, and it was so bright on the other side. In the doorway was a silhouette. An angel. Its eyes met mine. I knew this one. Josette.

She launched from the doorway like a rocket, her sword coming down on the hound lunging towards me. I hadn't seen it, would never have been able to stop it. Another angel came out of the door, then another. They assaulted the remaining demons. Josette was at my side.

"Fellow, I did not expect to see you again, much less find you here," she said.

She was an ethereal sight in a simple long white gown and sandals. She knelt and put her hand on my forehead. The world began to clarify. The other angels were dispatching the second hound, and now they were attacking Rebecca?

"No," I cried, reaching out for anything I could and sending it banging into the angels. It distracted them enough to allow her to duck around them and run towards us.

"Don't hurt her," I said to Josette. I didn't know if she could or not, but she had six hundred or so years on the vampire, so I assumed she could.

"This one is yours?" she asked, confused. She floated to her feet and held her hand up to the angels. "Stand down," she said to them.

Rebecca reached my feet and turned. She hadn't been running from them, but running to reach me, to protect me from them. She hissed when they approached.

"Stand down," Josette repeated, placing herself between the angels and Rebecca. The angels pulled up. One was older, his hair long and grey, his bare chest lined with scars. The other was younger, with a fresh face and delicate features. He reminded me of the angel I had found dead in the snow.

"Josette," the older one said. "We've discussed this."

Josette was agitated. "We have done no such thing," she said. "This man has come here to help us, and you would destroy him and his companion?"

The seraph glowered. "He is no man, Josette. He is a diuscrucis. You know the laws. You have agreed to abide by them."

They were talking to each other like Rebecca and I weren't even there. As if they could just decide to kill us and make it so. As if we couldn't resist. I tried to stand, my legs shaky. Rebecca caught me before I could fall.

"Look at him," Josette said. "Man, diuscrucis, whatever he is, he just about killed himself to save us. I did not agree to return such benevolence with violence, regardless of our laws. The law is short-sighted and flawed if that is how it is intended to be interpreted."

The comment infuriated the angel. "How dare you," he cried, the power of his voice shaking the Monastery further, and causing Josette to shy away. "Do you still not understand?" he continued, his voice back to a normal volume. "After all of the time we have spent over the last three days speaking of such things? The life a diuscrucis saves today is the life it barters for power tomorrow. That is their history, that is their truth."

I didn't appreciate being called 'it', and I didn't appreciate being judged on someone else's merits.

"Excuse me," I said, trying to get into the conversation. The younger angel looked at me, but the elder was preoccupied with browbeating Josette.

"How do you know they are the same?" Josette asked. "What if you are wrong? Moses, the demons almost broke into our sanctuary! You know what that means. The sanctuary is more important than my life or yours. Landon is a savior."

It must have been a bad choice of words, because the older angel, Moses, looked ready to tear Josette apart with his bare hands. He raised his sword in front of his face. It was different than the others, older, larger, and simpler. It looked more like a medieval broadsword, and it had few runes along its surface.

"Josette, don't make me do this," he said, his voice heavy with regret. "You have been granted clemency for your years of loyal and honorable service to our Lord. Please do not turn your back on His forgiveness, on His love. No matter what this diuscrucis does today, if we allow him to survive he will be our destruction, as his predecessor almost was. Please."

His eyes pleaded with her to join them on their side. Josette looked at me, hanging from Rebecca's arm. I was only conscious because she had shared her energy with me.

"Josette, it's okay," I told her. "Just let the vampire go," I said to Moses. "She is little threat to you."

He looked at me, his face empty of emotion. "No demon will leave this Monastery," he said.

In that moment I realized why Heaven was having such a hard time. It was so ordered, so unbending. It couldn't adjust. Good was white, and evil was black, end of discussion. Now Josette was caught in the middle because she dared to see gray.

"I'm sorry," Josette said, still looking at me. Tears poured from her eyes. She stepped away from us, and towards Moses.

"The Lord will forgive me, for he knows my true heart," she said to Moses. She pulled her sword from the ether and held it out before her. "I do not wish to fight you Moses, but I will not allow you to slaughter those who have done you no harm, and in fact have saved your life. The only perfect being is God, and He did not write this law. We did. I challenge its validity according to the rights bestowed upon me by my consecration."

Moses took a deep breath and sighed. "Your rights were lost when you Confessed. You know that. You cannot make a formal challenge for seven years. Please do not do this."

Josette cast one last glance back at us. "You have given me no choices," she said to Moses, her voice filled with sadness. "I will not let you kill them."

"Then that is your choice," he replied.

He wielded the broadsword as if it were a toothpick, holding the massive blade one handed, cutting and slashing with speed, grace, and precision. Josette danced around the older angel, her body a blur as she twirled and twisted away from the sword. She didn't make any effort to fight back, at least not yet, her size giving her a distinct advantage on the defense.

The younger angel approached us. He handed me a simple white linen robe, which reminded me of my nakedness.

"Thank you," I said, sliding it on over my head. I was sure Rebecca had noticed me. What did she think about what she had seen? Why did it matter so much?

"My brother," the angel said. "He was outside."

I knew the angel had looked familiar. I shook my head. "I'm sorry," I said.

"I believe you," he replied. He paused to think. "You will help us?"

I nodded. "I'll help you until the balance is restored. After that, I make no promises."

"Then let us hope Josette wins," he said. "For I am willing to take my chances."

The battle was still raging, Josette and Moses continuing their angry dance. Josette had joined the fight in full, adding her weapon to the mix. Their swords were silver rays of light, whistling through the air, crashing into one another, throwing up a shower of sparks. It was impossible to say who was the better fighter, impossible to guess what the outcome would be. The rage shared between them was obvious, their mutual dislike apparent. In a way, it was good to know that even the warriors of God were not immune to such emotions. As Josette had said, they were not perfect.

For every bit of strength the older angel possessed, Josette made up for in agility. The huge broadsword came in at her from every conceivable angle and speed, followed by a foot, a fist, or a knee, and she would dip and dodge and parry without breaking stride, without making a mistake. Moses pressed the attack hard to keep her on the defensive, like he knew that once she had a moment to breathe, she would overtake him.

Just when it seemed as though the fight would continue forever, that is exactly what happened, and a moment later it was over. Moses reached out a little too far, a little too high, and left himself a little too off-balance. Josette pounced on the opening like a cat, springing forward and planting her sword in his stomach and pushing him over with the weight she bore down on it. He hit the earth hard, Josette straddling him like a surfboard, holding the blade in position to prevent him from continuing the fight.

"Yield," she demanded.

Moses coughed and glared up at her. "You are making a mistake Josette," he said. "I will not yield."

She twisted the sword, leading the older angel to wince in pain. "You have lost. Yield, and we will leave this place. The sanctuary will remain safe."

"I will not yield," Moses yelled.

He grabbed Josette's sword by the blade and threw it out of his body, sending the slight angel tumbling backwards. His hands trailing blood, he pounced on her, wrapping his arms around her neck. Josette struggled under his weight, her arms flailing. She sought to gain leverage to get him off, finding it difficult on the blood-slicked floor. Sickened, I pushed against Rebecca, trying to find the strength to come to her aid.

"This is their fight," Rebecca said, holding me in place. "You cannot intervene." I stopped squirming.

"I'm sorry Josette," Moses whispered, barely loud enough for me to hear. Her laboring had ceased, and I wasn't even sure she was still alive. That was when I noticed the knife.

It was a demon's blade, obsidian and serrated. It was lying just on the outside of the pentagram that had been scratched into the floor, near a pile of decayed ash that had once been a fallen angel. Josette's hand was inching towards it, trying to get a hold on it without drawing Moses' attention. It seemed surreal that it would come down to this, a scene that had been played out in movies that was happening now for real. I focused on the blade, and with the little energy I had left I pushed it, an inch or less. It was enough.

Josette's fingers wrapped around the handle, and she jerked the blade up and into the back of Moses' shoulder, burying it deep in his flesh. He cried out in shock and pain, giving her the chance she needed to get her arms under his chest and shove him away. He landed on his feet, pure animosity pouring from him. Josette staggered to a stand.

"How could you?" Moses cried, his bare chest already beginning to show signs of the poison. He turned to the younger angel. "Thomas, holy water."

Thomas raced back through the doorway into the room Josette had referred to as the sanctuary. Josette walked over to the stricken seraph.

"I'm sorry," she said. Her eyes were wet with tears.

"You should be," Moses said. He spat blood at her feet. "Your soul is tainted Josette. Since you met this crossbred demon-spawn you have lost your way. Do you think he is the solution to our problems? Do you think he deserves to live while I die?"

His anger turned Josette's sorrow into an equal rage. Her voice boomed in the gigantic room. "No one deserves to die for no reason other than being." She pointed at Rebecca. "Not even a demon."

Thomas returned from the sanctuary, racing by us to deliver the holy water to Moses. The older angel's' poison was spreading, but he remained strong enough to continue his vitriol.

"You are filth Josette, a sorry excuse for a servant of the Lord. You turn your back on Him because you don't trust in His plan. You should be grateful to Him, for showing mercy on you after what you did with your own brother."

It was as though in that moment all of time and space came to a screeching halt. Thomas hit the skids, stopping a good ten feet away from Moses and Josette, his eyes like saucers in response to the elder seraph's words. Josette's face drained of all color, and a frightening darkness flashed in her eyes. I remembered what Josette had told me about her brother. I could piece together what she hadn't. The vampires had thought she was a virgin, and in a sense she was, but for their intents they were wrong.

Josette wrenched the demonic blade from Moses' back and without hesitation reinserted it into his heart. She pulled it back out, and stabbed him again, and again, and again, the fury of her hurt, guilt, and shame overcoming all other rational thought, overwhelming her spirit of goodness. She sobbed as she punctured him, over and over, brought to a stop only when Thomas grabbed her from behind and held her to him with her back pressed up against his chest. Moses coughed up some blood, his face cracking with poisoned veins, and passed without another word.

"Josette," Thomas whispered, trying to calm her. "Josette, please it's me, Thomas." She flailed and fought, trying to break away, to continue her assault on the now empty form. "Josette."

I looked at Rebecca and motioned with my head. "We have to help her," I said.

Rebecca helped me walk over to Josette. Her face was feral, her growls incomprehensible. I reached out and put my hand under her chin, making sure her eyes were in line with mine.

"Josette," I said, my voice as soft and warm as I could make it. "It's Landon. It's okay. You're going to be okay."

I sank my gaze into her eyes, searching for her in them. She was seeing right through me, blinded by her pain. I leaned in and kissed her forehead. In response, a whine poured from her lips, a flat, straight, painful, powerful sound that felt as though it had her whole existence wrapped up in it. It continued for uncounted minutes, her sorrow heartbreaking. When it tailed off she collapsed into me, and I lowered her to the floor.

"What have I done?" she said. "Oh Landon, what have I done?"

I lowered myself next to her and put my arms around her. "You saved my life," I told her. "Mine and Rebecca's."

She squeezed my shoulder. "For that I am glad, but the cost was so high."

"Moses?" I asked her.

"No," she said, pulling back away from me. She looked up at me, and I understood.

"I'm so sorry," I said. It wasn't the pair of light, golden, heavenly eyes I had been so mesmerized by looking back at me. They were different now, changed, a simple brown that could have passed as human.

Chapter 22

"I don't understand," I said. "How could this happen?"

We had moved from the center of the room closer to the sanctuary door. We were all sitting on the floor. Josette was propped up against my shoulder. She looked worn, beaten, and tired.

"She used a demon's blade against another angel," Thomas said.

"He was going to kill her," Rebecca replied. "She had every right to defend herself. Is it her fault that the demon's dagger was the closest means to do so?"

"It does not matter," Thomas said. "The laws do not make circumstantial exceptions."

"Maybe they should," I said, unable to disguise my disgust.

Josette shifted on my arm to look at me. "Landon, do not be concerned." Her brown eyes were taking time to get used to. They looked so ordinary. She turned her attention to Thomas. "Our Lord knows my heart. He has cast me down as He must, for His rules are not arbitrary, yet He has not cast me to evil.

My heart is not filled with hate. Perhaps He may allow me to earn my redemption."

"What do you mean?" I asked.

"True fallen angels are demons," Thomas said. "They are the angels that have been seduced by evil, and have committed one or more of the seven sins with selfishness in their heart. Josette is not a demon, yet also not an angel. I do not know what she is, for I have never heard of such a thing."

"No angel has ever killed another without a self-serving motivation," Josette said.

"In all this time?" I asked. "That seems hard to believe."

"Why would it be?" Thomas replied. "Angels cannot kill one another with anything but a demon's blade. An angel using such a weapon is unheard of, unless it is obtained with the intent to harm. Such premeditation is always self-serving."

"What does it mean to fall?" Rebecca asked.

Josette cast her gaze to the floor. "I can no longer reach Heaven," she said. "I cannot return there. Maybe one day, but not now. My spirit is broken, cracked. I can feel the loss in my soul, and yet I feel alive. It is a different alive, but it still is."

"You must be of Purgatory now," Thomas said. "The place between."

Josette was silent. Then she stood and walked over to Rebecca. "Cut my wrist," she said, holding out her arm. Rebecca looked at me. "Do it," Josette insisted.

Rebecca reached out and ran her fingernail along Josette's wrist. Her blood began to well up through the cut, a thin stream of it pooling and dripping down onto the floor. No black veins of poison formed around the wound, but it didn't heal either. Josette looked at it in amazement before Rebecca reached down and tore a piece of cloth off the bottom of Josette's dress and wrapped it around the cut.

The fallen angel looked at the demon with tears in her eyes, nodded thanks, and approached Thomas, her other wrist held out. He didn't wait for her to ask. He took his sword and pressed it into her flesh, just enough to cause her to bleed. Again, the blood dripped to the floor and the wound did not heal.

"Mortal," she said. *"I'm mortal."* Her lips didn't move the second time, but I heard her voice in my mind.

"No," I said, projecting the words. She snapped her head around to look at me. *"Your power has shifted to this world, to Purgatory, to me."* I was trying to be comforting. I failed.

"No," Josette said aloud, her voice bitter. "I am not like you. I wish to be a seraph. I wish to fight for good, for God. You are kind Landon, but you will do what you must to be what you are. I must also be what I am, regardless of what has happened. I will help you against the demons, against Reyzl. I will not do evil for any purpose."

"I don't expect you to, and would never ask it of you," I replied. "If I can help you be restored, I will." I turned to Thomas, so serene despite losing his brother to the attack. "What about you? We have a few openings we're looking to fill."

"I am sorry diuscrucis, but I cannot. I am the only angel left to guard the sanctuary."

I looked over to the gigantic door that the demons had been trying to obliterate. It bore the scar of war, a crack that ran from the top corner down towards the center. It was open just enough, but behind it I could see a bright light, the beacon, reaching up through a hole in ceiling. I could also see an altar and pews, as well as racks of swords lined up against the wall.

"What is the sanctuary?" I asked.

"It is a conduit between this world and Heaven," Josette said. "The light is a beacon which draws us..." She bit her lip. "Draws angels to it, so when they are moving between the planes they do not get lost. An experienced seraph can travel without a conduit, but the novices need the light to find their way. "

"You said Heaven wasn't up, but the light stretches out into the sky," I said.

"It's a side effect," she replied. "The beam passes from this plane to the next, and reflects upward as a result."

"Without the sanctuary and others like it, we would not be able to reinforce our numbers," Thomas said. "The demon

Reyzl was hoping to capture it, to slaughter the angels coming into this world, or to destroy it. Thanks to you, he was unsuccessful."

"It is also a place of healing," Josette explained. "The light can purge demon poison more effectively than holy water. The light can also help us... angels regain themselves when they are tempted by evil."

"You mean Confession?"

Josette nodded. "Yes. After I left you the other morning, I came here. I was conflicted by my dealings with you, and I sought clarity. I had intended to meditate, but when I told Moses about what had happened, he believed that you had tainted my mind. He brought his concerns to the other Elders, and they insisted that I step into the light and Confess. I was compelled to tell them everything." Her eyes began to tear up again as she recalled the experience. "Things that I had never told anyone, things that I had denied for myself. He used my worst pain against me." Her tears were flowing again and I was going to comfort her, but Rebecca beat me to it. She took Josette in her arms and held her close.

"Yet they call me the demon," she said. Josette pulled away and looked up at her.

"You may bear the mark of the Devil," she said, "But you have embraced the freedom of choice granted to you and used it to forge your own path."

"Josette," Thomas said, placing his hand on her shoulder. She turned to face him. "I am sorry for the actions of Brother Moses, he had no right to treat you as he did. He was not the same since the betrayal."

"Thank you, Thomas," she replied. "You and your brother are two of the finest fellows I have had the pleasure of knowing. I understand what happened to Moses when Charis betrayed us, but this quest for vengeance has led many astray. I believe that our Lord has a plan for me, and that this is a part of it. I do feel the pain of this loss, and I long to see my home again, but I believe in His wisdom."

I listened to Josette speak with a new respect for her. I couldn't imagine what it would be like to dedicate so much of my existence to something only to be discarded for holding fast to the same morals and beliefs that had brought me there. It was amazing to me that she held no ill will towards God for his abandonment. She believed that what He had done was right, and that He held some grand design for all of us. I didn't get it or believe it, but I respected her unwavering faith. Our work here was done though, and we needed to get back to the city.

"Thomas," I said. "I don't suppose you have a car?"

Chapter 23

An angel had no need for a car, but a Touched warrior monk did. They needed to eat after all, and somebody had to make runs for groceries. The car was a powder blue 1970 Chevy Suburban, a beast of a vehicle that had been well maintained by the monks, and came equipped with its own snowplow. Despite its age and lack of interior creature comforts, it was a more solid performer than the Rolls Royce had been in the crappy mountain weather we had driven into.

As Rebecca had predicted, losing their Commander had caused the Rift, wherever it had been, to close, and the demons that were summoned from Hell couldn't survive long here, especially in the cold. We did come across a few of the scouts as we headed back down the Monastery's long driveway, but none of them looked like they had much more time to exist.

Rebecca and Josette were in the front of the car, with Rebecca behind the wheel. I was exhausted from the battle, and they had both insisted that I do my best to shut my eyes and recharge my batteries. I was so weak I hadn't even had the energy to change the simple white robe into something a little less drafty, and my head was spinning soon after I laid it down on the long rear bench seat.

The vampire and the angel, Josette might have fallen but I still thought of her as an angel, were both silent, lost in their own thoughts as we drove. All three of us had gone through some major personal stuff in the last twenty-four hours, and we all needed a chance to do the mental computations. In an effort to create a calming environment, Rebecca had found a classical music eight track in the glove compartment. I fell asleep to either Bach or Mozart. I always got them confused.

I wasn't surprised when I found myself back at my Source. As my mind had succumbed to the soothing sounds of the symphony I could feel my soul calling out to my consciousness, pulling it into this place. I was standing inside the Museum of Natural History, right in the spot where I had died. I don't know how I knew it was the spot, because the whole area was under reconstruction, nearly ready for re-opening post – 'terrorist' attack. Ancient Egyptian artifacts, sculpture and jewelry and dioramas with paper mache pyramids and little plastic Egyptians surrounded me. There was a shadowy figure standing in the corner.

"Ulnyx," I said, beckoning the Great Were to step into the light. He did so without hesitation, his will broken by my own. "Do you know why I'm here, of all places?"

The demon's hair was gone, replaced with a smooth bald scalp. He had traded in the rock star look for something more upscale, a tight black suit and a shiny blue tie.

"That's where it started," he said, motioning at the spot I was standing on.

"Where I died," I said.

"Yes sir," he replied. "Your power has grown, but you still aren't ready yet."

"Ready for what?"

He smiled. "You know what. You can't win that fight, not yet. You haven't let go."

"Enough riddles Ulnyx. Let go of what?" I looked at him, and he dropped to his knees.

"I would tell you if I could," he said. "It's not something you can be told. You just have to do it."

I walked over to him and knelt down so we would be at eye level. "Tell me," I commanded, shouting right in his face. He didn't react.

"I'm sorry sir."

I got back to my feet and looked around the room. I was supposed to let go of something, but what? I had accepted who I was, and why I was. I was comfortable with my role in this fight. What else did I have to do, or prove, or think? I had died here, in this room. It had something to do with that.

Just beyond the spot where my body had landed was the main exhibit space, where the Chalice had been before the Demon Queen had claimed it. I half-expected to see the Grail sitting there in its tamper-proof, bulletproof case, mocking my ability to locate it. Instead, there was a large block draped by a blue velvet blanket. Was it part of the new exhibit? It looked out of place with the other Egyptian artifacts.

I walked over to the block and took hold of the drape, pulling it off so I could see what was underneath. I was surprised to see a block of marble with the Chalice engraved on the top, along with a short message and a list of names. I started reading them until I got to my own. I read it four or five times to be sure it said what I thought it did, then looked at Ulnyx, waiting on his knees.

"I already know that I died," I said.

He shrugged. "Don't look at me boss," he said. "This is your Source."

My Source, right. I looked at the memorial again. My soul was still trapped by my memories of mortality, of being human. My name on the stone was just a reminder that I had once been part of the world of man. The power I possessed was limited by what I had learned from that existence, but that part of my being had ended. From the beginning Dante had said that I would need to move beyond my past self in order to succeed in holding the tide of human desolation at bay. I had learned so much in the past few days, and now all of my experiences were coming to a head.

How could I just let go of being human? I reached out and ran my finger along the embossment of my name on the stone. Landon Hamilton didn't exist anymore. He had been a mortal who had been killed by a demon. I held his memories, but I was something different, something more. I was Divine.

"Landon." The voice was soft and warm. Josette.

"What are you doing here?" I asked, turning to look at her.

She was standing at the bottom of the steps up to the memorial, wearing the white coat and boots she seemed to favor. Her eyes were their more human brown, but she still bore an ethereal glow.

"You called for me, and I came," she said.

It was the same thing Sarah had said when she had appeared here. Did that mean Josette was asleep too, resting in the front passenger seat of the Suburban?

"How did I call for you?" I asked. There was so much I still didn't know.

"I felt you in my mind, and then there was a door. Your voice was carrying through it, whispering my name. I opened the door and stepped through, and you were here. What is this place?" She looked around the exhibit hall, her eyes wide with wonder. When she saw Ulnyx, she gasped. "This is your Source?" she asked.

I nodded. "Don't be afraid of Ulnyx. He's under my control." I saw the Great Were bristle at the statement, but he could do no more.

Josette stepped up to me. "Do you know what this means?" she asked.

"The world is my Source," I repeated. "I should be able to draw power from it when I'm awake, but so far I haven't been able to. Josette, you were once alive. How did you learn to let go?"

She held up a hand. "Landon, you've misunderstood," she said. "This is not your mortal world, your Earth."

I looked around. It sure looked like the world I was familiar with. "What do you mean?"

"Do you remember what I told you of the realms, and how they are organized?"

I remembered. Heaven, Hell, and Earth were stacked on the same plane, separated by dimensions of... I don't know what. Belinda Carlisle hadn't been totally wrong, but it was actually Purgatory that was a place on Earth.

"Yes. What about it?"

As soon as I asked her, I knew. Her response verified it for me.

"I've fallen," she said. "That's why I could hear you calling me. That's why I can reach you in this place. Most of us never reach our Source. For those of us who do, it is often a single room, for the powerful a garden perhaps. I have been to my Source once. It was my childhood bedroom, the place where I always felt the most at peace and the most safe. This world is your Source, as amazing as that is. Purgatory is your Source."

In that moment I felt it, and I knew it. I don't know if I would have had Josette not been there to open my eyes. Did Dante know? I suspected he did, but he would never have told me. I had been thinking of Purgatory as a location in the mortal realm, like a Fantasy Island hidden in the Pacific somewhere, or the lost city of Atlantis. I had never considered that it was another dimension so close to our own that it rested just out of reach, in close enough proximity that I could use its power to alter my familiar universe.

That was what I had to let go of. Not my prior mortality, but my understanding of where I was, where my Source originated, the power that I had at my command. I could change things as I saw fit here. I could make this world as I decided it to be. When I focused, I was reaching into my Source and changing this world. What happened in the mortal realm was in many ways a side effect, similar to the light of the sanctuaries' beacon.

A thought, and I was standing right next to Josette, no bipedal motion required. I put my arm around her tiny waist and with another thought we were outside. One more thought and I launched us into the sky. This was my place, my rules. Here, I was as close to a god as I could ever hope to be.

The ground was a blur beneath us as we rocketed forward on wings of thought. Josette was an experienced aviator, but she was filled with a new sense of wonder in sharing the rush of flight with me. She giggled and hooted while I looped around the Museum a few times, enjoying the sensation of being airborne, then shot off into the sky like a cannon. I knew where I wanted and needed to go.

We never made it. We were headed in the right direction, a dark streak cutting through the night air, when Josette gasped and vanished from my arms. A split second later I felt a sharp pull within my chest, and the ground disappeared from beneath me. The hard metal roof of the Suburban greeted me instead. My body slammed up against it, then dropped back down to the seat.

"Dammit," Rebecca cried, her arms fighting with the wheel of the truck to keep it on the road. I could feel the mass of steel slipping and sliding along the snow-covered surface.

"What's happening?" I shouted, reaching out to wedge myself between the roof and the seat. I heard a sharp cry from outside the car, and then saw a gout of flame pour over the windshield.

"Fire demon," Rebecca said, throwing me forward as she slammed on the brakes. I saw a tremendous torso flash by in front of us, then heard crashing in the trees. "I don't think Reyzl was too happy with us ruining his conquest." Rebecca slammed back down on the accelerator as heavily as she dared, sending the Suburban lurching forward again.

I couldn't help but smile. "Good," I said. "Josette, are you okay?"

She leaned over the seat to look at me. "For now," she said. I saw she had a cut on her forehead that was threatening to run into her eye. She was too vulnerable like this.

"Did you have a nice dream?" Rebecca asked. I could see her look back at me in the rearview mirror. Was that jealousy? What had Josette been saying in her sleep?

"It was interesting," I replied.

I grabbed onto the car again when a massive shoulder pummeled the side. Rebecca's hands worked the wheel, and she somehow managed to keep us on the road. She wouldn't be able to do this forever.

"I wouldn't think a fire demon would do too well with snow," I said.

"It wouldn't, if the snow could touch it," Rebecca said. "It evaporates before it has a chance."

I looked out the window, hoping to catch a glimpse of the thing, but it was just too dark. There was another shrill cry, and I could feel the heat pummeling the roof of the Suburban. Josette cried out in response, ducking down into the passenger compartment as far as she could go.

Rebecca slammed on the brakes once more, throwing me against her seat as the car skidded forward. The demon was standing in front of us, illuminated in the headlights, a twenty-plus foot tall winged monster coated in red and blue flame. Its muscular frame looked like dull red steel, its head a red, chiseled humanoid face with a pair of curled horns. It was holding a huge jagged edged cleaver that was dripping heat onto the roadway, where it sizzled and dug into the cement. I may have been able to heal from burns, but I wasn't invulnerable, and that thing didn't need to be precise to cut us all into pieces.

The demon raised the blade as we approached, the car doing nothing but sliding along the icy roadway. Just when its arm reached its apex, the car hit the wet pavement melted by the demon's fire and jerked to a stop. We were sitting ducks. I closed my eyes and focused my will, reaching for the power that I now knew was just a micron thin film of existence away.

It was as though I were diving into an ocean, feeling the ripples of energy spread around me, envelope me, and cleanse me as I submerged myself. I raised my hands and pulled the snow from the sides and rear of the car, gathering it up and hardening it to ice over the top us. The crack of the demon's cleaver sinking into the ice shield echoed through the night like a massive thunderclap. I felt the pressure in my mind, but I pushed back, drawing the strength I needed from my Source. It was enough.

The fire demon roared out in anger, bringing its weapon down on the shield again and again. The defense was holding for now, but I couldn't maintain it forever. When the monster raised its arm to strike, I threw the block of ice up at it on a tremendous gust of air. It managed to get through the flame and slam into the demon, causing it to cry out in unimaginable agony. It tumbled backwards to land with a terrible crash.

Massive amounts of steam poured off it, the flames of its body dimming and pulsing, fighting to stay lit. I took the opportunity to throw open the rear door of the truck, grab one of Rebecca's swords, and jump out. Rebecca and Josette both reached back to try to stop me, but I evaded their efforts. The second I was clear, I pulled more of the snow and moisture to me, encasing the Suburban in ice. This was one fight they couldn't help me win. I walked to the front of the car, lit from behind by the car's headlights reflecting through the ice. I looked back and could see Rebecca and Josette both watching me with frightened concern.

I raised the blessed sword in front of me and focused my will on the air around me, pulling the heat out of it and making it colder and colder. My skin crawled with the tingling numbness of threatened hypothermia, my Divine nature keeping me in an uncomfortable but survivable homeostasis.

The fire demon's flames had sputtered back to life, and it pulled itself to its feet. I stood before it, a mouse against a lion, certain only that I wasn't about to let it toast my friends.

It regarded me warily, yellow eyes peering down on me from above, not sure what to make of the puny thing that had knocked it on its ass. We stared each other down for a minute or more, and then it reared back and belched flame, leaning down and in at me as it did so.

I sucked the heat from the air around me, pushing it away and off to the landscape on either side of the road. The trees around us ignited, lighting up the scene as if we were battling in Hell itself. The blade followed the gout of flame; its size creating more of a scream than a whistle.

I brought up my own sword to block, holding tight on my Source and pulling in more and more power to steel my body against the blow. I caught the edge of the blade with my own, feeling the vibration through my limbs as I pushed back against the force.

My feet dug into the pavement, pulling up cement while I slid backwards. I pushed harder, feeling the heat of my muscles, the heat of the cleaver's flames, then turned the weapon aside.

I leaped forward on impossibly strong legs, my body carried up, up, up, right into the face of the surprised demon. I focused once more, taking the cold of the frigid air around me and pumping it all into the sword. A nasty set of teeth bent and snapped at me as I rose towards them, but I planted my free hand on the demon's small, wide nose, switched my grip on the blessed blade, and sank it deep into the monster's forehead.

The length of the weapon steamed and hissed, the cold breaking through the barrier of heat, the icy metal a powerful poison. Veins of ice spread out from the insertion point, and the demon screamed in pain. I held on while it shook and thrashed, reaching up to try to pry the metal splinter loose.

It took almost three minutes for the demon to stop fighting to dislodge me, and I held tight to the sword the entire time. The ice ran down from its head to its neck, from its neck to its shoulders, out and down towards its feet. The flames that coated its body snuffed out, it dropped to a knee, and then fell forward to the ground. When it hit the earth it shattered, breaking into millions of pieces of frozen ash. Its head was the last to smash against the road, and it landed just feet from the front of the Suburban.

While the skull was being reduced to icy dust, I waved at Rebecca and Josette, a surfer making a clean break to the shore. Back on terra firma, I pulled the protective shell away from the car, and then let go of my hold on my Source. At once I was overcome with a wave of heat, nausea, pain, and light, and I don't know what happened next, because I wasn't awake to witness it.

Chapter 24

I woke up in bed at the Waldorf, my naked body frigid to the touch, shivering with chills, and sweating profusely despite being buried under a mound of blankets. Josette was sitting cross-legged on the end of the bed, keeping an unblinking watch on me. She had traded in her angel robe for a pair of blue jeans and a leather jacket, looking ever more the human than I could have anticipated. Still, the look suited her.

“Hey,” I said, my voice little more than a meek whisper. I tried to lift my head and was rewarded with a massive throbbing.

Her face lit up when she saw I was awake. “Fellow, you are revived,” she said. “Thank the Lord.”

She was forgetting herself, and she looked embarrassed for it. I was going to ask her what time it was, what day it was, but somehow, I knew. I could feel a trickle of energy flowing into me from Purgatory like a leaky faucet. The innate connection between the two realms was undeniable. I guess it had to be that way in order for Mr. Ross' so-called 'processing' to run without a hitch.

I had been unconscious for about six hours. It had been long enough for Rebecca to get us back into the city in the takes-a-lickin-keeps-on-tickin Suburban, get me back to the Waldorf, take off my clothes, and bury me under these blankets. I had opened myself too much to my Source. There was a part of me that was still, and would always be human, and it couldn't absorb that kind of Divine energy without consequence.

Neither could this world. Dante had warned me, and I hadn't been careful. It was like a spinning top, too much flow from Purgatory, too many changes and alterations, and it would begin to wobble and potentially topple over. I had to be more careful, more precise - a surgeon instead of a linebacker, for everyone's sake.

"It's good to see you again," I said. "How are you holding up?" I shook a bit as a wave of coldness washed over me. I really needed to be more careful.

She smiled. "I am well. As well as can be. I do not need to understand God's plan to have faith in it. I've found I am still able to adjust my wardrobe, which is something I guess." Her blue jeans turned black before my eyes, then shifted back to blue. "I didn't feel right about wearing white. Not now."

"I'm sorry Josette," I said for the second or third time. She waved her hand at me.

"There is nothing to apologize for, as I have already said. The Lord has decided our paths lie together, and I do not begrudge Him for that. I enjoy your company."

That statement succeeded in stopping my shivering for a few seconds, and brought some heat to my face.

"We make a good team," I replied. "Where's Rebecca?"

"She went back to her apartment to retrieve something she called an Obi," Josette said. "I am not familiar with the term."

I couldn't help but laugh. This conversation was making every part of me feel better. "An Obi is an Awakened human, he's my..." I stumbled for a moment trying to think of the right word, something Josette would get. "... Squire? For lack of a better word."

She furrowed her eyebrows in a super cute way. "He carries your sword?"

I laughed out loud that time. "Maybe squire wasn't the best word. He's a friend," I said. "We didn't bring him to the sanctuary because he's mortal. He would have been killed."

"Why do you not Touch him?"

It was my turn to be confused. "Touch him?" I asked.

"Where do you think the mortal servants of God come from?" She floated to her feet as though she were lighter than air. She walked up the bed, leaving the smallest impression in the mattress, then turned and flopped down beside me. "For angels, you Touch a mortal by dousing their head in holy water, saying a prayer, and laying hands on them. It's very much like the Catholic Baptism ritual, but with a little more power behind it. Of course, I wouldn't know how a Purgatorian would do it."

We sat together in silence for a minute while I thought about it. I had this new tap of energy flowing into me. What would happen if I flowed some of it into a human?

"That wouldn't make him invulnerable," I said.

"It would make him resistant," she replied. I was convinced, but I wouldn't do it without asking Obi for permission first. He might not want to be that tied to my power.

"Have you ever fought a fire demon before?" I asked. That thing had been ridiculous, and it amazed me to think of her standing toe to toe against one.

She shook her head. "Never alone," she replied. "That Great Were we fought was a toy in comparison. Thankfully, they are denizens of Hell, and are rarely summoned to this realm. They are difficult to control, and very unstable here. The amount of power needed to keep the Rift open would be immense."

Reyzl was powerful, but by the way Josette spoke of the fire demon, I didn't think he was that powerful. "Reyzl didn't summon the demon alone," I said.

Josette agreed. "He would have needed at least two other demons of his equal to maintain the Rift. It is bad sign if they are already working together to stop you."

"How many demons of Reyzl's power are there?"

"Reyzl is what is known as an archfiend. There are three in North America, four in Europe, one in Japan, one in Australia." She started counting on her fingers as she listed their numbers. "Two in Russia, six in the Middle-East including three just around Jerusalem, and probably a few others who have gone undocumented. They are very territorial, though they will join forces if the need is great enough."

That was an awful lot of evil running around. I still felt like I knew so little about how this war operated, even though I was finding myself deeper and deeper into the thick of it. Still, I wasn't convinced that Reyzl had done this with the help of another archfiend. I just didn't think I'd been in play long enough or proven myself strong enough for the demon to ask for help from his peers. That left me with just one other possibility.

"What about the Demon Queen?" I asked.

Her reaction was one of shock. "How do you know of her?"

"Da.... The Outcast told me," I replied, remembering not to upset her by using his name. "Did Rebecca tell you anything about our goal?"

"No, she said she would leave it to you to explain."

I spent the next hour or so telling Josette everything I knew about the Chalice, the Demon Queen, and the Knights Templar. Everything Dante had told me to steer me in this direction. She knew most of it, but from a different perspective. The angels wanted to find the Chalice, to bring it back to the sanctuary, and to use it. She wouldn't tell me what effect it would have on a seraph. I didn't think it was that important, so I didn't push.

While I was talking, I could feel my body normalizing, recovering from the damage I had done to it. I stopped shaking soon after, and my physical form didn't feel so lifeless to touch. I would survive this, and learn from it.

"The Demon Queen could have summoned the fire demon herself," Josette said, answering my earlier question. "She would have no need of Reyzl to do such a thing."

That's what I was afraid of. "How powerful is she?" I asked.

"She is the most powerful demon currently in this realm," she replied, as if that would answer the whole question.

"Okay," I said. "You said currently. How do demons get here? Rebecca said that the ones summoned from Hell couldn't survive here long."

"All demons derive their power from the First Fallen, either through his minions here in this realm or from the power contained within Hell. He divvies this power most sparingly, as he is loathe to part with it, but does reward exceptional service as he sees fit. Demons rise in power by making deals with one another, and they rise to the top through backstabbing and betrayal, ever hoping to destroy the one above them and claim their souls. It is the nature of evil to covet power in this way."

I couldn't help but wonder if mankind was that much different. The whole organization of it made perfect sense. "So the Demon Queen was once one of the Devil's human creations, and she ascended to her position?"

"No," Josette said, surprising me. "What I have told you is a vast simplification to the processes by which this war maintains its armies. Demons can also come from Hell on their own if they possess enough power and motivation. These are the descendants of the Second Fallen, the army of seraph who followed the First when the truce was declared and my Lord granted him Hell."

"Why don't they come?" I asked. "Wouldn't the war end that much faster?"

"No. Think of it in comparison to man's invention of nuclear warheads. Were the strongest of the demons to enter this realm, my Lord would have no choice other than to grant His disciples leave to join the fray. The result of such a clash would incinerate this world and everything in it, leaving nothing for either side to claim."

Complete Armageddon, instead of a Rapture. "So the Demon Queen came from Hell?"

"That is the only possibility," she replied. "We would have known of her many years ago if she were accumulating power as Reyzl has. She arrived unannounced only weeks before the Chalice was lost."

It was a lot to think about. I closed my eyes and tried to picture what Hell must be like, filled with creatures of untold power that could obliterate the world in a furious firestorm. I was glad most of them chose to stay there.

"You are courting Rebecca?" The question broke the silence, shattering it into a million little pieces.

"Courting?" I asked, trying to fight against my embarrassment. "I thought you were a modern girl?"

She grimaced. "I don't know what the correct term for this is nowadays. I haven't had much inclination to explore such things."

Did angels even have an interest in relationships? It didn't seem like it, though even if they did I could understand why Josette would be disenfranchised.

"Courting is good enough I guess," I said. "No, we aren't courting. Why do you ask?"

She shrugged. "It's the way she looks at you. There is a... hunger."

I laughed. "She's a vampire. There's probably a part of her that thinks everything with two legs is food." I decided not to tell her I had already provided Rebecca with a potent meal. Let that be our little secret.

"Landon, be serious. She likes you."

I wasn't sure about where this was going, but I found comfort in being able to talk to Josette about it. "I like her too. I think we connected, as friends I mean." She had kissed me a few times, and I had liked that, but it didn't make us an item.

"Friends?" She raised her eyebrow. "She doesn't look at you as a friend looks upon a friend."

"The hunger?"

"Yes."

She had looked at me in a strange way when I woke in the Suburban, but it had been more of a visceral, chilling look. It was not an intimate look at all, and I had taken it for jealousy. Then again, why be jealous unless you already thought there was something there and you didn't want anyone else butting in?

"What do you think?" I asked.

"What do you mean?"

"Rebecca and I?" The thought was both exciting and frightening. I took a deep breath to calm myself.

"As you said, she is a vampire. A demon. I don't think my opinion is the best one to go on."

"I thought you respected her choice to join me?"

"I can respect her, that doesn't mean I have to trust her," she said. "Whatever good intentions she has, her kind, her family, perhaps even her have intentionally caused pain and suffering to others. That is a difficult thing for me to resolve. Remember, I have been battling vampires for hundreds of years. She is unique in her views, which to me makes her more dangerous."

"I'm not exactly a saint," I pointed out. "You like me anyway."

"You don't exist to fuel evil," she said.

"Neither does Rebecca, if she chooses not to."

Josette pursed her lips and thought for a moment. "I will trust you," she decided. "She is very attractive."

I could feel my body heating up again. "She has a powerful soul Josette. She told me you were in trouble and suggested we go to your aid. Plus, she won control of her family from her father. I'm sure you knew him, Merov Solen."

Her face darkened. "I knew him. He was a cruel nosferatu. Thank God he has been destroyed." She tilted her head, her expression softening. "The rescue was her idea?"

"Yes."

She was silent for a minute. "She is a rare creature indeed. Yes, I think you would do well to court her."

Chapter 25

By the time Rebecca had returned with Obi, I had showered and morphed the seraph robe into something a lot more comfortable - a pair of jeans, a pair of black Keds, and a faded polo shirt. Her face lit up when she saw I was up and about, and she rushed over to wrap me up in her arms. Considering what Josette and I had spoken about, I couldn't help but get a little thrilled by the gesture.

"Hey Becca," I said into her hair, returning the hug. Her familiar smell was comforting, in a different way than Josette's company had been.

"I'm glad you're feeling better," she said into my chest.

It was a little weird that this beautiful creature that could rip through a stack of gargoyles without pause was so small and delicate in my arms. She pulled away so Obi could get in, holding out his arm in greeting. We did a proper man hug, the ex-Marine all smiles.

"Man, I was worried I wasn't going to see you again," he said.

"You know I'm not so easy to get rid of," I replied. "Did you take care of Cathy?"

He laughed and nodded. "That girl was crazy. She didn't remember anything that had happened to her though. She just kept going on and on about how her mother messed up her whole life, how she would never meet someone special or get married. Man, I know why. Oh yeah, we've got something for you."

Obi reached around and brought his bag to the front of his body, unsnapping it and pulling out a laptop. It was a super thin, slick black slab of coolness that must have cost a fortune.

"Merov's," Rebecca said.

"It has VPN access to the main servers," Obi said. He was like a kid on Christmas. "Merov had a killer setup, and one of the biggest pipes in the city."

"He used it to do automated stock transactions," Rebecca explained. I was familiar with the latency wars being fought on and around Wall Street. He who had the best ping wins.

"I take it we can use it to get the information we need?" I asked.

"You bet," Obi replied. He walked over to the sofa and plopped down on the end next to Josette, seeming to notice her for the first time. He gave her a big smile and held out his hand. "I'm Obi," he said. "You must be Josette. I recognize you from the pictures. It's awesome to meet a real angel."

Josette hid her pained embarrassment well, taking Obi's huge hand into her own tiny one. "Thank you," she said. "It is fine to meet you fellow. What pictures are you speaking of?"

She didn't know. Obi stammered out a reply. "Uhh... I'm sorry. I thought you knew. Merov had a lot of eyes on you. He wanted you to uhh... your blood and umm... being a virgin..."

She didn't mask her pain as well the second time, casting her eyes down and clenching her jaw. I had to stop Obi before he stuck his foot any further down his throat.

"Obi, can you get us booted into the mainframe," I said. He hadn't been oblivious to her reaction, and he jumped at the chance to get out of the awkward situation.

"Sure," he said, flipping open the cover and losing himself in the screen.

I turned back to Rebecca. Her blue eyes were dazzling looking up at me, and I could feel myself getting lost in them.

"You said before we left Merov's that you had a lot more to tell me," I said, my voice cracking a little.

Her eyes sparkled at my discomfort. Why was it that just admitting there was a real attraction and interest had made her existence so much more deliciously unbearable?

"Can we talk about it in private?" she asked.

She grabbed my hand and started pulling me toward the bedroom, causing my whole face to start heating up and turning red. I had never been good with this sort of thing, as

Carly Lane could attest. I was interrupted from the alone time by the bell. The doorbell. Who could that be?

Everyone was on high alert when I let go of Rebecca's hand and approached the door. "Who is it?" I asked, trying to catch a glimpse of the visitor through the peephole. I don't know why I was so on edge. I doubted that Reyzl or the Demon Queen would bother knocking.

Nobody answered. The door clicked and then swung open, almost smashing me in the head in the process. I didn't get to see who was there before I was thrown backwards and onto the floor, sliding back until I reached Josette's feet. I gazed over to the side to see Rebecca had been thrown as well.

"Buongiorno Signore," Dante said, bursting into the room.

He was wearing a gaudy red suit, holding a black cane with a large red diamond on the end, his white hair making him look like a pimped up Santa Claus. He looked pissed as he took in the four of us, piled together en masse against the sofa.

"I leave you alone for a few days, and when I come back you have a veritable Army of." He paused as he tried to find a word to describe what he saw. Failing, he gave up. "Didn't I warn you about working with our enemies," he said.

I tried to get up, but my body was frozen solid. "They aren't our enemies," I murmured through petrified lips.

Dante raised his eyebrows. "Not our enemies?" he asked. He walked over and slammed the cane down between my legs.

"Not our enemies." He looked down on me like I was a misbehaving kindergartener. "Not our enemies. It is the nature of good and evil to be the enemy of balance," he shouted. He pointed the cane at Rebecca, lying motionless next to me on the floor. "Her kind especially. They cannot survive without murder and destruction, and the wanton manner in which they fulfill their base needs is sickening."

I looked to Rebecca, her face sweating and muscles tense as she tried to move. The bonds that held us were too strong, Dante's power too great. He aimed his cane at Josette next, the angry look in his eyes exploding in ferocity at the sight of her.

"The seraph, the servants of God who wouldn't even let me in to see Him when I discovered the truth. All of my years of loyalty and servitude, I asked for no more than a conversation, for understanding. Instead I was turned away. They play at righteousness, but their end game is not so much."

I tried to move again, feeling the force pushing back against me when I attempted to bend my fingers. Dante was from Purgatory, his power had to be the same. He had said that Purgatory was mine to make as I saw fit, that my bloodlines and life had made me special. If that was true, he shouldn't be able to hold me here. I closed my eyes and focused on the flow of power I could feel bleeding into me. I focused my will on bending my fingers, pulling the power in to aid me. I strained to make a fist, to conquer Dante's hold. I failed.

Dante had moved on to Obi, who sat there in silence, his eyes glued to him, not even trying to move. Ever the soldier, he was conserving his strength, waiting for his opportunity. Dante looked him over, then reached out and poked him in the chest with the cane.

"You are Awake, but mortal," he said, all of the anger fading from his tone. "What are you doing here?"

He must have let go of Obi's mouth, because the former Marine was able to speak. "I'm fighting for my people," he said. "I'm not afraid of you."

Dante's face exposed his huge smile. "No, you aren't. Nor should you be my friend. This is your fight, and you have every right to be part of it."

"So you'll let me go?" Obi asked, motioning to the rest of his body with his head.

"Ahhh, most assuredly so, Signore. But not yet." By Obi's reaction, I could tell Dante had frozen him again.

I reached for the flow a second time. I couldn't use it to make myself strong enough to move, but maybe that was a clue. If all I was doing was trying to counter force with force, it was a zero sum game. Whatever hold Dante had on me, I couldn't remove it physically, and so I stopped trying. What I needed to do was understand the power, and counter that.

"I am happy, Landon, that you have found one reasonable ally, though I find it unlikely that he will survive much longer."

Dante turned his attention back on me, looking down with the smile still on his face.

I maintained my calm, my senses questing forward to try to discern his Divinity, to test his power. I focused, watching in fascination as his form lost its solidity, fading away and becoming almost ghostlike. He tilted his head, observing me. I focused harder and literally made his visage split in two, one atop the other but just the tiniest fraction off, as if I were watching a 3d movie without the glasses. I looked past him around the rest of the room, and I could see the same double vision effect. My excitement grew when I realized that I had uncovered his secret.

"Signore," Dante said, still looking down on me. "We should speak in private."

I looked down at myself, my single, solid self. Yes, we should. I felt the flow of power pounding in my soul, and I opened it up into a stream and followed it back to its origin. I watched my body shift, one world superimposed over another.

In Purgatory I was free, and I reached out with my will and lifted Dante away from me, holding him in midair with ease. I floated to my feet, noticing with awe that the entire other world was frozen in time.

"You wanted to talk," I said to him. "Talk." I lowered him to the ground, but I summoned Ulnyx. "Keep an eye on him," I ordered the Great Were. Ulnyx bowed and went to stand at Dante's side.

A solid mountain of laughter erupted from Dante then. It was so strong and loud that I almost lost my hold on the tether of energy that I was using to keep myself there. Before I even knew what had happened, he had grabbed Ulnyx by the throat and thrown him to the ground, stepping on his neck with a fine Italian leather shoe.

"Excellente Signore," he said, his voice booming. "You have surpassed every one of my expectations for what you could become. I am a proud papa." His face turned serious. "Still, do not think that any of your toys can control me. I will forgive your error this once." He stepped off Ulnyx and allowed the Were to rise, sputtering, and slink back behind me.

He had been hoping for this, I realized. Every word and gesture in the Waldorf had been to push me, to test me, to find out what I could do.

"How did you know?" I asked him.

"I can see it in you," he replied. "I can feel it like a geyser bubbling up from your soul. It is the power I always knew you had, but I did not expect you to master it so soon."

It wasn't as though I had a choice at the pace. Even with my success, I had almost died a half dozen times. "What you said about my companions?"

He shrugged his shoulders. "Mostly true," he replied. "But I didn't send you back as my puppet, I sent you back as man's Champion. The decisions you make are yours to make. I may give in to my discontent at times, but do not be dissuaded by my biases."

"Did you see the seraph's eyes?" I asked him. I wanted to find out what he knew about Josette's situation.

He nodded. "Yes. She has fallen to you, which is a most fortunate event. She is a powerful ally, though I would expect her to refuse to fight against good. The other one, the human, he is a rare and unexpected find."

"It's like I've been blessed," I said. Dante didn't laugh. "Lost your sense of humor?" I asked him.

"Mr. Ross has provided me with some information," he replied, ignoring my question. "It's the reason I came to visit you. We're running out of time, Landon. As you know, the North American archfiend has already launched the first of a series of attacks against seraph strongholds. Their goal is to cut off the angels' sanctuaries so that they cannot reinforce their numbers. Once that is done, they will hunt down the remaining forces one by one until they have shifted the balance enough to gain complete control of the mortal world. The power of the Grail makes them close to unstoppable."

"The holder of the Chalice has power over the amulets," I said. "We can stop it if we can get the Grail."

Dante nodded. “That is so. We know the Demon Queen is in possession of the Chalice, but even Mr. Ross has been unable to discover her location. Demons would rather be tortured to death than give her up.”

If the Demon Queen had the power to summon the fire demon on her own, I could only imagine what she could do to squealers. I would have chosen torture too.

“Rebecca, the nosferatu, has the information we need to track her down. How much time do we have?”

“According to Mr. Ross, all sanctuaries are to be attacked at midnight in their respective time zones. New York was not supposed to be attacked until then either, but the archfiend Reyzl chose not to wait, likely so he could claim glory for being the first to victory. It’s too late to save Australia, but the sooner you find the Demon Queen, the better.“

I had been shortsighted to think that the goal of destroying the sanctuary had been to create a single foothold of power in New York. I had underestimated the Demon Queen, not realizing that her play was for a quick and decisive victory versus a strategically staged attack. To be honest, I hadn't thought about any of that. I had been more concerned with saving Josette, not even considering the ultimate motives. Now more seraphs were dead, and the balance was sliding further and further towards Hell.

"Okay," I said. "I'll find out where the Demon Queen is, hunt her down, get the Chalice, and save the world." It sounded so simple, and somehow I managed to say it as if I thought I could pull it off. To think that six months ago I was just an ex-con security guard. "What are you going to do?"

Dante shook his head. "There is nothing I can do. This fight is for the world of mankind. The way you draw your energy to return here, I must do something similar to walk in your world, and neither one of us can do so forever."

I looked back at my body in man-space, still frozen in time. "One last question," I said.

Dante raised his eyebrows and smiled. "Yes?"

"What would you have done if I hadn't been able to transport myself here? If I hadn't discovered the secret of my Source?"

Dante didn't hesitate to answer. "Of course, Signore, I would pray."

Chapter 26

When I regained my body, Dante was gone. Rebecca was snarling with her fangs bared, and Josette and Obi sat on the couch and shook out their arms in disbelief that they could move them again. I jumped to my feet and turned to Obi.

"Obi, fire that thing up and see what you can get. We need to move fast."

"What's going on?" Josette asked. "The Outcast?"

"I'd like to rip the Outcast into tiny little pieces," Rebecca said. She relaxed her posture and looked at me. "Where did he go?"

"Back to Purgatory," I told them. Then I gave them the rundown of what he had said to me.

"Even if the New York sanctuary is the only one standing, it will not be enough," Josette said. "With all of the angels forced to travel to one location, it will be very easy for Reyzl to keep them boxed in. Archangel Michael will know this, and will be forced to enter the battle himself."

"Global thermonuclear war," I said.

"Which means we have to find the Queenie before they have time to take out the rest of the sanctuaries," Obi said. "If the archfiends are orchestrating this whole thing, then they have to know where she is, don't they?"

"Not necessarily," Rebecca said. "She could be sending everything along over an encrypted online channel, or using familiars. There's no guarantee what Merov knew will be of any use to us, but it's the best we've got right now."

"What's the password?" Obi asked. Rebecca reached out for the laptop. He handed it to her and she keyed it in.

"It's too complex to say it," she explained, handing the computer back to Obi.

His fingers flew over the keys as he worked his hacker magic. "This is going to take some time," he said after a few minutes. "There's just so much data here."

Rebecca reached out and took my hand. "We still need to talk," she said. "Holler when you find something." She pulled me towards the bedroom again, and this time there were no interruptions.

She kissed me the moment the door had closed, wrapping her arms around my shoulders and pulling my face down to hers. I could feel my pulse quickening at the sensation of her lips against mine, the sweet smell of her, the soft firmness of her body pressed against me. It was a moment I didn't want to end, a moment that I wanted to get lost in, to hold onto forever, to forget about the consequences if we failed to find the Demon Queen. It would be so much easier to stay here, to hide in the Waldorf Astoria with Rebecca and enjoy one another until the demons came for us. Until we were forced to fight, were overwhelmed and destroyed. It was the last part that caused me to break the embrace, to end the kiss.

"You are incredible," she said to me.

"So are you," I replied.

I had so many thoughts circulating through my head, but I didn't know how to express any of them. They all coalesced in the same spot. I wanted her to stay with me, to stay by my side, to be my girlfriend? It seemed a naïve and simplistic way to describe the relationship I hoped we could have. Girlfriends were for humans. I didn't know what it was for us. She was here, now, so that would have to be good enough.

"Whatever happens," she said, "I want you to know that I'm so happy that I met you, and that we got to spend the last few days together. You've changed my life in more ways than you can imagine."

Saying the premature goodbyes like this, it was like Casablanca or something. "Here's looking at you, kid," I replied. She laughed at my bad humor. "Seriously, I'm not giving up until I'm dead. If I have to take on all of the demons in Hell, so be it. They'll be after me anyway, and it's not like there'll be much else to do once Hollywood has been eaten."

She smiled. "We'll fight together," she said. "You're mine. I'm not about to let some other demon take you."

"That's super sweet of you," I said. "There was something else you wanted to tell me. Something you learned from Merov."

Rebecca's smile faded. "It doesn't matter now," she said. "If we make it through the next twenty four hours, we can talk about it then."

I was reluctant to just drop it, but it wouldn't matter anyway if we failed to stop the Demon Queen. I pulled Rebecca close again and kissed her, initiating the intimacy for the first time. Her response was passionate, ferocious, her mouth hungry for mine. The hunger. It was as Josette had named it. I would have let it continue for who-knows-how-long, but Obi was way too good at cracking computers.

"I've got something," he shouted from the sitting room. I gave Rebecca one last kiss, and we dashed out to see what Obi had discovered.

"What do you have?" I said, sliding onto the sofa between Obi and Josette.

Rebecca took up the space on the arm of the chair on the other side. Obi had his face planted against the screen, his finger tracing a line of numbers across it.

"This is an encrypted e-mail Merov received about where to pick up the amulets for the assault," he explained. "It was deleted, but I managed to pull it from the drive and decrypt it."

I laughed. "Obi, we were only gone for five minutes."

"That's what you think," he replied.

I hadn't realized I had been so busy with Rebecca. I had totally lost track of time.

"Anyway," he said, "Reyzl and Merov were exchanging emails about the attacks on the sanctuaries. As far as I can tell, the dude was planning to carry out the attack, then join forces with the other lead demons to go after the Queen, your standard double-cross. He knew he would need control of the Chalice first or they would lose the power of the amulets and she would kill them all."

He scrolled down a bit and pointed at a line of garbled text. "Here, he's telling Merov that he found out how to reach her, and that once the sanctuary has fallen he'll send him the location and time that they are going to converge on it. As near as I can tell, he was going to go talk to her in person and distract her while his minions stole the Chalice, then once it was out of her reach they would bring in an army of thousands through a series of Rifts that the other big bads would create."

"I wonder if it would be enough," I said. I looked at Rebecca. "You don't have this in your inherited memories anywhere?"

She shook her head. "What time was it sent? Maybe Merov never saw it."

"Hang on one sec," Obi said, using his finger to trace the line of code across the screen again. "Yeah, this was sent about an hour before we went in. He never read it. So.. we know that Reyzl knows where the Chalice is, and that Merov didn't know. Now what?"

I didn't want to say it, but there was only one answer. "We have to get Reyzl and make him talk."

"How are we going to do that?" Josette asked.

"We bring him to us," Rebecca said, her blue eyes twinkling. "We make a deal with him."

"What kind of deal?" I asked.

"We want the Chalice, he wants the Demon Queen. If we take the Chalice, then he has his chance to attack her."

That must have made sense to her in some kind of demon-logic, because it evaded me. "Why would he do that?" I said. "He already has his plan to go after the Queen, he doesn't need us."

She looked at me as though I was to be pitied for my lack of understanding of the complexities of deals with devils. "Landon, you have to think more like a demon. Think with your evil side."

She was right. I was thinking too much like a human. Reyzl had the potential to live forever. He was hundreds of years old.

He didn't need to do anything based on the immediate reward. He could plot and scheme for years to see a single thread reach its completion.

"There are a few possibilities," I said. "The most important part is that if we do the dirty work for him, his risk is reduced, because if we fail she'll never know he had anything to do with it and he'll get rid of some of the thorns in his side." I looked at Josette as I said it. She had been his greatest adversary for who knows how long. "If we succeed, he'll either renege on the deal and try to take the Chalice by force, or he'll let us go with it, but he'll make sure he does everything he can to know its whereabouts and go after it when our guard is down. A thousand years or two is nothing to him."

"He's already waited more than two thousand," Josette agreed. "He was not an archfiend then, but he predates Christ."

I hadn't known that. I looked at Josette in shock. "Seriously?"

"Reyzl was known by another name once, before the First Fallen returned him to this world. He was Pentawere, son of Egyptian King Ramses III, last of the great Egyptian Pharaohs. He plotted with his mother from her bed, and slit his father's throat, murdering him in cold blood. He was hanged for his treachery, but he always hungered to return to this world and claim the power that he still believes is his. The First granted him his wish, and he has spent the last three thousand years building his strength through deceit, destruction, and orchestrated chaos."

"Three thousand years," Obi said. "That's a heck of a lot of deceit, destruction, and chaos."

Josette nodded. "Yes, it is. I have spent the last two hundred years working with my fellows to keep his power neutralized. He has almost reached the point that he will be unstoppable without intervention from an archangel. The Chalice will give him the power he needs."

"So the likelihood that he won't double-cross us is pretty much zero," I said.

"I wouldn't be too sure," Rebecca said. "He'll have to decide if he wants to take on the Demon Queen immediately, because she's sure to come after the Chalice as soon as she knows it's gone. It may be to his advantage to let us go with it and recapture it later."

There were so many possibilities. It was enough to make my head spin. "Either way, we need to be ready to fight back. I think I'd rather deal with Reyzl than the Demon Queen."

"I think we're all agreed on that," Josette said.

The idea of making a deal with Reyzl was crazy, but it didn't seem we had any other choice. We had to get the Chalice. We could worry about everything else once that was done. "Okay," I decided. "Rebecca, do you know how to get a message to him?"

"Of course," she replied. "I just need to make a phone call."

Perfect. That would give me some time to take care of something else. "Make the call," I said. "Obi, can I talk to you in private for a minute?" The former Marine lifted his head from the laptop.

"Sure man," he replied, closing the lid and putting it onto the end table next to him. He got up and followed me into the bedroom. "Look man, I like you, but I'm not going to make out with you," he said with a laugh when I closed the door.

"I had something else in mind," I said. "I was talking to Josette, and she suggested that I promote you."

Obi laughed. "Promote me? I didn't know we had ranks."

"It's not that kind of promotion. I want to... I don't know what a good word is... *enhance* you."

"Like Robocop?"

I couldn't stop myself from smiling. "I was thinking Steve Rodgers," I replied.

Obi's smile faded as he accepted that I was being serious. "What do I have to do? What are you going to do?"

"You don't have to do anything," I said. "You've seen what I can do. How I can do it is a little complicated, but the important part is that I can pull some of that power out, and push it into you. I can make you stronger, faster, more resistant to damage, fatigue."

"Steve Rodgers," Obi said, his expression thoughtful. "What's the catch?"

"You'll be tied to Purgatory. If you die, you can never go to Heaven, but you can also never go to Hell. Other than that, no uniform, no shield."

It was obvious that Obi was torn. It was an easy decision to make if you were a devout believer or a serial killer. Join your team and be assured that the life after your life would be what you wanted or deserved. It wasn't so simple for someone like Obi. He had a strong desire to help his fellow man; almost his entire life had been dedicated to it. At the same time, he believed he was a good person, and he wanted to see Heaven one day. From what Josette had told me about getting souls to come back to fight, I couldn't blame him.

"Do it," he said, lifting his eyes and looking right into mine, burning into them with the strength of his conviction. He was a soldier first. "You aren't going to make it through this without me."

"No, I don't think I would," I replied. "Kneel down."

Obi dropped to his knees in front of me, still looking up at me with proud confidence. I reached out and put my hands on his forehead, then closed my eyes. I could feel the soft heat of his flesh against my palms, and I held onto that sensation as I reached down into my soul and took hold of the flow of my

Source. I pulled it up with care, not sure of how much I needed, and certain that I didn't want to harm Obi.

As I gathered the power, I focused my will on the former Marine, telling his body to be stronger, tougher, healthier, more powerful - superhuman. His forehead grew hotter under my hands, and I could feel the sweat beading and running along the outside of my fingers. I pushed more of the energy into him, each moment of thought and will increasing his endurance. When his mouth opened and he began to moan, I ebbed the flow and dropped my hands from his forehead. The second I did, his body fell backwards onto the floor.

"Obi," I said, kneeling down over him. "Obi!" I was going to put my hand to his throat to check his pulse, but I didn't need to. I could sense him lying there below me. I could feel the Divine energy that I had implanted in him, the same as I could sense it in others. I knew he was alive, I just hoped he wouldn't sleep too long.

His eyes flicked open, and he threw out a surprised fist. It connected squarely with my gut, the blow cracking my ribs and lifting me four feet off the ground. I landed back on my knees with grunt of pain.

"Ah crap," Obi said, realizing it was me. "I'm sorry, man."

"I guess it worked," I said. "How do you feel?"

"Ready to go kill some demons," he replied.

I stood and held out my hand to him, but he used his new strength to push himself up off the floor to a stand.

"Thanks man, but I got it," he said with a grin.

We went back out into the living room. Josette and Rebecca were sitting on the sofa, facing each other and talking as if they were old friends. When they noticed we had returned, they both looked at us and giggled.

"What?" I asked defensively. I had gotten the giggle treatment a lot in my youth, and I knew from that experience it was never due to something flattering.

"It is of no concern fellow," Josette said. Her eyes examined Obi. "It is done," she stated.

"I'm a new man," Obi replied.

"You Turned him?" Rebecca asked, surprised.

"Enhanced," Obi corrected. "I'm not a demon."

"Reyzl?" I asked, with a little more force than I had intended.

"Let's go up to the roof," Rebecca said.

Chapter 27

"What were you talking to Josette about?"

I had been needling Rebecca for the contents of her conversation with the seraph the entire way up to the roof. We had left Josette and Obi behind, and had taken the emergency stairwell up, bypassing the door lock that was supposed to keep guests away from the top of the building. She had been ignoring me until we stepped out onto the blacktop.

It was a dark, dreary, drizzly day, the kind that I had always hated when I had been a kid. I was thankful for the weather now, because it meant Rebecca could be out here without risking her health.

"Landon," she said, giving me that same look of inferiority that I was getting used to. "You destroyed a fire demon single-handed, and you're worried about girl-talk?"

"Girls are a lot more intimidating than fire demons," I replied, shrugging.

She laughed, and then sighed. "If you must know, Josette thanked me for bringing you to her, for helping save the sanctuary and her life. She said thank you in the truck on the way back, but whatever you said to her while I was gone, she was a lot more exuberant. Anyway, as we were talking about it I made a comment about the way you lost all of your clothes in the flames, and she admitted with much embarrassment that God gifted you with a fine physique. You should be flattered to have an angel say that about you."

My face had turned beet red by then, and I couldn't make eye contact with her. "I didn't think Josette thought about me that way."

She tilted her head to the side to listen, then led me away from the stairwell and over towards the huge air-conditioning unit. "Don't get too flattered," she said. "She doesn't think about anyone that way. But she does believe in you, which is much more important."

"What about you?"

When we reached the back of the unit she stopped walking and kissed me on the cheek. "I believe in you too. He'll be here in a few seconds."

I was going to ask her who, but I felt the presence approaching for myself. It wasn't Reyzl, but it was familiar. A moment later, a small demon popped up over the side of the roof. He grinned when he saw us.

"Ahh yesss, the vampiresss and her toy."

Rebecca bared her fangs at the demon. "Yuli, I suggest you show some respect, or my toy will break you in half with a thought."

Reyzl's messenger stopped laughing and looked at me with a frightened expression. "My apologiesss Mastersss... whatss your namesss?"

"Landon," Rebecca said. "Diuscrucis Master Landon. If Reyzl doesn't remember him, remind him that it was Landon who killed his servants at the Catskill sanctuary."

I didn't think the demon could look more afraid of me than he already had, but somehow his posture took on an even deeper level of fear. He was shaking as he spoke again. "You havess a message for Mastersss?"

"I want to make a deal," I said. "Tell him we know his plans, and we want a piece of the action. We'll retrieve the Chalice from the Demon Queen, and keep his amulets in play so he can launch his attack against her. In exchange, he'll tell us how to reach her. He'll also agree to allow us to keep the Chalice and take it off the table."

"If he accepts he's to meet us on Liberty Island in an hour," Rebecca added.

I wondered if we had overloaded Yuli's tiny mind, as he hovered silent and motionless for over a minute. I looked at Rebecca, wondering what was going on, but she was reacting as if the activity were normal. Finally, he nodded. "Yesss, yesss. Masterssss acceptsss your dealsss. He will meetsss you."

"One hour," Rebecca repeated. We were going to have to move fast to get there in such a short amount of time.

"One hoursssss," Yuli said. He gave me one last frightened glance and darted away, disappearing around the corner of the air conditioner.

"Can all demons communicate telepathically?" I asked her, once I could no longer sense Reyzl's messenger.

"No," she replied. "Yuli is Reyzl's familiar. They have a blood bond that allows them to communicate without regard for distance, among other things. His messages are the only ones Reyzl trusts completely, which is why I called for him."

"Well it looks like the deal is on," I said. "An hour isn't much time."

"Then we better get a move on, worm."

"What about the Touched coming up the stairs?" I asked.

There were four of them total. I had noticed them approaching as the familiar had left, but Rebecca must have caught their scent sooner. That was why she had positioned us out of sight while we had taken care of our business with Reyzl.

She looked at me with black eyes. "We could use a few more swords," she suggested.

I heard the door groan as it opened, and four pairs of boots stomped out onto the rooftop. I could sense them standing there, uncertain.

"I know I saw it stop up here," I heard one of them say. "It looks like it's gone."

"Let's look around, just to make sure," another one said.

They had come up here looking for Yuli. Now they were fanning out, going over to the sides of the building and looking out and down to see if they could catch a glimpse of where the demon was headed. One of the Touched was headed for our not-so-hidden hiding spot.

"Landon?" Rebecca asked.

I didn't want to kill them. I wish my reasons were more kind, but it was mostly because I didn't want to upset Josette, or risk doing any more damage to the balance.

"Can you disable them without hurting them?"

She didn't look pleased, but she nodded. Her clawed fingers retracted back into normal hands, and she reached into a pocket and removed a pair of gloves. She couldn't cut them without the poison killing them. Then again, I was sure she had done this plenty of times before. It wouldn't be very helpful to kill your prey before you could drain it of its blood.

Rebecca padded over to the corner and waited for the Touched to approach. I could sense them moving, and knew they were getting closer. I had just enough time to see half a head of long brown hair move past the edge of the HVAC when Rebecca reached out, grabbed the Touched, twisted her around and slipped a hand around her neck and mouth. I looked her right in her frightened eyes while Rebecca constricted her throat until she passed out.

"She has a dagger," Rebecca said, finding the small thin blade beneath a black down jacket.

"If it'll hurt a demon, we'll take it. Come on," I said, picking up the unconscious woman and taking us out from behind the air conditioner. When we got to the center of the rooftop I called out to her friends. "Hey," I shouted.

The other Touched were still peeking over the edges of the building, searching for Yuli, but they turned to me when I spoke. There were two men and another woman, all wearing the same black down jacket. Seeing one of theirs in my arms, they stayed motionless while waiting to see what I wanted.

"She's alive," I told them. "You can all go home alive, and you can take her with you, but I need your weapons."

"What does a demon need with a blessed dagger?" the woman asked. Her voice was a mixture of fear and anger.

"Look closer. I'm not a demon," I said. "But I do need to go and kill one, and I'll need your knives to do it. Please don't make me take them by force."

The woman stepped towards me. "If you hand me my sister, we'll drop our weapons here and leave."

I nodded, and started walking towards her with her sister cradled in my arms. When I had reached her, I saw she had tears running down her face. I had been so callous in my consideration of their mortal lives. What was I becoming? I put the woman down and held her so her sister could support her. She used her free hand to reach into her jacket and take out her blade, handing it to me hilt first.

"If you're killing demons, I wish you good hunting," she said to me. "Come on fellows," she shouted to the two men. I could hear their daggers clatter onto the blacktop. A moment later the door groaned again, and they were gone.

"The Order of the Blessed Virgin," Rebecca said after they had left. "They take a vow of celibacy when they're Touched. They're servants, not warriors, which means the angels must be getting desperate to send them out into the fray."

"They have to be getting reports of the other attacks. We need to get to the Statue. Let's grab the daggers and go."

Chapter 28

Getting from the Waldorf to Battery Park before the last possible outgoing ferry made its departure proved to be a challenge of its own, even without any hiccups. After meeting back up with Josette and Obi, we decided on public transit, hopping a couple of subways and walking a bit to get down to dock with only a couple of minutes to spare. I had covered us all in a simple disguise as Japanese tourists, and the rainy weather was helpful to hide the two swords as umbrellas. We had also each claimed one of the Blessed Order's daggers. There had been a moment of tension when Rebecca and I had returned from the roof with them, but Josette had been elated when I told her that nobody had been killed in their acquisition.

It was the middle of the afternoon when the ferry docked at the Island. I looked up at the Statue, and couldn't help but think about the night Mr. Ross had dropped me off on the torch; cold, scared, and confused. It had only been a few days ago, but I felt like it had been an eternity. I had learned so much, experienced so much, changed so much in that short time.

I looked at Rebecca, remembering our first encounter. The way she had pummeled the closet I had been hiding in, toyed with me like a cat, and in the end let me go. She had been frightening in her raw, violent power. That fear had turned to admiration and affection. She wasn't a mindless killing monster, but a beautiful, intelligent, thoughtful creature with her own free will, her own power to make her own decisions. She caught me looking at her and winked. It was like she could read my mind.

The rain had kept some of the visitors away, but the Island was still crowded with people. We disembarked from the ferry and headed up towards the Statue itself. I kept my senses focused on the area around us, staying alert to any Divine that might show up. I wasn't picking up anything.

"Where are we supposed to meet?" Obi asked. He had spent the entire trip marveling at his newfound resistance to cold, and had removed his heavy wool pea coat in response.

"I don't know," I replied. "I just figured we'd know it when he showed up."

"I know where he is," Rebecca said. "Follow me."

We made our way into the pedestal, back into the lobby, and then to my surprise back to the storage closet where I had spent my first night returned to the mortal world. Rebecca cast a sidelong glance in either direction to make sure we weren't being watched, then slipped a key into the door and swung it open just wide enough for us to squeeze through. Once we were in, she slammed the door shut and locked it again.

The room was pitch black, but I was able to see without too much difficulty, my world illuminated in grayscale. "Here?" I asked.

"You'll see," Rebecca said. She motioned with her arm to move us even further together against the back wall, pressing us up against the shelf that had been knocked over when we had met. Judging by the way Josette and Obi were stumbling in the darkness, they weren't as fortunate with their sight.

Rebecca knelt down and put her hand against the solid cement floor. Except it wasn't solid, it had just looked that way until she pulled up a simple brass handle from beneath the glamour. A glamour I hadn't even been able to see through.

"This passage was added in secret by a powerful demon named Silza," Rebecca said. "His goal was to provide a refuge for those who were looking to make the most of the opportunity to subjugate this country, and in doing so bring them under his control. He was killed by Reyzl." She pointed at a messy scrawl of runes on the underside of the door. "These runes hide this passageway from the eyes of any who don't know the command to enter. They also protect those inside from being sensed. There are six beings in existence that know this place exists, and we are four of them. Even the Demon Queen could not find us down here, which is why Reyzl has chosen this place to meet us."

It was also her nest. Her home. I tried not to let it bother me that Reyzl knew where she lived, especially after what she had said he wanted to do to her. There was someone else who knew. Who?

"I don't have any lights," she told me, holding the door open so we could climb down.

Why would she? She didn't need them. I looked around the storage closet until I found a can of turpentine. All I needed was something to ignite. I opened it and focused, forcing the chemicals to combust, then pulled the flames out of the can and wound them into a dancing ball of light. Josette and Obi looked grateful to have their eyes back.

"Let's go," I said, leading them down into the darkness, holding the light over the back of my shoulder.

Rebecca closed the door behind us as we descended a ladder about thirty feet down through a small round tunnel. The entire length of the shaft was covered in the same scrawled runes, and I could feel a pressure against my head while I climbed downward.

"Angels cannot enter this place," Josette said. "I have seen runes like this before, in a sewer below Paris. When I tried there was such pressure, I felt like I would drown."

"I don't feel anything," Obi said.

My feet touched down on an old, thick rug whose center had been worn away by the many feet that had scraped against it on their way up or down over the years. The passageway continued through a circular stone archway that traveled another thirty feet before opening up into a larger space. I could just make out the vague shape of a bed resting near the back end of the area. I could also hear the faint sound of...singing?

The voice was a smooth baritone, the melody old and unrecognizable to my modern ears. Even from here I knew whose mouth was producing the sounds, whose breath was being expelled into the air in the shape of the rough, sad notes. Rebecca hopped off the ladder, cocked her head, and frowned.

"Looks like you were right," I said to her.

She nodded, looking more fearful than I had believed she could look. I hadn't expected her to be apprehensive about the archfiend after she had already put a dagger through his heart.

The room was large, with a high arched ceiling and a mosaic floor. Against the back wall was Rebecca's bed, an intricately carved four-poster that in other circumstances I might have spent hours pondering, wondering how it had come to be in this location without anyone having seen it. Towards the southern wall a rack of blades of all shapes and sizes, thick blocks of wood with plenty of nicks taken out of them, and a mat to separate the training space. To the north a refrigerator whose contents needn't be guessed, and an antique-looking desk with a laptop sitting on it. Did she really have Internet access down here?

Sectioned off near the center of the room was a small sitting area with a leather sofa, a couple of end tables, a rocking chair, and a large flat-screen television. Reyzl was sitting in the rocking chair, his eyes closed, his legs pushing him back and forth. He was wearing a simple pinstriped suit and a pair of wire rimmed glasses, and he didn't even bother to open his eyes when we entered. Being able to examine him up close, I could see that his features were more akin to the Egyptian sculpture I had seen in the Museum than they were to any of the Indian's I had come across around town.

"You're late," he said, his voice holding a hint of a British-English accent. During our first meeting he had seemed so powerful, so malevolent, so in control of everything. Now, he didn't even register as being evil.

"That depends on your concept of time," I replied. For someone who could wait forever, there was no such thing as late.

Reyzl opened his eyes and turned his head. I could only imagine the black orbs were focused on me, looking me over for a second time. "You are a resourceful one," he said. "Your success against my angels was unforeseen, and most unfortunate."

I glanced over my shoulder, surprised to find Rebecca hiding behind me. Not wanting to show them I was afraid, I walked over and sat down on the sofa, turning to face the demon.

"It was nothing personal," I said.

Reyzl laughed. "Personal," he repeated. "No, it wasn't, was it? Just as Ulnyx wasn't personal." He smiled. "It is of no matter," he said. "I will destroy you when it suits me. Or perhaps you will come to work for me, as your predecessor once did. Either way, you will fall under my dominion as all things are destined."

He turned his head to look back at where Rebecca, Josette, and Obi were still standing, trying to keep as much distance between themselves and the demon as possible.

"Rebecca, will you not join us? And Josette? It is a pleasure to see you here. It tickles me that after all these years you will be helping instead of hindering. You have made excellent choices in friends, Landon."

I suspected his words were intended to intimidate. Instead, I found myself amused by his self-importance. He was a powerful demon, but I had power too, and right now I refused to let him get the best of me.

"You do understand," I said, trying to mimic his quiet bluster, "Time is important in consideration of our endeavor."

Reyzl's head whipped back to look at me, his blank expression showing signs of life as he reacted to my mocking tone. Just as soon as it had appeared, it was gone, replaced with his calm emptiness.

"Of course," he said.

He rose to his feet and walked over to the exercise mat in the corner. He knelt down on it and started scratching out runes in the vinyl, his finger cutting through in precise, rigid lines. A minute later he had completed a circle with the runes, and with a guttural exultation they began to burn.

"This is a transport Rift," he said. "It connects to an identical circle in the home of the Demon Queen. You will step into this circle, and step out of that circle. You will retrieve the Chalice and return. At that time, I will open a second Rift to Hell through which my legions can travel through the circle and launch the assault on the Demon Queen."

I walked over to the circle and looked right into Reyzl's eyes. "I've got it," I said. I motioned to the others. "Let's go."

Reyzl's hand was a lightning bolt, lashing out and attaching itself to my shoulder, his claws digging into my skin. "Just you," he said, letting go before I could retaliate.

Just me? "We had a deal," I said.

"A deal that you would get the Chalice from the Demon Queen. Your companions are my insurance that you will not sell me to her in exchange of your own life. This Rift connects both locations. Should she come through the circle, my soul would be forfeit."

"What if she kills me and then comes through?"

"I will know if she kills you, and destroy my side before that can happen. If you die, your companions will be executed as well. Consider it an added incentive." His head tilted downward towards my groin. "You must leave the weapon here," he said. "You cannot pass through the Rift while you are carrying it."

By myself, unarmed. This was getting better by the second. I should have known that making a deal with a demon wouldn't be a straightforward thing. I looked over at Rebecca, her expression a mixture of anger, sadness, and fear. Josette and Obi seemed to be hiding their emotions better, though neither looked very comfortable with the situation.

"We had a deal," Reyzl reminded me.

I could almost sense the hint of mirth in his voice. He had trapped me perfectly, leaving me between a three thousand year old Egyptian rock and an even harder place. Resigned, I nodded my understanding to the demon, slipped the dagger from my belt and dropped it to the floor. I took a deep breath and stepped into the Rift.

Traveling through the Rift was identical to what I had experienced in Purgatory when Mr. Ross had led me off of the beach. One moment I was one place, the next I was someplace else. There was no wormhole, no weird wavy lines, no churned stomach or headache. One step brought me into the Rift under the Statue of Liberty. The next step brought me onto a stone floor.

The first thing I noticed was that it was super bright. So bright that part of me felt like it was shriveling under the intense glow. The second thing I noticed was the Grail. It was sitting right in front of me, about forty feet away. It was resting on a simple stone pedestal, looking as though it were still in the Museum of Natural History, as though the entire thing had been a dream and I was back to my actual life.

That illusion didn't stick long, because the third thing I noticed was that I wasn't alone. To the right of the Chalice were two simple white metal folding chairs, the kind they use at outdoor weddings. She was sitting in one of them, smiling at me.

"Landon," she said with a gentle voice not befitting the Queen of Demons. "I've been waiting for you."

Chapter 29

So many images passed through my mind in that moment as I relived every second of my existence since the woman sitting so patiently in the chair across from me had killed me.

I should have been afraid, because the Demon Queen knew who I was, and was waiting for me, and was going to destroy me once she had finished with whatever conversation it seemed she wanted to have - there were two chairs after all.

I should have been angry, because she had caused such wanton chaos and destruction, had left such evil in her wake.

Instead, my mind was distracted by how beautiful she was sitting there, her lustrous long black hair falling over her right breast, her perfect white smile so inviting, her feline yellow eyes sexy and dangerous in a way that Rebecca could only dream of. A black collared coatdress with a deep neckline and low boots rounded out the vision. What the heck was I thinking?

I took a deep breath and swallowed, trying to get my stomach back down where it belonged before I made a mess of her clean stone floor. I could see the source of the light now, spotlights arranged around the perimeter of the room, casting so much brightness and heat that any demon not wearing an amulet would be hard-pressed to do much of anything caught in the trap. Yet there she was, sitting bathed in the light, oblivious to the damage it should be doing to her. I could see the plunge of her dress down into her cleavage. She wasn't wearing an amulet.

"Waiting for me," I stuttered, trying not to sound overwhelmed, and failing miserably.

"For longer than you know," she replied. "We have a lot to talk about."

I started walking towards her, my legs feeling shaky beneath me. Dante's voice echoed in my mind, describing to me how this woman had slaughtered the Knight Templar who had defended the Chalice for over two thousand years, along with a whole contingent of seraphs. What could I have that she wanted?

"I need the Chalice," I said, feeling stupid right after I said it.

No doubt she knew I needed the Chalice. She had been waiting for me. Did she take it not for the demons, but to draw me in? How could she, if I had still been a mortal then? Had she known what I would become when she killed me? That one was too much to wrap my mind around.

"Take it," she said, motioning to where it sat on the pedestal. "On one condition."

One condition. I should have known. No demon would give up anything without making a deal. "What condition?"

"A few minutes of your time. That's it."

I stood there, trying to think of the trick, the angle she was using to take advantage of me. I looked at the Chalice, and then looked back at her. She didn't need to take advantage of me. There was nothing I had that she couldn't take. I walked over to her, pulled the other folding chair around so I could sit across from her, and planted myself in it.

"I'm listening," I said.

"Like I said, I've been waiting for you for a long time. Since before you even existed in fact. That day at the Museum, the day I took the Grail, I didn't know that it was you, the too polite security guard, who would be the one. I had thought I would be stalling the archfiends for years, perhaps centuries while I waited for you to arrive."

"Why were you waiting for me?"

"I want your power," she replied. "I need your power, if I am to do what needs to be done."

"I have a feeling you could just kill me and take my power," I said.

She smiled, a warm sweet smile that confused the heck out of me. She was evil, right? "It's not a power that can be taken," she said. "You have to share it willingly."

"Why would I ever want to do that?" I asked. "You're the most powerful evil in this world. You used the Chalice to arrange the devastation of mankind."

She reached out and put her hand on my leg. I could feel the warmth of it through my jeans. "You of all people should know that evil is subjective," she said. "Is it evil to kill in order to save? Is it evil to lie in order to protect?"

I couldn't really argue with that. "So you're saying you aren't really evil?"

She took her hand away. "What I'm saying is that the word evil is just that. Look at the seraphim. The reason Hell exists is because they hold the capacity to do bad things, just as some demons have capacity to do good things - your friend Rebecca for instance. I have done things that you would call evil, but I had also done my share of good. What I need from you has a purpose that I believe is good, even if others might disagree."

"What purpose is that?" I asked.

"To end the war, of course."

"You can end the war with the Chalice. You can end the war by sitting here, talking to me. The archfiends will destroy the sanctuaries and all mortal life will cease to be."

Another smile. This one was much more placating. "That's only true under the assumption that I want the demons to win. That's only true if we are speaking of the same war."

I was lost. Who did the Demon Queen want to win, if not the demons? What other war was there?

"I don't understand," I said.

"Balance," she said. "It's all about balance. You. Me. This world. Heaven. Hell. Purgatory. Good and evil. Every one of these things is a gyroscope, turning and spinning in a perfect choreography of chaos and order. Yet, if that is true, then why do you exist? Why do I exist?"

It was back to the question of why I am? "Balance," I replied

"Yes, that is part," she said. She waited for me to tell her the rest.

"I don't know," I said. I looked over at the Chalice. Time was not a luxury I had right now to be partaking in her riddles. "Is there a purpose to this?"

She pursed her lips, looking thoughtful. "I was afraid I might be moving too fast. That it was too soon." She was talking, but not to me. Her yellow eyes dilated and focused, as if there were someone else in the room with us. "I can't be sure I'll have another chance." It was like sitting with someone while they were on the phone. "You're right. It's a risk, but I have to take it."

She blinked once, then leaned forward again and put her hand up to my face, moving too fast for me to pull away. Her soft, cool palm pressed against my cheek.

“There isn’t much time,” she said to me. “I will tell you this once, and I need you to remember it.”

Her eyes locked onto mine, and I found that I couldn’t pull away. The black slits resting inside the yellow orbs captured me, held my soul in a way that left me powerless, and defenseless. While I had feared the Demon Queen and her power, I had still badly underestimated it. She could have taken my head from my shoulders and I wouldn’t have noticed.

“I do not know how long it will take. It may be days, it may be years, it may be millennia. The day will come when you will no longer eat, no longer sleep, and if you aren’t careful you will no longer feel. You will sense the balance in your soul, and what was once familiar will become alien. You will question the balance, question the war, and question yourself and everything you see around you. You will search for answers. You will scour the world to find the true purpose of who and what you are. Some you will find, and some you will need to determine for yourself. Remember that you are free, that you have your own will and your own choices. Remember these words, search for your answers, and then find me again.”

She pulled her hand from my face, keeping her eyes locked with mine. I had so many questions, but only one of them managed to find its way from my brain to my lips.

"How will I find you again?"

She leaned forward, keeping her eyes on mine until she was too close for me to focus on them. Warm lips brushed against my cheek, then slipped back to my ear. "When you are ready, you will know. I will be waiting."

My eyes closed of their own volition as she whispered, my body and soul absorbing as much of her essence as it could manage. "Reyzl," I said, fighting to speak above the chaos churning through my being.

"Let him send his army. I am prepared. Take the Chalice, and hide it as Dante has asked." I felt her hand lift mine, push open my fingers, and place something in it. "Pour this into the Chalice before you step into the Rift. It has been blessed by an archangel and will permanently negate the power of the crystals. Once you step through the circle be prepared. Reyzl has betrayed you."

She backed away from me. I opened my eyes and looked down at the object she had placed in my hand. It was a vial of blood. Her blood.

"Who are you?" I asked, looking up. Gone. I should have known.

I jumped out of the chair and raced over to the pedestal, grabbing the Chalice from the platform and running back towards the Rift. I had expected that I would have felt something from holding an object of such power, but it could have been a Chinese knockoff for all I knew. I laughed when it occurred to me that maybe it was, and the Demon Queen had just played me for an even more complete fool than Reyzl had. This whole thing had gone from crazy to crazier over the last few minutes, so I wouldn't have been too surprised.

I stopped right before the circle, taking the vial of blood the Demon Queen had given to me and holding it over the Chalice. I hesitated to use it, unsure if I would be doing the right thing or just falling for another demonic trap. She had said an archangel had blessed the blood, and she hadn't been lying, but Josette had told me all of those guys were staying up in Heaven, and I trusted her, so how could that be? Still, it was such an unbelievable statement that I found myself believing it. After all, the Demon Queen had let me live and I knew Reyzl wanted to kill me. It was a flimsy bit of logic, but it was all that I had.

I used my thumb to push the cork out of the vial and dumped the contents into the Chalice. The moment it touched the wood it began to hiss and steam, leaving a smell of sulfur and incense behind. I felt a shockwave that ran through my entire body, and deep within my soul I understood that I hadn't been deceived. Now I just had to somehow deal with Reyzl.

I closed my eyes and took a few deep breaths, taking hold of my Source and pulling its power to me, preparing it for use. I had no idea how I was going to use it, but I had been warned of the impending ambush and I needed to be ready.

I took one last gulp of air and stepped forward.

Chapter 30

It was one step into the circle, another step out of it. I didn't wait to get my bearings before I tried to propel myself away from the Rift, to put some distance between Reyzl and myself and get a better idea of what I was up against. It was a wasted effort. As soon I had cleared the circle a pair of hands wrapped around each of my arms, and a knee came down on my back to push me to the ground and hold me in position. My assailants bent me backwards, twisting me upwards at an awkward and painful angle. It caused me to drop the Chalice, sending it tumbling to the ground a few feet away. Reyzl bent over from the waist and scooped it up into his hand. He held it up over his head, admiring it in the light of the flames coming from the Rift. His eyelids fluttered minutely. I could only guess he was realizing what I had helped the Demon Queen do.

He recovered from his discovery and turned to me. "Thank you, Landon," he said with a surprising sincerity. I suppose he was grateful I had done his dirty work for him. "I had suspected that filthy hell-spawn would be expecting me to stab her in the back again. That being the case, I just need one more thing from you." He started walking towards me.

I tried to focus my will, to make myself stronger so I could break free of my captors. Another wasted effort, I was in too much pain to get my mind where it needed to be. I glared up at Reyzl as he approached.

"You're in for a surprise if you think killing the Demon Queen will be so easy," I said.

He crouched down in front of me so we were at eye level. "Since she was expecting my betrayal, I can only assume she's prepared for my arrival," he said. "Don't worry about me. I'm aware of that bitch's tricks. That's why I couldn't let you keep the Chalice. That's why I need to do this."

His arm whipped out, the blessed dagger I had dropped gleaming in the firelight. I felt the coldness of the blade as it dug into my neck, and then the warm wetness when my blood began flowing from it. Reyzl placed the Chalice under it, collecting my plasma.

"With your blood, I have no need to waste time with crystals," he said.

I closed my eyes, trying to convince myself that I didn't need to breathe. The wound was already healing, but my trachea was still wide open. I knew I had to stop Reyzl from doing whatever it was he planned on doing with my blood. I tried to focus again, reaching for my Source and coming up empty.

"Having trouble concentrating?" Reyzl asked, laughing. He stood and whispered something to whoever was holding me. I couldn't see them, but I could see the archfiend dip his finger into the Chalice, could hear the sucking sound as he fed my blood to each of them.

"Delicious," one of them said. I knew that voice.

"I've never tasted anything like it," the other agreed in the same voice, confirming their identities. I had run into them once before, when they had tried to kill me before I had ever left Purgatory. Mephistopheles's Collectors. What were they doing here?

Reyzl crouched down again, dipping his finger in my blood and taking it into his own mouth, making a show of the violation. "You have no idea how powerful your blood is when combined with the power of the Chalice. If you had, you would never have made the deal with me in the first place. I'm so glad you did though. I would have been happy enough if the Queen had taken care of you for me, but everything has worked out more perfectly than I could have dreamed."

What power did the blood give him? Whatever it was, it couldn't be good for the balance, or for me. I struggled against the fallen angels that held me, but their grip was iron.

"Now if you'll excuse me," Reyzl said. "I have an army to summon and feed." He stood, kicked me in the face, and started walking away.

"What should we do with him?" one of the angels asked.

"I have what I need. Kill him," he replied.

When one angel released my arm, and the other one grabbed it, jerking me to my feet. I could see him now, his silver hair falling over his elfish face. He was wearing the same leather duster, though there was no sign of his wings. He circled around in front of me and drew his sword.

"*Landon. I can feel you are here. What is happening?*" The voice in my head was forceful, powerful. Josette. She was still alive!

"*Are you okay*?" I asked.

"*For the moment*," she said. "*We are chained to the ladder by the entrance. Obi is injured. Reyzl said he has plans for us.*"

I already knew what kind of plans the archfiend had for Rebecca, and I could imagine what he would want with his longtime nemesis. Why he wanted Obi, I didn't know, but just the thought of what the demon was going to do to them was the worst torture imaginable.

"*I'm so sorry this happened*," I said. "*I'm so sorry. Reyzl has me. I'm going to die.*"

"*No*," she replied, her voice commanding. "*You cannot. Not yet.*"

The angel held his blade back, preparing the blow that would remove my head. "You were lucky the Outcast saved you the first time," he said. "You won't be so lucky again."

"There's nothing I can do," I shouted back to Josette, even my mental voice panicked at my imminent decapitation.

Then it hit me. In my current state I couldn't focus enough to pull my Source to me, so instead I pushed myself to my Source, feeling the shift from one realm to another. The world faded into a translucent mess. My current location on Earth had no counterpart in this dimension. Instead there was only pure white, the absence of everything, like the wall at the end of the beach. I could see the fuzzy transparency of the mortal world frozen in time, moments away from the end of everything.

"Landon."

I turned, and she was there, in all of her heavenly glory. Not the fallen Josette, but the angel Josette, in lustrous white robes, her ivory wings stretched out wide from her back.

"Josette. I don't understand what's happening," I said. It was all too much. She floated over to me and put her arms around me, holding me as I cried. "I've failed," I told her. "You, Rebecca, Obi, the sanctuaries and the balance. I can't stay here forever, and when I go back, I'm going to die. It will all be over, and it's all my fault."

She stroked my hair, and kissed my forehead. "It isn't over," she said. "You will not die. It is not my Lord's will."

I looked up at her, my vision blurry with my tears. "There's nothing I can do."

She used her finger to wipe the droplets away from my eyes. “There is something you can do,” she insisted. “Summon the Beast.”

The Beast? She must mean Ulnyx. With a thought, he was there. He laughed when he saw that I was crying, my state of hopelessness leaving me too weak to control him.

“I knew you would blow it,” he said. “When you die, my soul will be free to find another host. I doubt your sidekick will be able to resist me.”

His words snapped me out of it. I reached out with my power and constricted it around his neck, lifting him off the ground and choking him. “Your soul will never be free,” I shouted, my anger flaring.

“A demon can absorb the power of another demon,” Josette said. “You trapped his soul when he tried to take your body. You can take his power for your own.”

Ulnyx's expression turned fearful.

“How?” I asked.

“Kill him,” she replied.

So I did. I wrapped him in my power, twisting and crushing and pressing in on him, watching as his body was compressed into nothing more than dust. He had no chance to speak, no chance to beg. My power was unequaled here, and he didn't stand a chance. I could feel his soul floating unhindered by his shell, but unable to escape. I pushed it toward me on a gust of air, a small black cloud of energy. I brought it to my face and took a deep breath, taking it in for the second time.

Memories flashed before me, years and years of memories. Ulnyx was born a werewolf, killed his parents, and slaughtered his brother, the leader of his pack. His thirst for blood and destruction was insatiable, his need to destroy unending. His power was the power of pure evil, and I brought it into me, absorbed it into my soul and took it as my own. It wasn't a painless process, the inherited memories vile and disgusting, threatening to drive me mad. I released a guttural growl, an angry howl. I could feel myself changing, losing control. I looked at Josette.

"Why?" I asked her, feeling betrayed.

"There is no other way," she said. She continued to float before me on her angel wings, her beautiful, calm, loving existence the only thing keeping the demon's evil from overwhelming me. "I will protect you fellow. I will save you, so that you can save your world. I believe it is His will."

She reached out and took my hand, which I now saw was the clawed hand of the Great Were. I could feel the pressure building in my soul, could feel the darkness creeping in on me. I was only part demon. I was never meant to do what I had just done. I couldn't survive it and keep my sanity.

She took the hand and put it to her face, kissing the grotesque, demonic palm. "Godspeed, Landon Hamilton," she said. She took my evil claws and raked them down her face, cutting deep into her flesh. The black lines of the demon poison blossomed across her skin.

"No," I cried, the passion of my emotion holding the darkness back for the moment at least.

"I love you brother," she said. "Look after my daughter."

She opened her mouth, and a burst of light shot out of it, catching me off-guard and splashing against my face. It blinded me with its brightness, and pressed hard against me like water from a fire hose. I couldn't. No, shouldn't turn my head. I opened myself up to it, opened my mouth wide and accepted the flood. Again, I was overcome with memories and images, Josette's childhood, her mother and father, her brother, the pain of her violation, her death, her hundreds of years as an angel walking among the mortal, her unrequited service to God.

Then, the unexpected: her brother an archfiend, her capture, her torture, her pregnancy, and her daughter. Sarah.

I fell to the ground, my mind a battleground between good and evil, Ulnyx and Josette. I could feel them both vying for control of my soul, their memories conflicting and washing through me: death, destruction, love, charity, anger, selflessness, Heaven, Hell. Somewhere in the mix I rediscovered myself, regained my own identity, and stepped between them.

"Enough," I cried to nobody, looking up and seeing I was alone in Purgatory, in my Source. I could feel them in my soul, could hear their voices, see their memories, pull the smaller flow of their power and mix it with my own. The balance. Josette had sacrificed herself so that I could absorb the demon and not go mad. She had saved my life to stop Reyzl and protect her daughter. Sarah had thought her mother was dead. Now she was. She had done it for me.

I pulled at the new sources of power, letting the feeling of it flow through me. I looked over at my still form, held by one of the fallen angels, about to be beheaded by the other. Josette had been training for hundreds of years. She knew how to escape from that hold. Now I did too.

The sword was already whistling through the air when I retook my body. Faster than I could ever have moved before, I snapped my head back to where I knew the angel's to be, feeling the crunch as the force shattered his face and loosened his grip. In the same motion I dropped to a knee and threw my upper half forward, lifting my captor up and over, into the path of the blade. He cried out in pain as it dug into his back. His grip destroyed, I sent him into the air to slam hard into his counterpart.

Neither angel stayed down long, rolling to their feet once their kinetic momentum had been broken. The one who had been holding me looked like he had already healed from the sword strike, and he pulled his own sword with a grin.

"Thanks for the blood," he said, flexing his back. "Delicious, and nutritious."

My blood. Whatever Reyzl had done, it had made them not only impervious to damage from blessed weapons, but had increased their healing rate beyond my own. I dropped into a defensive crouch, waiting for the attack that I knew would come.

They struck together, their swords thin white lines of steel arcing toward me. I ducked and dodged, twisted and danced around the blades, somehow matching the impossible speed of their motion as I circled around the room. I could see that they were pushing me, herding me towards the wall. I couldn't play defense forever.

I reached in and found the Great Were's power. I felt the strength surge through my limbs, felt myself growing and changing. My hands stretched out into gigantic claws, my clothes tearing as my mass increased. The angels' swords whistled towards me.

I caught the first with a massive paw, the edge of the blade sinking into my flesh but nowhere near deeply enough to harm me. I closed my grip around it and held it, then sidestepped the other attack and lashed out with my other claw. It caught the angel in the face, the razor sharp fingers ripping and tearing, removing most of the head in one swipe.

No sooner had I brought my hand back when I could see the intense wound beginning to heal, the face rebuilding, the mouth opening to laugh. I wrenched the sword from the other angel's hand, flipped it in the air to take the hilt, caught it with a smaller human hand, and delivered the killing blow, removing the mutilated head before it could regenerate.

"No," the other angel cried, seeing his partner's headless corpse topple to the ground. I let the transformation reverse completely, shrinking back to my human form, reknitting my tattered clothes together, remaking myself as whole. Armed, I turned to face him.

"My condolences," I cursed, darting forward, slamming him in the face with the hilt to knock him back, then whipping the blade around and through his neck.

I didn't wait for him to fall, instead spinning around, looking for Reyzl. I found him near the Rift, speaking under his breath and scraping out another circle. He hadn't noticed what had been going on behind him and probably believed I was already dead. This would be easier than I thought.

My plan was to dash in and remove the archfiend's head before he had any idea I was still alive. It might have worked too, if he hadn't finished the circle at the same time I started towards him. The runes burst into flame and the first of Reyzl's army stepped through. A humanoid female with scaled red skin and bright yellow eyes. It saw me as soon as it entered, letting out a cry of alarm and shoving Reyzl away from my attack.

The archfiend rolled to the side, somehow keeping his hold on the Chalice, and rose to his feet as I decapitated the demon with the cursed sword. If he was surprised to see me alive, he hid it well.

"You continue to impress me with your persistence diuscrucis," he said with a smile. "However, I'm afraid you're in the way."

A second demon stepped through the Rift, then a third, a fourth. They hissed when they saw me, springing forward to attack. Reyzl bent over and placed the Chalice on the ground, then began to unbutton his suit jacket.

I did the one thing that made sense. I couldn't fight Reyzl and an army of demons on my own, so I ran. Not to get away, but to get help. Rebecca. I raced down the corridor, the demons chasing behind, still streaming in through the Hell Rift. I heard growling as hounds joined the devils.

She was standing next to the ladder, pulling against the handcuffs that bound her, the demon Yuli perched above. He was cackling at her futile attempts to escape, hopping back and forth on the rung. They both turned to look at me as I rushed in, Yuli freezing in fear, Rebecca baring her fangs in a half-snarl, half-smile.

"Hey," I said to her, cracking the sword down on the chain of the cuffs. Freed, she grabbed the sword from my hand.

"Hi handsome," she said, her eyes fading to black. "Nice eyes." She leapt forward and tore into the devils behind me.

Nice eyes? I wasn't sure what she meant, but I didn't have time to think about it. I heard flapping wings, and saw Yuli flying away up the shaft. He wasn't worth chasing. I started to turn back towards the fray when I saw Obi. He was lying on the ground behind the ladder, his eyes closed, a huge bloodstain on his stomach. He was still alive, but he was out of the fight.

My anger flared and I hurried to catch up with Rebecca. I used Ulnyx's strength to throw around the devils like rag dolls, leaving them broken for her to dispose of. I had already lost Josette, and I didn't know how long Obi would last without help. It was time to end this.

Reyzl was waiting for us when we reached the main room. He had removed all of his clothes except his underwear, having placed them in a neat pile next to the Chalice. His body was taut with lean muscle and covered in dark scars that formed more of the demonic runes. They burned on his skin, the flames bathing him in a red glow. His hands had morphed into talons, the ends dripping demon fire.

"I've grown weary of you, Landon," he said. I felt his power all around me, pressing on me in an effort to freeze me as he had done before. I pulled on my own flow and pushed myself free, feeling his efforts dissipate from the force of my will. He observed his failure without emotion, and then launched himself at me.

I almost didn't move in time, skipping to the side as a clawed hand raked across my abdomen. I felt the tips of his hands scrape against my skin, the demon fire burning worse than any real flame. I winced in pain as I dodged a second strike and blocked a third with my forearm. The wound wasn't healing. In fact it was growing more painful as I moved.

"Does it hurt?" Reyzl asked. "You aren't as impervious as you believed."

I grunted in response, catching his arm when he threw it forward, twisting it and hearing a satisfying crack as it shattered. Reyzl moaned and backed away, his snarled lip defying his nonplussed expression.

I pressed the attack, but the arm healed almost instantly, twisting back into the proper position and coming up in time to block my punches. Each time my hand hit one of the runes I felt the pain of the demon fire biting into me. Each time I felt the pain I grew angrier. The anger made me sloppy.

An overthrown, off-balance punch later I found myself slammed up against the wall, four deep punctures in my chest and lungs, gasping for air and trying to get back up. Reyzl stood ten feet away, allowing himself just the slightest smirk while he watched me struggle.

My whole body was burning up, my soul was crying out in despair. Josette had given herself up for me, given herself up for nothing. My anger fell way, replaced by acceptance and a sudden calm. I had done my best, hadn't I? There had never been any guarantees.

I looked around for Rebecca, finding a mass of demons near the opening to the corridor but not seeing her anywhere. I wanted to tell her I was sorry, that I wished we had more time together, that I thought she and I could have been something special. I swallowed with a dry throat and licked my lips. Reyzl was still standing there, just looking at me, watching me die.

The demon fire. It was burning me up, preventing me from healing. I almost laughed when I thought of it, not that I could laugh with the holes in my lungs. I closed my eyes and relaxed, pulling on my Source and letting my focus fade. The air held moisture, moisture meant water, and water doused fire. Could it put out demon fire? There was one way it could. Josette hadn't sacrificed herself so I would know how to fight like her. She had given herself to me for another reason, to provide me with something she knew I would need. After all, who knew the archfiend better than she did?

I reached for her power, picturing her bedroom, her simple straw doll, her carefree and safe life before her brother had become evil, before her mischief had brought down her parent's ire. I mixed it with my own, sent it out with my will, demanding the vapor in the air to condense, demanding that it rain.

My eyes were closed, but I felt my body cool and heal as the air around me began to cry. This wasn't just any rain, but holy rain, holy water, Josette's tears. I finally took a deep breath, opening my eyes to glorious chaos. In front of me, Reyzl was hunched over, trying to escape the water, his skin sizzling wherever it touched him. Behind him, the demons were rushing back towards the Hell Rift, but the rain had extinguished it. With no escape, they shrieked and howled in pain as the flesh washed off of them like dirt. Where was Rebecca?

"How?" Reyzl asked, trying to straighten up. The runes on his body had been extinguished, but he had drank my blood from the Chalice, and he was healing as fast as the water could wound him. I knew from experience how much it must hurt.

I caught the motion out of the corner of my eye. With a thought, I stopped the rain. "Something you can't begin to understand," I said to him.

"And what is that," he growled. His strength was returning, and he started moving towards me, his fury obvious despite his blank black eyes.

"Friends," I said.

He caught on too slowly, sensed her too late. An instant later Rebecca was on his back, a hand on each end of the cursed sword. She winked at me, and then pulled the blade towards herself, slicing through Reyzl's neck.

The black fog of his soul poured from the top of his headless corpse as it fell. Rebecca opened her mouth to accept it, her head tilting back in ecstasy as she absorbed the immense power of the archfiend. I sat against the wall and watched it happen, waiting for it to be done.

Then it was. The last of the black fog vanished down Rebecca's throat, and she fell to her hands and knees, her breathing heavy. I rushed over to her and put my arms around her waist, holding her steady.

"Are you okay?" I asked. She didn't respond right away. "Rebecca?"

"Just give me a minute, worm," she replied. "I think it was something I ate."

It was the perfect release. I closed my eyes and gave myself up to the joke, my laughter strong and loud. A moment later she joined me, laughing weakly, then coughing, then laughing again.

"Help me up?" she asked.

I let go of her waist and circled around in front of her. She reached up and took my hand, and I pulled her to her feet. She stumbled as she rose, so I wrapped her arm over my shoulder to support her.

"Nice work," I said.

"You almost killed me with that rain," she said. "I was lucky to duck under the sofa before I got too beat up."

"I'm sorry Becca," I replied. "I couldn't think of anything else."

She shifted her weight so she could drag my head down to hers. She kissed me hungrily. "Apology accepted," she said. "It all worked out."

"Reyzl?" I asked.

"I took his power," she said. "Let's grab the Chalice and get out of here."

We walked over to where the Chalice sat on the floor next to the Hell Rift, surrounded by the wet ash of the demons killed by the holy water, and filled with the water itself.

"I've got it," Rebecca said, bending over to pick it up. She couldn't reach it with her arm around me, so she pulled away to bend down further.

"I know this is going to sound corny," I started saying as she grasped the Chalice by the stem and turned it over to dump out the holy water, "and the timing kind of stinks, but I was thinking maybe you and I could, you know, be together. See how it goes?"

"I'm sorry, Landon," she replied.

Huh? I wasn't expecting the rejection. "I don't understand," I said. No reply. "Rebecca?"

That was when I noticed the flames of the runes around the Hell Rift had reignited. She turned to face me, her eyes as black as night, her expression sad but strong. She shifted forward and the pain in my stomach was renewed. Her claws made a sick sucking sound when she removed them from my gut. Blood ran down over my wet clothes, down into the Chalice.

"What are you doing?" I asked her. I didn't even see her other hand sweep up behind me, her claws digging into my neck. My spinal cord severed, I dropped to the ground like a sack of potatoes.

"I'm sorry," she repeated, lifting the Chalice to her mouth and pouring the contents down her throat. After she swallowed, she dropped the Chalice to the ground.

"Why?" I asked.

"Survival," she said. Without another word she stepped into the Hell Rift and was gone.

Physically, I couldn't feel anything. Emotionally, I had just been ripped in half. She had saved my life more than once. She had been my friend, my companion, and I had hoped she would be something more. I had trusted her with my life, trusted her despite the fact that she was a vampire, a creature of evil. I had told Josette she was different. She was supposed to be different. I wanted to believe that absorbing Reyzl's soul had done something to her, that there was no other explanation. As much as I hated it, I was having trouble with that. When she had said she was sorry, she had been lying.

I lay there alone, waiting for my body to heal, not knowing if I would ever see her again. The tears ran unabated from my eyes, and I didn't think they would ever stop.

Thank you!

It is readers like you, who take a chance on self-published works that is what makes the very existence of such works possible. Thank you so very much for spending your hard-earned money, time, and energy on this work. It is my sincerest hope that you have enjoyed reading!

Independent authors could not continue to thrive without your support. If you have enjoyed this, or any other independently published work, please consider taking a moment to leave a review at the source of your purchase. Reviews have an immense impact on the overall commercial success of a given work, and your voice can help shape the future of the people whose efforts you have enjoyed.

Thank you again!

About the Author

Michael Forbes is mobile and web application engineer and author of science fiction and fantasy. He has a degree in fine art, and loves good user interface and industrial design. Michael lives in the Pacific Northwest with his wife, a cat that thinks she's a dog, and a dog that thinks she's a cat. Although he has been reading and writing voraciously since childhood, Balance is Michael's debut novel. If you like what you've read, he'd love to hear from you!

To keep up with Michael, please visit him at: http://www.mrforbes.com/site/writing.

About the Cover

Credit goes to the following for the royalty free stock imagery used in the creation of the book cover. All graphics licensed under Creative Commons 3.0 Attribution:
http://creativecommons.org/licenses/by/3.0/

Statue of Liberty:
takashiirie.com
http://www.freevector.com/free-vectors-graphics/

Wings
www.artshare.ru
http://www.freevector.com/wings/

Landon Silhouette
123FreeVectors.com
http://www.freevector.com/club-people-silhouettes/

Grunge Background
ImaginaryRosse
http://imaginaryrosse.deviantart.com/art/Grunge-Textures-117555400

Cityscape
Stockgraphicdesigns.com
http://www.freevector.com/cityscapes-vector-graphics/

CPSIA information can be obtained
at www.ICGtesting.com
Printed in the USA
LVHW051452120219
607279LV00019B/804/P